THE
CUMAL
FILES

James Keegan

SLEUTH HOUND BOOKS

THE CUMAL FILES
ISBN: 978-0-6484856-3-6

GLOSSARY

Koori – a non-derogatory term for an Australian aboriginal person

Kookaburra – native Australian bird with a call that sounds like laughter

Drongo – Australian slang for 'fool'

Fair dinkum – Australian slang for 'serious'

I had a Barry Crocker – rhyming slang for 'I had a shocker...'

Two-bob crook – police slang for 'a low-level criminal, an amateur.'

You've lost your marbles – slang for 'you're crazy'

Wider than the Nullarbor – the Nullarbor Plain covers a huge area in southern Australia

Could eat the crutch out of a low-flying duck – slang for 'very hungry'

Ned Kelly – legendary Australian bushranger

Tell a porkpie – slang for 'to tell a lie'

Pharlap – a champion Australian racehorse

For my son,
My sun

ONE

The target skipped along the road in school uniform, seemingly in love with the world and oblivious to the presence of evil.

Corporal KA72 scoffed at her naivety as he twisted a dial on the console to zoom the CCTV camera in. He turned a separate dial to focus the picture then studied the target on the screen. She was a rare beauty, well-developed for fourteen, with charcoal coloured skin.

KA72 smiled, proud of himself. Proud because he'd planned the entire operation and would secure the perfect target. A target who would fetch a substantial fee from one of the perverted, mega-rich clients who collected teenage girls the same as they did luxury supercars. And because those clients had decided that Aboriginal girls were flavour of the month, the upturn in sales had provided valuable funds for his organization. Profits in the millions would buy support from corrupt politicians and help loyal members already entrenched in parliament to achieve the organization's ultimate objective - the absolute control of a far-right government.

KA72 read information at the top of the screen. *Camera location: northern entrance to King's Park, Redfern. Tuesday 6th of August. 15:26 hrs.*

It was time.

He turned to the guard seated next to him. They worked for the same private contractors, monitoring public security cameras for South Sydney Council.

"Joel, mate, it's okay if you wanna go for a smoke. I'll keep an eye on your screens." He waited for Joel to stand. "Can you grab us a Starbuck's while you're out? Maybe an éclair from the bakery too?"

Joel nodded then left the control room.

KA72 locked the door behind him. He returned to the console and pressed three buttons. The screen split into four smaller pictures showing the view from each of the cameras mounted around the park. He concentrated on the picture at top-left. The target stepped from the road and onto a concrete cycleway.

He grabbed his cell phone and dialled a number, let it ring once then ended the call. A few seconds later the phone buzzed and he pressed the screen to answer.

The caller grunted as though clearing his throat. "Verify, soldier...What's the target number?"

"She's AF14-104," KA72 told him.

"And I am?"

"You're Captain KA43, team leader of acquisition unit thirteen."

"And you are?"

"Corporal KA72, in position as required."

"Good...We have eyes on the target and will grab her once she's further inside the park. All clear to go ahead?"

KA72 stroked a thick, red beard. His ample gut pressed against the console as he leaned forward and squinted. "You're in the white van with a logo on its side...Correct?"

"Yes. Hurry the fuck up."

Eyes scanned the screen again. "There's nothing coming up the street behind you, and no-one but the girl in the park. Proceed."

KA43 ended the call.

KA72 watched the white van speed along the cycleway towards the target.

The target glanced back as though suddenly spooked. She turned onto a section of lawn and hurried towards a row of thick bushes by the nearest exit.

A KA soldier leapt from the van and chased her. He wore black combat fatigues and a full-face balaclava. The van followed.

Her backpack seemed to hamper the target as she ran. She stumbled then waved arms above her head. Was she calling out? To who?

The soldier tackled her to the ground forty metres from the exit. He flung her over his shoulder, ran to the van and threw her into the rear compartment. He jumped in and slid the door shut. The van made a u-turn then sped back in the direction it'd come.

KA72 noticed movement on the picture at bottom right. A small truck appeared from behind bushes the girl had ran towards. It drove across lawn then stopped on the cycleway. He selected the nearest camera and zoomed in. A council truck with two men seated in the front cabin...Witnesses?

"Shit." He grabbed the cell phone and called the last number.

"What?" KA43 answered.

"There's a problem. Go back."

"Why?"

"Two council workers in a truck probably saw the whole thing. Eliminate immediately before they report it, or cops will swarm from everywhere..."

KA43 swore then barked orders for his driver to expedite to the park. "Listen 72, we'll take care of the council guys and transport the girl. You contact the boss and get another crew called out. Pronto. Have them clean up the bodies and the truck once we're done. Got it?"

"Understood. Just follow the same route out of the city that you came in on. There are no cameras."

"Good. So, no-one but you watched this...Right? And no-one else will see it, and no copies are made?"

"Only me, and no hardcopies...I'll delete everything that shows you, the girl, the workers, and the other crew. Cops will come to view the footage at some stage but don't worry...By the time I'm finished with it, it'll look like the park's been empty since midday."

"Good. I'll buy you a beer if you're at the High Council ceremony later."

"Hey, I've heard all about the fun and games that go on at those special ceremonies." KA72 grinned. "This will be my first, and I wouldn't miss it for the world."

KA43 gave a wicked laugh then ended the call.

Before he set about doctoring the CCTV footage, KA72 copied the digital recording of the abduction onto his personal USB memory stick then hid the stick in his rucksack. Most within the organization would have considered his actions a betrayal of trust, because retaining such evidence placed all members at risk. But he understood the nature of his relationship with its leaders better than most. He was a soldier in an army like no other, loyal to the cause, yet essentially an assassin for hire. And KA's High Council were anonymous and ruthless men, who at any moment might decide that he knew too much.

The memory stick was more than insurance. It was KA72's lifeline.

TWO

"Porter, Nadia's gone missin' and it's your frickin' fault."

Harsh liniment fumes filled the closet sized office and whacked Dan Porter on the nose. He stopped typing and blinked stinging eyes then peered over the monitor towards his accuser.

Eddy Tindall stood in the doorway, sheened in sweat and hissing like a peeved cobra. "You hear what I said, Porter? I thought you're different from other cops," he shouted above the ruckus behind him. "But you aint. You're just another useless pig who don't give a shit."

Porter frowned as guts churned. Nadia was Eddy's younger sister, a gem of a girl who brought him homemade biscuits whenever she came to watch Eddy train. "She's been missing since when?"

Eddy jammed boxing gloves into black thighs. "Since she finished school this afternoon. I wanted to pick her up because of what's going on." His face flushed purple. "But I couldn't, 'cos you pricks made me come here."

Porter blew hot air through vibrating lips. He stood and stretched his back then strolled to Eddy. He looked past him, to the boxing ring in the middle of the gym. Tugger Walford leaned against the ropes wearing a faded blue singlet and white shorts. He held a punching pad in one hand and phone against his ear in the other.

"Calm down, champ," Porter said. "Tell me wh--."

"Nah, stuff your program." Eddy ripped the gloves off and threw them at Porter's feet. "Don't care if you lock me up. I'm outta here…" He turned and ran.

Porter stepped into the grey gym and watched him shove the exit door then slam it shut. The other boys stopped training, a flock of laughing kookaburras. He told them to get back to it, beckoned Tugger to join him, then trudged into the office and fell into a chair. He rubbed his jaw and stared at the biscuit jar on the desk. When Nadia had given it to him she'd blushed and giggled. Had the bastards taken her too?

Tugger ambled in, sat opposite and rested hairy arms on a pot belly. An ex-boxer with a mangled nose to show for it, he helped Porter run a boxing program for juvenile offenders at Redfern Youth Centre every Tuesday afternoon. He was a dark-skinned sexagenarian with a resemblance to Danny DeVito, with tufts of white hair circling a bald crown and a comical face that made others smile. His official title was 'ACLO Walford', as the Aboriginal Community Liaison Officer for City of Sydney police command. He'd held the position for a year but had played peace-keeper between cops and kooris for decades.

"Sorry about that, Port," Tugger said. "Not makin' excuses for him, but Eddy's frantic. Just spoke to his mum and they've no idea where Nadia is."

"No worries, been called much worse. And that tantrum just now isn't why I've decided to take him off the program."

"What? Thought you were on his side?"

"Cut that bullshit, mate, you know I am. But he's nearly eighteen and needs to start helping himself. And it's probably out of my control now…"

"How's that?"

"I just read the latest lab report. He's tested positive to crystal meth again."

"Bugger…Will Juvenile Justice want him locked up this time?"

"Reckon so, with his record full of petty thefts then three armed robberies in a month…He was lucky to be here."

"I've told him that, to pull his head in. Even tried gettin' him to church."

Porter smirked. "I bet that went down like maggots in a meat pie…"

Tugger folded arms. "Wouldn't hurt you either, comin' to Sunday mass now and again."

"Reckon I'd rather be at a Justin Bieber concert, and that's saying something…"

"A non-believer eh?"

"Nah, there's a few things I believe in."

"Well, Eddy weren't real keen on the church invite either. He's been hangin' with that Neilsen grub just to spite me."

"I reckon he'd be dealing too…"

"Then doin' a bit of time might be good for him? It could get him off the gear and away from Neilsen."

Porter glanced at the biscuit jar and saw an image of Nadia's smiling face. She seemed happy. Strange, because a stabbing pain in his chest told him she was far from it. He checked his watch. "It's only just gone six…They sure Nadia's not with friends?"

"She always says if she aint goin' straight home. Friends aint seen her. It's a worry."

"Too right…" Porter draped a navy-blue tie around his neck then buttoned cuffs of a turquoise business

11

shirt. "I've got a meeting later with the new Police Minister and a few other pollies about Azelia, the missing girls taskforce I've been working on. But I'll be out searching for her afterwards…"

"What's the new fella's name again? He took over from that Abercrombie fella who died in the car crash last month, right?"

"Yeah…Ken Moorecroft. And word is, he hates cops. He reckons we don't work hard enough…"

"Hah, well you tell him that it's you lot and the nurses and the ambos who are out there twenty-four-seven wipin' society's smelly arse. Not him and his gutless mates…Am I needed at the meetin'?"

"Nah, it's only political bullshit…"

Tugger nodded.

"Steve Williams is worried Moorecroft's gunna pull the plug on Azelia," Porter said. Detective Superintendent Steve Williams was his boss at City Central police station. They'd been good mates for ten years since playing in police rugby teams together.

"You're kiddin'?" Tugger unfolded arms and leaned forward. "How many girls we up to now?"

"Forty-six in three months. Steve says that Commissioner Delaney, John Sinclair, and Bonnetti the Immigration Minister are all pushing for Azelia to get canned."

"Why?"

"I can understand Delaney's motives…That shopping mall bombing in Bankstown last week has got the public worried. There's mounting pressure on him to nab the ISIS blokes who've claimed responsibility, so he wants to move our funds and resources over to his anti-terrorism squads. But I thought the other two would be fighting to keep Azelia going..."

"Honestly, what hope have we got when Sinclair the frickin' Aboriginal Affairs Minister doesn't give a toss? You'd all be crazy to stop investigatin'."

"Yeah and it's getting worse...There's been a spike, with another fifteen missing in the past week. Let's hope Steve's wrong."

"Bloody oath...How do I tell families around here that their girls are vanishin' but you coppers can't be arsed lookin' for 'em?"

"I don't reckon the Asian and African communities will be too impressed either."

Tugger scoffed. "That supposed to make us kooris feel better, 'cos a few Asian and Somali girls are missin' too? More than thirty of these girls are Koori, Port. No wonder family's like the Tindall's are pissed. They know your mob aint doin' enough."

"Eh don't forget, you work for the cops now. My mob is your mob...But you're spot on, and we can't blame 'em for being angry."

"They'll show just how angry if Moorecroft ends the taskforce...They're scared 'cos nothin' like this has happened before."

"Yeah, two of the girls are from Amber's school and Jane's beside herself."

Tugger lowered black eyes. "I shouldn't rant, not when you've got your own girl to worry about. Just frustrated..."

"I get it...But cops on Azelia have been flat out, working hours of unpaid overtime. It's piss-weak bosses skimping on resources that let us down."

13

"Yep, and I bet they'd find the overtime money if young white girls were missin'…"

Porter couldn't disagree.

"Listen, Port, kooris are talkin' of protests and riots and they want change. And they still don't trust you fellas, despite your bosses' tellin' the media different."

"But they trust you, mate, kids through to the elders. If you ask for calm they'll listen."

"Nah, it's like you said…I'm workin' for the cops now and trouble-makin' kooris don't like it..." Tugger reached into a pocket and threw a red pamphlet on the desk. "They're listenin' to fellas like him."

Porter scanned the pamphlet. "Where'd this come from?"

"They're all over the city. He's put ads in papers too."

"Who?" He paused to read from it. "This…Lionel Roberts?"

"Yep, he's the new Aboriginal rights fella for Legal Aid. Based here in Sydney."

"I didn't know Legal Aid had human rights advocates…"

"Some judge created the positions back in '07 after those interventions up in the Territory. Every State's supposed to have one. It's only taken twelve years to get ours…"

"You know this Roberts bloke?"

"Yep, since he were a pup...He grew up here in Redfern, a good Koori kid. I haven't seen him for a bit 'cos he's been out west."

"Roberts?" Porter scratched a cheek. "I know most Koori families around here. But not them…"

14

"Lionel don't have real family around here, not that we know of. He were only days old when the nuns found him dumped on the steps at Saint Francis. Father Roberts, bless his soul, took him in and raised him."

Porter had attended police funerals at Saint Francis, the oldest church in South Sydney. "When was that?"

"Around '79 I guess, 'cos Lionel's forty this year…"

"Same here. Reckon I've spent a lot less time in church though."

Tugger chuckled. "Lionel, or Lio as we call him, was always of strong faith. Takes his job real serious and from what fellas tell me he's a jet. Made a name for himself out bush and is lookin' to do the same here."

Porter read aloud from the pamphlet. "Police must do more to find Sydney's missing girls. The incompetent police hierarchy has failed to protect our sisters and daughters. Trust me to save them. Any information helps. Stronger, together, let's bring them home. Contact my office at daa, daa, daa…Confidentiality assured. Lionel Roberts, Bachelor of Law with honors, University of Sydney…"

"Like I said, he's full of gusto with plenty of support already."

"Incompetent police hierarchy." Porter sniggered. "No argument there...But why Legal Aid? With honors in law he'd make squillions at a private firm."

"Money's never been an issue."

"Yeah?"

"Other orphans at Saint Francis went to state schools. But Lio went to posh, private ones. He didn't work during uni…Someone outside the church sponsored his education. No small change…"

"Who?"

"No-one knows. Not even Lio, I've asked him."

"Strange…" Porter read aloud from the pamphlet, imitating the baritone bravado of his childhood hero, Roger Ramjet. "Trust me, to save them…" He chuckled. "This bloke's on a one-man crusade. Bit naïve isn't he?"

"No, Port, he's different…"

"Well, reckon I'll come across him sooner or later. And he's spot on, that we're not doing enough." He waved the pamphlet. "But this breeds mistrust. It's hard enough getting info from kooris without sprouting paranoia…"

"Or the truth? Now you're being naïve…Kooris are born with paranoia about your mob."

Porter smirked and returned the pamphlet. *Your mob.* He knotted the tie then finger-combed his dark-brown fringe to the left. He scratched the scar that ran two inches down the middle of his forehead, the permanent reminder of a knife-wielding junkie's attempted lobotomy, then yawned as he bent to straighten trousers over polished black shoes.

He stood and hauled an imitation-leather briefcase from the desk. "Get Roberts on side, Tugger, for the girls' sake."

"Leave it with me…"

"Good man."

"And you talk some sense into them politicians tonight. Tell 'em they'll lose the streets if they scrap your taskforce and have more blood on their hands."

Porter turned in the doorway. "We're fighting an uphill battle against these drongos but I'll give it a crack…And don't fret, because Nadia will be okay."

The pain in his chest stabbed again. Why would Tugger believe him, when he didn't believe himself?

"You said that about them other girls, months ago, and they haven't come home yet."

"Yeah, but I will find 'em." Porter nodded. "If it kills me..."

THREE

Lionel Roberts sipped a cool drink and appreciated expensive gin as it slid down his throat. He placed the glass on a side table, sank into the leather armchair, and hummed along to the Bob Marley tune sounding overhead while he glanced about the soft-lit room. The African-themed 'Rhino Bar' in the heart of Sydney's law district had become the watering hole of choice for its elite. On this Tuesday night it was packed with a young and beautiful clientele of lawyers, solicitors, clerks and prosecutors. They buzzed in animated chatter.

He checked his phone. 10.17pm. Fred Klose had said he'd arrive an hour ago. Doubt thudded against his chest and he sensed his friend wouldn't show. But surely Fred had forgiven him? The passing of time usually healed old wounds. Maybe it hadn't?

He looked up from the phone and realised his questions would soon be answered.

Klose strode forward in a tight-fitting shirt and jeans. He was a lean 6'2, with a dazzling smile as wide as his broad shoulders.

Lionel rose to meet him. They hugged and thumped backs then sat opposite each other.

"You slack son of a bitch, it's about time you invited me for a drink." Klose grinned. "Is it true you've been back in the city for months?"

"Thanks for coming on such short notice...And sorry, I've been so busy in this new job."

"But aren't I your best buddy? Told me so in your text message, only two hours ago…"

Lionel knew to ignore his sarcastic sense of humor. "You always have been, and always will be…" He called a waitress and ordered two gin tonics. He waited for her to leave, noticed Klose's bulging biceps and remembered how to feed his ego. "Been working out, Fred? You're still looking fit..."

Klose smirked and leaned back in the chair. "And you haven't changed one bit either…Still long and gangly, with your wild Jimi Hendrix hair and that piss-poor excuse for a goatee hanging from your chin. And hell dude, what's with the all the grey bits?"

"I'm el naturale…" He pointed at Klose's head. "Unlike some, I don't ask my barber to lather me in peroxide…"

Two middle-aged men, they giggled like they had during their time as law students at Sydney University. They'd bonded from the start, drawn together by common interests and similar life stories.

Klose, like Lionel, had never known his Aboriginal mother. He'd shown Lionel a few pictures over the years and told what he knew of her. She'd been pretty, with a thin nose and fairer skin than most kooris.

Klose had been raised by his father, Josef, a German immigrant who'd arrived in Australia in the late 1950s. With blond hair, honey-colored skin, a prominent nose and chiseled jaw, Fred resembled a Scandinavian snowboarder. Few picked him as a half-caste Koori.

On completing their law degrees they'd gone in separate directions. Lionel practiced law. Klose had joined the Federal Police to enforce it. They'd kept in touch through emails and the odd phone call but hadn't seen each other for five years. Lionel knew the reason they'd drifted apart, but now wasn't the time to discuss it.

"How are the Feds treating you?" he said. "Still working security detail for the Attorney General?"

"Nope, I'm off that."

Lionel sighed under his breath. It wasn't the answer he'd hoped for. "Permanently?"

"Yep, bored stiff in our Sydney office for now." Klose smirked. "Does have some benefits though…"

"I'm sure it does…" Lionel hesitated, unsure how to proceed. "Do you know Karen Flintoff from the AG's legal section?"

"Yep…" Klose locked hands behind his head. "Why?"

"How well do you know her?"

"Not very, and don't see her much these days. She's attached to the Pitt Street office."

Lionel frowned. "Yes, she is."

"What's the problem?"

"Nothing…"

Klose leaned forward. Brown eyes probed Lionel's face. "What's going on, Lio? You're being weird."

"Okay…I need your help and don't know how to ask. It's complicated, a very sensitive matter."

"Bud, sensitive's my middle name…Tell me."

Lionel sucked a breath then let it out slowly. "Alright. Not long before I messaged you earlier, I received a call from Senator Nick Galios. Heard of him?"

"Yep, leader of the Greens, been around for ages. Always fucking up the policies of the major parties,

20

right? Anti-police, anti-government. A bleeding-heart refugee lover, from what I've read..."

"I can't agree with that...He's a great man and one of the few politicians supporting the indigenous. Anyhow, he contacted me regarding an issue of great concern, and seems keen to shame the government once again."

"In relation to?"

"Kate Bonnetti told him she attended a meeting earlier where police terminated their investigation into the missing girls."

"The Azelia taskforce? Fuck me, that's insane."

"Yes, it seems that Commissioner Delaney is more interested in slaying imaginary terrorists...Nick is furious, and fears they'll start targeting all Muslims. He says we need to hold the government and police accountable for neglecting these girls."

"Damn right...Through a public inquiry?"

"Yes, but as Nick rightly says, the Human Rights Commission won't grant us one on the basis of missing girls. It's too easy for the cops, in the current climate, to suggest that terrorism is the greater concern..."

"Then how?"

"There's been a significant increase in the reported abuse of Koori children in far-western communities, especially in the past year. We'll focus on that."

"You've lost me, bud... How does that help find the girls?"

"In the short term, it doesn't. But if we can show that the government and police have failed to deal with issues out west, we can secure a parliamentary inquiry to delve into it. From there we can broaden its scope, and paint a picture of wide-scale neglect that puts pressure on the government to resume Azelia and do more to locate those who've disappeared."

"It's a solid plan…"

"And hopefully, going forward, it'll promote positive changes to government thinking. We can make a real difference here, Fred."

"I agree…So, why'd you ask about Karen Flintoff?"

Lionel hesitated, aware of the risks in trusting anyone but himself with the task. But what choice did he have?

"I need someone to dig for dirt on her," he blurted.

Klose's eyes narrowed. "Why? What's she been up to?"

"Don't know. That's my problem. I thought you were still guarding the Attorney General and had access to her…"

"Ah, now I get it. But isn't she small fry?"

"Indeed…Yet somehow she's on the AG's panel that assesses all human rights related submissions. The requests for public inquiries and so on…"

The waitress returned, smiled and handed them drinks.

They watched her saunter away.

Lionel clicked fingers in time to an unknown reggae song then turned back to him. "What were we talking about?"

"The AG's assessment panel…Who are the others on it?"

"Retired Judge Charles McKinlay's the Chairman. And there's John Sinclair."

"McKinlay? He'll be a bitch to get past, he loves the cops. Is Legal Aid supporting your submission?"

Lionel scoffed. "My boss is gutless, he'd never support it, and I don't intend to inform anyone there about it. I'm a realist, Fred, who's lived in this skin long enough to know certain people there despise me and will do anything to see me fail."

"I know what you're saying, bud. People hate what they fear. And you're their worst nightmare, a koori bush lawyer looking to rock a boat that's been anchored in calm waters for eons…"

Lionel smiled at the imagery. "Yes, ignorance is bliss…But luckily there are those like Galios to hold the powers that be accountable. He didn't say too much, but seems confident he can get Sinclair on our side. As you say, McKinlay's opposition is a given. It comes down to Flintoff's vote. We get her, we get the inquiry."

"Which is where I come in with the dirt?"

"Yes…Can you help me, Fred?"

Klose said nothing, face stern as a terracotta warrior.

Lionel waited. He'd soon know if he'd been forgiven.

After what seemed an eternity, Klose's face broke into a smile. "You're my brother from another mother, and you know I'll do what I can."

Lionel exhaled towards the African sky. "Thank you…"

Klose continued with child-like exuberance. "Luck happens to be on your side."

Lionel leaned forward. "How so?"

"Yours truly is banging a hot little secretary from Flintoff's office. And she's the worst gossip in the department, hands down."

"Sounds good, but won't she wonder why you're asking questions and go straight to her?"

"Don't worry, bud, she's under my charming spell. And if there's dirt to use on Karen Flintoff, she'll know it."

"Wait a minute…I said, dig, for dirt. Who said anything about using it against her?" Lionel cleared his throat to mimic a nineteenth-century English Lord. "That, my dear boy, would be blackmail, the pastime of scoundrels…"

"You serious?" Klose held his stomach as though holding back laughter. "Your powers of manipulation are legendary. How else did you trump me at uni?" They both laughed. "Who digs for dirt without wanting to bury someone in it?"

Lionel spoke slow and deliberate. "You're a special friend. I appreciate it. Find what you can, the more shocking the better…And thanks again."

"For what? Haven't helped yet…"

"For your forgiveness. I know you loved Megan. We never meant to hurt you."

Klose's face reddened. "That was what, six years ago? She's old news, bud, and I've had plenty warming my bed since then. She chose you, simple..." He held arms out. "And now neither of us have her."

"I heard she's married to a rich French guy in Paris…"

Klose stood and avoided eye contact. "I'll be in touch…" He started to leave.

"Thanks…And Fred, one last thing."

Klose's eyebrows arched as he turned to face him.

"When it's all over you'll remember this day with pride." Lionel smiled. "Because it's the day we started to change this world for the better..."

FOUR

Porter woke earlier than he wanted to on Wednesday morning. His red brick, two-story house in the heart of western-Sydney's suburbia had never been insulated, and the chill of winter filled his lungs and made him cough. His head throbbed as though eyeballs had been drawn out through ears. He stumbled into the bathroom to urinate, recoiled at the sight of blood-shot eyes in the mirror then headed downstairs.

He yawned, dawdled to the kitchen counter and turned to face the middle of the room. "Good morning ladies."

Jane sat at the table. Her eyes remained fixed on a magazine. "Guess so…"

Amber jumped up from her seat and pecked his cheek. "Morning Dan, the kettle's boiled," she said in a cockney accent with an Australian twang. She wore a pink robe over mocha skin and long black hair in a ponytail. Taller than most fifteen-year-old girls, she had legs up to her armpits.

He opened a coffee jar, smirked and nodded towards Jane. "What's up with Rhianna today?"

Jane despised the nickname her fellow nurses had given her, and Porter knew it. She had an uncanny resemblance to the famous RnB singer – tall and sexy, with a similar cute nose and pouting mouth.

Amber giggled into her cereal.

Jane kept her head down. "Not funny, da both of you." She glanced up at him then back to the magazine.

26

"Don't know what's worse? Da girls at work calling me that stupid name, or them calling you 'Russ'?"

The younger nurses had swooned over Porter at the hospital's most recent Christmas party and told Jane he resembled Russell Crowe. Handsome, they'd said, in the same rugged way.

He smiled. "C'mon babe, is it my fault I'm a dead ringer for Maximus Meridius?"

She studied him. "These days you look more like da raggedy Russell, da one in Body of Lies. You sure aint no gladiator…"

"You obviously forget about when you seduced me? You said my deep, husky voice sounded just like Maximus…" 'Gladiator' had long been Porter's favorite movie. He held a fist high as though wielding a sword. "On my command, unleash hell!"

Amber laughed and coughed up cereal.

Jane scoffed. "I seduced you? You're still drunk…"

Amber giggled. "And you've woken half the neighbors."

"You came home late again, Dan…" Jane sighed. "Guess I should be grateful though, at least you made it past da couch this time."

He took a deep breath and prepared for battle. "Had a mongrel of a day then worked past midnight searching for the girls. And yeah, I had a few beers with Betts afterwards. Was only two or so when I got in, right?"

"Four thirty-three a.m…" Jane's eyes darted over him. "And from da state of you, it was more than a few."

He made a coffee then sat next to her and placed feet on Amber's lap. "Well, I feel like crap too if it cheers you up any…"

"It would be nice for Amber and I to eat dinner with you once in a while."

Amber huffed. "Geez, don't bring me into this. I'm going to watch tele..."

Porter waited for her to leave the kitchen. "Babe, if I wanna have a beer after work, I will."

"Oh yes I know, it helps you coppers unwind. To deal with da stress, right?" Jane's face contorted in a scowl. "Wah di rass mun!" She flung the magazine across the kitchen.

He frowned and tried to decipher the abuse she'd hurled in Jamaican slang. Then he grinned, because only Jane could sound that cool and angry at the same time.

She growled. "Don't you smile at me like that, Dan Porter."

He realized he'd pushed too far and tried to pull her close.

She leaned back. "Don't touch me…" Her voice rose. "Think you da only one who has terrible days at work? Well, I did too…

"Babe, I'm sor--."

"But I came home and cooked your dinner, that's still in da fridge, ironed our clothes and helped Amber with homework…And guess what? Didn't need one beer to help me through it." She stood, brown eyes glazed, her gorgeous face furrowed.

He held her wrist. "Sit down. Please?"

She shook her head as she sat. "Can't go on like this. You're drinking way too much. Amber's been through it already and I won't put her through it again..."

He leaned in to kiss her and she pulled away. "Again, I'm sorry babe..." He put a hand on her knee. "Can't sleep sometimes and I dunno why..." His conscience groaned at the lie. He knew the reasons he couldn't sleep and they'd multiplied since Sydney's girls had started disappearing. But he would never burden her with his problems. "The booze helps..."

She gazed into his eyes. "Hate when we fight like this...I know you're tired and not sleeping well. I hear you every night..."

"Hear me?"

"Yes, when you do sleep. Talking, yelling...Screaming, kicking, punching. Some nights I swear you're gunna knock me out of da bed. It's like you're having nightmares."

He sipped coffee and stared at the fridge.

She leaned closer. "Will you let me help?"

He had to give her something. "Just feel like my career's going nowhere. It's getting me down..."

"Why don't you put yourself up for promotion?"

"They'd never promote me. I've rubbed too many bosses the wrong way. They want pimple-faced social science grads these days, not old hard heads. It's just a phase, babe...I'll get over it."

He kissed her cheek, brushed away silky black hair and ran soft kisses down her neck. She chased his lips with her own.

"Amber?" he called out. "Where're my pancakes you promised?" He stood and stretched.

Jane pulled her satin nightie over ample bosom then studied him over the coffee mug. "Dan, we really need to t--."

"I don't wanna tell Tugger what happened at the meeting last night. You won't be too over the moon either..."

"What are you talking about?"

Amber walked into the kitchen and draped an arm over Jane's shoulder. "Heard yelling. Everything okay?"

Jane smiled.

Porter ruffled Amber's hair. "All's good...Was just about to tell your mum, that pompous idiot Moorecroft has scrapped the taskforce I've been working on."

"What?" Jane's mouth stayed half open as she took hold of Amber's hand.

"Don't have enough money they reckon, and Delaney convinced them to prioritise his anti-terrorism squads...The Missing Persons Unit is taking over, which is a worry 'cos those stooges struggle to find a stray coffee mug. Steve's leaving me and Betts on the missing girls' cases, but that's it..."

"Only two plain-clothes investigators for such an important job?" Jane scoffed. "How do those bastards live with themselves?" She turned to Amber. "You're staying home, no school."

"But mum, I've gotta go...The netball team trials are on today."

"Nope, it's too dangerous. Crazy sickos are plucking pretty young black girls from da streets, and they're not taking my baby girl."

He winked at Amber to let her know he'd take care of it. Her eyes sparkled in reply.

"I'll drive her to school and bring her home," he said. "Until this is over."

Jane groaned. "Okay, okay…And days you can't, I will."

Amber pecked her cheek. "Love ya."

"Don't leave da school grounds until Dan's there to pick you up. Clear?"

Amber saluted. "Yes, ma'am."

Jane faced him. "I see what you mean about Tugger now…" A phone vibrated on the table. "It's yours." She glanced at the screen. "Claire Duggan?"

He picked up the phone. "She's the intell analyst on Azelia…"

Amber had a mischievous glint in her eye. "Hmm, Claire…She pretty?"

Jane glared at her.

Porter pressed the 'answer' button. What couldn't wait until he started work later in the day? "G'day Claire…"

"Sorry to bother you at home Dan, but I was asked to pass this on right away."

"No worries. Go ahead."

"We've got a solid lead on Nadia Tindall."

"Yeah?"

"Two council gardeners didn't return to their depot in Redfern last night. There'd been no sign of them, or their truck. Where do you think they were working yesterday?"

"Surprise me…"

"Kings Park."

"In Redfern? The one her mum said that Nadia walks through on the way home?"

"Yep. Crime Scene guys combed the area at first light this morning but unfortunately found nothing worthwhile. You won't believe this…"

"Reckon I will…"

"Twenty minutes ago, close to seven, the council truck was found burnt out. Near Newcastle's shipping terminal."

"Newcastle? It's two hours away, a fair hike in a stolen truck…And the missing council blokes?"

"Inside it. Fried…"

"Bloody hell…" Porter scratched behind his ear. "Does Steve Williams know?"

"He told me to call you, and wants you and Bettsy to check it out asap…And, oh, another report came in that we didn't have access to at the meeting last night… An anonymous caller reported a vehicle of interest. A white van of unknown registration with a red logo on the side door, not further described. It was last seen leaving Kings Park at high speed, at approximately 3.30pm yesterday."

"Anything from CCTV?"

"Redfern Detectives checked it out late last night. There's nothing of Nadia, so we're assuming she walked around the park, or got taken before she reached it. The footage shows the council truck coming and going throughout the morning, but it's not seen in the afternoon. We've got nothing more regarding possible suspects…Anyhow, I'll send you the location of the burnout truck."

"Okay, cheers. Catch up later." He sensed Jane's eyes on him as he ended the call.

"We're not chilling out together today, are we?" She placed hands on his shoulders, made a sad puppy face and circled him with seductive swagger. "I was looking forward to some alone time when you got back from taking Amber…"

Amber pretended to vomit. "Mum. Gross..."

He took Jane's hands and kissed the back of each. "Sorry babe, I've gotta get to work. Something humungous has popped up." He hurried from the kitchen.

"Hah, I wish it would, Dan Porter," she called out. "I wish it would…"

FIVE

Who murdered the two council gardeners? And if the same mob have Nadia, where is she? Those were Porter's questions to himself when he jolted awake in the passenger seat. His partner, Senior Constable Ian Betts, managed to find another pothole as he steered the sedan onto the freeway exit towards Sydney.

Porter glanced at his watch, 1.26pm, then out the window. He'd slept for most of the trip south from Newcastle. He caught a whiff of a foul odor and turned to accuse Betts of farting, then pulled the shirt collar towards his nose. It reeked of death, of charred human flesh.

He'd seen plenty of dead'uns in his time and forgotten the look of most, but their rancid smells stayed in his nostrils, hair and mouth for years. His nose twitched as he remembered the first 'deceased person' job he'd attended more than fifteen years ago. Gas had billowed from the old lady as he scooped loose body parts from a murky bathtub. They'd looked like rotten eggs floating in a stagnant creek, and had smelt even worse.

"Yep, you do stink to high hell…" Betts said. "Welcome back to the world. Good nap by the sounds of it, you were snoring like a trooper."

Porter yawned. "Serious? Sorry mate, I'm shattered..." He sniffed at his collar again. "Hope there's a fresh shirt in my locker, I smell like a frickin' cremation pit. And I noticed you didn't go anywhere near that truck..."

Betts chuckled. His neck wobbled like a turkey's. "What, and reek like you do?" He rubbed a fat cheek. At thirty-eight, a year younger than Porter, he hadn't aged well. "Whoever roasted those gardeners did a thorough job of it."

"Not wrong. They've left us sweet fuck all."

"A few tire tracks and some wind-blown boot marks...Doubt they'll find prints or DNA."

"No chance. That crime scene's as clean as two blokes inside a chargrilled Isuzu can be."

"Stop making me hungry. Barbequed chook for lunch?"

"Sick bastard...What's your take on the tire tracks?"

"That none led out of the clearing? They torched the truck then took off out of there..."

"Yeah, in a helicopter...And from the lack of markings on the ground, I don't reckon it touched down."

"I'm guessing it wouldn't be easy to board a copter that's hovering like that?"

"It's not, which means these blokes are well trained. Probably ex-military. And if Nadia was with 'em she could be anywhere by now..."

Betts thumped a palm against his forehead. "Shit, I forgot to ask that Newcastle boss about their canvass."

"Good thing I didn't..." Porter took a battered notebook from breast pocket. "You were too busy flirting with that probationary constable."

"You've gotta admit, Port, she did have a sensational rack on her..."

Porter laughed then read from the notebook. "The forensic blokes reckon the truck was torched between 2 and 3am this morning. As you saw yourself, there was nothing but industrial estate surrounding the crime scene. A nearby service road runs past a deserted army base then through to Newcastle's shipping terminal. The nearest residents are three clicks away. Ones they've spoken to saw and heard nothing."

"Any cameras on the service road? They usually keep tabs on trucks coming and going from the terminals…"

"No cameras, or any other means of knowing who used the road during the night."

"What's with the army base?"

"It's an abandoned world war two barracks. They're waiting on military clearance to search it later today."

"Good…Check your phone, it vibrated a while back."

Porter took his phone from the console and selected the first missed call.

"Dan?" Claire answered. "On your way back?"

"Will be at the office in ten. What's up?"

"I've just noticed a job that's been allocated to you guys. Computer dispatch, not for broadcast…"

"What is it?"

"Deceased female at Central Morgue. Thought I'd call and let you go straight there."

"Bloody hell, we're just returning from a smelly friggin' funeral pyre…"

"I told radio that…Want me to try giving it to another crew?"

"Nah, seems they want us to go…Cheers." He ended the call with a frustrated sigh.

"So?" Betts said.

"Another dead'un. Central Morgue."

"Why us?"

"Must be related to the missing girls…" Porter's gut knotted as he said it. He turned and grabbed a blue folder from the rear seat. It contained profiles and photos of forty-seven missing girls. Would he find one of them at the morgue?

"Fair enough. We can grab a bite to eat after it. I'm starving..."

"Yeah…" Porter said, distracted by a message Jane had sent at 10.15am. *'Call me, soon as you can.'* He saw she'd called eight times. Strange, because she rarely contacted him at work. He cursed the missed calls. He'd been too busy yacking to Betts or other cops when Jane had needed him.

Worry punched him in the guts. He pictured Amber giggling into a cereal bowl, and Nadia blushing as she handed him biscuits. He heard Jane howl. In pain, or in mourning?

His hands trembled as he called Jane's cell phone. It rang five times then diverted to voicemail. He tried the home phone. No answer. He gazed outside. Visions of Jane and Amber flashed through his head faster than the concrete jungle flew past the window. Jane's busy and can't answer, he tried to convince himself. Amber's safe at school, there's no need to worry.

Betts glanced at him. "You alright?"

"Yeah…" Porter lied. "I was just thinking, I've got a stack of paperwork to get done. The Neilsen brief's due next week and I haven't even started it." He rubbed an itchy armpit. Sweating, in the middle of winter? He closed eyes and stretched his forehead with index fingers.

"Neilsen…Armed robs?"

Porter opened his eyes. "Yeah, him and Eddy Tindall."

"I heard about Eddy losing the plot at boxing yesterday. You should've belted the cheeky prick..."

"Bit harsh isn't it? He was worried about Nadia…"

"Ah, got no time for those kids. Off their heads on ice and running around like they own the town."

"Was gunna take him off the program. Now I'm not sure. First his old man, and now his sister…"

"You're too fucking soft sometimes, Port. That kid was a waste of space long before his dad shot through."

"Eddy's not a bad kid. Just needs a bit of direction."

"A bullet's what he needs." Betts sniggered. "Would do us all a favor..."

Knots in Porter's gut tightened the closer they got to the morgue. Convinced the deceased female would be one of the missing girls, he whispered their names as each innocent face flashed through his mind. He tried Jane's phone again. No answer. Tight knots became a stabbing pain.

"Bloody hell, can't stand it, hurry up," he blurted.

Betts eyed him sideways and frowned. "Chill, mate, we're here…"

A few minutes later, Porter pressed an intercom button outside Central Morgue's rear entry.

"Hello?" A lifeless female voice crackled.

Porter announced them in his most serious baritone. He opened the glass door after it buzzed and unlocked, then led Betts down a grey corridor. They entered an office. Its furnishings were as dull as the lights were bright. A middle-aged woman approached, face frozen in a frown. She wore a white surgical gown, and her dark hair bundled under a net.

Porter presented a silver police badge.

She turned her nose up at it. "Diane Smith, morgue attendant on duty. You guys took your time as usual...Here for the deceased female?"

"Well, we're not here for a live one...." Porter matched her icy tone. He prided himself on being civil whenever possible but knew a bitch when he met one. "And it's not like she's got somewhere else to be..."

Smith scoffed, unlocked another door, and beckoned them to follow.

Betts prodded Porter's ribs then pointed at her. "We've already found the stiff."

"I reckon you're right..."

Porter rubbed his scrunched nose as they followed her into a narrow room. It reeked of disinfectant, as pleasant as death could be. Two rows of refrigerated steel cabinets hummed. Lined along opposite walls, they rose to the ceiling and were divided by a concrete walkway. Morgue drawers filled each cabinet. Ten drawers across, three drawers high.

Smith stopped in front of drawer number eleven, placed a gloved hand on the handle and turned to Porter. "I don't know a lot about this one..."

He noticed the name tag on the drawer. His chest heaved and his heart fell to the floor. Mind numb, he opened his mouth to speak but nothing came out.

Betts read the name tag aloud. "Unidentified black female..."

In Porter's mind, he saw Jane smile. He shivered and turned to Smith. "Someone brought her in with no idea of a name?" His voice croaked. "Doesn't make sense…How old is she?"

Betts put a hand on his shoulder.

Smith frowned at Porter. "You're shaking. Can't cope with the sight of a cold little corpse by now?"

Betts glared at her. "Listen you patronizing moron, he's seen more blood and gore than you ever will." He waved a hand around the room. "Think it's all clean and tidy like this when we find these bodies? When they're mangled in cars, drowned in rivers, hanging from fucking trees…"

She shrugged, wide-eyed.

"Porter's got other things going on, so wipe that smug look off your face and open the fucking drawer..."

She recoiled then searched through a set of keys. Betts stood over her and breathed loud. She inserted the key into drawer eleven and turned it. The drawer rolled out.

"Wait!" Porter lunged forward and pushed it back inside the cabinet. "I need to make a phone call first."

She opened her mouth to protest. Betts held a finger to pursed lips. She backed away.

Porter stared at the phone and tried to focus the blurred images in his head. Jane kissed him. Amber jumped on the bed in her favorite pink pyjamas. Nadia Tindall cheered when Eddy knocked another opponent to the canvas. More than forty other faces flashed through his mind, of the missing girls whose photos filled the folder he clutched to chest.

He called Jane's phone and her voicemail message greeted him. He tried their home phone and let it ring for two minutes. He glanced at Betts, feeling more

40

crook in the guts with each passing second. It rang out so he called her cell phone again. He rammed a shaking finger onto the 'end call' button when he heard her voicemail message and turned back to Smith.

She placed a hand on the drawer. "Now? I have other things to do you know?"

He moved opposite her. "What you mean, you don't have much on this one?"

She pointed to the name tag.

"That's it? No paperwork from body handlers?" Betts said. "They brought her in from…?"

She shrugged, grabbed the handle and pulled. The drawer rolled out to reveal a black plastic bag.

Porter clamped a hand on her wrist and stopped the drawer from rolling further. He leaned closer with eyes fixed on hers. "Bullshit, where'd she come in from?"

She shook her wrist free. "I answered the rear buzzer at eleven-thirty this morning. This bag was on the driveway, outside the delivery door. No paperwork, tags, nothing. Spoke to my supervisor, body handlers, and the security guys. No-one knew anything about it."

Porter checked his watch. "It's nearly two…When did you report it?"

Smith sighed. "Straight away. Knew it wasn't the average stiff in a bag. The woman on the phone told me to leave it there until police and forensics arrived."

"Why didn't you?" Betts said.

"Members of the public could see it, and we keep the back door clear for deliveries. She said to secure the body and not touch it. I haven't…Well, except for a quick peek to determine gender. Wish I hadn't really. It's quite disturbing, even for me…"

"How'd you move her?"

41

"Security guards helped me...The woman on the phone said special police would come to check it out, said it related to a missing girls' case or something." She looked them up and down. "I guess standards have slipped?"

Betts grunted. "What's disturbing about it?"

"You'll see, if I can open the damn bag?"

He glanced at Porter. "Leave us mate, I'll do this alone..."

Porter swallowed. Bile burned his throat. His pulse quickened. "Nah, I'm okay, open it."

Smith pulled the handle. The whole drawer rolled from the cabinet.

Porter studied the bag. Two meters in length, half a meter wide. Crumpled. A hump near the middle. Which end was the head at? He bent closer and his eyes traced an imaginary outline of the body inside. It was too short for both Jane and Amber, he tried to convince himself. And maybe Nadia as well...

"Wrong end..." Smith sniggered then pointed. "Or do you have pictures of feet in your folder there?"

Porter flashed his best 'fuck you' glare and stepped to the other end of the drawer.

Smith ripped the zipper sideways. The body-bag fell open.

SIX

Lionel Roberts gazed down from the office to the wondrous expanse of emerald-green water that sparkled as sunshine burst through cotton-like clouds. The view from the Circular Quay skyscraper left him with tingling skin every time he saw it. His previous workplace, an oven in far-west Galargonville, had a faded picture of the Opera House on its wall. Now he worked in a modern office block in the city, with air-conditioning and a view of the real thing.

He watched the green and yellow passenger ferries rumble to all corners of Sydney harbor. Faster vessels skimmed past them. Catamarans glided. Luxurious yachts held anchor in calm bays. Years away from the city had given him a greater appreciation of its beauty. And of its contrasts. From the busy yet tranquil harbor, to the CBD's concrete chaos far below him.

He'd always called Sydney home, in a physical sense at least. It was the place he'd lived most of his life. But in his heart and deep within his soul, he sensed his real home was in a far-away place. Ghosts of ancestors would visit his dreams, urge him to follow and then quickly disappear. It troubled him, not knowing who they were and where they wanted to take him.

The daydream ended when his phone's ringtone blared the chorus of 'Treaty' by Yothu Yindi. He checked the time before answering. 2.02pm. "Lionel Roberts speaking…"

"Lionel, it's Nick Galios…Calling about our conversation last night."

"Mr Galios, thanks for getting back to me so soon."

"But not with what you want to hear I'm afraid…"

Lionel frowned. "In what way?"

"I rang Judge McKinlay first thing this morning. His response when I explained the increased abuse in the far-west and your proposed inquiry into it, was icy, to say the least…"

"You presented the full facts?"

"Of course, those I knew." Galios scoffed. "He said to come back with concrete evidence and not, in his words, pie in the sky rubbish."

"Ouch."

"Yes. His disdainfully dismissive nature is unique, even for a retired judge."

"Did he give reasons for rejecting it?"

"None. Apparently, you and I are a disgrace to society with purely selfish agendas."

"Wow, he didn't hold back, and strange that he commented on my motives. I know all about him and have followed his career. He knows nothing of me…"

"Don't bet on it, that old fox knows everything."

"You're probably right, and his opposition is no surprise. Every state's Police Commissioner supported his nomination for Chair of the Human Rights Commission. They can't afford another inquiry into police neglect and have entrusted him with ensuring it never happens."

"And then there's his well-documented hatred of terrorists…We're wasting our time on him…" Galios' tone became despondent. "In fact, have I made a mistake by contacting you about this issue?"

"What do you mean?"

"Last night I was angry. And in truth, it was a result of the increased focus on terrorism more than anything else…I've been asking myself…What will yet another parliamentary inquiry into police neglect actually achieve?"

Lionel huffed. "Accountability and transparency, for a start."

"I have my doubts…"

"Yet you didn't have any regarding the inquiry in '96...Have you stopped caring?"

"Everything was in our favor back then, Lionel. International pressure, a nation with a growing conscience, the national reconciliation convention being held the next year…We were always going to get what we wanted."

"Okay, granted…But what's changed since then? Not a lot…My ultimate goal, Mr Galios, is to achieve constitutional recognition."

"A noble pursuit. However, it's far removed from the inquiry you're after. Isn't it?"

"I don't agree. It's all related. I must seize the opportunity that the abuse and missing girls case presents, terrible and sad as it is, and bring to the front what is continually being pushed to the rear. Out of sight and out of mind…"

"Look, Judge Mills made fifty-four recommendations in the 'Bringing them Home' report. As far as the Human Rights Commission and international observers are concerned the government has met every requirement. Australia's past wrongs have been righted, whether we agree or not."

"On paper, Mr Galios, yes. But not in practice…I've been out in the far-west, have seen the neglect and abuse first hand. The government and the police continue to ignore it."

Galios sighed. "I'm sorry Lionel, I must withdraw my support…"

Lionel tugged at curls. How could he make Galios reconsider? He smiled when he found the answer. "You do realize, that if I get my inquiry and force the government to resume Azelia, they'll have to take staff from their anti-terrorism strikeforce. Matilda. Which means there'll be less police to harass members of the minority groups you represent."

"I told you those concerns last night, but since then Commissioner Delaney has assured me there'll be no racial profiling by officers attached to Matilda."

Lionel laughed into the phone. "Mr Galios, I thought you'd know better than to trust Delaney. My source within the police says the targeting of young Muslim men will be the main strategy employed by the anti-terrorism squads."

"What source?"

"I can't say…" Lionel lied, because he didn't have one. "But they've proven to be extremely reliable in the past."

Galios said nothing for ten seconds. Lionel imagined his mind ticking over, precise as a Swiss watch.
"You're right, Lionel, we must hold this government more accountable. But without concrete evidence, and plenty of it, they'll simply deny there's a problem in the far west, or blame a shortage of resources and budget limitations. The world evolves around priorities…"

"And the level of media coverage on any issue seems to determine a politician's priorities…But how do I get the media interested?"

"You need a face, someone the public can relate to. Not anonymous victims living a thousand miles away in the Outback. Find someone who'll stand up and tell the nation their story. They'll become the media's darling."

Lionel blew hot air at the phone. Kooris in far-western communities were too afraid, too shy to discuss such matters. They'd refused to do it with him when he worked there, let alone in front of a white man's court. And most of them accepted the way things were and had shown bemusement when he'd told them differently. "Such a witness will be near impossible to find out there…"

"I agree, and that's why I suggest you forget the media and concentrate on securing Karen Flintoff's vote."

"And Sinclair?"

"Oh, don't worry about him. He was always a given. You've got his vote already."

Lionel smiled. "That's incredible. So quickly…How?"

"I simply mentioned that as Minister for Aboriginal Affairs it would be political suicide for him to oppose such an inquiry." Galios chuckled. "And I may have reminded him the federal election's only months away, and that his lot hold a fickle majority won on my party's preferences. I made it very clear that our continued allegiance is dependent on him supporting you. He really had no choice…"

"Fantastic, thanks very much."

"You're welcome…Now do your part, put someone to work on Flintoff and get her on side. But discretely, because it will only agitate McKinlay if he learns you've tried to influence her."

"Good advice…And I already have someone on the job."

"Let's hope they do it well. Your submission depends on it. Your career perhaps…"

"I realize that."

"Is it someone you'd trust with your life?"

Lionel thought of Fred Klose. "Yes, more than any other…"

SEVEN

Porter gripped the morgue drawer. Veins on forearms bulged. He gasped at the sight of the bloody mess inside the body bag. "Oh, fuck. No!" He clawed at it and searched for anything to disprove his eyes.

Betts wheezed. "Jesus…"

"Told you it's not pretty," Smith said.

Porter fought the urge to vomit. Nadia Tindall's severed head lay on top of her bruised stomach, black eyes wide and glazed with horror. Her tongue jutted from a half-open mouth and rested on blood-stained teeth. A crater of gristle, where her nose should've been, sparkled under harsh light. Hair tangled with dried blood covered her dark forehead and framed a once angelic face.

Porter shook the drawer. "No, fucking, no!" He fell to knees.

Betts pulled him to his feet and told Smith to leave them. She scowled then retreated to the office.

"This is my fucking fault," Porter shouted. "I'm the bloke who insisted Eddy come to boxing yesterday…" He swung his head from side to side in denial of what he saw. Why had he reacted this way? He usually treated death with nonchalance and typical cop bravado. But it had wrapped merciless hands around his throat and threatened to choke him.

"Port, listen…Port?" Betts squeezed his shoulder with a strong hand. "Deal with that bullshit later…Right now, let's do our job and take a good look at her. Alright?"

Porter closed eyes and breathed deep through his nose. He opened them, blew air out in a hiss and dipped his head.

Betts bent over the corpse. "There's gotta be something here to help find this mongrel…"

Porter watched him pull the bag tight over the drawer's edges. He grimaced at the gruesome cavity between Nadia's shoulders then leaned forward to examine it. Shredded tendons. Protruding bone. He moved to the other end of the drawer. Thick welts circling her calves and ankles indicated she'd been tied. Similar welts circled her left wrist. Her right arm had been hacked away below the elbow and pushed inside her vagina. Its hand hung limp between purple thighs. His gut swirled, he swallowed acidic bile. Some sick bastards had played a cruel, demented game.

Betts put on plastic gloves. "Get ready to turn her over, eh?"

Porter nodded and pulled gloves on.

Betts yelled instructions to Smith.

She returned with a digital camera and took close-up shots of Nadia from different angles. Then she laid the camera down, took a clear plastic bag from her pocket, lifted Nadia's head and dropped it inside. She sealed the bag, her expression colder than the refrigerator she placed it into.

She moved back to the morgue drawer. "Can't say I've done that before."

They turned Nadia's headless corpse onto its stomach.

Betts bent towards it. "What the fuck?"

50

Smith angled her head to one side. "What's that…Writing? Carved into her skin?"

Porter's eyes stung, transfixed. "It's a branding," he told them, because he'd helped his father mark cattle the same way. "It's been burnt into her..."

"Motherfuckers..." Betts straightened. "And what the hell does 'KA' mean?"

Porter shuddered at the agony Nadia had endured. The letters '**KA**'; bold and crisp, two inches by two inches; had been branded on her lower back. Pink letters, in contrast to her dark skin.

Four lines of text ran under the branding. They'd been scored into her skin, were smaller and shallower than the branded letters.

"*Impure in Body, Impure of Soul,*" Porter read in a grave whisper. "*You have denied her, the right to grow whole.*" His head rocked back.

Betts stared. "Never in my life…"

Smith smiled as she took photos. "Mine too."

Porter staggered from the room in a trance then slumped into a chair in the office. He closed eyes and saw Nadia's haunting face, her butchered body and the brutal text. Another surreal nightmare…He opened his eyes.

Betts sat opposite, face wrinkled with concern. "We'll have to tell her mother."

"I'll ask Tugger to bring her here." Porter stood and exhaled. "Need to make phone calls..."

Betts rubbed his gut. "I'll speak to security and check the CCTV. Then I'm ordering pizza."

Porter rang Jane's cell phone and she finally answered. She'd been at the hairdressers for hours without access to her phone. When she questioned the multiple calls, he said he'd responded to her urgent message and was concerned about Amber. Jane laughed and said she'd forgotten who'd agreed to collect her from school. She told him not to worry. She had Amber in the car.

He left her oblivious to the torment she'd caused and phoned Tugger. He struggled to tell him about Nadia and omitted all horrific details when answering questions. Tugger said he'd inform Debbie Tindall in person and bring her to the morgue.

He then phoned Claire and asked her to arrange for forensics staff to examine Nadia prior to autopsy. She told him that Azelia's termination had made front page news. Opposition political parties and community groups were outraged.

Porter ended the conversation with Claire. Betts returned from the security office.

"How'd you go, mate?"

Betts scoffed. "Typical useless morons…Security guards and all other staff on duty saw nothing. Wasted my time asking for surveillance footage…"

"Weren't there cameras above the driveway on the way in?"

"Yeah, but they haven't worked for months…" Betts flung a dismissive hand at the ceiling and sat. "General duty crews are canvassing for witnesses. Will check surrounding businesses for any camera footage later. Doubt we'll find anything worthwhile…"

Porter phoned Steve Williams and gave him a summary of developments. He described the state of Nadia's corpse.

Williams groaned. "Tell you, Port, branding is a first for me. Are 'KA' the crook's initials? Of one person, or a group? What the fuck do those letters, and that message, mean?"

"No idea yet, but I'm certain that Nadia's killers are with the mob who did the council blokes. Reckon they witnessed her abduction and had to be taken care of…"

"Agreed. But why risk dumping her at the morgue and exposing themselves? Why cremate the council guys and not her too?"

"They could be protecting a location…Or trying to confuse us, and want us to think they're separate mobs."

"Possibly…Or did they simply want you and Betts to see the message? As investigators who worked Azelia."

"Reckon you're onto something there, given the timing of it getting canned. Maybe they wanna lay blame and hold us responsible for Nadia's death?" He pictured the message scored into her back. '*You have denied her.*' Were they referring to 'you,' as in, the entire police force? Or 'you,' Dan Porter, have denied her? He tried to shake the image but it lingered like a thief in a dark alley.

"Is this a serial killer we're dealing with, Port? Or a one-off psycho with a vendetta, someone out to disgrace us?"

"As you said, I reckon they've used Nadia to send a message. Hope it's a one-off…"

"You and I both…What's clear from their brazenness is that these pricks consider us incompetent."

"I'll be happy to prove 'em wrong."

"They're daring us to find them, Port, playing a game."

"Well, bring it on…How have locals reacted to the Azelia news?"

Williams sighed. "Koori leaders are meeting as we speak. You know Sam Cartright's gang? Fucking troublemakers, spoiling for a fight. We're in for a rough old ride…"

"It scares me, mate."

"Me too, the whole city's on edge and I'm not sure the force is prepared for it."

"Nah, not that…The mongrels abducting our girls have started to kill 'em. And we've no bloody clue who they are, or how to stop 'em. That's what scares me…"

EIGHT

Lionel Roberts forced a smile as his assistant Wendy placed a cup of coffee and a newspaper on the desk like she did at 8.30am every work day. A country girl with old-fashioned morals and a degree in political science, she'd been a wonderful asset during his short time at Legal Aid. When she'd interviewed for the position, he realized her passion for Aboriginal justice and culture was equal to his own. For that reason, and not her pretty smile, he gave her the job.

"It's terrible..." She pointed to the front page of Thursday's newspaper. "They mutilated the poor girl...Not a good look for the cops is it?"

Lionel read the headline aloud. "Sydney horror: Missing girl brutally murdered as police scrap taskforce." Devastating news, a koori girl taken from once safe streets and slaughtered. But, and he hated himself for the thought, it was the horrific story he'd waited for. It would grab public attention. Media coverage would stir raw emotions in blacks and whites alike. And with police announcing Azelia's cessation on the same day, tensions would rise beyond boiling point. At least he hoped they would...

"It's tragic," he said. "Any mention of a name?"

She gulped. "No, but my cousin knew her. Was Nadia Tindall, only fourteen..."

Lionel winced, because he knew the Tindall family. The father's name he'd forgotten, a drunken deadbeat. But the mother, Debbie, was a proud koori who'd always worked several jobs to support her kids. He would send a card to offer condolences.

"I can't believe the police ignore this like it's not happening."

She over-exaggerated raised eyebrows. "Lionel?"

"Okay, I believe it…Mutilated? Does it say how?"

"Nothing specific, thankfully. The thought's bad enough."

"Indeed…" He sipped coffee. "Perfect, thanks." He pushed the newspaper aside then grabbed a bundle of mail from the in-tray. Wendy left the office.

It had been a fortnight since Lionel flooded the city with pamphlets seeking information regarding Sydney's missing girls. His post office box overflowed. Wendy had told him to be encouraged by the response, despite ninety-nine percent of it being hate mail.

Obscure political parties accused him of dividing society. Fanatical white supremacy groups, Neo-Nazis and the National Socialist Alliance, condemned his prejudice against whites and warned him to watch his back. Police Associations demanded he stop bad-mouthing their members. Asian and African community groups suggested Aboriginals sought preferential treatment. Religious leaders asked he place trust in Jesus, Mohamed or Buddha. Peace activists expressed fear he'd start a civil war. And there were pictures of kidnap suspects with obscene notes attached. Suspects ranged from famous movie stars to a horde of Ku Klux Klansman on horseback.

Lionel took an envelope from the pile and opened it. He chuckled at the picture that slid out. Ronald McDonald's hair and nose had been colored black. A caption read 'It's you, Lionel, you're the kidnapper!'

He opened another twenty letters and discarded nineteen. In the one he kept, an anonymous source alleged a convicted child rapist living in South Sydney had abducted the girls. He would copy the letter and send it to the police as he'd done with a hundred others. But he hadn't received a reply and wasn't expecting any. If police couldn't bother investigating the missing girls, who would read anonymous tip-offs?

Bored with hate mail, he toggled the computer mouse and the monitor flicked into life. He opened the email inbox. Near full. Judging from recent days most of it would read similar to the paper mail. He scrolled down the page and skimmed over the 'subject' fields. He reached the bottom and prepared to click to the next one when then noticed a 'subject' written in capital letters near the top of the page.

He read the line in a whisper. 'IMPORTANT INFORMATION RE MISSING KOORI GIRLS – PLEASE OPEN' He opened the email and read it in a blur. After reading it a second time he sat back and played with his goatee. The third time he leaned towards the screen and read slower.

Dear Mr Roberts,

I'll stay anonymous, my nickname's Shirley. I'm a koori woman living in Sydney. I saw your message in the paper before I came away (I'm on holiday in the UK) and like you, I'm sickened by the disappearance of so many koori girls. Just now I've read on the internet about the murdered Tindall girl being found.

It's horrible and something must be done to stop it. You sound like you care so I'm willing to give you a chance. You see, I know of bad things that've happened. I've been scared and afraid for a long time and there are those I need to protect. That's why I can't tell you everything from the start. Make some progress and let me trust you and maybe I'll tell you more.

My history teacher used to say, 'To deal with the present, we must first understand the past'. It's one of few things I remember from school because I think it's true. I don't know who exactly is taking these girls, but go to Crooked River mission. I'm sure you'll find some answers there.

Please don't reply to this. If you do, I will ignore it and cease communication. Don't try to find me, and keep this email to yourself. Good luck, and trust no-one.

A shiver of hope ran down the back of Lionel's neck. "Yes. Finally…"

'Shirley' had provided anonymous, unsubstantiated information. But if he could confirm she'd sent the email from the UK it would lend credibility and help him believe in her the way he wanted to. He jotted down the internet provider number in the email's header, opened an address search tool from the computer's desktop and entered the digits. He hit the enter key and waited for the search to complete.

After a few minutes the 'Geographical Location' flashed on the screen. The email had originated from Scotland, United Kingdom. Lionel grinned. Could 'Shirley' be genuine? He printed her email and locked it in the desk drawer.

His cell phone rang. He read the caller ID and answered. "Fred, good to see your ESP's still working. Just the man I need to talk to."

Klose sniggered. "Thought you'd be waiting on my call…"

"I was…You remember that email search program you gave me?"

"Aha…"

"Is it accurate?"

"Has been for me. It playing up?"

"No, I've just used it to confirm a location. It seemed to work okay."

"Location of who?"

Lionel hesitated. 'Shirley' had requested complete secrecy. But what did he have to hide from Klose? "I received an email from a koori lady this morning. It relates to the missing girls."

"And?"

"Told me she's in Scotland. The search confirmed it."

"Excellent…Who is she? What info did she give?"

Shirley's words echoed in Lionel's head. *Trust no-one.* "Ah…None yet. Says she may have something later, and wants to stay anonymous." He hesitated. "Might be nothing, but I checked her location anyway."

Lionel listened as Klose clicked his tongue for five seconds. He swore under his breath, because no-one detected his lies better than Klose did.

"She, might have something later?" Klose said, tone sarcastic. "She sends an email from Scotland to tell you nothing?"

"I know, it's frustrating beyond belief. Really hope she makes contact again…"

"Yep…" Klose paused. "Hey, about Flintoff…"

Lionel jumped all over the change of subject. "What?"

"I've come through on this one, bud."

"What did you find?

"You wanted dirt. I got you sewerage."

"What?" Lionel almost yelled. "You're killing me..."

"Okay...According to Jenny, my secretary friend, Karen Flintoff is having an affair."

Lionel prayed for her lover to be a well-known celebrity and not her local plumber. "With who?"

"This, bud, is your deal breaker...Flintoff is fucking Rothwell, and has been for years."

Lionel leaned back, mouth half open. He lowered the phone and scenarios presented by the revelation played out at light speed in his head. He raised the phone to ear. "As in, Attorney General Rothwell?"

"Yep. Unbelievable, eh?"

"And she's certain?"

"Has no reason to lie...She caught them in the act once and ever since gets a day off work whenever she wants it...The girl's a hopeless gossip, but with a secret as damaging as this I believe her."

"Good enough for me...Thanks, Fred, it's amazing, more than I'd hoped for. Pressure on Flintoff and Rothwell. Perfect... I'm confident of getting my inquiry."

"But not too confident?"

"Not at all...And even if McKinlay does oppose it, he'll have to abide by the majority vote and follow Rothwell's direction. Transparency goes out the window with careers at stake..."

"What if Rothwell leaves the final decision with McKinlay and calls your bluff?"

"Would you risk the international controversy? Married, with a reputation to uphold..."

"You're right, it's perfect."

"And I owe you…"

"Yep, a steak dinner three times over." Klose laughed before his tone darkened. "Listen bud, be careful, and don't let this come back to bite you…How do you plan on using this info?"

"Not sure yet…There'll be no mention of the source, you have my word…Will they suspect Jenny?"

"Don't worry about her. Apparently there's plenty close to them who know of the affair. Flintoff's popular and they protect her. It's the best-kept secret in politics..."

Lionel smiled. It used to be the best-kept secret in politics. "Fred, if I'm successful with the submission there's a chance I'll be taking an investigation team out west. Would you be interested in joining it?"

"Sure bud, I'd love us to work together…"

Lionel thanked him again and ended the call. He rocked back in the chair and gazed out the window. An hour earlier he'd felt jaded, had doubted himself and wondered if he'd taken too much on. Weeks of abusive mail, ignorant police and dead-end leads had taken their toll. But now, what a day…Potential witness 'Shirley' had emerged. He had Rothwell at his mercy. Bit by bit the plan came together.

He decided he didn't have time for a face-to-face meeting. He opened the computer's phone directory and called the Attorney General's Sydney office. When Jenny answered he smiled at the irony. She diverted the call and he waited, heart beating louder than the trilled ringtone.

A confident voice answered. "Karen Flintoff."

He hesitated. An inner voice urged him on. "It's Lionel Roberts, Ms Flintoff. I'm an Aboriginal Human Rights Advocate with Legal Aid."

A slight pause. "How may I help?"

"I've an urgent matter to discuss. Extremely important."

"Go on."

"It's of a personal and sensitive nature, perhaps more suited to a meeting…But I'm sorry, time is of the essence."

She huffed. "You're being very strange, Mr Roberts. If it's urgent just tell me."

"You're comfortable discussing it over the phone?"

"My line's secure. Get to the point."

"Okay…Please listen carefully, Ms Flintoff. What I'm about to tell you requires your complete and immediate attention."

NINE

Porter parked the unmarked police sedan against the curb and listened to Ian Betts' phone conversation with the Forensics Unit doctor. He hoped for good news, that Nadia Tindall's killer had been identified.

Five minutes later Betts ended the call and dropped his phone into the center console. "We've been driving around the CBD like chooks without heads for two hours. Have seen a hundred white vans and stopped more than twenty. Is Williams fair dinkum? He really thinks we'll find our crooks this way?"

"You're right, it's harder than finding a pork chop in Tehran...But it's the only lead we've got."

"A waste of fucking time...Head to Mickey D's can you, I'm craving a Big Mac."

Porter glanced at the dashboard clock. "It's only five-thirty...Didn't you eat lunch?"

"Four hours ago. Not my fault you never eat, skinny bastard."

Porter gasped in mock disbelief. He shielded eyes from the setting sun with one hand and steered the sedan into peak-hour traffic with the other. "What did the doc say about Nadia?"

"Sure you wanna know?"

"Mate, I had a Barry Crocker yesterday. All's good now," Porter lied. "Tell me..."

"Alright...She was messier on the inside than out."

Porter winced. "Fingerprints?"

"Nope, spotless."

63

"Same as the truck in Newcastle. It's gotta be the same mob…"

"Yep, and they're bloody good at what they do."

"Raped?"

"Several times. The doc had never seen internal trauma like it."

"DNA?"

"Multiple profiles found. No matches yet."

"Mongrels…" Porter increased volume on the police radio. "We'll get one, these blokes are bound to have form."

"Yep..."

"City 15 or any car in the vicinity." A female voice crackled over the police radio. "Check bona fides...Anonymous informant states two men, not further described, acting suspiciously in a white van in the Cinema City carpark, corner of Lane and McGowan streets, Surry Hills. Informant says the van's circling the carpark with teenagers congregating. City 15, any car in the vicinity."

Porter nodded at Betts and threw the sedan into a sudden U-turn.

Betts snatched the radio handset. "City 106 copy that," he blurted. "Five minutes...Anything else, radio?"

"106, five minutes, copy," the operator said. "Nothing further on the van. White is all we've got..."

"106 copy..." Betts replaced the handset then gripped the 'Jesus' handle above the passenger window.

Porter drove his foot onto the accelerator pedal and weaved the sedan through traffic. "These are our crooks, mate, I can feel it," he yelled above screeching tires.

"Fair chance. Let's ho--."

BEEP! BEEP! The police radio sounded through the speaker again, loud and piercing. "Any car in the vicinity," a male operator said this time, "corner of Cleveland and Pitt streets, Redfern. Raja's mini-mart. Confirmed armed robbery in progress, knife produced. Two Aboriginal males in late teens, wearing white hooded jumpers, not further described. Informant is the store attendant. Any car in the vicinity..."

Porter scanned the road ahead. They traveled east on Cleveland street, towards Surry Hills, three hundred meters from Raja's minimart. "We're on top of that, we've gotta take it."

"No, keep going past it. We want the white van."

BEEP! BEEP! "Any car in the vicinity," the operator persisted. "Confirmed armed holdup, Raja's minimart, corner of Cleveland and Pitt streets, Redfern. Suspects have left the store, last seen running east on Cleveland towards Chalmers Street. Armed and dangerous. Any car in the vicinity."

The speaker crackled as numerous police crews acknowledged the job.

"There!" Porter pointed ahead to the right. Two males in white hooded tops darted across the road and avoided an oncoming car by inches. He followed them with a hard-right turn into Chalmers street. Traffic squealed to a halt. Car horns blared.

"Fucking hell, Port!" Betts grabbed the handset. "City 106 in pursuit, radio. Two suspects from Rajas are on foot, east on James Street."

Porter swung the sedan into a right-hand turn then slammed the brakes. "Shit, bollards..." The suspects hurdled steel posts that blocked vehicular entrance to a narrow lane then ran down it. "I've got the porty and torches…Call for a dog." He grabbed the portable radio and two torches.

Betts wheezed a hurried breath. "Foot pursuit, radio. Suspects south on…" He spun to search around them and squinted. Day rapidly became night.

"Elizabeth Lane," Porter told him.

"South on Elizabeth Lane…" Betts said. "On portable. Request a dog, and for responding crews to cordon the perimeter."

"Copy 106," the operator said. "Foot pursuit south on Elizabeth Lane. Proceed with caution. Both suspects armed with knives and dangerous. Dog and backup on the way."

Porter sprang from the sedan, pressed the remote lock as he ran and tossed a torch to Betts. Fitter and faster and thankful he wore sneakers, he pulled ahead of him.

He flicked the torch on and lit up the lane. Deserted, bordered by rubble where torn down apartments hadn't been replaced. At the end of it a brick wall surrounded a construction site. The hooded males ran to the left when they reached a T intersection.

"They went left towards the building site," Porter yelled over his shoulder. He heard an angry grunted reply behind him. He sprinted towards the corner where they'd turned. Wailing sirens got louder. He urged himself to run faster because he wanted to make the arrest before backup arrived. He rounded the corner at a sprint. His shoulder scraped a brick wall.

A steel bar struck him flush across the nose. Bone snapped as his head whipped back. He skidded across the road with momentum, heels first. The back of his head thudded against concrete and flopped to the side. The portable radio clattered to the ground. The torch rolled then stopped. Its bright beam lit up the construction site.

Porter moaned. He closed dazed eyes for a few seconds then forced them open. *What the fuck?* A deafening crescendo of whizzes and whirls rang in his ears, the sounds of alien spaceships from childhood cartoons. He tried to lift his head from the road but it would've been easier to heave a hippo from quicksand. Blood flooded his face and stung his eyes. His hand shook while he wiped it away. A finger brushed his nose and he stiffened. Teeth gritted. He rolled onto his side.

He stared down the lane, blinked and tried to focus blurry images. When he did, two koori boys in hooded jumpers stood over him holding steel bars. Eddy Tindall glared with eyes full of hate. Ben Neilsen snarled.

"Eddy?" Porter said with a metallic, bloody gargle in his throat.

"Like that pigeee?" Neilsen's high-pitched squeal echoed along the lane. "Bam!" He swung the steel bar like a baseball bat. "C'mon bro, do it," he shouted at Eddy, "finish this dog."

Eddy moved closer. He hissed down at Porter and raised the bar.

Porter mustered the last of his energy and tried to stand. He couldn't. He stared up into Eddy's bloodshot eyes.

Neilsen jumped up and down like the drug-crazed clown he was.

"Don't…" Porter pleaded with Eddy.

"Fuck you pig! For my sister, you cu--."

"Stop! Drop it!" Betts yelled. He panted loudly. He aimed a Glock at Eddy and shone the torch in his face.

Eddy dropped the bar and raised a hand to shield his eyes.

Neilsen grinned. "Yay, another piggy to play with." He swung the bar then pointed it at Betts.

Betts crouched into a combat stance three meters from Neilsen. He shifted his aim onto him. "Put it down," he shouted. "Won't tell you twice..."

"Ha, ha, ha, ha, ha." Neilsen waved the bar above his head and danced in a tight circle. "Piggy, piggy, pi--."

BOOM! The hollow-point bullet tore between Neilsen's eyes and took half his head out the other side. He thudded to the ground next to Porter.

Eddy looked at his dead friend, eyes and mouth wide open. He snarled at Betts.

"On the ground dickhead," Betts shouted at him.

Porter struggled to his knees. "Fuck...Betts. Why? You didn't have to--."

"Shut up," Betts snapped at him. He aimed the Glock and torch at Eddy. "I said to get down, boy...Do it!"

Sirens stopped wailing in adjoining lanes. Car doors slammed shut. Dogs barked. Excited voices called out.

Eddy lowered his chest to the ground and eyed Porter, a cocky smirk on his face.

Betts stepped towards him, holstered the Glock and took handcuffs from a belt.

In an instant, Eddy pushed up and landed on his feet. He shoved Betts in the chest, spun and ran.

Porter swayed as he stood. He watched Eddy sprint down the lane.

"Run you little bastard," Betts yelled. He raised the torch and Glock in one smooth motion. Wrists and elbows locked at shoulder height.

Porter saw him close one eye to take aim. "Betts! No!" He staggered towards him.

BOOM! BOOM! BOOM! Betts fired and kept the torch aimed. Three bullets struck Eddy in the back. He collapsed against concrete in a crumpled mess. Betts smirked then frowned when uniformed police ran into the lane.

Porter glared at him then picked the torch up and stumbled forward.

Eddy lay on his side and sucked at the cool air. Porter knelt beside him and cringed as he watched Eddy's guts slither through the hole in his back. He lay the torch down and it lit up the road. It resembled a butcher's floor, littered with bits of flesh. Bloody rivulets zigzagged over it.

He cradled Eddy's head in one hand and patted wet hair with the other. "Sorry champ..."

Eddy wheezed as though desperate for a final breath. Crimson bile spilled over his trembling lower lip. Moist black eyes darted back and forth between Porter's then froze, eyelids wide open.

Porter's fingers shook as he closed them.

He searched Eddy's pants and found a sharpened ice cream stick. *Knife, my arse.* In one jumper pocket he found a zip-locked bag of white crystals. *Ice.* In the other he found crumpled banknotes. *Thirty bucks...Fuck, he died for thirty bucks?*

Porter tried to stand but his conscience weighed him down. First Nadia, now Eddy. He'd failed them both. Eyes flickered before the time bomb in his head exploded.

TEN

After the productive phone conversation with Karen Flintoff on Thursday morning, Lionel Roberts had turned his attention back to the email from 'Shirley'. He'd sat at his desk for an hour and pondered the best course of action. Crooked River was an insignificant, outback town. Why had Shirley told him to go there? If he did take an investigation team and found no evidence of neglect and abuse, to what extent would his proposed inquiry suffer from it? He wanted to reply to her email and ask questions. But he couldn't because she'd made it very clear. If he did, she would cease all correspondence.

At 10am he'd called Wendy into his office. He told her bare details of Shirley's email and tasked her with gathering information from State Archives regarding Crooked River's township and greater district. He wanted copies of everything on record about its history, residents, and the Aboriginal mission within it.

Wendy returned at 6.30pm, dropped a manila folder onto Lionel's desk and collapsed into a chair opposite him.

He smiled. "Busy girl, were gone all day…How did it go?"

She pointed to the folder. "That's all there was."

He flicked through pages inside the folder then squinted at her, unable to hide his disappointment. "Ten pages? Certain you found everything?"

"Yes, went through all sections of the relevant archives." She rubbed her eyes. "Four times over..."

Lionel frowned. "Crooked River's mission has been there since the early twenties. The Aboriginal Welfare Board was required to file the names and birthdates of all who lived on it. I don't see any here dated after..." He paused to skim over the second page. "None after mid-1963?"

She covered a yawn with a hand. "I'm aware of the AWB and records they were supposed to keep. I've studied them the same as you, and all government archiving systems. Remember?"

He huffed at her uncharacteristic sarcasm. "Then why couldn't you find the old Welfare Board files?"

"Told you, Lionel, I searched for hours. That's the lot."

"Nonsense." He sat back with arms folded. "Guess I'll have to find them myself..."

She hesitated. He wouldn't have blamed her for calling him an arrogant pig. Her eyes glistened. "I'll go back tomorrow."

An awkward silence.

"Sorry, shouldn't speak to you like that," he said. "No excuses but it's been a draining day for both of us."

She broke eye contact and nodded.

"Record keeping during the stolen generations was notoriously lacking, but this is ridiculous..." he said. "I need those records. They can't have vanished without a trace?"

"Michael at Archives agrees…Thing is, they didn't vanish, because there never were any AWB records filed for Crooked River after 1963. As you know, all nationwide record keeping ceased when they abolished the board in '69. For kooris living on Crooked River mission between '63 and then, it's like they never existed."

He scratched his temple. Could there be substance to Shirley's advice regarding Crooked River? "How'd the AWB get away with that? Crooked River was one of the more populous missions…"

"Yes, with more than four hundred families at its peak."

Lionel smirked. She knew her stuff. "So where are the records of those families now? How can Michael be certain they never existed? Removed from the archives, perhaps, or deleted?"

"I asked him if they'd been deleted and he said it's impossible. All records in the archives, old and new, get filed electronically. Few people have access to their maintenance. He opened the database and showed me the file history. Nothing's been deleted. Like the printout shows," she gestured to the folder, "record keeping ceased in '63."

"So according to government archives, Crooked River mission was unpopulated for six years, when all other historical accounts we've studied show otherwise…Is this the first time you've come across this in the archives?"

"Yep, and as you said, government record keeping during the '50s and '60s in particular, was terrible. But when I sifted through the archives today, every mission had hundreds of pages of information, with every year covered. Except for Crooked River. Why hasn't anyone noticed until now? Michael certainly hadn't…"

"No-one's cared before now."

"Likely…Something's dodgy about it."

"Or corrupt? Crooked River's had the usual problems over the years but no more than other towns and missions considering its size. Definitely nothing that justifies deleting a chunk of its history…"

"Where to from here?"

"Let's keep the missing records to ourselves at the moment. Michael will do what he has to, we can't control that. But someone's taken significant risks to tamper with AWB files relating to those six years. I intend to find out who, and why. The fewer know of our discovery, the easier it'll be."

"I can ask Michael to sit on it?"

"Good idea. But discreetly, and don't jeopardize his position."

She dipped her head. "You seem quite the expert on Crooked River, considering you've only read a few history books…"

"I spent a week in its local court last year, filling in as the Legal Aid rep. Defended a young koori guy accused of punching a cop. Not sure why, because the koori had come off much worse."

"Just the norm…They're friendly cops then?"

"Think yanky rednecks with thick Aussie accents…The kooris in town are barely tolerated. Definitely not accepted…When I lost the court matter a police car followed me out of town to make sure I left. They didn't want no black human rights lawyer sniffing around their hick town."

"Rednecks alright…Sounds like a horrible place."

"The town itself is lovely…Colonial, sandstone buildings. A couple of 19th-century churches. The pub's okay. Ancient trees line bright red streets."

"And the river?"

"It's brown but clean, deep and wide. Runs through town then into hills. The mission's set on it."

"What's it like, the koori community there?"

Lionel made a mental note to stop calling it a 'mission'. "It's in a wonderful location, surrounded by hills. The residents seemed happy enough. New houses, a modern school. To be honest, Crooked River wasn't a place I planned to investigate."

"But it is now?"

He hesitated. Wendy was the only person within Legal Aid who knew of his quest for a public inquiry. The only colleague he trusted, to an extent. "Maybe, because of the missing records. Makes me wonder…" He glanced at the ringing cell phone, picked it up from the desk and answered. "Nick, excuse me for a second please…" He placed a hand over the phone. "Thanks Wendy, brilliant work today. See you tomorrow."

She waved and left the office.

"Nick, I've got fantastic news."

Galios' laugh crackled through the phone's speaker. "Hey, I'm the one who called. You'll want to hear mine first."

"I'm listening."

"Well, allow me to gloat. I've been busy making phone calls…Have you seen the papers, and TV reports?"

"I'm impressed. Azelia's termination dominates all media. And how'd you get your story into this morning's paper, at such short notice?"

"Aha…A desperate journo, hungry for a scoop, is either a politicians' worst enemy or closest ally.

Thankfully, my favorite hack was starving. Do you like the story?"

Lionel sniggered as his admiration grew. "Couldn't be more anti-police if you'd written it yourself…It's exactly the coverage we need to get the right people asking questions."

"Must say, I do love seeing that useless old prick Delaney getting caned by the press."

"And rightly so…His police force turned its back on those girls."

"What I really rang to tell you is this…Charles McKinlay called me ten minutes ago…"

"And?"

"He was abusive at first, accused me of going over his head and straight to Rothwell. Then, from nowhere, he says Rothwell's directed him to make an immediate decision regarding your submission."

Lionel's chest heaved. He recalled his conversation with Karen Flintoff. She'd acted as instructed. "That's fantastic news, that they're considering its merits at least…"

"McKinlay will speak to Sinclair and Flintoff tonight and ask them to vote on the matter. You've got a meeting with him tomorrow at nine, at his office in Martin Place. He'll give you the panel's decision then."

Lionel realized he had a sleepless night of worry ahead. "With only him?"

"Yes, it's very unusual, and these things rarely move this quickly. Someone's watching over you, Lionel, you're blessed."

Wise men who often visited Lionel, spirits of his ancestors, hovered in front of him. "Not blessed…Someone watching over me? Maybe…"

A long pause.

"You know, I had to refrain from laughing," Galios said. "Charles seemed genuinely bewildered that Rothwell expects Flintoff and Sinclair to cast a vote without even reading your submission."

"I can imagine the look on his face when Rothwell told him…"

Galios chuckled. "Indeed…Well, my work's done. What did you want to tell me? Have you worked a miracle with Karen Flintoff?"

Silence for five seconds while Lionel considered telling him about 'Shirley.' "Yes, I managed to speak with her this morning, and explained the situation in the far west."

"Great. What was her response?"

"I'm confident she'll vote in my favor."

"Really? How could you be, after one conversation?"

"Certain you want to know?"

Galios snorted a laugh, as though enjoying the game. "Considering the sudden directive from Rothwell, and McKinlay's backflip, I don't know if I do."

"Yes, perhaps it's best you don't…"

He must've been worried by the mischief in Lionel's voice because he continued in a serious tone. "Lionel, be very careful how you handle this situation."

Lionel pulled away from the phone. Why the sudden concern for his welfare? What did Fred Klose and Nick Galios know, that he didn't? "Whilst I appreciate your advice, I do know what I'm doing."

"I hope you do…Because there'll be serious consequences if you get it wrong."

ELEVEN

Four hours after he'd passed out in a Redfern laneway, Porter stopped behind Superintendent Steve Williams outside an interview room in City Central police station. He peered over Williams' shoulder. Two Internal Affairs investigators sat at a table in the middle of the room. One, close to sixty, had a round head and jowls like Jabba the Hut. The other, in his mid-forties, had the face of a ferret. They wore identical suits with identical hairstyles. Black with pin-stripe. Slicked back and parted at the side.

Williams stepped into the room. "Gents, we've just returned from the hospital. The doctor said Dan's been badly concussed and isn't fit for interview. But he wants to do it now and get it over with."

Jabba the Hut peered up at Williams. "We've finished with Betts. He's having a quick debrief with the psych then going home."

"Excellent…Any point asking how it went?"

"No, but I worked Fraud Squad with him a few years back. He's a good fella, a good cop. It'll sort itself out."

Williams stepped aside to let Porter into the room. "Blood samples were taken, and they shouldn't be a problem. Port's only a rotten drunk off duty, right mate?"

Porter didn't reply and watched Williams leave the room. He stumbled on an electrical cord and fell into a chair opposite the investigators. He adjusted the plaster strip across his nose. They ignored him, heads down. An electronic recording machine with a built-in video camera stared at him from the table.

Jabba the Hut straightened in the chair. "Don't think we've met? Detective Inspector Ron Jacobs from Internal Affairs, heading this critical incident investigation." He turned to ferret face. "This is Detective Senior Sergeant Brian Little, assisting. Our contact details..." Jacobs pushed two business cards across the table.

Porter noted the registered service numbers listed on their cards. He'd been in the cops four years longer than Little and tried to ignore the fact. He couldn't contain himself. "Nothing like a job at IA to hurl you up the corporate ladder, eh Sarge?" He smirked at Little.

Little jerked his nose.

"Do you have an Association rep to sit in with you?" Jacobs said.

"Don't reckon I need one?" Porter wiped sweat from his neck and rolled the shirt's sleeves to elbow length. The business shirt Williams had lent him hung loose at the shoulders. Strange, because he'd always been broader than him. He tightened the bandage around his head.

"Your nose must be sore?" Jacobs said.

"Clean fracture. Not the first, won't be the last." Porter heard his own voice. His usual baritone sounded nasal and mid-pitched. "Drugs have worn off, got a prick of a headache. We getting on with this?"

Jacobs flicked the electronic recording machine on. Three green lights flashed. A long beep. He pointed to Little, who readied pen to paper.

Jacobs cleared his throat. "This is an electronically recorded interview betwee--."

Porter rocked forward on the seat. "I haven't agreed to this. Won't…"

Jacobs sat back with brow furrowed.

Porter out-stared him.

Jacobs flicked the machine off. "Didn't want to tell me that, prior, to commencing the interview?"

"You didn't ask…"

"What's your reason for declining?" Little said.

"Won't sit here like a two-bob crook and talk into a machine. Done nothing wrong, and I'll prove that…And is this a criminal or internal interview?"

"Nothing wrong? That's yet to be determined…" Little mumbled as he wrote.

Porter began a reply then stopped, mouth half open. He massaged the back of his head and felt warm blood oozing from stitches. A dull ache at the hospital had become a chisel chipping away his skull.

"You alright, Porter?" Jacobs said.

Porter stooped towards the table and tried to focus on stained carpet.

"It's an internal interview only at this stage," Jacobs said. "We need your version of events…Two koori kids have been shot by cops, and the world's asking our bosses why. Our job is to supply them answers."

Little sniffled. "If you're innocent, it's best to co-operate…"

Porter straightened. "I'm here, aren't I? Crook as a dog…Co-op-er-ating…You need my version of events…For what? To load bullets for the firing squad?"

Jacobs frowned. "No-one likes a smartass, Constable, and I don't like your tone."

"Well, excuse the cynic in me you blokes but we're talking about the fucking police force here." Pressure built at his temples. Porter winced. "This might be internal for now, but we all know anything said can come back to haunt me...Guaran, fucking, teed."

"You're obliged to answer our questions," Little said. "You'll face disciplinary action if you don't."

"Two kids are dead 'cos I chased 'em. And you reckon the threat of disciplinary action worries me? Fucking drongo…"

Jacobs raised an open hand. "Calm down, Dan. Brian's trying to help."

"Like fuck he is…I'm not new to critical incidents, unlike some who spend careers hiding behind desks…" Porter glared at Little. "I know my obligations...To provide a statement. Or you blokes can write q's and a's in your notebooks like real cops do." He folded arms and licked the blood trickling from his nose.

Jacobs squinted at him. "Betts shot Neilsen, to save your life. Tindall was a dangerous, fleeing felon."

"That's not how I remember it…"

"Listen, corroborating's easier for both of you. If you don't support Betts he'll be charged, and probably do time." Jacobs leaned forward. "He's your partner, Porter. A good man with a wife and kids to support."

Porter heard Betts say it again. '*A bullet's what he needs…Would do us all a favor.*'

"Betts is a good bloke sometimes. Not always…" Porter said. "I joined this job to put killers away, not protect 'em."

"Look, maybe Betts did fuck up," Jacobs said. "He'll have to deal with the consequences. But, so will you..."

"That sounds like a threat...Thought it's your job to protect the honest blokes?"

"Simply advice, from someone who's seen it all before...You'll be treated like a leper, because no-one's got time for a cop who rolls on his mates. What'll people think? He saves your life and you put him in it..."

"Deep in it..." Little said. "And why the sympathy for shitbag junkies? They would've killed you."

Porter covered eyes with hands. He tried to dismiss images of Nadia's mutilated corpse and Debbie Tindall's distraught face. He sighed and took the hands away. What was the point of trying to explain?

"Would you prefer we do this tomorrow?" Jacobs said. "You've been concussed, you're tired and not thinking straight...Go home and sleep on it."

"Nah, I'll make a statement. Now."

Little huffed as he wrote.

Jacobs' face soured like a homeless drunk who'd spilled the last drop of wine. "If you provide a conflicting statement, public prosecutors get involved. Which means there'll be one hell of a media circus and kooris baying for blood. Are you prepared for the worst scenario?"

Visions of Nadia, her distraught mother, and Eddy's desperate last stare swirled in front of Porter. After the past few days what could be worse? He shrugged.

Jacobs sighed then pointed to the computer and printer on the desk in the corner. "Set those up, Sergeant, for the Constable to write his statement."

Five minutes later, Porter sat alone in the interview room. A burning sensation rose from chest to throat. He cursed himself for initiating the pursuit. Then Betts, for needlessly taking two young lives.

What had Betts said in his statement? He would've had to admit to shooting them. Ballistics would prove it...But how had he explained the, 'why'? Why did he shoot Eddy in the back? An unarmed boy with no chance of escape...

He'd typed two lines when Jacobs entered the room, placed a copy of Betts' statement on the desk and left without saying a word. He stopped typing and shook his head at the audacity. They'd want him to support Betts' version of events no matter how fabricated, and leave the police faultless in all legal and procedural aspects of the shooting. They'd pretend to care for them both whilst only protecting the force.

He started typing again then glanced at Betts' statement and stopped. He heard Betts chuckle and watched him devour a Big Mac. Ian Betts, his partner, the bloke who'd saved his arse on countless occasions. The one who made him laugh to lighten the mood. The one who tolerated his foul temper. The bloke who'd given him strength, like recently at the morgue when he'd felt weak.

He fingered the keyboard. *Make the right decision, Porter. It's the most important of your life...*

He could tell the truth and became an internal witness. Worlds would turn upside down. Life, both private and professional, would never be the same again. And would guilt forever haunt him if he destroyed another cop's career?

Or he could lie and support Betts' version. Turn the nightmare into a dream. Life would go on as though the shooting had never happened…But could he ever look in a mirror again?

An hour later he'd printed and signed a four-page statement. He handed it to Jacobs when they returned to the room.

Jacobs read the statement, blank-faced. He slid it across the table to Little then studied Porter. "Are you happy to stick with that?"

Porter said nothing. He took his copy from the table and left.

Steve Williams waited for him in the adjoining briefing room. He suggested Porter take a seat then went to speak with the IA men. He returned to the briefing room when they'd left and smiled at the attractive woman who hurried past them into the interview room. He sat next to Porter. "How'd it go?"

"Mate, I don't wanna talk about it. You'll find out soon enough."

"Whatever happens, you have my support. Okay?"

Porter shrugged.

Williams inclined his head towards the interview room. "That was Deidre Sharpe who just walked past, our top psychiatrist. She wants a chat…"

"Nah, not gunna happen." Porter stood. "Can hardly keep my eyes open, head's fucking killing me. Haven't spoken to Jane. Heading home…"

"Told you already that Jane knows you're okay. I called her from the hospital."

Porter inhaled then blew air at the ceiling. "Don't need a chat…I'm all good."

Williams rose to lock eyes with him. "You don't look it…I'm worried as your mate, not your boss."

"I've just had enough bullshit for one day…"

"I told Deidre to be quick. It's critical incident protocol. Mandatory."

"Yeah, the force covering its arse for later when I've blown my brains out…" Porter clenched his jaw. "Bloody hell, mate, why are you pushing this? You know I hate talking to these people."

"Understood…But this shooting, and with what's happened in your past…Things catch up. It won't hurt to tal--."

Porter eyed him sideways. "My past? Fuck, don't go there…" He headed for the fire stairs.

"Superintendent Williams, it's very late, and I've still several officers to get through," Deidre Sharpe said from the interview room's doorway. "Is there a problem?"

Williams grabbed Porter's elbow. "Hang on, I'll sort it out."

Porter shook his arm loose and leaned against a table.

Williams followed Sharpe into the interview room. Five minutes later he came out smiling. "Deidre's reluctant but I've vouched for you until Monday."

"I still have to see her?"

"Yes, there's no avoiding it…" Williams grinned. "Just don't neck yourself before then, 'cos it's my job on the line…"

Porter laughed then grimaced from the effort. "Better for her anyway, not having to deal with me right now."

"I told her the same…"

Porter searched for the question he'd wanted to ask. His head rocked back when he found it. "We were heading to another job when the robbery went down. Check bona fides of a white van at City East cinema..."

"Yes, heard you acknowledge it…"

"Anyone check it out?"

"All crews headed to the robbery once you called pursuit…One finally got to the cinema a couple of hours later. Van was long gone…"

Porter forced air through gritted teeth. "Should've listened to Betts and ignored the robbery. Boys would still be alive and we could've had that van..."

"Don't lump that crap on yourself, you made the right decision." Williams walked to the elevator and pushed a button on the wall. "Come on, I'll run you home. Then I've gotta get back to Redfern..."

The doors opened and Porter stepped into the elevator. "You're not finished at the shooting scene? What's going on?"

Williams followed him and pressed a button. The doors closed and the elevator descended. "Locals are running amok. Lighting fires, trashing cars and buildings. Gangs of koori and islander kids roam the city, bashing the crap out of any whiteys they get their hands on. Have six in intensive care already."

"Bloody hell..."

"Your mate Tugger's in the thick of it, trying to restore calm. But it's useless. 'Doing it for our murdered brothers' they've told him. A hundred cops and the whole riot squad's fighting for control of Redfern. It's full-blown mayhem."

Porter ran a hand over sticky hair at the back of his head. "I knew the locals would go off…"

"They were bound to. It's been brewing for weeks. First the pricks abducting the girls wanted to humiliate us…Now pissed off kooris want revenge, the blood of dead coppers on their hands. And I fear they won't stop until they get it."

TWELVE

Lionel Roberts entered the National Human Rights Commission's waiting room in Martin Place, Sydney on a chilly Friday morning. He wore a black Armani suit with a white shirt and red tie underneath it. He'd shined his best shoes, cut wayward curls, and trimmed his goatee. The receptionist asked him to sit and wait. A grandfather clock in the corner showed 8.55am on the most important day of his life.

He yawned and rubbed aching eyes. He'd worked till the early hours on the submission paper he'd present to Charles McKinlay and had found it difficult to concentrate after learning of the boys murdered in Redfern. Koori leaders had kept him informed throughout the night about the riots and brawls that had spread across the city. Part of him had wanted to join them and vent his anger. But he'd resisted, because the meeting with McKinlay was contingent on him staying out of a police cell.

The grandfather clock chimed nine times. Charles McKinlay opened the office door and told Lionel to join him.

Lionel stepped forward with briefcase held to the front in two hands like a bashful schoolboy. McKinlay had been a God-like figure in the courtroom, perched high in his leather throne. But up close the hunched old man seemed a mere mortal. He stood half a foot shorter than Lionel and the grey suit hung from his skeletal frame.

Lionel met his intense gaze and was mesmerized by fluorescent blue eyes. He had to look away as the whirlpool in his stomach threatened to pull him under. He offered a sweaty hand. "Mr McKinlay, thank you for seeing me, sir." He heard his own voice, soft and trembling. He wriggled his nose at the rich smell of leather and antique timber furnishings.

McKinlay took his hand in a weak grip, shook it once then closed the door. "Take a seat." He shuffled to the opposite side of a mahogany desk.

Lionel placed the briefcase on the floor then sat and watched him. McKinlay had been hard but fair throughout his career, a High Court Judge intolerant of those who'd wasted his time and the taxpayer's money. As he'd made his way up through the lower courts his support for the police had been a rarity. He believed in public order and had dealt out justice accordingly, unperturbed by civil rights protagonist who'd cried foul over the lengthy sentences imposed. He'd recently turned seventy-eight, and judging by the gossip Lionel had heard in legal circles, his razor-sharp mind hadn't blunted with age.

"Can I see your submission documents, Mr Roberts?" McKinlay said in a well-practiced, dreary tone.

Lionel took two folders from the briefcase and laid them on the desk. Folders thick as a yellow-pages phonebook bound in dark leather. The imprinted gold font on each cover described their contents.

McKinlay reached forward to pick up a folder and weigh it in bony hands. "The Commission requires a paper that outlines your proposal, Mr Roberts. Not an encyclopedia…"

Lionel shifted in the chair. "The issue's too important for lack of detail, sir."

McKinlay eyed him with nonchalance. "I shall get straight to the point…I can see you have spent many hours on this submission. However, at present, there is no need for me to read it. My fellow panel members have already voted in your favor. Against my advice…"

"That's wonderful news."

McKinlay groaned. "Calm down, you do not have your inquiry yet…Rothwell wants me to grant you an investigation phase, fully sponsored by the Attorney-General's department. I want you to tell me. Why should I?"

"The details are in my submission, sir. Multiple reports suggest Koori children are being abused and neglected in the far-western districts. Police are aware of the problem and have identified suspects, yet not one arrest has been made. These children's human rights are being ignored, and that's why you should…Sir."

McKinlay stroked wispy white hair at his forehead. "How does such an investigation, so very far away, aid the situation here in Sydney?"

"Positive action in the Outback can influence what happens in the city, sir. Kooris will take note and realize they aren't being totally ignored. It's all related…"

"If you are referring to the missing girls' cases, surely Senator Galios has made you aware of the reasons for taskforce Azelia's termination? You will never convince me the police have neglected the human rights of a few by favoring anti-terrorism measures that protect millions…"

"It's not my place to argue the point, sir, but the murder of those boys in Redfern last night is the spark kooris were waiting for. It's lit a fire of discontent that threatens to burn out of control...Grant this investigation in the far-west and support any subsequent inquiry. Let it be the positive action that can extinguish the fire."

McKinlay's thick eyebrows jumped. "Have you spoken to Rothwell? It is exactly what he said..."

Lionel resisted a smile. "Attorney-General Rothwell's a wise man, sir."

"No, he is a typical politician...A weak fool, spooked by media coverage of Azelia and the murdered Tindall girl, who considers it too hazardous to ignore you."

"Sir, if I don't find evidence, it works in your favor. Observers would say you acted in the best interests of human rights. And your police buddies will be happy..."

"I shall ignore the reference to my, 'police buddies'." McKinlay glared at him. "And what if human rights abuses are detected out there? Even then, a parliamentary inquiry would not be a given...Rothwell and other politicians prefer to protect the public, and themselves, from such revelations."

"As Mr Rothwell seems to agree, protecting the public's one matter. Ignoring them is another?"

McKinlay sneered. "You lot had your inquiry in '96 and achieved the desired outcome. Why drag the State and this great nation through the same muddy bog, over and over again?"

Lionel rocked back in the chair. *You lot?* He leaned forward, emboldened by a sudden, unknown force within him. "Mr McKinlay, sir, my people continue to drown in that muddy bog. It hasn't disappeared…"

McKinlay dismissed the statement with the flick of a hand. "An interesting debate for another time…You forget though, that unlike Rothwell I am not influenced by public sentiment. Nor the media…" He hesitated. Eyes bored into Lionel. "Tell me about Sinclair and Flintoff…Why did they support you without having any detailed knowledge of your proposal?"

"I've no idea, sir."

McKinlay squinted as he grunted. "I am convinced there was foul play, that they were somehow influenced…I shall find out who is responsible, Mr Roberts, and there will be harsh consequences."

"What exactly are you referring to, sir?"

"Ah, you give your arrogant smile, as though enjoying a victory over me…You, a Koori kid, barely out of law school." McKinlay scoffed so hard he coughed. His eyes sparkled. "Are you aware that as Chairman, under the Act, I set the time-frame for the investigation phase?"

Lionel took a deep breath to calm himself. He exhaled through pursed lips. "I am, sir…How long will I have?"

McKinlay clasped hands on a child-like belly. "I grant you a three-month investigation period. You will appear before me at its conclusion when a final decision regarding an inquiry will be made."

"Three months?" Lionel's voice quivered. "It could take weeks just to form a team…I have multiple locations to visit and hundreds of witnesses to interview…It's impossible to complete it in three months."

"It is simply a matter of prioritization, Mr Roberts. And surely you wish to finalize it as quickly as possible? I imagine you will then be eager to start building your bridges, having found the, solutions, to our nation's problems?"

Lionel refused to take the bait and held his nerve. "I'll return in three months with sufficient evidence to support a parliamentary inquiry, and I'm extremely grateful for the opportunity the Commission affords me. Thank you, sir."

McKinlay's face crumpled in a picture of confusion. "Very well...Karen Flintoff will provide the details you need. Are you conversant with investigation protocols under the Act?"

"I am, unless they've changed?"

"They have not...You will lead an investigation team of three, and can interview witnesses and so on. Your primary role is to coordinate the police investigators." McKinlay waited. Lionel gave a confident nod. "Two Federal Police investigators are required. I shall contact Federal Police Commissioner Watkins to arrange the secondment and ensure their integrity. One investigator will be seconded from the New South Wales Police Force."

"Must I arrange that?"

"No, I will personally send a request to Commissioner Delaney...Questions?"

"Yes, one...Is it still a requirement to nominate a home-base, a secure residence for the safekeeping of evidence, etcetera?"

McKinlay tapped his temple with an open hand. "Silly of me...It is, and this being the official first day, tell me...Where will that home-base be?"

"The Crooked River district…The townships and Aboriginal communities within it."

"Out near the South Australian border is it not? Far north-western corner of the State?"

"That's right."

McKinlay leaned forward. "Interesting…Why Crooked River?"

"It's the logical choice."

McKinlay's forehead wrinkled as he opened the folder in front of him. Eyes skimmed over the submission document. "And yet there is no mention of it here, on page nine, where you have listed the top ten districts of interest. I do hope you have not ignored relevant statistics in making that choice. If I find that to be the case, I shall reject your proposal outright and cancel the investigation."

Lionel frowned at the change of tact. "Sir, statistics only reflect official complaints. Based on my own observations over recent years, the Crooked River district has an alarming number of unreported incidents. Of abuse and neglect…" He broke eye contact to tell his lie. "I'd always intended to start there..."

McKinlay's fingers formed a tepee under his nose. His piercing eyes darted over Lionel's face for what seemed an hour. "Mr Roberts, as I would say to my son when he was a boy…Have your fun stirring the wasps' nest, but do not come running to me when they bite."

THIRTEEN

Lionel Roberts finished the mixed grill with extra bacon, the usual Saturday brunch at his favorite eatery on George Street. He sipped a cappuccino then opened the newspaper and closed it again, unable to think of anything but his pending investigation. He glanced at the phone. 10.45am. He had a grand performance planned for 11am and didn't want to be late, so he called the waitress and paid his bill.

He'd made numerous enemies since returning to Sydney, with those on both sides of the justice system who didn't appreciate his forthright manner. But Sam Cartright, the self-elected president of 'South Sydney Rights for Aboriginals', was one of few allies. He'd always been like a big brother, someone who shared Lionel's passion for Koori justice but delivered it by more violent means. When Sam had asked for assistance, Lionel had eagerly agreed to support the Hyde Park protest rally.

He left the café, turned his jacket's collar up to protect from August winds and turned towards the park. A group of boisterous teenagers swept him along the footpath with them. They thrust homemade banners in the air and chanted. Cops are kiddy killers! Pigs don't care! They reminded him of student days when he'd supported causes he didn't fully understand while insisting he did.

He dipped his head to a horse-mounted policewoman as he rushed past. Sirens whirled. Car horns honked. Traffic police shouted instructions and tried to clear cars and pedestrians from gridlocked streets. He glanced to the opposite side of the road where hundreds of protestors surged towards the rally. Armed with song and banner, an army laid siege to the heart of Sydney.

He entered Hyde Park and saw a stage up ahead. Sam stood on it and spoke into a microphone.

Lionel shuffled towards the stage and studied the faces of those jammed tight around him. They were aged from teens to old age pensioners, with white skin, dark skin and all shades in between. Whether they were there to support kooris or simply hated the government, he didn't care. Angry crowds made for nervous politicians.

He squeezed his way to the front and Sam sent security guards to escort him onto the stage. He acknowledged Sam's introduction with a quick wave to the fifty-thousand strong crowd then took the microphone from him.

Lionel was a gifted public speaker and soon whipped the crowd into a frenzy. He told them how the police had failed every citizen of the State. How the government didn't care about Sydney's missing girls from minority groups. Yet they'd poured money into anti-terrorism resources because two Caucasian women had died in a recent hostage situation. The crowd jeered the name of each politician he slandered.

He then told the story of Eddy Tindall and Ben Neilsen, two respectable Koori boys, future boxing champions who'd been cut down in their prime by trigger-happy cops. Killed in cold blood for committing a petty crime…And the cops who'd done it? Betts the shooter, Lionel told them, had been charged with two counts of manslaughter overnight. They cheered.

"But what about Senior Constable Daniel Porter?" Lionel asked them. They booed. "He forced them into a corner…Was there a choice for those frightened boys but to fight back?"

"No!" they replied with fury.

"Do we want them both to rot in jail?"

"Yes," they roared as one.

Lionel paused to let the noise subside and continued in a calmer tone. "We will prevail in this battle, but please, stop fighting amongst yourselves and hurting the innocent. Save your fury for the government, and the police, the real enemies." They roared. He pumped a clenched fist above his head and yelled into the microphone. "Stop police brutality, the neglect of human rights. Stop it now!"

Hyde Park erupted in a chorus of defiance. Signs bobbed up and down. Banners flew high. "Stop it now! Stop it now!" thousands chanted, over and over.

Lionel's chest heaved as a wave of euphoria washed over him.

Sam took the microphone and placed an arm around his shoulder. "Awesome job bro, they love you," he shouted above the noise then put the microphone to his mouth. "Let's hear it for Lionel Roberts, our number one human rights lawyer. A seeker of Koori justice. No, all justice."

The crowd roared their admiration. Lionel waved to acknowledge them, hugged Sam, then walked to the back of the stage. He spotted a gap in the crowd, an exit route from the park. He stepped down the stairs.

When he reached the bottom, Tugger Walford grabbed his elbow. He marched him into a cordoned area behind the stage. Lines of riot police with shields stood close by.

"What the hell you doin'?" Tugger said, face crimson.

"Let go of my arm." Lionel glared at him. "Is this how you treat an old friend?"

Riot police turned towards them.

Tugger presented the ID card hanging around his neck. When they turned away, he prodded Lionel's chest. "We are friends…But after the rubbish I've just heard, aint sure for how much longer."

Lionel hesitated to compose himself. His heart thumped, still flooded with adrenaline he'd sucked from the crowd. "You can't shove me around like this, Derek."

"Only mum and me enemies call me Derek, and you aint me mum…Look, I've spent the last two days tryin' to calm this mob. And now you've gone an' blown it all up again."

"The riots must continue until our demands are met. Why aren't you angry those boys were murdered?"

"I'm sad as the next fella, and maybe it coulda been different bu--."

"That's the point, Derek…It, should, be different. They were petty thieves."

Tugger scowled. "Call me Derek again, see what happens…Since when is armed robbery a petty crime? Did you even know 'em? They sure weren't the saints you spoke of…"

"Never met Eddy. Know his mother. Didn't know Neilsen."

"Not sayin' they deserved to die, but you left some important details out of your speech."

"Such as?"

"Them boys were meth addicts. They sold drugs to use 'em. Funny you didn't mention that…"

"You're taking their side?" Lionel pointed to the riot police. "And who says they were dealing?"

"Ask your mate Sam, they were workin' for him."

"Nonsense…"

"Is it? I read your newspaper ads and pamphlets, and figured you'd matured into a fine fella. Still got the same dorky walk, but I saw confidence up on that stage that weren't there before. And y--."

"I'm not the kid you knew."

"Wrong. Still wide-eyed with your head up your own arse…"

"I have work to do…" Lionel started towards the police lines.

Tugger blocked him. "Aint finished with you yet…How you gunna fix it? How you gunna end this bloody race war you've started?"

Lionel stepped back and shrugged. "You heard, I asked them to stop the violence. But you know what, part of me wishes I hadn't. Some dead white kids might be what's needed to get their full attention. Maybe a few politician's sons?"

"Don't play the tough hombre, it doesn't suit you…Father Roberts taught you violence aint the answer, be rollin' in his grave hearin' this. What's happened to you?"

Lionel gazed over Tugger's shoulder towards Saint Mary's Cathedral. "I grew up and started thinking for myself. The church doesn't have the answers anymore. Not to my questions…"

"Thinking for yourself aint a bad thing. Dismissin' your faith is."

"I question religion's power to heal..."

"It still can…And it will."

Lionel frowned as he shrugged. He threw arms to the front with palms facing up. "It causes most of the conflict in the world, and always has. Think about it...Hatred in Asia, between Buddhists, Catholics and Muslims, and amongst themselves. Genocide in the name of religion…And the Middle East, being destroyed again by Christians and Muslims on modern-day crusades. Just two examples…Mass death and destruction. For what?"

"You forgettin' young fella…Father Roberts taught us that faith brings peace."

Lionel scoffed. "I loved Father Roberts, and he was well-intentioned. But wasn't he a hypocrite to preach that religion is peaceful when he knew its violent history?"

"No, he weren't, and belief in it can stop violence."

"Not anymore…It's become an evil that divides mankind more than skin color."

Tugger hesitated as though waiting for more. "You're serious? And God?"

"He's the white man's God. I'm guided by our spiritual fathers now, and they watch over me, help me follow the path they've set…"

Tugger sniggered. "You've lost your bloody marbles..."

"I have to get home." Lionel patted his shoulder and turned to leave.

"Okay, you aint bonkers. Well, maybe a bit…" They both laughed. "Give me one more minute to explain somethin'?"

Lionel huffed. "What?"

"Dan Porter. You're wrong about 'im."

"Isn't he the same as Betts, a racist pig?"

"Both them fellas worked this city for years and never had problems with kooris…"

"Why defend them? Betts showed obvious contempt for blacks. I assume Porter's the same?"

"You're wrong. His girlfriend's Jamaican you know?"

"You've never seen a racist with a black girl fetish before?"

"You aint listenin'. Port's a good fella who helps Koori kids. He's one of the few coppers been lookin' for these girls."

"He worked Azelia?"

"Yep, and the poor bugger's shattered about Nadia Tindall. He cares, he aint no racist…"

Lionel rocked his head from side to side. Had he condemned Porter without knowing the facts? "I trust your judgment of character. But Porter initiated the pursuit and he can't be guilt free?"

They'd moved closer to the riot police. Tugger leaned towards him. "How'd Betts get charged with manslaughter," he whispered, "when his partner's the only witness? Weren't nobody else about…"

Lionel stroked his goatee. "Porter?"

"Yep, and Betts would've got off otherwise. That's what the bosses wanted…"

"No doubt, this murder's their worst nightmare." Lionel paused. "The pressure on him to support Betts' story...Yet he told the truth?"

"And blames 'imself for the whole lot...I called 'im at home this morning. He's gettin' death threats. Car was vandalized last night. Has mongrels abusin' his missus and daughter. He don't deserve it."

"I'll speak with Sam and convince him to drop the smear campaign against him."

"Ta, I'd appreciate that..."

Lionel walked towards the buzzing crowd. He turned when he reached the police line and waved goodbye.

"Hope them ancestors of yours are takin' you on the right journey," Tugger shouted. "I'll pray for ya..."

FOURTEEN

Porter stopped outside the open doorway of Deidre Sharpe's office on the 9th floor of Police Headquarters and peered inside. She sat in an armchair in the room's far corner with a tinted window behind her and a coffee table in front. She held a file in her left hand and a coffee mug in her right.

In a moment of boredom during the half-hour taxi ride from home, he'd Googled Deidre and read her police employee profile. She'd been the NSW Police Force's chief psychiatrist for nine years and had run her own private practice before that. She specialized in psychological trauma and working with frontline police daily, she saw plenty of it. Her team of junior counselors conducted most of the force's standard, mandatory counseling sessions.

Deidre personally conducted the psych assessment interviews of those officers involved in major critical incidents such as police shootings. According to her profile, she deemed them integral to her studies of Post-Traumatic Stress Disorder.

Porter stepped into the doorway and coughed. She smiled, told him to come in and close the door. He dawdled across the room in rubber flip-flops and dropped into the chair opposite her with a loud sigh. He pulled a wrinkled t-shirt over the top of fleecy tracksuit pants, sat back and crossed arms.

She had long legs covered by a full-length pant and wore a pale-blue blouse that revealed toned arms from the elbows down. A pleasant face, peach colored and smooth with minimal makeup, topped by a bun of honey-blonde hair. Intelligent olive-green eyes flecked with hazel.

He rubbed the three-day growth on his jaw and watched her as she watched him.

She placed the file on the table then sipped from the mug.

Porter sniffed the air and savored the coffee's rich aroma. "You like yours strong?"

"It has to be for these Monday morning blues...Can I make you one?"

"Nah, she's right." He glanced at the file. "Mine?"

"Yes, and it's more interesting than most service histories I've read." She set her face in stone and leaned back to study him.

"Wanna know how I'm feeling, don't you?"

She smirked as though she'd won the first battle. "Why don't you te--."

"Bloody awful and don't wanna be here."

"Well, I knew that..." She leaned her head to the side. "Your body language typifies the hardened cop who detests my 'warm and fuzzy' world. And, I overheard your conversation with Superintendent Williams the other night..."

"Listen, why don't you just ask the questions designed to cover their arses, I'll answer, and we can both get back to doing something useful."

"Daniel, you and I talking, is useful. And mandatory... But you decide what you'll take from it." She pointed at his nose. "That must have hurt? Always thought it fascinating how the eyes bruise as well..."

"It's Dan, not Daniel…And I don't need sympathy, or a friend, so cut the bullshit and ask what you wanna know. Has the shooting fucked me up or not? What?"

Her eyes sparkled. "First of all, I'd like to know more about you."

"You read my file. It's in there."

"You're right, it is," she said in a calm voice. "But it only tells me what you've done and when you did it. You've seen and done things most people can't imagine, Dan. I need to know if, and how, those events have affected you."

He glared at her. "Isn't this a debrief session?"

"Yes, we're here to discuss the shooting. But, as I've explained, I can't begin to understand how it's affected you, without knowing how your health's been before the shooting, compared to now, after it."

"Same as always…"

"Have you noticed any changes?"

"It's only been four days…Like what?"

She hesitated. "You seem tense and on edge. Have you always been?"

"You're a mind reader now? Not tense, I feel fine."

"You've been wringing your hands and pumping your left leg since you sat. It's understandable that you're tense, Dan. You've been through a terrible ordeal."

He unlocked hands and held his leg still. He turned away from her, towards the window. "If you reckon so…"

"Any physiological changes?"

"Such as?"

"Problems sleeping? Loss of appetite?"

"Nah…"

"Please be honest, Dan, you don't look like you sleep well."

"I sleep fine..." He rubbed under eyes. "Next."

"Shallow breathing? Heavy sweating?"

He turned back to face her. Had she climbed inside his head? She'd described his symptoms to a tee…He placed hands over wet armpits.

"Sudden mood swings? Feeling down?" She persisted. "More aggressive than usual? Abnormally emotional?"

He dismissed the guilt surrounding his recent behavior. It was none of her business. He'd talk about the shooting and nothing else. "Nah, I'm fine."

"Do you smoke? Are you a heavy drinker, Dan?"

"Never smoked, and don't drink much…Try to keep in shape and it gets harder at our age, doesn't it? You look like you work out?" He flashed his most charming smile, hoping she'd drop her guard and change the line of questioning.

She wrote in the notebook then gave him a look of pity that left him in no doubt she'd seen through his pathetic flirtation. "Be aware of your feelings over coming weeks. Call me if you experience anything I've mentioned. Okay?"

He dipped his head.

"Are you in a relationship, Dan? Do you have family and friends you can talk to?"

"Yeah, to the girlfriend and family. Friends? Judging by messages left in emails and on social media, stuff all…" He smiled because he wanted to show he didn't care that all his best mates, except Steve Williams, had turned their backs on him. Didn't care that the entire police force had labeled him an internal witness 'dog', a whistle-blower. But he did care, and it crushed his soul more than he'd ever admit.

"Tell me about your support network. Your family and girlfriend…"

Porter sighed because Deidre Sharpe wasn't going away. He was trapped in her web until she'd heard enough and decided to set him free. A reluctant narrator, he told her what she wanted to know.

He'd met Jane in London eight years ago during a police rugby tour of the UK. He'd suffered a facial gash during a game and she was the nurse who'd taken care of him. Born in Jamaica, she was the eldest of three girls and now thirty-four. She'd moved to England aged ten and had been widowed at twenty-five when her husband died of liver disease. She had one child, Amber, who was now fifteen. After two years of long-distance romance Porter had asked Jane to move to Sydney. She and Amber had lived with him since.

He told Diedre that his father Les and mother Irene, both sixth generation Australians of Irish descent, were alive and in good health. They still lived in the house he'd been raised in, set on three hundred acres of prime South Coast farmland. Les had closed the dairy years ago but still kept a few potty calves and horses to keep busy. Irene loved to bake and help at the library. His younger brother, Craig, worked overseas and hadn't been spotted for ten years. Deidre didn't ask where or why, so he didn't tell her.

"Sounds lovely, a farm by the sea." She wrote while she spoke. "Perhaps you and the girls should visit your parents for a while?"

Porter smirked. "That coming from you or Steve Williams? He's tried to get me away from Sydney since the shooting. Might send Jane and Amber down for a while, be safer for 'em."

"Steve's concerned, and I won't lie, he mentioned the farm. Time off work would be beneficial."

"Nah, wouldn't do it to mum. Besides, couldn't relax knowing what's happening up here. Another five girls were taken over the weekend. I need to get back to work."

"Yes, I heard. Horrendous...I read that you worked on Azelia. How has that case affected you?"

"It hasn't, was just another job." He pursed lips, as he'd done as a kid whenever he told porkpies to his mum.

She cocked her head. "Have you had thoughts of self-harm, Dan? Or similar?"

"Nah, never."

She paused to observe him for what seemed an eternity. "I don't wish to force you off work but please consider the farm...Do you need medication to help you relax? To sleep?"

His demeanor turned from lukewarm to frozen in an instant. "Don't do pills..."

She sank into the chair while she wrote then stopped and stared at the floor. All of a sudden, she sat upright and plucked his service file from the table. She read it for a half a minute. "You were, twenty-three when you joined the police...Did you work before that?"

He watched her. Did she already know the answer? He couldn't remember if his file contained previous employment history. "I was in the military," he blurted.

Her eyebrows arched. "Really? Army? Navy? From what age?"

He swore to himself. She hadn't known. "Army. Was too young..."

"How interesting."

"Nah, not at all. More of a past life forgotten..." His mother cuffed the back of his head. He'd told another porkpie.

Deidre held the pen against her chin. "I'd like to discuss that."

"I'd rather not."

"Tell me at least, why did you leave the army? Was there active service?"

He blew hot air through lips to release pressure and whistled like an old-style campfire kettle. "You still haven't asked me about the shooting. Again, isn't that why I'm here?"

"You said you're okay with the shooting, for now?"

"And I've answered your questions…Reckon it's time to go?"

She glanced at her watch. "Yes, it's eleven already. We'll discuss the shooting next week."

He leaned forward, chin cradled between thumb and forefinger. "Next week? Serious?"

"Next Monday, Dan, same time." Her eyes examined his face. They both stood. "You, may think you're okay. But I, must be certain of it."

He rushed for the door. "I can hardly wait…"

FIFTEEN

Porter sat on the lounge room sofa as he swallowed the last piece of a ham sandwich. He craved a neck massage after his torturous session with Deidre Sharpe and Jane was happy to oblige. Her velvet hands on his crocodile skin melted away tension. After ten minutes of bliss he thanked her with a peck on the lips. She turned it into a deep French kiss, her tongue hot and moist in his mouth. Amber had netball practice she reminded him, was getting a lift home with her coach and wouldn't be home for hours.

Despite his protests, she dragged him up to their bedroom. She ripped his clothes off and threw him onto the bed. She jumped on, pinned him down, and ignored claims that the stitches on his nose would burst.

For the first time in months they made love. Afterwards they snoozed, bodies entwined, sweat-drenched and naked.

Porter stirred after fifteen minutes and shifted onto his side to watch her. He chuckled at her cat-like purring and the way her nose wriggled while she slept. When she woke an hour later with a contented glow over her face, he kissed her forehead and drew her close.

She stroked his chest hairs. "What da hell took so long, Dan Porter? Been waiting months for that…"

"You saying I had a choice?" He grinned and caressed her back. "Worth the wait though, wasn't it?"

She pressed a finger to her mouth and squinted. "Hmm…"

"I'll give ya, hmm..." He reached under the sheet and tickled her firm stomach.

She wriggled and kicked and begged him to stop. When he did, she propped herself on one elbow.

"Why you staring like that?" he said.

Her face crumpled in a frown. She began a reply then stopped.

"Jane?"

"Okay, okay. It's your eyes, babe…Once da brightest green and full of life. Maybe it's because you're tired, but now they're dull and colorless..."

He said nothing.

"Are you still upset about da Tindall girl? And those boys? You've been so quiet, seem so sad…" She spoke in a hypnotizing melody and ran fingers across his forehead as though trying to wipe away worries. "Please, how can I help you?"

"I've been thinking about you, and us..."

She leaned over him. Long nipples brushed his chest. "Me? Us? You say that with a cold, blank look on your face…What am I supposed to feel?"

He sat up, back against the bed head. "Been thinking of our future..."

She pulled away from him. "What da hell?"

He dropped his eyes. How to tell her?

She poked a finger into his chest. Her face reddened. "Well, what's da story?"

"Babe, calm down…" He paused, troubled by the dread on her face. Was it best to let her go, knowing she and Amber would have a better life away from his moods and excessive drinking? Was he trying to convince her of it, too gutless to say it? "Just worried that I'm gunna lose you..."

She sighed. "You're crazy to think that."

"I've been such a bastard lately and wouldn't blame you for leaving…"

She covered herself with a sheet and sat up cross-legged, eyes level with his. "Nope, I'll always be here for you, babe…Amber and I, we aint going anywhere…"

"Hope so…Sorry, you know I'm a shocker with feelings."

She caressed him with kind eyes. "Don't be, or they'll punish you." She moved to cradle his head in her lap and stroked his hair. "What happened with da psychiatrist today?"

"Told her I'm okay."

"And she believed you?"

"Reckon so…"

"What else you talk about?"

"Usual psych bullshit…" He looked up into her face and smirked. "And you…"

Her eyebrows jumped. "Really?"

"She asked how we'd met, about mum and dad…" He paused. How to approach the subject? "She made a good suggestion…"

"What?"

"She reckons I'd be less stressed if you and Amber went down to the farm for a few weeks."

"And you agree?"

"Yeah, I do. It's not safe here."

She shook her head. "We're not leaving you."

Porter couldn't tell her the truth, that he wanted to stay and hunt Nadia Tindall's killer. "Do it for Amber, babe. Who knows what these mongrel vigilantes will do?"

"Come with us? We'll leave in da morning…"

He paused to search for an alibi and found a lie. "Can't, got another appointment with the police psych."

"When?"

"Thursday, then more next week. Drive down in your car, and I'll have one from the insurance company by Wednesday. I'll join you in a fortnight when the appointments are over."

"Two weeks? Nope, I'm not leaving you here alone, not with da way you feeling right now."

"Jane, please? You asked how to help. This will…"

Her eyes darted over his face. "Okay, okay. We'll leave tomorrow, on one condition."

"Yeah?"

"You're not to work. Rest at home, see da psychiatrist, then come to us."

"Deal. But I've gotta go to the office tomorrow, just once."

"What da hell for?"

"Dunno, but Steve Williams wants to see me. Will take a taxi and be home in no time."

"You'd better be…" She bent to kiss him.

He sat up, returned the soft kiss and stroked her cheek. He swept a strand of hair from it and smiled, grateful for the love of such a woman. "You're right, you know, about it being dangerous to ignore emotions…"

"Really? And what's brought on this sudden self-evaluation?"

"You're the most important person in my life but I've never told you that. I've taken you for granted…Sorry."

"Babe, no…You're da kindest, sweetest, most caring man I've known. That's why you feel so much pain. How can I not love you?" She giggled. "With your busted nose, black eyes and scraggly beard…Who could leave such an adorable man?"

He wanted to laugh with her but sensed a need to be serious. He said words that had never left his mouth. "I love you, Jane. You're my angel. Love you more than I thought possible. Marry me, babe. Let's finally do this?"

Her jaw dropped. She flashed a smile prettier than a thousand rainbows. "Babe, you sure? It's da first time you've told me that…And now you want marriage? Can hardly believe it..." She squealed and hugged him. Then she swayed back and her facial expression turned sour. "Don't you be messin' with me now…"

"Not messing, and sorry, don't have a ring yet…But what you reckon, will you marry me?"

She leaned close and held his face in both hands. Eyes locked, souls merged into one. She kissed him like he'd never been kissed. "Did that answer your question?"

He licked his lips. "Reckon that's, in the affirmative?"

She hugged him tight. "Yes, thank da Lord, you've finally done it. We're getting married."

They laughed together, drew apart to kiss then laughed some more.

She stopped, leaned her head to the side and eyed him. "When?"

"When what?"

"When are we getting married?"

"Babe, we've just agreed to do it…Don't know, when…"

"My family's coming to visit in four months," she blurted. "Perfect, we'll do it then."

He frowned and tried to unjumble thoughts. "Yeah, sure, why not? But won't you need more time, to organize everything?"

"Yay! Don't believe it's happening." She bobbed in front of him, like a toddler who'd drunk too much red cordial. "Don't worry, I'll plan everything."

"Mum?" Amber called out from downstairs. "Dan?"

Jane squealed. "Oh my god. Amber." She leaped from the bed and took her nightie from a hook on the wall. "I've got to tell Amber." She pecked his cheek, turned and ran. Then she stopped in the doorway and marched back. She planted herself next to him.

He'd never been on the receiving end of a such an intense stare. "What's wrong?"

"I'll marry you. But there'll be no secrets..."

His face twitched. Eyes blinked quicker than usual. "Like?"

"Your nightmares. You're keeping things from me. Secrets..."

"Not secrets babe. Only things from the past you don't wanna know."

"What happened?"

"Now's not the time…But I promise to tell you before the wedding."

"You'd better, or there won't be one." She kissed him and ran from the room.

He fell back on the bed and watched the ceiling spin. *Bloody hell, Porter, what have you done?*

SIXTEEN

Late Monday afternoon, Lionel Roberts sat in a waiting room outside Karen Flintoff's office in Sydney's CBD. She'd phoned earlier and told him to come to see her but hadn't said why. He chewed a fingernail and tapped his feet. Was there a problem with his submission to the Human Rights Commission?

His past few days had been hectic. After Saturday's Hyde Park rally, he'd spent that night, all of Sunday and most of Monday morning preparing for the investigation phase. As feared, because it contradicted what he'd told Charles McKinlay, the most recent reports of abuse in the far-western districts confirmed that only two alleged victims resided in Crooked River. Had McKinlay found the same discrepancy? Was Flintoff going to tell him that his investigation was over? Before it had begun?

His phone showed 5.40pm. Flintoff made him sweat. A text message from Wendy buzzed and he read it. Michael from State Archives had agreed to keep their discovery of the missing Welfare Board files a secret. He grinned at the news.

The office door opened and Flintoff told him to come in. He took a seat opposite, watched her across the desk while she shuffled papers and searched for any sign his investigation would go ahead. She was close to forty, attractive but not beautiful. She wore a navy business suit, and a white blouse buttoned up to her neck. Auburn hair hung to her shoulders.

She peered over brown-rimmed glasses and made brief eye contact. "Do you know Klose and Rhodes, the Federal police investigators on your team?"

Lionel closed eyes and suppressed a sigh of relief. He still had his investigation. He opened them. "Yes, Fred Klose's part Koori and will be a wonderful asset. Don't know Rhodes, but Fred says he's a brilliant investigator."

She watched him through dull blue eyes. "I can confirm the AG's department is sponsoring your investigation, with all expenses to be met by this office." She slid papers across the desk. "Read and sign each page."

He did as she'd instructed for the first two pages and frowned when he came to a section on page three. He read aloud. "Name of immediate supervisor and supporting comments."

"Dennis Bourke isn't it? Is he aware of your investigation? Will that be a problem?"

He saw from the glint in her eye that she hoped to make him squirm. "You could try to have Dennis stop me from doing this, considering he doesn't approve of it. But we both know you won't..."

She sneered with gritted teeth. "It's despicable what you've done, Roberts, especially the way you've done it. Blackmail's the lowest of the low and I'd love more than anything to stomp all over your ambitions..." She huffed. "Dennis Bourke owes me. He'll sign and make supporting comments tomorrow."

Lionel smirked, unable to disguise delight at his triumph.

She squinted at him. "You think this is over? It's only just beginning..."

"Meaning?"

"I can't hurt you, but you've made enemies with two of this nation's most powerful men. Rothwell's incensed and hates you more than I do. McKinlay's been humiliated and vows revenge. Can't honestly believe they'll just let you carry on and get away with it?"

"I'm at war with the established order of things…I expect to make powerful enemies and I'm prepared for them."

"Listen to you…You've no idea what these men will do. Their stubborn pride will eventually defeat all reason, and then they'll make their move. Be careful if I were you…"

"Your friendly advice is appreciated." He leaned closer and held her gaze. "I can't control what actions Rothwell and McKinlay decide to take. But if I were you, Karen, I'd ensure your assistance continues if and when called upon." She averted her eyes. "Do we understand each other?"

She snatched the papers from him and flicked to the next page. "Regarding the New South Wales cop…We've had nothing back on that request, have you?"

"Not yet. They've tried seconding another investigator of Koori descent without success. Told me I'll know by tomorrow afternoon."

"Rental accommodation's organized and paid up for three months. Have three vehicles waiting for you out there, office equipment and supplies have been ordered. The driver taking you to the airport on Wednesday will give you credit cards and the expense account details. Questions?"

"Must I inform local police we're coming?"

She kept reading. "Inspector George Barrett, Chief of Detectives for the Crooked River command, is your contact officer and has already been notified. Requests for assistance will go through him."

"Sounds good." He placed a palm on the desk and prepared to stand. "Anything else?"

She flipped to the final page. "Read the declaration, sign, then fill out section 34." She slid the papers to him.

He read, signed his name, and dropped eyes to section 34. He smiled then read aloud. "Proposed name of Investigation Phase."

"It's okay if you don't have one, the department will name it…" She pulled the papers towards her.

Lionel did have a name. He'd had it for years, since he'd followed the 'Bringing them Home' inquiry. "Carinya," he told her as chest swelled. "It'll be known as the Carinya investigation."

She held pen to paper. "Spelt with a C?"

He nodded. He wanted her to ask what it meant but doubted she cared.

"Stop in the waiting room," she said without looking up. "I'll get copies made for you."

He strolled to the door, opened it halfway and turned back. "A happy, peaceful home."

Her forehead crinkled. "What?"

"Carinya, it's from an Aboriginal language…The word for a happy, peaceful home." He gave a courteous nod. "Thanks for your assistance, Karen. Until next time..."

120

She scoffed like a hangman ignoring pleas for mercy. "Are you really that naïve?" He flinched at her hateful glare. "There won't be, a next time."

SEVENTEEN

Porter's pulse went into overdrive as he stepped from a taxi then stood in front of City Central police station. He clicked his tongue against the roof of a dry mouth and studied the dark, angry sky. Rapid exhalations formed steam clouds that floated away on a numbing breeze. Only on his first day as a probationary constable had he felt such apprehension arriving at work. What confrontation awaited inside the concrete monstrosity? What did his boss, Steve Williams, want to tell him?

He ignored the stares and snide remarks from uniformed cops smoking in the forecourt and scurried through automatic doors into the entry foyer. He ducked left to avoid front-desk staff then swiped his ID tag to unlock a glass security door. Once inside the ground floor's secure area he bypassed the elevators. He rushed to the stairwell and side-stepped into it.

He pushed the fire door shut and flung his back against the wall. Heart pounded his ribcage. His brain spun out of control on its axis. He waited a few seconds and listened for movement above him. Convinced the stairwell was empty, he leaped up three stairs at a time. When he reached the fourth floor he pulled the fire door open. He turned a corner and hurried into Steve Williams' office. He closed the door then flopped into a chair opposite him. Panting. Skin moist.

Williams stopped typing and recoiled. "Christ, what happened to you?"

Porter fought to regain his breath. "Nothing...You said 10am, Tuesday. Here I am."

Williams frowned and rested hands on the desk. "That's a mangy beard you've got if I've ever seen one. And did you run from home? You look like crap..."

Porter agreed. He'd gasped at his reflection in the mirror that morning. "So everyone keeps telling me..."

Williams chuckled. "Sorry. How you going? Any problems downstairs when you came in?"

"Nah, no-one said a word...I feel beaut and ready to get back into it." Porter wiped his forehead with a handkerchief then scratched wet circles under armpits. "Took the stairs, needed the exercise. Been sat on my arse watching footy and drinking beer all weekend..."

Williams lowered his eyes. "I shouldn't have asked you to come in. Hoped it'd do you good to get out and confront the haters. But I can see it's done the opposite..."

"What?"

"It's stressed you out, Port. You're shaking and sweating. Your face is still swollen and bruised. I fucked up, and should've come to see you at home."

Porter said nothing.

Williams sighed as though disgusted with himself. "How'd you find it with Deidre yesterday?"

"I'm not going back there, mate. Waste of time."

"She said it went okay?"

"So much for confidentiality..."

"Don't worry, she didn't tell me the juicy bits."

"Were none, she didn't even ask about the shooting."

"She will...Look, I asked her to suggest that you get away. Or the girls at least..."

Porter smirked. "Wasn't easy convincing Jane, 'cos we're getting married. They're driving to the farm now."

"Good, glad they're out of harm's way..." Williams' mouth fell open. "Wait a minute, did I hear...? You're not?"

"Yeah, mate. And sooner than later, according to Jane."

"Dan Porter getting married. Don't believe it..."

"Bloody hell, neither do I..."

Williams reached across the desk and they shook hands. "Congrats, she's a top girl, you've done well."

"Yeah..."

"So, you're heading to the farm after this too?"

"Nah, mate. Like I told Deidre, gotta get back to work and find the mongrels who killed Nadia. The blokes taking these girls..."

"I've already transferred those cases to Missing Persons unit."

"Yeah, figured I'm here for the handover...But no need to take me off the investigation altogether. Can still search for the white van."

"We need to discuss that..." Williams hesitated. Porter sensed he had bad news and delayed giving it. "Speaking of white vans, we had a close call overnight."

"Yeah?"

"They tried to grab another Koori girl, in North Sydney this time. She managed to jump from the van and get away."

"Serious? She okay?"

"Few scratches...She's only twelve but cluey for her age. Said their heads and faces were covered and could only give a basic description. Three men, all dressed in black. She did remember a partial rego though…"

"And?"

"I'll admit, we got excited. She described a white van with red markings, and the database search came ba--."

"The same?"

"But too good to be true…"

"Stolen?"

"It was reported to have been stolen an hour before the attempted abduction. Was found burnt out in the Harbour National Park, around five this morning."

Porter scratched a cheek. "A white van with red markings. Nadia, and now this girl. Hope we've sussed out the owner?"

"Van's registered to an international company…" Williams took a printout from the in-tray and read from it. "Kennard Atkins Mining Corporation. They own several mines and quarries around the country. They export mining equipment, mainly through Hong Kong and onto China, and Singapore towards the Middle East. Hi-tech tools small enough for shipping containers."

"Wait, KA's an abbreviation of Kennard Atkins. And KA, the letters branded on Nadia's back. Strange coincidence, or something in it?"

Williams' grey eyebrows arched. "I noticed that too. But why would a mining company want to brand girls with its logo?"

"Suppose…" Porter frowned. "Van was stolen from where?"

"Their warehouse near the airport, reported by the night manager. He checked out okay but let's face it, anyone can make a false report over the phone these days."

"I've said it for years, it's a fraudster's paradise…Hope you plan to interview more staff at Kennard Atkins? Are you gunna check out their bosses and see what business they're doing?"

"Detectives will meet with executives from their CBD office this afternoon. But I'm not expecting much to come of it. It's a massive company with thousands of employees. And you ever known kidnappers to use their own vehicles? On multiple occasions? I've no doubt the van was stolen…"

Porter cocked his head. "Maybe…I'll head out tomorrow and speak with workers from the warehouse. Has anyone viewed their surveillance footage? Anyone checked to see if the reported stolen time is legit? Have analysts gone over all reports of stolen vehicles in the past few months, checked to see if there's a pattern in MO and the type of vans being stolen?"

Williams sighed. "It's all been covered, Port. And I'm sorry, you're off this job. Completely."

"What? I know these cases inside out, much better than the fools at Missing Persons."

"Call came from the top. It's out of my hands."

"From who?"

"Delaney wants you out of the media spotlight, gone from the city if possible. Says it's too damaging for the force. And dangerous for you, with the death threats and other dramas you're having…"

"Too damaging? And you agree? You're only protecting the force, don't give a fuck what's best for me…"

"Bullshit…And right now, are you well enough to know what that is?"

Porter ignored the question because Williams was right. "Mate, every night when trying to sleep, I see Nadia and Eddy's faces. If I'm ever gunna forgive myself for what happened I need to find these bastards and put 'em away. Can't you give me a chance to do it?"

"I spoke with forensics guys regarding Nadia this morning…Nothing came from DNA or other tests. We've got no suspects, and fuck all hope of finding any."

"There'll be less hope if you send me away?"

"Listen, I've tried to keep you here but for the immediate future you can't work in the city. Delaney's adamant. He's giving you two options."

"Fuck Delaney. You blokes are all the same…"

"You know that's not true. I'm only the messenger…"

Porter massaged his forehead with stiff fingers. "The options are?"

"He wants you off work until after Betts' first court appearance. Special leave with full pay."

"They've refused his bail for a reason, hoping the riots will die down. It could be a month until he's in court…"

"Best you take the paid leave then…Delaney will suspend you otherwise."

"He can't suspend me…Haven't been charged, criminal or internally. And can't force me to take leave. Not unless Diedre Sharpe says I'm gunna neck myself. And she won't…"

"I told Delaney you'd say that. And you're right, we can't force you off work." Williams pressed a button on the desk phone and spoke to his assistant. "If he's here, send him in."

Porter stared at him. "And?"

"Wait, someone's joining us..."

Three knocks on the door. Williams told the visitor to come in and take a seat.

Porter turned to the man who'd sat next to him. He squinted, because he looked familiar. "Who are you?"

Williams cleared his throat. "Port, meet Lionel Roberts. Knew you wouldn't want time off, so I answered a request from the Attorney Generals' department. Lionel's proposal is your second option..."

Porter huffed at Williams. He glared at Lionel.

Lionel shifted in the seat and offered a hand.

Porter ignored it. "Roberts? The bloke who's been calling for my head in the papers?" His face tingled, hotter. "That's where I've seen you, on the tele…At that Hyde Park rally? Calling me a kiddy killer and trying to throw me in with Betts…You're that Lionel Roberts?"

Lionel withdrew his hand and turned to Williams. "You said he'd know I was coming."

Williams opened his mouth to speak.

Porter leaned forward. He raised a hand to cut him off then stared at Lionel. "Ignorant bastard. Don't you fucking talk like I'm not here…Tugger Walford says you're switched on, but you're the last bloke I wanna see right now so you can't be too smart…What the hell are you doing here?"

Lionel's eyes pleaded with Williams. Hands fidgeted in his lap.

"Port, calm down," Williams demanded. "This was my idea."

Porter slouched in the chair and slowed his breathing. Still. Then in an instant he sat upright. Veins at temples throbbed. "Calm down? Bloody hell, my girls have been scared shitless 'cos of this turd and his henchmen. Had hoons at our door, threats day and night. And you expect me to calm down?"

"Okay, I fucked up. Again..." Williams said, tone impatient. "Lionel has an offer to make. Can you hear him out?"

Porter folded arms.

Lionel faced him. "I understand that you're angry. Tugger, whom I respect greatly, changed my opinion of you. I apologize..."

Porter blew air at the ceiling. His lips vibrated like those of an exhausted trumpeter.

"You've been nominated for secondment to an investigation team I'll be managing," Lionel said. "I was uncertain considering your involvement in the shooting, but Mr Williams spoke highly of your skills and convinced me you're the man for the job."

Porter grunted. "You're a bloody human rights lawyer... Reckon you'd know sweet fuck all about investigation management?"

"We will look into violations against Koori children in far-western townships. Two federal police officers, and you, if you agree."

"Violations by who?"

"That differs from town to town...Some are police officers, government social workers, medical staff. But sadly, most offenders are Koori men, living in the same communities as the victims."

129

Porter scowled at Williams. "Investigating cops? Can't be serious? Half the force's labeled me a dog, and now you want me locking up more? Nah, no way."

"Port, the investigation's a prelude to an inquiry Lionel's hoping to get before parliament. You'll be taking statements, interviewing witnesses…Won't be locking up cops. This way you keep working." Williams glanced to Lionel.

"I know you mourned Nadia's death, that you care about kids," Lionel told Porter.

Porter eyed him. "You've focused on the city up till now. Why shift to the Outback?"

"I'm hoping for a swift, positive result out there. That will put pressure back on politicians, and hopefully force the government to resume Azelia and give these missing girls the attention they deserve. Consider this a chance to make a difference, in more ways than one…"

Porter sat back to ponder his options. He prided himself on being a hard worker, and work was what he wanted to do. "When would I go, and for how long?"

"We fly out tomorrow morning to Crooked River. It's sixteen-hundred kilometers to the north-west via Broken Hill. A three-month secondment at this stage."

Porter pictured Jane in her wedding dress, saw her sparkling eyes and radiant smile. She'd been hesitant to part for two weeks, let alone twelve. But she'd have to understand if he were seconded without a choice? He could fly back to Sydney for visits...Maybe a break would do them good and give him time to get his head sorted before they spent the rest of their lives together?

But the dread of investigating other cops and the rotten stigma attached to it nagged him. "Dunno if I can go," he told Lionel. "I'm getting married..."

"When?"

"Four months from now."

"As I said, the initial investigation phase is only three months. But if it's extended beyond that, I can't guarantee time off."

"Can I think about it?"

"Afraid not. Another guy's on standby. I need to know now."

Porter sighed. Jane had waited long enough and he couldn't let her down. And other things played on his mind and urged him to reject Lionel. Could he cope with such a challenging investigation in his current state? How would his dependence on alcohol sit with his workmates, those he'd have to live with?

He chose the wedding as the best excuse and resigned himself to weeks of boredom on the farm. "Nah, can't go, have made a promise to a great girl." He turned to Williams. "Will take a month's leave then come back and nail the bastards who took our girls."

Lionel straightened in the chair. "Our girls?" he said to Porter. "You just referred to them as, 'our girls'..."

Porter looked at him as though he'd just farted. "So?"

"I've never met a cop with your passion. I want you on my team."

"And the wedding?"

"You'll get time off if needed and I'll put that in writing. We'll be staying in a large house. There's enough room for your fiance to visit if she wants."

"Port, I'll be glad to have you back once you've finished out there," Williams said. "But c'mon, this is perfect for you right now."

They both sold it well, but Porter realized he couldn't work with Lionel. He'd caused too much pain. "I've gotta run the boxing program at the youth club. Can't turn my back on those boys…"

Williams smiled. "I've spoken to Tugger. He's happy to take over and has already lined up a young constable to help him. Don't worry about that."

"Nah, still not interested. Take the other bloke…"

Lionel's black eyes fixed on Porter. "What if I told you we intend to pursue leads that have direct links to the missing girls?"

"I'd say you're feeding me bullshit you reckon I wanna hear…" Porter scoffed. "Could you be further from the problem, out there in the middle of nowhere?" He held his palms up towards Williams, to suggest he end the meeting.

"No lies…" Lionel said. "I can't explain how this investigation will lead to the missing girls, because I'm not sure myself. But it's a feeling, a sense, that you'll have to trust me on."

Porter ran a hand through hair. He scraped nails on scalp as he brought it back to the scar on his forehead. Was a bloke he'd wanted to punch in the head five minutes earlier, now asking for his trust? He whistled as the pressure valve in his chest popped. "Bloody hell, you have a feeling? That's the best you can come up with? Don't know why Roberts, but I wanna believe you…" He turned to Williams. "One question, mate…"

Williams sat forward. "Sure."

"Working with Roberts, I'd be way, way out bush. Wouldn't have to come back for psych appointments with Deidre…Right?"

Williams laughed. "No, not even she could pull that off…"

The back of Porter's neck tingled with hope. If Lionel's investigation provided the tiniest link to the missing girls, he had to embrace it. And not having to face Deidre Sharpe again was a deal breaker, the chocolate mousse after a rump steak with veggies. He addressed Williams. "Not happy, mate, but I'll go…"

"Fantastic," Lionel said. He offered a hand. "Welcome to the team."

Porter ignored it. He dipped his head to Williams and left the office. Lionel Roberts would have to earn his respect and forgiveness. Like most in the modern world, he'd expected it much too soon.

EIGHTEEN

KA2, the organization's Chief of Staff, stood at the head of a marble table in a dank and candlelit long-room. "I declare this High Council meeting for August, open. May the Gods protect our kingdom. Magnus est Alba!"

"For the kingdom of Alba is great," chanted the four men sat around the table. They wore purple gowns. Ivory masks covered their eyes.

"Might we fill our cups before we continue?" The thick-set Master of Espionage, KA9, sniggered. "Thirsty work this slave business…"

KA2 sat then clapped his hands twice.

Two naked teenage girls came forward to fill each man's pewter cup with red wine. Task complete, their feet shuffled over smooth stone as they withdrew to shadows.

"Right, down to business," KA2 said. "Our Supreme Leader, KA1, can't be with us. The Secretary, KA6, gives his apologies but has supplied the latest financial report. Apologies also from KA3 and KA7. I realize that Tuesday nights aren't ideal for meetings, so thank you for your attendance."

KA5, Keeper of Slaves, groaned. "I agree, Tuesday nights are far from ideal. And can we not we hold these meetings in Sydney, closer to home? The drive up north in peak hour traffic is beyond tedious…"

"KA5, always complaining…" KA2 laughed as he said it. "These underground chambers have served your slave keepers and us well, while the deserted barracks above provides the perfect cover. And there are very few nosey cops here in Newcastle, whereas Sydney's infested with them…"

KA5 bowed his head. "Right you are, Chairman."

"Any urgent matters?" KA2 asked the group.

"Yes," KA8, the Chief Abductor said. "A rather disturbing incident last night. The failed abduction…"

"Ah, yes." KA2 sipped wine. "Are we all aware of what happened in North Sydney?"

They nodded. KA2 gestured for KA8 to continue.

"I'm worried the Sydney abductions have become too risky," KA8 said. "This afternoon we had detectives sniffing around and questioning our managers. Why do we continue using our own vans? It will eventually lead them to us…It's crazy."

"The fact that it's crazy is why cops won't suspect our employees of being involved. In all the abductions we've done, it's only the second to go wrong," KA2 said.

"We've been lucky…With increased media coverage, the public's become more vigilant. They're taking notice of suss looking guys in vans. We should suspend our operations in Sydney until things cool a bit."

"I disagree," said KA5. "We have countless orders for Koori girls we've yet to fulfill and Sydney's the best place to find them."

KA8 scoffed. "It's not the only city with pretty young Koori girls. What about Brisbane? Perth? Melbourne?"

"Pretty, yes. In the same numbers? No."

The Lord Adjudicator, KA4, stooped over the table. He addressed KA2, voice calm. "I have to agree with KA8, Mr Chairman. Sources tell me that police are searching for white vans with red logos. It's the only lead they have and they won't let it go easily."

"Not to mention a near disaster when Newcastle detectives asked to search the barracks last week," KA8 said. "Lucky our high-ranking military friends convinced them that soldiers had already searched for the missing girl, and assured them this place is empty and abandoned. Our holding cells, the ceremonial cavern, this very meeting room…All would've been discovered."

"I suggest we move into other cities and markets," KA4 said. "Search for gems in, New Guinea, for example. They are not dissimilar in appearance to Koori girls, and our customers love a new, rare species…"

KA2 tilted his head to the side. "Wise words, Lord Adjudicator… KA5, you will shift operations away from Sydney. Inform those waiting on orders they'll be filled as soon as possible. Suggest 'alternative' options, as KA4's alluded to..."

"But Chairman," KA5 protested, "the Supreme Leader wants all orders filled as soon as possible. Upcoming elections require maximum funding."

KA2 huffed. "The risks in Sydney far outweigh the benefits, and I've seen the secretary's financial report. We've enough money to buy crooked politicians and our seats in parliament ten times over…KA5, you will do as this council instructs. KA1 will be informed of the reasons in due course…"

"Very well, Chairman. As the council wishes..."

"Any other urgent matters?" KA2 said. "No? Good...Well, this talk of federal elections leads us nicely into our first agenda item. The pain in our collective arses. Greens' Senator, Nick Galios."

"Aye to that," KA9 said. "If only the stupid wog and his family had stayed in Greece where they belong..."

The others sniggered and drank.

"As you're well aware, our sleepers in parliament wait to fill vital positions in the new government," KA2 said. "Millions will be spent to ensure it. From there, only one obstacle blocks our policies from becoming legislation."

"Galios is that obstacle..." KA4 held his hands out. "But how to deal with him?"

"It's not only within the Senate he's making waves," KA5 said.

KA2 turned to him. "That so?"

"I spoke with our contact at the Human Rights Commission...The Koori lawyer, Roberts, got his investigation approved on the back of support from Galios and the Greens. Rothwell's obviously concerned about a media backlash."

KA4 tut-tutted. "It would be diabolical if it leads to an inquiry. Would place our sleepers, and all our plans and years of hard work in jeopardy."

"Why did Sinclair support the investigation? Isn't he on our payroll?" KA2 asked KA5.

"No, he's not, and unfortunately cannot be corrupted. We tried to get at him but Galios had beat us to it. Sinclair needs the Greens' preferences."

"Can't we replace Sinclair?" KA9 said. "As we did with Abercrombie when we got Moorecroft in..."

"No, it's too close to the election," KA4 said. "On a positive, yesterdays' dismissal of Kate Bonnetti from the Immigration portfolio got our man Sean Jenkins into the job. He's now only one step from leadership."

"Our man Jenkins, eh…" KA8 chuckled. "Hardly a political bone in his body yet will soon become the Prime Minister of Australia. Amazing, the power of the dollar…"

"Indeed…" KA2 prodded the table with a thick finger. "Greed helped us achieve our objectives in '68, and it will again."

"Very true, Mr Chairman," KA4 said with his usual grandeur. "From all reports, Roberts has nothing. His investigation's been granted to appease the media and welfare groups. He will find nothing out west. There's naught to concern yourselves with."

KA9 laughed. "Wish I knew what you fellas do in your civvy lives, when you're not here playing High Council. It's annoying, not knowing who can do this and that…"

KA2 scratched his buzz cut, grey head. "It's been that way for centuries. Only our three highest ranking members and KA6 know the true identity of all members. It's for your own protection, KA9."

The others mumbled their agreeance.

"We've still not solved the problem of Galios," KA2 continued. "I believe what KA4 says. However, the investigation's a distraction we can do without. Nothing good comes from those like Roberts sniffing around. You never know what they'll stumble across…"

"I assure you, Mr Chairman, there's nothing to find," KA4 said.

"What's completely assured in this world, my dear friend? Galios must be removed from the equation…We'll kill two birds with one stone."

"How?"

"One, Galios will no longer disrupt our plans. Two, he's inspiration for Roberts, and that boy will lose all resolve without guidance. His death will be a warning."

"Is it not a significant risk to assassinate him?"

"I see no alternative. Our interests in parliament must be protected."

"And Roberts?"

"We deal with him if and when he becomes a threat…"

"I suggest that Galios be eliminated well before the elections."

"Agreed KA4. I'll request the Supreme Leader's approval immediately. KA9, do you have assassins in mind?"

"Yes. KA72, a newly promoted team leader. He and his team are perfect for the job."

"Ah yes, he ran quite a few successful operations in South Sydney…Excellent."

"We aren't the only ones appalled by Galios' pro-immigration policies," KA9 added. "From what I'm hearing, others may take care of him first."

KA2 sat back in the chair and spread arms wide. "You see my friends, there's no need for concern. Senator Nick Galios will thwart us no more."

NINETEEN

Porter heaved open the homestead's front door and gawked at the pink sky. The sun glowed orange and sank into a shimmering horizon. His sniffed at the air and caught the unmistakable scent of eucalyptus. An angry magpie squawked in the distance.

The man standing in front of him on the wide veranda cleared his throat. In his mid-sixties, of medium height and thin as a marathon runner, he wore a crisp Police Inspector's uniform. He'd combed grey hair from front to back.

"Inspector George Barrett..." Barrett offered a hand. "Chief of Detectives and acting Local Area Commander of Crooked River." He pointed at Porter's face. "Nasty bruise. Did you lose a fight?"

"Yeah, with a baseball bat..." Porter shook his hand and introduced himself.

He glanced to the woman next to Barrett. He guessed she was close to thirty. Taller than average, she had a healthy glow and athletic leanness. She wore a white blouse, and a grey skirt that covered her knees. Her golden hair, thick and shiny like her lips, she'd tied in a ponytail.

"G'day," Porter said to her.

Her eyes, deep turquoise pools, met his as she dipped her head.

Porter led them down a hallway, through the kitchen and into a family room at the rear. The spacious family room adjoined the kitchen and had been set up as an office. Flames crackled from an open fireplace in the corner.

The Carinya team chatted on sofas. They stood when Barrett entered.

Porter waved a hand towards him. "Inspector George Barrett, the local boss…This is Lionel Roberts, the Investigation Manager. Sergeant John Rhodes, and Senior Constable Fred Klose, from the Feds."

Barrett shook their hands then turned to his female colleague. "Chaps, meet Detective Senior Constable Lyn Foster." His strong voice with its far-west inflection reminded Porter of macho voice-over blokes from 1990's beer commercials. "Lyn's the liaison officer between our command and Carinya, your first point of contact for any needs."

"Good to know…" Lionel said. "Nice to meet you."

"Likewise. I'll be happy to help any way I can." Her voice was confident and smooth as velvet.

"Well, welcome to Crooked River chaps," Barrett said. "How was your flight? Trust your accommodation's suitable, I recommended it for you. And I see you've got three shiny Landcruisers sitting in the driveway…"

"No problems getting here," Lionel said. "The house is perfect, and the river frontage is lovely."

"This place is a beauty alright, over a century old, heritage listed…There's something about these old girls with their sandstone brick and rustic exteriors. High, ornate ceilings." Barrett looked down. "The smell and feel of solid timber floors…"

"Location's fantastic too, halfway between the mission and town."

Barrett's eyes narrowed. "You already know the way to the mission?"

Lionel nodded. "I've visited once before... How's it going out there?"

"Personally, can't say, because I haven't been for years. But we've had very few reports of abuse on the mission, and it seems an unusual choice to base yourselves here." Barrett cocked his head. "I'm sure you have your reasons…"

"Few reported incidents, yes. It's the unreported ones I'm interested in…"

Barrett turned from Lionel to the three policemen. "You'll be ditching those suits before long, chaps. Nights remain cool but the days are already stinking hot."

The group chatted for twenty minutes. Barrett checked his watch. "Five already…Must be off, I've a meeting to get to."

"Pleasure to meet you both," Lionel said.

Barrett and Lyn walked towards the front door. Barrett turned back. "Almost forgot…Lyn's hosting your dinner tonight, on me. Our pub's a grand old thing. You'll love it." He smirked. "Be your first chance to meet the locals..."

"Sounds great, thanks," John Rhodes said. Nuggety as a pit-bull terrier but with a gentleman's demeanor, his bald head and greying mustache made him appear older than forty-three. "What time, and how do we find it?"

"Let's say, seven?" Lyn smirked. "Drive down the main street and look for a pub. We've only got one..."

By 8pm, Porter and the others had finished their meals at the Crooked River Hotel. He remained in the dining area with Lyn. Lionel, Klose and Rhodes had moved to stools along the bar. A cloud of cigarette smoke hung over the room. The stench of stale beer rose from stains in faded, lime-green carpet. Packed in like sheep in a shearer's pen, rowdy patrons failed to hide their curiosity of the four outsiders who dared drink in their pub.

Porter noticed a group of locals that stood out from the rest. Six men dressed in training gear, with matching t-shirts and shorts, sat around a circular table and watched him over the top of beer glasses. "I'm guessing those blokes in the corner..." he pointed with his eyes, "are the local footy team? What's with the filthy looks? You'd reckon I stole their teddy bears..."

Lyn snorted as she ran a finger over a wine glass. "Yep, the footy team. Always here on Wednesday night's after training."

"And the filthy looks?"

"That's every male detective in the Crooked River district, excluding Barrett. They know of you, and why you're here."

Porter gritted teeth and pushed air through his nose. He'd only been in the outback for half a day but the crisp country air and open spaces had refreshed him. He'd decided that escaping Sydney's demons would do him good. But the detectives' suspicious stares winded him, worse than the time a female junkie had kicked him square in the balls. Could he ever escape memories of Eddy Tindall's shooting and the subsequent events? Would others ever forget?

"You know what happened in the city. And you're still sitting here. Why?" he asked her.

"I've only been here two years. I worked in Sydney's outer-west before that…" Lyn's tone matched her kind face. "I'm nothing like this lot, and won't judge you. We've all made mistakes."

He sculled the rest of the beer, unsure how much she knew about him and which of his mistakes she referred to. "Off to the bar... Another wine?"

"No thanks, early start tomorrow."

Porter joined the service queue and waved to acknowledge the Carinya blokes at the far end of the bar. They raised their glasses and continued their conversation. He noticed one of the footy team ahead of him in the queue, the detective who'd stared at him the longest. He towered above the crowd. Spiky blond hair added an inch to Shaquille-like height. His shoulders were wider than the Nullarbor.

Porter ignored the whispered gossip around him and stepped alongside the spikey-haired giant at the service counter. A cute brunette in her early twenties smiled at him as she poured a beer. A dark-skinned bloke cleaned glasses behind her.

"Ronny?" the brunette called to the bloke cleaning glasses. He turned to her. "I'm busy over here. Serve this guy…" She indicated Porter with a tilt of her head.

Ronny wiped hands on a black AC/DC t-shirt and trudged towards the service counter. With a face as chubby as his round body, he had rusted steel wool for hair and a thin nose. He stopped all of a sudden, a vicious scowl on his walnut-brown face. He leered at Porter with black eyes. "Sa, sa, sorry, Emma," he stuttered. He turned back to the cleaning bench. "I don't sa, sa, serve kid killers."

Porter forced a laugh. He had another admirer.

Emma spun to face Ronny. "Get over here and pour this guy a beer. Now."

Ronny cleaned a glass, head down. "That pig killed my friend, Emm. Can't look at him."

"Ronny." Emma moved beside him to shout in his face. "You'll lose your job if Gary hears of this. Get your arse ov--."

"Emma, you heard him." The spikey-haired giant spoke slow and deliberate, like Crocodile Dundee on valium. "He doesn't serve child killers, and I don't blame him." He snarled at Porter. "You've got a hide. This is a copper's pub..."

Porter winked at him. "Good thing I'm a copper then."

"Fucking smart arse eh? Judging from your ugly swollen mug, you've already copped a floggin'. Don't make me give you another."

Porter turned and met his grey stare. He stood 6'3 and weighed two-twenty pounds, but he guessed the spikey-haired giant had four inches and fifty pounds on him. He felt bullied for the first time in his life. A strange sensation... "Problem, mate? What was your name?"

Patrons around the bar dispersed. Emma retreated from the service counter and folded arms as though she'd seen it all before. Ronny watched on, eyes wide as a bloodthirsty UFC fan.

"Name's Jim Thompson. You'll call me Detective Sergeant. No problems here for me... But for you, can bet on it." He didn't flinch and kept his eyes on Porter. Detectives who'd rushed to stand behind him sniggered, a pack of hyena.

"Why's that?" Porter looked Jim up and down and smirked at his tight-fitting shorts. He noticed muscles in his right forearm bulge as his hand clenched into a rockmelon-sized fist. A knotted cross tattoo, red and green in color, covered the forearm. "Those are nice snug shorts you Aussie Rules boys wear…Is it because I prefer rugby that you blokes don't like me? Because I like to let my balls breathe a little?"

Jim's face flushed crimson as he brought his chin within an inch of Porter's nose. "No Porter, it aint 'cos you're a rugby poofter. You're a lying, scheming, IA dog, who turns on his mates and can't be trusted. That's why you're not welcome here…"

"Too bad, champ, 'cos I'm thirsty." Porter turned to Emma. "Schooner of VB thanks sweet."

The bar fell silent. No-one said a word.

Porter braced himself for a punch and planned his first move. He'd go for Jim's knees, if he could get off the floor. He glanced down at the long black fingers gripping his shoulder.

"Dan, ignore him," Lionel said. He turned to Jim Thompson. "I'll be speaking to Inspector Barrett. We've been assured of your assistance. Not this, harassment."

Jim grunted at him then locked eyes on Porter. "Awh, aint this sweet boys. The snitch has his blackie mate watching out for him. Awh…"

The Detective hyenas laughed as one.

"Don't you have any Koori boys to bully today?" Lionel asked Jim. "Getting braver now, taking on men?"

Jim's yellow teeth glistened as his upper lip curled. "I remember you…You're the Legal Aid bush lawyer who represented that cheeky blackie last year?" He turned to share the joke with his detective mates. When he turned back to Lionel his eyes shimmered with hatred. "We've already led you out of town once. Guess we were too friendly, 'cos you didn't take the hint. Best you and these city poofters leave town. Now. 'Cos I tell you, we'll be far from friendly a second time."

Porter's jaw clenched. Hands became fists. He focused on Jim's square chin, determined to unleash erupting aggression in one telling blow. A firm hand gripped his elbow. He turned to see John Rhodes beside him. Fred Klose stood on the other side.

"Here's your beer." Klose handed Porter a full schooner glass.

Porter tasted the beer. He licked cool froth from lips then smiled at Jim. "Catch you later, this being the only pub and all…"

"You can bet on that, dog." Jim shot him a look of disgust, growled at Emma, and led his pack from the pub.

Porter and the other Carinya blokes shared a moment of victorious banter then joined Lyn at the dining table.

"What was that all about?" she said.

Porter groaned. "What do you reckon? Like you said, the local cops know me. I expected crap from them. But the dark bloke behind the bar…Ronny? What's his problem?"

"Ronny's nearly fifty, with the brain of a ten-year-old. He cleans the pub and drives the delivery truck. Sorry, should've warned you about him."

Porter frowned at his failing memory, uncertain if he'd had dealings with Ronny back in the city. "He's not too dark and doesn't have typical Koori features. Half-caste?"

"Maybe…His surname's Goodwin. Only been here six months. Nice guy, just a bit simple." She giggled like an embarrassed teenager. "Said he loved me the first time we met, and every time since."

Klose made his eyes whirl. "That's a bit weird."

"Was kind of sweet, until he started threatening every guy I talked to…"

Rhodes chortled. "You've hit the cupid jackpot there, Lyn."

Porter watched patrons filter back into the hotel. "He's not the only simple one around here…I know Goodwin's in Redfern, but not Ronny. Does he reckon I killed his friend?"

"He knew the Neilsen kid and others around Redfern," Lyn said.

"Where did he grow up?"

"Hasn't said…Only that he fell in with the wrong crowd, had a bust-up with his family, and came out here to escape bad influences."

"Reckon he's easily led astray…" Porter said.

"Yep, and I'm sure the detective guys told him all about you. They control him like a puppet the poor bugger."

"Could've done without another enemy this first day, but understand him hating me. He reckons I've killed his mate and now trying to steal his girlfriend…" Porter shook his head at the stupidity of it. "Girl behind the bar seems alright…Emma?

"Yep, Emm's lovely. Her dad Gary Rowe's the publican. He's out of town hunting with Patto, the usual barman. Both nice guys…"

"And the albino gorilla… Jim?" Rhodes said.

She scrunched her nose. "Jim Thompson's the Detective's team leader and captain of the footy team. All-around wanker, chauvinistic womanizer and racist arsehole…And, Bill Thompson's son."

Klose laughed. "Chauvinistic womanizer? You speaking from experience, Lyn? C'mon, a gorgeous girl like you has to expect a heap of attention out here?"

She sneered at him. "Jim put the hard word on me in my first week. Knocked him back, said he wasn't my type. And married…The prick's made my life miserable ever since."

"Who's Bill Thompson?" Rhodes asked. "You said his name as though it means something."

"It does, around here at least…The Thompson's have been the richest and most influential family in this district for decades, going back to the early nineteen-hundreds. They own thousands of hectares of prime river frontage, most of it taken from Aboriginals, and make a fortune selling it off to investors…Bill Thompson was the Senior Sergeant here back when they were gods, as were his father and grandfather."

Porter warbled with puffed cheeks, loud and deliberate, bored by stories of local reputations. "He, was, the Senior Sergeant here. Once a god or not, a retired cop, aint a cop. There's no need to fear that bloke…"

"I'm not sure if that's true," she said. "Bill's the Mayor now and has more control than ever. No doubt you'll meet him before long. Word is, he's ropable that

149

Carinya's in his town. He says you're bad for business…"

TWENTY

Mid-morning on Thursday, Porter sat in the passenger seat as Lionel drove the Landcruiser along a bumpy, red dirt road. He struggled to forget events from the night before. The hatred towards him at the pub had been insane. But this was a new day, he told himself. He had to harden the fuck up and move on. The Mayor and local cops didn't want him in Crooked River because they had something to hide. What? It was time to get out and about, and find it.

Two hours earlier he'd sat at the kitchen table while Lionel briefed the Carinya team. He'd explained it would be difficult enough for him and Klose to gain the trust of local kooris, and near impossible for Porter and Rhodes. He separated them into two teams with one Koori member in each, then allocated a list of victims, witnesses and locations for each team to investigate. Lionel would work with Porter, Klose with Rhodes.

Porter had contemplated asking to work with Klose instead, unsure if he could forgive Lionel for putting Jane and Amber at risk. He'd decided not to. Lionel had earned respect by confronting Jim Thompson at the pub, and deserved a second chance. Besides, was there any point holding a grudge, out in the middle of nowhere?

Porter gazed out the window as the road weaved through towering eucalypts. Vast wheat-colored plains stretched to the horizon littered with mulga bush, coolabah trees and purple wood wattle flowers that

151

glowed beneath an azure sky. Grey kangaroo grazed by the road. They stood to watch the approaching vehicle then bounced away over parched earth.

Lionel turned the Landcruiser left onto Crooked River road and drove south towards the Aboriginal mission. He began whistling another tune, Bruno Mars', 'The Lazy Song.'

"You whistle more than the seven dwarfs," Porter said. "Why so chuffed?"

Lionel stopped whistling. "Look around, who wouldn't be happy? It's gorgeous, away from that miserable city and all the miserable people living in it. Feel closer to the land, closer to my people."

"Are these your ancestors out here?"

"No, these lands have belonged to the river people for thousands of years. Crooked River's their lifeline."

Porter remembered discussing Lionel's background with Tugger Walford. "Where are your people then?"

Lionel sighed. "Don't know…"

Porter waited and hoped he'd tell him more. "Why's it called Crooked River you reckon?"

"That, I do know…The first white explorers got frustrated trying to survey all its twists and turns. They named it accordingly."

"Lifeline? The land's drier than a priest at an AA meeting…Where's the life?"

"It's always there if you know where to look. A local story from the Dreamtime tells us - Long after the dry has set in, what water brings, the land remembers…"

Porter paused to think. "Fair enough…"

The Landcruiser slowed.

"We're here…" Lionel pointed to the left. "See that sign?" He drove through a narrow entrance where a rotted wooden gate had fallen aside. "It's the original one."

Porter read the sign aloud. "Crooked River Aboriginal Mission. Established nineteen twenty-three."

They parked in the shade of river gums then strolled to the edge of the brown, tranquil river.

"I can think of worse places to live…" Porter said.

Lionel pointed along a dirt path to a row of white weatherboard houses with neat gardens. "Stumble out your door to swim or catch a fish, surrounded by these gorgeous hills."

Porter counted fifteen houses then followed Lionel's gaze across the river. Red and white mottled hills lined it. When he turned back to the houses a Koori elder approached them on the path. He stopped a meter away and reeked of liquor.

In his early eighties, Porter guessed, the man resembled a beer keg with arms and legs. Snow-white hair curled around ears. His nose was broad and wrinkled, the same as his forehead. He wore a stained cowboy shirt. It failed to cover an ample gut. Dirty blue jeans hung to bare feet that scraped grey mud. He gulped clear liquid from a plastic bottle as he watched them through glazed eyes.

"Flashy suits and car," the man said with a slur. "Are ya gov'ment fellas?"

Lionel offered a hand. "Hello uncle, my name's Lionel Roberts. I'm a lawyer, an Aboriginal rights advocate from Sydney. This is Dan Porter. And we're not with the government. Well, not exactly…"

The man ignored Lionel's hand, took a swig from the bottle and squinted at Porter. "Porter? I seen the news…Aint you that whitey who killed them Koori boys in the city?" He turned to Lionel. "Why you bringin' this fella out 'ere? Tryin' ta get 'im shot?"

Porter stepped forward before Lionel could answer. "I didn't kill anyone…" He moved closer and towered over the elder. "And you are?"

"Tommy Davis, the boss man 'round 'ere, born and raised," he said to Lionel. "What you fellas want?"

Lionel peered over Tommy's shoulder. "We'd like to speak with the residents."

"Kids are at school, others are out. Talk 'bout what?"

"I'm sure you know why we're here, uncle. We're investigating the alleged abuse and neglect of Koori children. Don't be suspicious, we're here to help."

Tommy burped.

Lionel grimaced then cupped a hand over mouth and nose.

"Aint been no abuse," Tommy said. "Not by coppers or anyone. We're happy out 'ere, they leave us alone. It's you city fellas comin' 'ere that makes problems." He took another swig.

"Well, we'll talk to the residents anyhow. To make sure…"

Tommy snarled and bared all four teeth. "Think you're one of us, callin' me uncle and pretendin' ta care? You aint nuffin' like us…Think you gunna come out 'ere and impress us stupid country fellas with ya fancy legal talk?"

"I'm sure someone here needs our help?"

"Like I told ya, aint nuffin' ta save us from."

Lionel raised the briefcase in his left hand. "A report in here says otherwise. Only a few months ago, a young girl living here was allegedly molested by a local policeman."

Porter moved forward. "Being the 'boss' man, you'd know about it? Right, Tommy?"

Tommy stepped back. "It's all crap, nobody touched no-one. Tilly Johnson tellin' stories ta get attention."

"Tilly, that's the girl," Lionel said. "Which one's her house?"

Tommy gave a devious smile. "Johnson's don't live 'ere no more. Moved on, ta don't know where…"

"We'll find out…The report doesn't name the officer involved. Who was it, Tommy?"

Tommy shook his head.

"Tell ya who hurt Tilly Johnson…" The harsh, crackling voice behind Porter startled him. Lionel jumped. They turned towards the riverbank. A frail Koori elder, darker than the shadows, sat on the rotting trunk of a fallen gum tree. "Was that bastard--."

"Simpson! Shut your mouth ya silly old fool," Tommy bellowed as he strode towards the elder.

The elder opened his mouth.

Tommy smacked him across the head and knocked him from the tree trunk. He hissed, the elder cowered and picked his tattered cowboy hat from the ground.

Porter ran to the elder and helped him to his feet. "You alright, mate?"

The elder said nothing. He looked ten years older than Tommy, his face a withered prune with a sparse beard hanging from it. He'd tucked a black and green chequered shirt into faded jeans and rolled it to the elbows. He wore rubber flip-flops on mud covered feet.

"Get inside," Tommy shouted at the elder then kicked him in the backside to push him past Lionel and Porter. The elder hobbled towards the houses and didn't look back.

"What are you doing?" Lionel said. "You've no right…"

"Got every right, young fella, and people 'round 'ere know it."

Lionel's face reddened as he prodded a finger at him. "You assaulted him. We should take you into the police station."

Tommy chuckled. "Police station? They'd laugh and kick ya skinny black arse back ta Sydney. Local coppers let me run this place as I need ta, it saves them comin' out. On this 'ere mission, I am the police."

"That old bloke wanted to name the copper involved in the Tilly incident, and you stopped him." Porter growled down at Tommy. "Who you protecting?"

Tommy pointed towards the elder, who climbed steps to the third house. "Him, Old Man Simpson. Drunken fool's about ta mouth off with his usual crap. That's who I'm protectin'..."

"You let us take care of that. I reckon he knows what happened to Tilly..."

"He knows nuffin', just likes ta play games and gossip." Tommy sculled from the bottle. "Troublemaker…"

Porter and Lionel exchanged a suspicious glance.

"We'll speak to uncle Simpson later, and the others," Lionel said. "You may think you're the law, Tommy, but you're wrong." His thick eyebrows arched. "Can bring Inspector Barrett out here to explain it…Do I need to?"

Tommy sighed. "Aah suit ya bloody selves. But my people have nuffin' ta say ta you fellas. Wasting ya time…Now rack off back ta town and leave us be."

"Next time we'll chat when you're sober." Lionel pointed to Tommy's bottle. "So please, go easy on the whiskey."

"Ha, it's gin ya fool. And look at ya, layin' down rules like some fancy school teacher…Ya in my country now, young fella." Tommy's black eyes held a wicked glint. "You'd be smart ta follow my rules..."

Lionel frowned. "A threat?"

Porter walked towards the Landcruiser. Lionel followed.

"Take it how ya want. It aint my problem," Tommy shouted out to them. "You fellas look clever and talk clever, but ya too stupid ta know where ya aint welcome…"

TWENTY-ONE

Wednesday morning, a week after his team's arrival in Crooked River, Lionel Roberts sat at the Carinya homestead's kitchen table and nibbled honey on toast. It had been a frustrating week where his team received a cold reception in each Koori community they'd visited throughout the district. Hostile residents refused to talk. He'd wasted precious investigation time, and neglected districts he knew to be rife with the abuse of Koori children.

He leaned back in the chair and studied the ceiling's ornate cornices. Had he made a mistake basing Carinya in Crooked River? Had he placed too much faith in Shirley's information? He waited for a vision and hoped for guidance from the wise elders who'd brought him this far. When they failed to appear, he sucked on his bottom lip and stared into the coffee mug. He had to decide whether to stay or go, and soon.

"You're quiet, Lio," Klose said from the chair opposite. "Alright?"

Lionel sipped lukewarm coffee then told the team of his predicament. They discussed the matter for five minutes and agreed they'd give it one more day before deciding their fate in Crooked River.

Lionel watched Porter devour a pile of bacon and scrambled eggs. He smiled because Porter's mood seemed to improve each day. He'd started to open up and looked nothing like the mess of a man he'd first met in Steve Williams' office. He was clean shaven and had a fresh buzzcut courtesy of John Rhodes. Both the keen glint in his eye and his appetite had returned. He was drinking less beer and jogging every day.

"I could eat the crutch out of a low flying duck," Porter said. "Loving these morning runs…The clean air's beaut."

Rhodes washed dishes in the sink. "And you're looking better for it too…"

Klose poked Porter's gut. "Don't eat too much, bud, won't fit into your wedding gear."

"The wedding's still months away, and reckon only Jane needs to worry about that." Porter grinned. "Us blokes can always make last minute adjustments…"

They laughed together.

Lionel addressed Porter. "Speaking of Jane…You said she and Amber might visit?

"Hopefully, in the next couple of weeks…"

"They still at your parents' farm?"

Porter moved to the gas cooktop and threw more bacon into a frypan. "Yeah, and reckon they'll stay a while yet. Amber's fallen in love with dad's horses."

"She'll enjoy it out here then. Have seen groups riding along River road."

"I know, I'm always dodging horse shit during my run…" Porter's phone vibrated on the table. He rested tongs in the frypan then took the phone from Lionel. He pressed its screen then placed it on the benchtop. "Claire, what's up?"

Lionel strained to hear the conversation above the sound of hissing bacon.

"Hi Dan, how's it going out there?" Claire's voice crackled through the phone's speaker. "What's that noise?"

Porter leaned towards the phone. "Cooking brekky. Got you on speaker."

"Ah, okay. Just got off the phone with Interpol guys in Singapore. They wanted to speak to you personally but I said I'd pass the info on to you. It's related to the missing girls…Your line secure?"

Porter glanced at the others. He turned off the gas, left bacon in the frypan, grabbed his phone and sat at the table. "Fire away, Claire. What you got?"

"Not good news I'm afraid. A Koori girl's been found dead in Singapore. Dumped in an industrial waste bin near shipping docks. They're sending her dental records and photos through to us. Good chance she's one of ours abducted from Sydney."

Lionel swallowed the lump in his throat.

'Sounds like it," Porter said. "Why'd Interpol ask for me? I'm off the case."

"That's what's interesting…She had the same markings as Nadia, the 'KA' branded on her back. And your report of Nadia's homicide is the only one they could find with the same MO…Which is unusual, given what she told me…"

"How?"

"These guys in Singapore have access to Interpol databases that we don't. They've sifted through hundreds of photos of dead girls and saw they all had the same 'KA' branding. But like I said, your report's the only one that mentions it."

Porter huffed. "You telling me Interpol had knowledge of serial killings with an MO the same as Nadia's and didn't tell us? That they didn't bother to disseminate it?"

"And it seems they've known for a while."

"That info would've made a huge difference to our investigation…"

"Yep, but for some reason Interpol insists on keeping it low key. According to the Singaporeans, all other Interpol offices have retained a 'missing" status on the deceased girls who've been located."

"Bloody Interpol mongrels…" Porter fumed. "What are those bastards hiding?"

Lionel took eyes off the phone and noticed that Klose and Rhodes were both enthralled by the phone conversation. "Or, who are they trying to protect?" he asked them.

Porter's face flushed red. "That's frickin' obvious…It's this 'KA' mob, whoever the sick mongrels are."

Claire sighed. "We're no closer to knowing that either…Singaporean intel analysts searched all databases for the letters 'KA,' hoping to find a link to known criminal organizations. Found nothing. They're in the dark regarding what the letters 'KA' stand for, and who they might be."

Porter gritted teeth. "Not the only ones…" He thanked her, ended the call, and discussed the missing girls' case with Klose and Rhodes.

Lionel trudged to his bedroom. He sat at the desk and rubbed a hollow chest. How many of Sydney's missing girls were already dead?

He opened his laptop and navigated to the email inbox. He gasped as he read the fifth subject title: **'More from Shirley**.'

Trembling hands fumbled with the mouse. He opened the email.

Dear Lionel,

It's me again, Shirley, writing you from bonny Scotland (although I'm sure you already know that ☺). I read on the internet about Carinya, and have to say, I'm impressed. Getting the backing of the Attorney Generals' office couldn't have been easy? And I see you've got Nick Galios in your corner, he's one of the good guys. I said I'd give you more information if you made progress. You have, so I will.

There are two attachments to this email. The first one is a copy of a letter I received many years ago from my best friend at the time, Cathy Inglis. Cathy lived with her family on the Crooked River mission. In 1968, when she was eleven, a white man from the Aboriginal Welfare Board came and took Cathy away. I'm sure you're well aware of the wicked powers the Aboriginal Protection Act gave the government.

Cathy's family thought she was going away to have a better life – a white man's money, a proper education and a better future. Read the attached letter from Cathy and you'll see this was far from the reality. Cathy was 'sold' to a Dutch man, Bleeker, and went to live on a farm in central Queensland with his wife and children. That man raped and beat Cathy every other day. She sent me the letter shortly before she killed herself.

The second file I've attached is a copy of a receipt. A welfare board fellow by the name of Alec Ferguson wrote it out to Bleeker, for the money he paid for Cathy. Cathy must've stolen the receipt from Bleeker, and it was attached to the letter she sent me. I scanned both documents long ago, and the originals are in a safe place.

Ten pounds, Lionel. My dearest friend was sold by the AWB for ten pounds! And she wasn't the only pretty Koori girl taken from Crooked River by Alec Ferguson. There were many others, not seen again. I've never dared to talk of this before. It's dangerous, and I've loved ones to protect. And who would've believed me? Or believed what Cathy wrote? But I know you will believe it Lionel, and you know what to do with it. PLEASE, tell NO-ONE of this email. Powerful men will do anything to protect a sordid past.

I trust you Lionel, so here is my mobile number, to be used in emergency only - +61056235143234. I prefer email contact, and check mine daily, so will reply asap if you need to know more. Good luck and please, be careful Lionel.

Shirley

PS – I doubt the elders at Crooked River mission will remember Cathy's story, her family were one of many who only stayed a short time. Mention another girl, 'Rosie', who lived there longer. She should get them talking. But don't mention her if Tommy Davis is around. He's an evil, evil man.

Lionel propped elbows on the desk and held his forehead in sweat laced palms. A sentence slapped him across the face as he read it again. 'Powerful men will do anything to protect a sordid past.' Like removing AWB files from State Archives? Or failing to file them in the first place? If true, Shirley's accusations provided strong motivation for a government to take such measures. A thousand scenarios whirled through his mind.

163

He rushed to the kitchen and sat, eager to share the latest development with his team.

"Why the big smile, bud?" Klose asked him.

Lionel tapped a finger on the table. "Can't say too much yet, but I'm certain Crooked River's where we need to be…"

Porter smirked. "Bloody hell, you've backflipped better than a gymnast…Didn't you say five minutes ago that you reckon we should leave this place?"

"Yes, but I've since received information that changes everything."

"Everything?" Klose said. "It must be good info if you're this confident?"

"I've got a name of an ex-Welfare Board employee. Not sure how he's linked to the missing girls, or what's happening out here at the moment, but it's a start," Lionel stated. He'd been concerned that the Carinya team doubted him as much as he'd doubted himself. "Dan, can you ask Claire for a background check and current address search?"

"No worries…" Porter rubbed his chin. "You wanna interview this bloke as a suspect, based on what your informant has said?"

"He's allegedly committed serious crimes against Aboriginal children. Why shouldn't we interview him?"

"We should. But it's best to first get a written statement from your informant."

Rhodes nodded. "It's how I'd do it. We've got contacts who can assist…"

Lionel tugged curls at his forehead. He hadn't considered getting a formal statement from Shirley but knew to heed the advice of experienced investigators.

"You're right, we need her story on paper…John, my informant's in Scotland. Is it possible for her to make a statement there?"

"Too easy, a mate with Interpol in Edinburgh owes me a favor." Rhodes winked. "Give me the contact details and I'll prioritize the request through Canberra. You'll have your statement in no time."

Lionel said nothing for half a minute while he considered the need to protect Shirley. She'd placed her trust in him. "No," he said to Rhodes, "my informant won't be comfortable with police contacting her. Send the request, and ensure your Interpol friend is assigned the job. Once he confirms receipt, I'll notify my informant. She'll contact him to arrange a time and place that suits her."

"Understood…Onto it."

"You trust Interpol, mate?" Porter asked Lionel. "After what me and Claire just discussed?"

Lionel held his hands out. "Do I have a choice?"

"Maybe not, but this aint a good one…"

"Rhodesy…" Klose stood and ambled towards the family room. "I'll do the request to Canberra. You call your mate in Edinburgh…"

Porter slid a pen and notepad across the table to Lionel. "Name and approximate age of this bloke you want Claire to find." He read from the notepad once Lionel had slid it back. "Alec Ferguson? Same as that famous soccer coach?"

Lionel sniggered. "No, that's Alex Ferguson…What's today's schedule?"

"Forgotten? You and me have a lunch date with Bill Thompson and George Barrett."

"That's today?"

"Yeah, worse luck…" Porter took Landcruiser keys from the bench. "I'm heading into town. I'll pick you up at midday on the way to Thompson's…"

Lionel gave a thumbs up as Porter left, then moved towards the whistling kettle. Nick Galios flashed through his mind and chuckled. He realized he hadn't spoken to him for a few days so decided to call him.

Galios' cell phone rang out. Lionel called his office. A secretary answered.

"Hi Dianne, it's Lionel Roberts. Put me through to Nick please."

A five-second silence. "I'm sorry Mr Roberts, but haven't you heard?"

"Heard…?"

"Such tragic news...Nick was murdered this morning. Shot as he left home…"

"What?" Lionel yelled into the phone. "Murdered? Who? Wh-…Why?" He dropped the phone.

Klose entered the kitchen and cuffed a hand around his shoulder. "What's up, Lio?"

Lionel brushed him away and scurried out the back door. He ran to the wrought iron fence and gripped it in two hands as he stared into the brown river. He shook it back and forwards. When rage exhausted him, he slumped against a fence post.

The back door squeaked. Klose approached him.

"They've killed Nick Galios…" Lionel's voice trembled. "I'm responsible…"

Klose sat next to him on the spinifex grass. "Not your fault, bud. He had dangerous enemies long before you came along."

"He didn't want to get involved in all this again, but I knew he couldn't say no…Murdered…In Australia? Why?"

Klose helped Lionel stand. "The scum of this world are threatened by men like him, and if it's any condolence, his death means we've got the fuckers worried… Rest easy, bud, we'll find them. And when we do, they'll pay."

TWENTY-TWO

Porter hummed his favorite U2 song as he drove the Landcruiser towards the Thompson homestead. Red hills dotted with grey granite boulders looked down on the dusty road. He increased volume on the car stereo. "It's a beautiful day!" His voice cracked as he strained to match Bono in the chorus.

With Lionel in no mood for socializing after hearing of Nick Galios' murder, Porter had decided to go alone to the lunch meeting with Inspector George Barrett and Mayor Bill Thompson. Curiosity motivated him. Was Detective Sergeant Jim Thompson, the blond gorilla from the pub, a chip off the old block? Wouldn't two massive wankers in one small town be a treat…And if Bill Thompson didn't want Carinya in Crooked River, he would ask the question. Why?

Fifteen minutes after he'd left the Carinya residence, Porter steered the Landcruiser through the Thompson's open front gates. A steel-picket and wire fence ran the length of the property's frontage and down both sides of the driveway. He drove past a wooden sign. Black letters on it read, 'Thompson Homestead, 1916'.

George Barrett waited at the end of the driveway and directed him to a parking space under an aluminum carport. He wore a red polo shirt, jeans, and sneakers. Porter wore a similar outfit, except his polo shirt matched the blue sky. They shook hands and strolled towards the house.

The Thompson homestead was ringed by majestic eucalypts. It had a wide timber veranda, sandstone veneer that seemed as solid as the day it'd been built, and a federation-red façade. Rays from the midday sun bounced off a rusted iron roof. Pink cockatoo screeched as they settled on it.

Porter nodded to the white-haired man who met them in the entry foyer. The man had wrinkled skin hanging from his chin and neck. He had an ugly nose- long, red and swollen; on an ugly, red and swollen face. He was sickly thin and 6'5 tall despite being hunched, with broad shoulders. He'd rolled a white business shirt to the elbows and tucked it into khaki trousers that fell to the heels of brown boots.

"G'day, son. Bill Thompson..." They shook hands. "Good to meet you..." He spoke like John Wayne, low and slow but with a thick Australian accent and a wheeze after each sentence.

Porter returned a 'G'day', surprised by the strength in Bill's bony hand.

Bill slapped his back. "Come in, son, come in."

He led them down a hallway with polished floorboards to a rectangular loungeroom. On the left side of the room, a beige sofa and matching recliners surrounded a sandstone fireplace. A well-stocked bar with marble bench top and shelves dominated the right side. Curtained windows covered the wall opposite the door.

Against the middle of the wall to Porter's left, a six- foot medieval knight in gleaming silver armor stood guard, holding a seven-foot steel lance perpendicular to the timber floor. He stopped a meter from the knight and leaned in for a closer look. The mannequin inside the armor had steel-blue eyes, frozen in a deadly gaze. "Impressive. The real deal?"

"Bloody oath, from 13th century Scotland." Bill ran a hand over the knight's armor. "A mate of mine owned a castle near Glasgow. He knew I loved this and shipped it over to me when he sold the place."

Porter fingered the steel lance's sharp tip. "This would've done some damage in its day.'

"Not wrong…" Bill moved to the bar and took a bottle from a shelf. "The missus is whipping up a feed out the back. There's time for a quick drink. What'll it be, son?"

Porter waved a hand. "Nah she's right, Thompson. Trying to stay dry."

"Call me Bill…A fine Scotch this, but suit yourself. C'mon George, I won't drink alone."

"Just one…" Barrett walked to the bar. He waited for Bill to hand him a full tumbler then turned to Porter. "What happened to Roberts? You were both invited…"

"Lionel got bad news this morning." Porter turned towards a section of wall covered in framed photos. "A mate of his died…"

"Nick Galios, right? I saw it on television. Assassinated, by the look of it."

"Terrible news indeed." Bill came alongside Porter and faced the wall. "The Greens leader, the fella supporting Roberts, wasn't he? Stepped on the wrong toes no doubt…"

Porter stood shoulder to shoulder with Bill and feigned interest in the photos. His hands trembled. For the first time since the confrontation with Jim Thompson, the hollow ache in his gut returned. "I've no idea whose toes Galios stepped on…But Lionel's a mess, and sends his apologies for not making it here."

He shuffled sideways along the wall. Mostly black and white, a few faded with time, the photos depicted Bill at various stages of life. Posing in his police cadet uniform, barely a man. Fishing by a river. Shooting rabbits. Winning a rugby premiership.

"It's not a problem, son,' Bill said. "Truth be told, you're the fella I wanted to meet. We need to discuss this Carinya fiasco…"

Porter faced him. "Why's that? Lionel's the investigations manager, the bloke wanting the inquiry. I reckon he's better qualified to answer than me…"

Bill's brief smile revealed tobacco-stained teeth. "That's not exactly what I meant, son. We're the same, different than Roberts. We, understand each other…"

Porter cursed him under his breath. He'd never liked being called 'son' by anyone other than his father. It was up there with 'young fella', a condescending term that blokes like Bill Thompson often abused. And he wasn't an idiot, he knew exactly what Bill meant because he'd made no effort to conceal his statement's racist undertones.

"We're the same?" Porter asked him. "What, because I'm a cop, and you were once?" His chest swelled. He'd fired back, and made it clear that Bill's retired rank didn't intimidate him. He turned to the photos.

"Yes, something like that, son." Bill chuckled. "Something like that…"

"Did you take these landscape pics? Not bad…" Porter lied to break the awkward silence.

"Thank you, son." Bill stepped closer to the wall and pointed to a series of colored photos. "I took most of them around here. A few up in the Territory..."

"Did you get into it after you left the cops?"

"No, photography's always been a passion of mine, capturing natural beauty. That, and whiskey of course..." He smiled and poked Barrett in the ribs. Barrett laughed, as though obliged to. "Got my own darkroom, and process the photos myself."

Porter played along. "Like a professional?"

"Hardly...But every man needs a hobby. Right, son?" He winked and nudged Porter's elbow with his own.

Porter pointed to a black and white photo. Bill as a young man, covered in mud, held a trophy above his head. "You were a bear of a bloke in your playing days. A front-rower?"

"I was, son, yes." Bill slurped whiskey then looked down at his body. "You wouldn't know it with this sack of bones. But ah well, was only twenty-three in that photo. Much has changed in fifty-five years...Time can't be kind to us all."

"Got that right," Porter said.

It annoyed him that he and Bill shared common interests. Photography. They'd both played in the front-row. Fishing...Was Bill a decent bloke, nothing like his obnoxious son? Then he remembered the contempt he'd shown for a dead Nick Galios and reminded himself not to be fooled.

Porter noticed the last photo. He bent to study it. A twenty-something Bill stood between two men of similar age, his arms draped over their shoulders. One was much shorter than Bill, the other of similar height.

All three wore black suits and grinned like naughty kids who shared a secret.

"What is it, Porter?" Barrett said.

Porter wobbled his head as he straightened. "Thought I recognized the smallest bloke in this photo. Face looks familiar but can't think from where. Bloody memory's shot these days…"

Bill pointed at the photo. "Little fella's Chuck, my best mate growing up. Taller one's an old workmate. Photo was taken in 1965, and they both moved overseas soon after, so doubt you'd know 'em. Well," he rubbed his hands together, "who's hungry?"

Porter followed Bill onto a rear veranda that was protected by insect screen. They sat at a pinewood table covered in trays of baked vegetables, jugs of gravy, and plates of scones with jam. Sweet aromas of home cooked food teased his nostrils and reminded him of his mum's Sunday roast. He pictured his parents' farm. Jane and Amber laughed while they rode horses. He smiled, conscience eased, content with their safety.

He looked to his left. The tallest hill in sight loomed beyond the northern fence line. In front of him, a hundred meters due east of the house stood a galvanized-iron shed. A hundred meters further on, Crooked River bordered the property. Away to his right, Thompson land stretched on forever.

The smell of sizzling lamb wafted to Porter's nostrils and shook him from the daydream. A kind-faced woman stood next to him. She wore a floral dress under a cooking apron, her grey-streaked hair tied in a bun. She appeared to be close to his mum's age, mid-sixties, and he guessed she'd been a stunner in younger years. He peered towards the shed.

"That's Bill's storage shed, where he keeps his toys," she told him, as though she'd read his mind. "Boats, bikes, guns and old cars."

Bill returned with a new bottle of whiskey. "Son, my wife. Kathleen…This young fella's Dan Porter…Senior Constable from the city, working that investigation I told you about."

Kathleen smiled at Porter. "Didn't need to hear it from Bill, you Carinya boys are the talk of the whole town." Her eyes sparkled. "Do you like lamb? Bill can't eat it anymore but it's George's favorite." She shifted her gaze to Barrett then frowned. "George dear, you look awfully tired. Those dark circles under your eyes…"

"I'm fine, Kath. Only the usual…"

Bill chortled. "Come on, son, don't tell us you're still having bad dreams? Not the bogeyman black fellas again?" He swilled more whiskey.

Barrett's face flushed red. He dropped chin to chest and lowered eyes.

Bill poured himself another glass and turned to Porter. "It's hilarious, son. George always sees things that aren't there. Says the ghosts of kooris haunt him and it's why he can't sleep." He scoffed. "Never heard such bullshit…Then again, you've always been a bit loopy…" He jabbed Barrett's shoulder. "Haven't you, son?"

Barrett sat silent.

Porter didn't laugh.

Kathleen placed a hand on Barrett's forearm and glared at Bill. "Leave George alone, you've embarrassed him." She turned to Porter. "Don't listen to Bill, thinks it's a big joke…George isn't the only one

174

haunted by Koori ghosts, you know? Others say the same, that they visit their dreams in all forms – crocodiles, eagles, snakes. Spirits of this land who'll never stop haunting us whiteys until we give it back…"

Kathleen cooked a mean lamb roast, and Porter piled a second helping onto the plate. She asked about his past. He indulged her with his life story, except the parts he always left out. When it got closer to recent events he ended it, and decided to make her the subject of conversation.

"So, Kathleen, how'd you and Bill meet?"

"Oh, that's not interesting at all." She waved a dismissive hand. "Our families were close. I was the prettiest girl and Bill the toughest boy. Was always meant to be…"

Porter sensed a hint of resignation in her voice. Bill had been the toughest, but who'd been her sweetheart? "Fair enough..." He turned to Barrett. "And you boss, what's your story in Crooked River?"

Barrett paused before answering. "Came here as an underaged cadet in '68 and been here ever since. Bill was my Sergeant. No exciting stories to tell. A simple country cop living a simple country life…"

"Must be close to retiring?"

"Yes, later this year."

Bill's neck wobbled as he shook his head. "No exciting stories? Bullshit…" He gulped whiskey. "Tell young Porter about the day I saved your skinny arse. There's a story…"

Barrett's face flushed bright red. Kathleen shook her head and carried plates inside.

"Right then, I'll tell the story." Bill leaned towards Porter, eyes glazed. "George was eighteen, mother's milk still wet on his lips. We were coming back from the mission and I sent him into the pub to get whiskey. Was dozing in the Cooper, wondering what's taking the bastard so long, when three Koori boys bolt from the pub. So, I head inside and holy shit, there's one hell of a brawl. Bottom of the pile with four shearers whacking the crap out of him, was young George." He chuckled and drank. "Tell him, son. Tell him why those shearers flogged you..."

Barrett moaned, as though he dreaded telling the story but had resigned himself to it. "Shearers were forcing the blacks to fight each other and taking bets. I tried to stop them..."

"Long story short, I threw them off in the nick of time. George went to hospital with more broken bones than a half-eaten chook...Did those Koori boys help when he's getting flogged to death? No, the weak mongrels left him for dead. Moral of the story, son...Do no favors for a black fella..."

Barrett sighed "... cos they'll do you none in return."

Bill clapped the performance then squinted at Porter. "How's your investigation coming along?"

Porter had expected the question and gave a prepared reply. "We've only been here a week...Locals in town and kooris on missions aren't saying a word. There have been no fresh allegations of abuse and we can't verify the existing ones. We've got nothing..."

A smugness spread over Bill's face. "That being the case, guess you'll soon be moving on?"

"Dunno, but Crooked River's our base and there's still a heap of witnesses to interview."

"Why you wasting time here, Constable?" Barrett said. "They've told you nothing because there's nothing to tell."

Porter looked from one to the other. "If you blokes reckon we won't find anything, why you so keen to see us leave?"

Bill leaned closer, reeking of whiskey. "What a stupid fucking question...Why would I want you in my district? Carinya's all over the national news. You're terrible for our image, and ruining our future."

"Don't you reckon that us leaving after finding sweet f all would be the best outcome for the town?"

"No, son, I don't. We've already had developers pull out due to the bad publicity you fellas bring, from projects that would've created much-needed jobs. There are still some in the pipeline, an Outback resort and theme park, planned for that land," he pointed south towards vast paddocks on his left. "Investors have made it clear...If Carinya stays in Crooked River, they go."

"It's Lionel's decision. We might be here three months..."

"Three months?" Bill said louder.

"Can't you talk some sense into Roberts?" Barrett asked Porter. "Can't you tell him to move on? Carinya will fail if he stays here."

"Lionel's his own man..."

Bill snorted. "Listen, son, I like you, you remind me of myself as a young fella...Yes, the local cops have labeled you a dog, bu--."

"I did what's right...Betts murdered those Koori boys."

"And I told Jim that, when he said you butted heads in the pub last week."

"I doubt the big bastard listened?"

"Ah, Jim can be a stubborn asshole but he's harmless. I'm helping you here, son, telling you what's best." Bill's face got redder. "Tell your friend Roberts to leave Crooked River. Take Carinya away and never come back."

Porter grinned. The real Bill Thompson had come to the fore. "Reckon you tell him yourself, face to face. A threat like that…"

Bill's head rocked back as he roared in laughter. "Hardly a threat, son. More like friendly advice, from an old head who knows a few things." He paused to gulp whiskey. "I'm just a Mayor trying to protect his district…Consider the assassination of Nick Galios this morning…"

"What about it?"

"You don't get it, do you, son? Men ten times more important and powerful than me, for whatever reasons, don't want Carinya here in the Outback. Galios' death is a warning. To you, and Roberts."

"I would've left the cops long before now if warnings spooked me…"

Bill's grey eyes chilled him. "You've never been warned like this, son. If you care to live much longer, I suggest you take notice."

TWENTY-THREE

At 6.30am Thursday, Lionel Roberts pounded on Porter's bedroom door and demanded he wake up. He strode into the kitchen to make breakfast, determined to make the day a success. He'd achieved nothing on Wednesday, unable to concentrate after learning of Nick Galios' shocking death, and couldn't afford to waste any more investigation time.

He thought about yesterday's email from Shirley while he waited for the kettle to boil. She'd mentioned a girl named Rosie. The spirits of wise ancestors had visited his dreams, and they too had urged him to find her. He decided he'd go and question the elders. Who was Rosie? Where could he find her, and what might her story reveal?

An hour later he parked the Landcruiser in the shade of river gums at Crooked River mission. He and Porter walked to the riverbank. Old Man Simpson sat on a fallen tree and chatted with two female elders. Lionel sat next to him, kicked black leather shoes off and rolled sleeves to elbows. Porter stood nearby with arms crossed over a tight polo shirt. He wore his favorite New Balance sneakers and Levi 501's.

"Good to see you again, uncle," Lionel said.

Simpson tipped his cowboy hat then pointed to the women. "This's Aunty Doreen and Aunty Mel. Both been livin' here as long as me, and nothin' they don't know 'bout this place."

"Nice to meet you, aunties. I'm Lionel. My friend is Dan."

The aunties smiled, shy and toothless. Thin grey hair fell to their swollen waists. Both wore floral dresses that revealed too much wrinkled bosom and too much vein-riddled thigh. Their bare feet and arms were darker than a moonless night, the same as their eyes.

"Not bein' nasty, but was hopin' you fellas stayed away," Simpson said. "Tommy says he'll belt whoever talks ta ya."

"Where is he?" Porter said.

"Went into town," Simpson told Lionel. "Said he had ta get away from 'ere, says spirits told 'im you fellas will bring bad luck."

Lionel studied Simpson's wrinkled face. Kind, with intelligent eyes. "The same spirits talk to me and say you're a wise man who wants to help…" He paused to let Simpson think on it. "You've been silent for too long, and don't need to fear Tommy. Okay?" He pleaded with his eyes. Did they know he fought for them? That they could trust him?

"Okay, Lionel," Aunty Mel said.

Simpson and Doreen nodded.

"Last week you wanted to tell us who molested Tilly Johnson," Porter said to Simpson. "But Tommy Davis stopped you…Who was it?"

Simpson straightened and turned towards the river. He turned back to Doreen, eyes wide, then faced Mel. Both women shook their heads.

"Dunno…" Simpson blurted. "And I aint afraid of Tommy…Was gunna give ya my guess, but truth is, I dunno who touched Tilly…"

Porter made googly eyes at Lionel.

Lionel agreed, Simpson was the worst liar he'd met. But he sensed the Tilly incident saddened him and was too recent to speak of. Koori elders preferred to discuss the distant past. With Shirley's email in mind, he tried to take them there.

"I've heard a story," he said, "about a girl who lived on this mission fifty years ago. Her name was Rosie." He watched their faces. "Do you remember her?" Aunty Mel flinched first. "Aunty Mel? You remember, don't you?"

Aunty Mel glanced over her shoulder to a clump of bush, a nervous twitch in her eye. "That's a name shouldn't be said 'round here," she whispered. "Tommy don't like it."

Simpson and Doreen shook their heads.

Lionel smiled and tried to ease their fears. "Why? What's Tommy hiding from us?"

"Rosie Davis were Tommy's niece," Simpson said. "Came ta live with his family when her parents died. Was supposed ta care for her but he made her life miserable."

Lionel detected disgust in his voice and pressed him further. "Isn't that more reason to tell us the whole story? If Koori children were harmed, past and present, we want to know."

"He's right," Mel said. "Us saying nothin' has only caused more sufferin'..."

Simpson dipped his head then turned to Lionel. "They'd come and rape all the girls, didn't matter how young. Rosie were the prettiest, and that sweet girl were only eleven when White Devil started on her."

Lionel swallowed. "White Devil? Who?"

"Them whitey coppers, a heap of 'em over the years…" Aunty Doreen whispered. "Never knew their names and hardly seen their faces, so we gave 'em nicknames. White Devil was worst of all. He'd bring the others late at night, all drunk, and send Tommy and other fellas down ta the river with gin and smokes." She cringed. "Then the coppers would 'ave their way with the girls."

"I remember one time when Malcolm, Tommy's nephew, tried ta stop the Devil from rapin' Rosie. He was only thirteen or so…" Aunty Mel's voice trembled. "Devil whacked him that hard he nearly went deaf in one ear. After that, Malcolm hid under the house when the Devil came, coverin' ears and bawlin' his eyes out."

Aunty Doreen scowled. "And that weak mongrel Tommy never raised a hand ta stop it."

"Malcolm still around?" Porter said.

Simpson ignored him and spoke to Lionel. "Poor kid went crazy when they kept comin' for Rosie. He just disappeared one day. Fellas said they'd seen him in the city. Then he went ta jail for robbin' fellas. Who knows where he ended up?"

Aunty Doreen shook her head. "Weren't ever seen 'round 'ere again..."

Lionel frowned. Was Malcolm yet another witness he'd never find? "And Rosie, what happened to her?"

"She disappeared too…" Aunty Doreen wiped a tear from her spotted cheek. "Fellas say whitey's from the gov'ment stole her. Was a lovely girl..."

Lionel gave Doreen a moment to compose herself. Government fellas? Shirley had mentioned Alec Ferguson from the Aboriginal Welfare Board. "Aunty, you say government men took Rosie away...Who were they?"

Doreen glanced at Mel. Mel nodded, as though willing her to continue. "Fellas from the city," Doreen whispered then peered towards the river. "Don't remember exactly, but they's from that lot, you know, who was supposed ta help us kooris..."

"Could it have been, the Welfare Board?" Lionel said.

"Somethin' like that..." Simpson said. "The same one always came. A tall, skinny fella in a fancy suit, drivin' a fancy car. Always took the youngest and prettiest girls away. Told us they bein' sent ta work and study, and that good whiteys would take care of 'em."

Aunty Mel sighed. "If the families kicked up a stink that skinny fella would just hand out chocolates, gin and smokes ta shut 'em up. Sometimes money..."

"Do you remember his name?" Lionel said.

Simpson shook his head. "Was long, long ago...And gov'ment fellas like 'im we've tried to forget."

Lionel paused to consider Simpson's words, aware of the painful memories evoked by his search for the truth. "I'm sorry but it's important we find him. Was he the same man who kept records for the mission?"

"What?" Simpson said.

"For example, did you report births and deaths to him?

"Yep, was the same fella for all of it...But after a while he stopped askin'. No-one cared who lived 'ere, so we never told 'em."

"Can you remember during what years no records were kept?" Lionel asked them but expected a negative response. As natives of the Outback, the elders had a very different perception of time to his own.

They gawked at him and shook their heads.

"Anyone complain when the girls were taken against their will?" Porter said.

Aunty Mel scoffed. "Complain ta who? No-one from the gov'ment listened, and you coppers were in on it…"

"They took my Yvonne when she's eleven," Aunty Doreen's eyes glistened as she told Lionel. "Fought 'em and fought 'em. Them coppers beat me ta the ground and dragged her away…Told me she'd gone ta live with whiteys in Western Australia. Few months after I got this letter from America, from a girl sayin' she's Yvonne and needed help…Skinny gov'ment fella laughed in me face when I told him." She glared at Porter. "Hah, complain…"

Lionel gulped. "Aunty Doreen, this removal of girls…How long did it continue?"

"Hmm…First started 'bout five or six years before they took Yvonne. She were one of the last. Whitey's only stopped comin' when their boss ended that protection thingy…"

"The Aboriginal Protection Act ended in 1969," Lionel said. "So, we're looking at a period from, say, 1963 until then…" *The timeframe matches those of the Welfare Board files missing from State Archives.* "Uncle, try to remember…The years that the government man stopped keeping records of this mission…Could they be the same years during which the girls were taken away?"

Simpson tugged a white beard. "Maybe…"

"You're certain you can't remember the names of the police who raped these girls? Or the name of this, White Devil?"

Simpson looked at the ground and said nothing.

Lionel had no doubt Simpson knew the men's names but didn't push further, he'd already gathered more information than expected. He thanked the elders for their bravery and asked that they keep the conversation to themselves. They all agreed it was dangerous to speak of it.

Five minutes later, Lionel drove the Landcruiser from the mission. He glanced to Porter in the passenger seat, who grinned while he studied his phone.

"What is it?" Lionel said.

"Good ol' Claire's come through again...She found this Ferguson bloke you wanna talk to."

"Fantastic. Where?"

"Broken Hill...She's sent an address and a photo. She says there're reports linking him to child pornography and sexual abuse of minors. But he's never been charged."

"Ewh, sounds like he could be the one...My informant's making her statement in Edinburgh today, and I should have it by late tonight. We'll fly to Broken Hill tomorrow morning and pay Mr Ferguson a visit."

"Fair chance he's the skinny government bloke the elders mentioned...But he's an old man who's kept whatever he knows to himself for decades. Why would he talk now? And if he does, what's he gunna tell you?"

Lionel appreciated the trust Porter had placed in him when joining Carinya and decided to make the trust mutual. But he wouldn't divulge everything he knew. "When they abolished the Protection Act all records were meant to go to the State Archives. There's none on file for Crooked River mission between 1963 and 1969."

"The same years that Simpson reckons no-one kept records…Bloody hell, mate, why didn't you tell me this earlier?"

"The importance of the missing files wasn't clear until now. But with the elders confirming my informant's info, I'm certain that if we can find them, they'll provide answers to some very dark questions."

"Reckon you're right…Ferguson never filed 'em to protect himself, and whoever gave him authority to remove those girls."

"Exactly." Lionel beamed. "I'm hoping that with your persuasion, Ferguson tells whose orders he followed. And if he has the records showing which girls were taken, we may be able to track them down. Aunty Doreen said her daughter ended up in America…Why?"

"And we've gotta interview all the cops who were stationed here back then, to work out which ones helped the crooked AWB blokes."

Lionel remembered what Porter had told him about his Wednesday lunch meeting. "Indeed…Starting with Senior Sergeant Bill Thompson and Constable George Barrett…"

"Carinya interviewing the Mayor and top cop of Crooked River…" Porter laughed. "Fuck me, that'll throw a dingo amongst the chooks…"

Lionel didn't laugh. He swallowed the vile tasting phlegm in his throat. Who was this White Devil, the policeman who'd raped girls and aided their illegal removal from the mission? He vowed to find him, to expose the monster and his evil deeds to the world.

TWENTY-FOUR

At 1.17am Friday, John Rhodes ended a phone conversation and rolled out of bed. He flicked on the light, ambled down the hallway to Lionel's bedroom and tapped on the door until it opened.

Lionel stood bare-chested and rubbed swollen eyelids. "John…What?"

"Sorry to wake you," Rhodes whispered.

"What's wrong?"

"I just spoke with McHendry, my Interpol contact in Edinburgh."

Lionel face crumpled in a look of concern. "And?"

"Bad news I'm sorry…" Rhodes yawned. "Your informant and her husband were killed in a car accident as they drove into Edinburgh this afternoon. A farmer saw them lose control in heavy rain, crash, and roll into a river. A messy scene, according to McHendry…"

Lionel's head rocked back. A hand covered his gaping mouth. "Oh, no, no…" He tugged at his goatee. "Nooo," he said louder. "Are they certain it's her?"

"Relatives living nearby supplied the cops with names. Shirley and Colin McMahon from Randwick, New South Wales."

"They've identified the bodies?"

"His. Hers hasn't been recovered yet."

"Then how can they know she's dead?"

Rhodes paused. "I'm only passing on what he told me… Apparently the farmer tried to rescue a female who floated face down, but the current carried her away before he could reach the car. She most likely survived the crash then drowned. Colin was already dead."

"Are they still searching?"

"They'll resume in the morning. McHendry thinks they'll find her body downstream, if wild animals don't take her first. Sorry mate…"

Lionel stared. "She'd resisted giving a statement. Afraid. I convinced her to do it…I promised to protect her and failed."

"It's not your fault, Lio. An accident…"

Lionel scoffed. "This was no accident…Nick Galios, and now Shirley. She's been murdered for what she knows and I'm the pathetic turd who put her at risk." He dropped a trembling chin to chest and broke eye contact. "I should stop this now, before more innocent lives are lost…"

"Look, McHendry's solid, and we're the only others who knew Shirley was driving into Edinburgh. She wasn't murdered. It's just a freak accident. And if you give up now, she and Galios have died for nothing."

Lionel nodded after a long silence. "You're right, I need to keep going and make Carinya's success their vengeance...And it starts today with Alec Ferguson."

Rhodes frowned. "It's not smart to interview him without a signed informant statement…"

"I really don't care for rules anymore. Our enemies don't play by them, so why should we?"

Later that day as the sun neared its zenith, Rhodes drove alone to Crooked River mission. At the briefing earlier, Lionel had tasked him with questioning Uncle Simpson. He was certain the elder knew more than he'd divulged. Rhodes had said he doubted Simpson would talk. Why would he trust a white policeman? Lionel had agreed but suggested that persistence was their closest ally. And Rhodes was the only Carinya member available for the job.

Lionel and Porter had left the house at 9.30am to fly to Broken Hill and were due to return late afternoon. Klose had paperwork to finish. After that he would locate Tommy Davis. He'd heard that Tommy was staying at a cousin's place near town, and once arrested he'd take him to the police station for an interview. Elders had made serious allegations. And as Lionel had said, the time had come for Tommy to answer them.

Rhodes arrived at the mission. He parked the Landcruiser and wandered down a narrow path towards the river. An elder wearing a cowboy hat sat on a fallen tree. A dozen women and their naked toddlers scampered towards the row of white houses, then stopped to watch Rhodes from a distance.

"Are you Uncle Simpson?" Rhodes asked the man in the cowboy hat.

"Yep, and you're one of Lionels' mob, aint ya?" Simpson squinted. "Same flash car and suit…Fellas don't give up, do ya?"

Rhodes sat next to him. "John Rhode's my name. And yes, I'm one of Lionel's mob…" He placed a bottle of gin between them. "For you..."

Simpson eyed him sideways. "Why?"

"In return for a friendly chat." Rhodes swiveled three-sixty degrees to take in the tranquil scene. "Nice spot, love these old river gums."

"It's home..." Simpson examined the gin bottle. "What ya want Rhodes? Tired of talkin' ta you fellas, and got nothin' more ta say…"

Rhodes leaned closer to him. "Lionel thinks otherwise. So do I."

"Told Lionel, I don't remember who them coppers were. No-one 'round 'ere does. Too dangerous ta remember and too dangerous ta talk to you fellas…" Simpson's eyes darted left and right, then to bushes near the river.

Rhodes turned to watch the bushes and listened until a gust of wind rustled them. He turned back to Simpson. "No-one's there..." He read the apprehension on his face. "Don't fear Tommy Davis. We'll protect you and your family…"

Simpson chuckled. "Fink Davis the only one tellin' what you fellas are up ta? There's plenty of others happy ta play lacky…They know what you've been told, and soon as you fellas pack up and leave, they'll make us pay."

"Who's 'they'? Who's Tommy working for?"

Simpson stared at the ground and dug a toe into grey mud. "Dunno, but they want you fellas gone. I know that much…"

Rhodes watched his hands tremble and sensed fear. "We'll move you to a safer place…"

Simpson raised his voice. "And I'm tellin' ya, Rhodes, I got nothin' more ta say…"

Rhodes stooped to make eye contact but the old man turned away. "Understood, you need to protect your family."

Simpson turned back and kept his head down. "I like you fellas and Lionel, youse are tryin' ta do good…But ya know what, Rhodes?

Rhodes answered by raising eyebrows.

"Whitey coppers 'ave been sayin' for years they gunna do us kooris right. But they never do…" Simpson scowled at two boys who'd wandered too close. Once they'd ran off he leaned towards Rhodes and whispered. "Can't tell ya which coppers hurt our girls all them years ago…But a fella with nothin' ta lose and no loved ones ta protect…He might tell ya."

"Who?"

Simpson turned his head towards the opposite side of the river. "See that biggest hill over there?"

Rhodes followed his gaze. One hill across the river mottled in red, white and grey, rose high above the others. "Yes."

"That's Bunyip Hill. Speak ta the fella who sits up there."

"Bunyip?" Rhodes had read Aboriginal storybooks as a boy. He pictured the bunyip as a giant, man-eating wombat. "As in, those mythical creatures from the Dreamtime?"

Simpson chuckled. "Mythical ta white fellas maybe…See them flat granite rocks on top?" He pointed towards the hill. "On the right's the bunyips' head, 'cos he's lyin' on his side. On the left's his body. See it?"

Rhodes squinted. "Ah, kind of…"

"People 'round 'ere are too scared ta go up there. They say that fella's a bunyip's evil spirit who sleeps all day and swims at night."

"Who is he?"

"No-one knows. He come from nowhere years ago and been lookin' down on us ever since. Talk ta him, he'll know who them bad coppers are…"

Rhodes thanked him and strode towards the Landcruiser. Halfway along the path, he realized he didn't know the quickest way to Bunyip Hill and walked back to ask. Simpson had gone. He turned towards the houses.

A female elder blocked the path. "I'm Aunty Doreen. Help ya?"

He peered past her. No sign of Simpson…And where had she come from? "Where's uncle Simpson?"

She glanced towards the river where bushes rustled in the breeze, then back to him. "He went for a kip…What you need?"

"How do I get to Bunyip Hill?"

She hesitated and played with her chin. "What ya want goin' up there?"

He grinned. "I like to climb…"

Her thick brows furrowed. "Up ta you…Turn right top of our road. First right again then over the bridge and turn right. Follow that and you'll come ta Bunyip Hill, just past the Thompson place…"

"Thanks." He turned and bounded towards the Landcruiser.

"Be careful fella," Doreen yelled. "There's bad spirits up there."

Rhodes acknowledged the advice with a wave over his shoulder. When he reached the car he called Klose's cell phone. He wanted to share what he'd learned from Simpson. No answer. He sent him a message telling where he headed then sped towards Bunyip Hill.

Tommy Davis crept up behind Aunty Doreen while the Landcruiser disappeared in a cloud of red dust. When she turned towards her house, she jumped and clutched a hand to heart. She tried to walk around him but he blocked her.

"What ya bin tellin' that white fella, Doreen?"

"Nothin' Tommy," she stammered. "He wanna go Bunyip Hill and I told 'im how…"

"That all he asked ya?"

"Yep…"

Tommy let her pass and watched her scurry home. He took a phone from his pocket and pressed a contact. The call connected but no-one spoke. He waited for an answer. When none came, he said, "Hello?"

"What do you want?" A male voice crackled through the phone.

"This here's Tommy Davis from the mission. Fella said ta call this number if there's troubles with them coppers from the big smoke."

"And the problem is…?"

"One's bin 'ere just now askin' uncle Simpson questions…I couldn't get close ta hear what they's sayin' but that silly old fool mighta talked…And the copper when he's leavin', asked how he gets ta Bunyip Hill…"

"Bunyip Hill. Why?"

"Dunno…"

After five seconds the man said, "Good work, you'll be well rewarded. And Tommy, I have two more tasks for you…"

"Tell me 'em."

"First, delete this number immediately…"

"Yep, right away…What's number two?"

The man explained the second task.

Tommy swore then ended the call.

TWENTY-FIVE

John Rhodes followed Aunty Doreen's directions from the mission and reached Bunyip Hill in less than ten minutes. He parked the Landcruiser off the road and tried Klose's cell phone again. Engaged tone...Was Klose on a call, or had the surrounding hills blocked his from getting through? He noticed the signal strength on his phone showed one bar and assumed the latter.

He stepped from the car and raised the shirt's collar to protect his neck from the harsh midday sun. He tightened the shoulder holster and checked the Glock was secure, then glanced to the quarry in front of him. It lay at the bottom of a sandstone cliff a hundred meters high. To his right, a red dirt path dissected Bunyip Hill and wound its way to the top.

He walked up the steep path and started to sweat within the first minute. He cursed himself for wearing trousers. The soles of his leather shoes were smooth and he took careful steps, grateful for chunks of jutting rock that helped him push on and upwards. Tufts of spinifex grass and clumps of olive-green mulga bush littered the hillside, their coverage sparser the higher he climbed. House-sized granite boulders defied gravity and clung to the slope, half-buried where they'd landed a million years earlier.

Three-quarters of the way to the top he stopped. Breathless. Trickles of sweat stung his eyes then ran down cheeks into his mouth. He smacked lips together. The liquid salt made him thirsty. His nose twitched at the foul stench of fresh animal dung. He looked down at green feces on his shoe and wiped it against spinifex to remove it. He scanned the hillside for the culprit. Bushes rustled to his right. A grey emu darted from its hiding place and trotted down the slope.

He swayed in a warm breeze as he took in the activity around him. Waterfowl splashed in Willy Wonka's chocolate river far below. Pink and white cockatoo shrieked in song from branches of red river gums. A wedge-tailed eagle glided through the pastel-blue sky, giant wings silhouetted against a fireball sun, a Lord watching over his brethren.

He shifted his gaze to the opposite side of the river and saw the mission's white houses through a gap in the trees. To his left beyond a row of hills lay Crooked River township. A typical outback town, its wide streets ran arrow straight. North to south and east to west, in a perfect square. Down to his right, a few hundred meters from the river, sunlight reflected from the Thompson homestead's roof.

Once rested he continued up the path towards the sleeping bunyip. After five minutes he reached the top and the ground leveled. He walked to the bunyip's body and wedged his foot in a crevice for leverage then dragged himself onto the giant granite boulder. He stepped over the smooth surface then jumped across a short gap to a smaller boulder. He landed on the bunyip's head.

He spun three-sixty degrees to study the shimmering horizon. He stopped and scanned the immediate surroundings. No evidence of human habitation…If a man did live on Bunyip Hill, where was he?

He looked straight down to where the bunyip's head met a dirt path. He noticed a rocky ledge that wrapped around a cliff face, to a path that seemed to lead to the far side of the hill. He decided to explore further and slid from the boulder.

The ledge was a foot wide and twelve feet long. Rhodes shuffled along it toes to heel and facing forward, not game to look at the quarry far below. Rock crumbled under foot. He slipped. Guts jumped to throat. He flung arms out to balance as his torso wobbled. He steadied, stumbled, then leaped forward and landed face first on the path. Safe. His knees trembled as he stood. He followed the path a few meters, climbed over a granite boulder then stepped his way through thick mulga bush.

A wall of rock confronted him when he emerged from the bush. It curved upwards, high above his head like a wave about to break. Unable to go left or straight ahead, he moved to the right through a ravine. He trod carefully. Dark caves at the bottom of the rock face down to his left would swallow him if he slipped and fell.

After fifty meters he came to a clearing. Rock walls rose three meters on all sides to form a natural amphitheater. He gasped when he saw the Aboriginal art, the hand-drawn picture stories that covered the walls. He took photos.

Rhodes checked the signal strength on his phone. No bars this time. He cursed Telstra and wished he'd listened to Lyn Foster when she'd told him Optus had better coverage. Unable to call Klose, he decided he'd drive to the Carinya residence and show him photos of the drawings. They would then return to conduct a thorough search for the man living on Bunyip Hill.

He ran back through the ravine, stepped through the mulga bush and scurried over the granite boulder. He hesitated when he reached the rock ledge. It seemed narrower the second time and the drop to the quarry seemed further. His right foot landed on the ledge. Heart bounced in his chest. Left heel lifted, ready to take a second step. A thud behind him. The sound of heavy boots landing on dirt? *Shit!* He froze like a tightrope walker with stage fright, unable to turn and look back. *What the fuck, was that?*

TWENTY-SIX

Detective Lyn Foster swore and slammed her phone onto a dining table inside the Crooked River Hotel. She'd been looking forward to lunch with her girlfriends from the Crime Scene Unit. She needed a long chat, an oily lasagne with garlic bread, and a few glasses of red. But Inspector George Barrett had just called and ordered her to investigate a suspicious death at the mission. He'd ruined her day off. When she'd protested, he told her that everyone else in their office was busy. Like hell they were…She snatched her handbag from the table, snarled at the male detectives perched at the bar and stormed out.

On the way to the mission she used the hands-free phone to call Fred Klose. She'd volunteered to help arrest Tommy Davis later in the day but Klose hadn't bothered to return her message. She frowned when his number rang out. Carinya staff had received constant threats since arriving in Crooked River, and she preferred to know where they were at all times.

She phoned John Rhodes. When they'd spoken earlier, he'd been en-route to the mission. Was he still there, and if so, could he wait for her? Did he know about the suspicious death? Her questions went unanswered because a sweet female voice told her - 'the number you dialed is not available.'

When she arrived at the mission the dashboard clock read 1.05pm. She parked then hurried towards a circle of kooris huddled near the river. Women and children wailed. Men blocked her path and refused to let her closer, then reluctantly parted to allow entry. Uncle Simpson lay dead on the cracked mud, gut bloated and face pale. Tommy Davis knelt beside him.

Lyn ignored the hysterical screams that demanded she leave. "What happened?"

"The silly old fool fell in the water 'bout thirty minutes ago," Tommy said. "He weren't like the rest of us, never learnt ta swim. I fished 'im out too late…" He dropped his forehead onto Simpson's purple chest and sobbed. After a minute he stood and pointed at Lyn. "See I told youse this would 'appen, that these white fellas from the city would bring us bad luck. Doreen saw Uncle Simpson talkin' ta one of 'em just before, and evil water spirits punished 'im for it…"

The gathering yelled at Lyn with growing rage. She moved to Aunty Doreen. "You spoke with one of the Carinya guys? How long ago did he leave?"

Doreen glanced at Tommy. He glared back, as though daring her to answer.

"Maybe, an hour?" Doreen said. "He was goin' ta Bunyip Hill…" She waved Lyn away, her voice got louder. "Leave girl, before them evil spirits take more of us."

Lyn looked down at Simpson. Her Coroner's report would say he'd drowned. There wouldn't be an autopsy because Tommy and the others would never allow the body to leave the mission. They would bury Simpson in sacred ground next to his ancestors.

With the investigation complete, Lyn turned her attention to finding Rhodes and Klose. Why hadn't they answered their phones? The mourning kooris threatened violence. She stepped out of the circle towards her car. "Doreen, why'd Rhodes go to Bunyip Hill?"

Doreen stared with sad black eyes.

Tommy pushed past her and stood in front of Lyn. He reeked of liquor. "Go! We don't want ya 'ere. You've caused enough bloody misery already..."

Five minutes later, Lyn drove fast towards Bunyip Hill. She phoned Klose, wanting to inform him that she'd seen Tommy Davis. No answer. She tried Rhodes' phone. What had Uncle Simpson told him? Again, no answer.

She passed the Thompson property then slowed into a corner. She braked hard as she came out of it, narrowly avoiding a red ute parked halfway across the road. Jim Thompson's private car? And was that a Carinya Landcruiser parked in front of it? She got out and strode towards the quarry at the bottom of Bunyip Hill. Where was John Rhodes? And what was Jim Thompson doing there?

Jim stood in the middle of the boulder-strewn quarry with his back to her. He wore a white polo shirt, khaki shorts, and flip-flops. She crept towards him then froze as a rock crunched under her heel.

Jim turned with a devious smile on his face. "Woah Foster, looking good. Love you in tight jeans...And your tits..." An obnoxious grin as he stared. "You should show 'em off more often. That skimpy top's perfect..."

She'd learned to ignore taunts from Crooked River's chauvinistic baboons. "What's going on?"

"Was next door saying g'day to mum when the job came through. Young fella from up the road called it in…He was walking his dogs when they ran over and found it."

"I didn't hear any jobs over the radio…His dogs found what?"

"The job wasn't broadcast, the station called me." He stepped aside to reveal what his massive frame had hidden.

She gasped and muffled a sob with hand. She stumbled towards John Rhodes' crumpled body. "Oh my God…" She noticed the blue rubber gloves on Jim's hands. "What happened?"

He peered towards the top of the cliff. "He fell, no doubt…Fuck knows what he was doing up there?" He sniggered while he wrote in the notebook. "Weird bastards this Carinya mob…"

She scoffed. "He was a cop, like us. And my friend…"

He shrugged and pointed to Rhodes' limp body with his pen. "A clumsy, dead friend. Climb in those shoes of course you're gunna come tumbling down…"

She gritted teeth. "The Carinya guys have been threatened, he didn't fall." She bent over Rhodes to examine bloody pulp at the rear of his skull. "How's this trauma to his head possible? When he's landed over the rock, and his back took the brunt of the fall?"

He kept writing. "His head hit first. Momentum pitched him forward and he stayed on his back. That's what my report's gunna say anyhow…"

She glowered at him, mouth open. "Look…" She knelt behind Rhodes and pointed at his sunken skull. "That's not been caused by a single blow on landing. He's been hit with a rock or something…" She bent closer to the ground. "Blood splatter patterns, in different sizes." She stood and scanned the red dirt. She ran ten meters then stopped and pointed to a blood-covered rock on the ground. "Look at this…Head was bashed in, then they threw this rock over here…"

He gave her a quizzical frown and continued writing. "I saw that…The blood could've come from anywhere. Dingo chewin' on his dinner? Who knows…?"

She huffed, strode to the plastic bag next to the body and picked it up to study its contents. Rhodes' wallet, police ID, iPhone, and Landcruiser keys…She fished out the battered phone.

Jim grunted. "Leave it. Don't want your grubby prints..."

She noticed the phone's open sim card holder. "No sim card." She glanced at him. "Did you take it out already?"

He didn't look at her. "Must've come out on impact. Look for it…"

She placed the bag down. Nothing could be recovered from the mangled iPhone. But if she could find the sim card, any data stored on it might explain why Rhodes had climbed Bunyip Hill. She stepped with caution and moved outwards in circles while she searched the ground. Five meters from the corpse she stopped and bent down. A boot mark in the dirt? A large boot with a serrated sole. The type found on police or military issued boots.

Her eyes followed the direction of the boot marks. Three more led to the road. She stood to full height and saw scuff marks in the dirt. Had more boot marks been kicked away? By the killer, or someone else? She piled rocks next to the marks to help Crime Scene staff find them.

She strode back to Jim. "Can't find the sim card…This is a crime scene, and it requires a thorough examination. Now."

He sighed as though bored by her. "The Crime Scene girls left town on another job twenty minutes ago. They can come out tomorrow…"

She marched up to him and hoped anger would mask her fear. "That's bullshit! There won't be a crime scene tomorrow…We can't leave his body overnight."

"You're right, dingos will get to him. I'll call the contractors out and have him taken to the morgue this arvo…"

"No, you need to get the Crime Scene Unit here…What are you hiding?" Hot blood flushed her face as she shouted. "A cop's dead, and you don't give a fuck."

"I'm the Detective Sergeant in charge. Don't have to explain myself to you, Senior Constable."

"And as the designated homicide detective for Crooked River, I'm saying it's murder."

"What you think aint worth shit. I'm your boss, you'll do as you're told…"

"I'll go to Barrett, over your head," she yelled. "I'm bringing the Crime Scene girls back from whatever bullshit job they're at, and giving this the investigation John deserves." She stormed towards the car then turned back. "I'm calling Barrett now…Will put you on the phone, let him tell you what a useless wanker you are…"

"Wasting your time, sweet lips…Already told George how I'm dealing with this. He agrees with my decision and says there's no need wasting resources on an obvious accident." He strolled towards her.

Her jaw quivered as she looked up to meet the glare of his grey eyes. The glint in them seemed a mixture of lust and rage. She backed away, unsure if he'd kiss or punch her. "It's pathetic what you're doing. This is no accident..."

"Well, best get your sexy arse out of here and tell a fella who cares. I've said it is, and that's all that matters."

She ran to the car, opened the door and turned back to him. "We'll see…"

A fiendish grin spread across his face. "Foster, be careful spending too much time with those city cops. I'd hate to see their clumsiness rub off on you…"

TWENTY-SEVEN

The Friday morning flight from Crooked River got
delayed and it was just past 2pm when Lionel Roberts
knocked on the front door of a miserable miner's
cottage on the outskirts of Broken Hill. Could the man
who lived there answer the many questions that puzzled
him? Could he help them find the missing records for
Crooked River mission? Or, did he still have them?

An elderly man opened the door and greeted him
and Porter with an angry grunt. Lionel introduced them
and resisted a triumphant smile. He recognized the man
from the photo Claire had sent. At 6'3 and wafer thin,
the man matched the description of the corrupt
Aboriginal Welfare Board worker the elders had
spoken of. The man who'd stolen girls from Crooked
River during the 1960s. Alec Ferguson, Lionel said
under his breath, atonement is nigh...

Ferguson led them to a dining room at the rear of the
house. The Carinya men sat opposite him at a square
table that was bare except for three glasses of water. A
silver clock with rusted edges hung on an otherwise
empty wall. Its tick-tock cadence sounded like a bass
drum in the awkward silence.

Lionel laid his briefcase flat on the table and waited
for Ferguson to speak. He said nothing, so Lionel took
out a notepad and pen. Porter had done the same. They
exchanged a glance that said, 'this'll be fun'.

"Thank you for seeing us, Mr Ferguson," Lionel
said.

"Did I have a choice? Sergeant Boulton parked out front said yar be coming if I liked it or not," Ferguson said with a faint Scottish accent. He ran a hand through white hair then sat back and stared at Lionel with pale-blue eyes. He had a pink face sprinkled with liver spots. A web of purple veins covered a fat nose.

"Let's get started…" Lionel said. "Mr Ferguson, is it correct you once worked for the AWB?"

"Aye, from '63 to '69…" Ferguson scowled. "What's this about?"

"Please explain your role with them."

"Was a record keeper under the Aboriginal Protection Act. I recorded populations and names of those living on missions. Identified children at risk and reported back to the Welfare Board."

"Children at risk?" Porter said. "In what way?"

"Not getting proper nourishment, suffering physical and sexual abuse from Aboriginal men." Ferguson glanced from Porter to Lionel. "Things like that…"

Lionel leaned forward. "What would happen to these children?"

"Were fostered out to white families, who took much better care of them." Ferguson gave an exaggerated sigh. "Listen, Roberts, I'm sure yar know what happened to those Koori kids in the 60's. Half the world knows of the 'stolen generations'…So why the hell yar harassing me with stuff the government's already dealt with?"

Lionel took a copy of the receipt Shirley had provided from the briefcase. He handed it to Ferguson. "Therein lies the problem, Mr Ferguson. The government hasn't dealt with the, stuff."

Ferguson's face lost all color while he read the receipt. Trembling hands dropped it onto the table.

"Tell us about the receipt," Porter said.

Ferguson said nothing.

"It's your signature on that receipt, Mr Ferguson, isn't it?" Lionel remained calm, despite the fire inside him. "A receipt you wrote to Bleeker for the purchase of Cathy Inglis. Eleven-year-old, Cathy, who you forcibly removed from her family at Crooked River mission."

Ferguson laughed like a wicked headmaster. "Look at yar." He glared at Lionel with bloodshot eyes. "Think yar scare me? Yar just a rich Koori kid in a suit, pretending to care 'cos yar guilty about having money. And yar…" He turned to Porter. His voice grew louder. "Yar shoot black kids for a livin' and turn on yar workmates…The hide of yar both, coming into my home and accusing me of things I know nothing about!"

Lionel wanted to applaud the performance but gave him a dubious smile instead. "You deny it's your signature?"

"Not saying another word to yar…"

"I can arrest your wrinkly arse and drag it to the station," Porter said. "If you prefer?"

"Arrest me?" Ferguson folded arms. "For what? A signature on a receipt yar can't prove I wrote? Give me a farkin' break…"

Porter glared at him. "Want a break? Arm, or a leg?" He winked then pulled a thick file from his briefcase and thumbed through pages.

"What's this?" Ferguson said with sarcastic defiance. "More dodgy receipts?"

208

Porter smirked. "Police intelligence reports detailing your inappropriate behavior with children in the park, and your love of surfing kiddy-porn sites. What will your daughters think? Doubt you'll be allowed near the grandchildren ever again." He swiveled in the seat to look down the hallway. "Where's your computer? Might check out your hard drive..."

Ferguson's cheeks turned red. "Yar can't touch it, don't have a warrant."

"Ah, but I'm already inside...You invited me in. Remember?"

Ferguson faked a laugh.

"Look, I've got more than enough cause to drag you and your hard drive outta here..." Porter's eyes bulged as he growled. "If you answer our questions, I'll let other cops deal with these intelligence reports, and we'll ignore your corrupt practices of the past. Dick us around, I'll be forced to show your wife, kids, family and friends what a grubby man you've been..."

Ferguson sank in the seat, a drunken gambler who'd lost his last bet. His face crumpled as though he would cry but he broke into laughter instead. "Still don't get it, do yar? I don't give a damn for reputation...If I tell yar anything, the repercussions will be far worse than any court's punishment."

Lionel frowned. "Repercussions from who?"

Ferguson sighed. "Look, they forced my resignation in '69 cos I knew too much. Men who threatened my family back then are the same I fear now. My family's alive because I never spoke of things I did and saw." His eyes pleaded with Lionel. "I must protect them. Talk to yar, they die..."

Porter reached across the table and grabbed Ferguson by the throat. "You vile piece of shit, wanna talk about death? We found out ten minutes ago that a mate of ours died this morning. A champion bloke, who I reckon was murdered by people 'you' know of. To protect secrets, 'you' know about..." He threw him back in the chair. "Don't expect sympathy because you're worried innocent people will get hurt. It's too fucking late for that..."

Lionel resisted the urge to laugh, amused by Porter's ability to switch between 'normal' cop and 'feral' cop. He waited for calm. "Alec, here's your chance to make amends. Name the people we're looking for and we'll leave you alone. You'll be protected and not named as an informant."

Ferguson rubbed his neck then scoffed. "They've eyes and ears all over, and they'd already know yar here talking to me. I'm good as de..." He stopped, as though his predicament had punched him in the face. "I'm dead already..."

Porter huffed. "Then do an ounce of good in your life, if only once..."

Ferguson twirled the receipt in his fingers. "Aye, it's my signature. What about it?"

Lionel told him the story of Cathy Inglis being sold for ten pounds to Bleeker. Ferguson gave them a long-winded explanation of the processes he had to follow for every girl sold.

"Don't understand..." Lionel said. "The Protection Act gave you the power to take the girls and give them to white families for free. Why'd they pay if they didn't have to? Cheap labor?"

210

"Hardly...Those girls had never worked a farm in their lives."

"Then why pay? Ten pounds was a fair sum back then...Why'd they want them?"

Ferguson's eyes sparkled. "Some white men had acquired a taste for the pretty ones. Well developed, lighter skin, straight teeth...Why yar think they wanted them?"

Lionel knew the answer but still grimaced. Cathy's letter to Shirley told what men like Bleeker had done to the girls. He wanted to hear Ferguson confirm it. "How could you do it, knowing those girls would be raped?"

"Ah, now, I didn't say that..."

"Let's pretend you didn't...How did you convince parents to let their daughters go, when they knew they'd probably never see them again?"

Ferguson shrugged. "Like yar said, ten pounds was good money in those days...Though they rarely got that much and there was my cut as well. Besides, they knew the power I had and didn't really have a choice. Some payment, a few little white lies here and there...They wanted to believe their girls were getting a better life."

Lionel cringed. "More like, big white lies? That were told often?" He inhaled to compose himself. He couldn't allow anger to hamper the interview. "Your job involved recording population data of Crooked River mission... But between '63 and '69, you didn't. Because you took girls you weren't authorized to, didn't you? And sold them for a substantial profit?"

"I got told not to keep records for Crooked River. But I did keep two, separate sets of files for the girls we removed...One for the girls taken under the Protection Act, who were integrated into white families. And a second set, for the girls we sold. I tried submitting the first set of files to State Archives, but again the bosses told me not to."

"Did you ask why?" Porter said.

"Wasn't my place to…Orders not to file records came from high up in government. The AWB Chairman maybe. Who knows?"

"I think you're lying," Lionel said. "You and Crooked River police had a terrific money spinner going, and filing the records would've led to discrepancies, to questions being asked by the AWB…"

Porter growled. "Answer Lionel's question…You took girls you weren't authorized to, didn't you?"

"No, yar wrong. Had approval from the bosses to take whoever I wanted. Who yar think the money went to? Look at this shitty house. Wasn't me…"

"If you didn't file the records with the AWB, and they're not in the State Archives, where are they?" Lionel said.

"I destroyed the first set of files relating to girls removed under the Protection Act years ago…The second set of files, the records of girls sold, I gave to the bosses. They're stored in a safe place with the rest of the…" Ferguson blurted the last two words, "Cumal Files."

"You keep saying, 'bosses,'" Porter said. "Government bosses?"

Ferguson hesitated, as though he'd come to a fork and was unsure which path to take. "The organization's bosses…"

"Wait." Lionel held up a hand. "I'm confused…You worked for a separate organization, that wasn't a government department? And, the Cumal Files…What are they? What are you trying to tell us?"

"Damn you, Roberts, I've said too much already..."

"No doubt," Porter said. "But being a dead man talking, why not tell it all?"

Lionel covered his mouth to muffle a laugh. Then he frowned at Porter and hoped he'd realize Ferguson might reveal more with some 'gentle' encouragement. "Go on, Alec..."

Ferguson sighed. "Two dangerous groups of men will want me dead after this…Those in government, for numerous reasons. But the men I fear most, as you should, run the 'organization'. They're powerful and mysterious. Even the richest and most influential dare not oppose them."

"Mysterious?" Porter laughed, loud and cynical. "But somehow, you know all about 'em?"

Ferguson inclined his head. "They recruited me and got me inside the AWB. I was one of them once…"

Lionel pulled his goatee. "Were they an organization of business men?"

"Not exactly, from what I saw…Junior members like me weren't allowed at meetings. It was said they had another name, some even said they were linked to a political party. I only ever knew it as 'the organization.'"

"What was your role within it?"

"I acted as a broker between them and the government. Bosses saw the Protection Act as a cash cow to be exploited."

"And the government turned a blind eye?" Porter said.

"Aye, that's where yar lack of record keeping comes in, and why nothing got filed in State Archives…It was a lucrative business, for politicians and the organization both."

"Yet you gave records of girls sold to the organization's bosses…" Lionel said. "Why keep such records when the paper trail leaves them open to scrutiny?" He pointed to the receipt for Cathy Inglis. "There's proof..."

"Yar have to understand, these men have strange ways and customs they've followed for centuries. Religiously, like a cult... Retaining the Cumal Files in hardcopy is one of those customs. Traditions they hold sacred demand it."

Porter frowned. "You've said, cumal, a couple of times…Gunna explain?"

"Cumal is an ancient Celtic word for a female slave. The Cumal Files are effectively ledgers that list the names, dates of birth, receipts and bills of sale for girls sold by the organization. Their traditions also demand that hardcopy lists of all members, associates, financial records and assets are kept within the files."

Lionel wobbled his head, thoughts muddled by intrigue. "Kept and maintained by who? Who did you hand your records over to?"

"The Secretary. He was part of the organization's High Council, the bosses if you like. He was, is, keeper of the files. I took them to a house north of Sydney."

"Where exactly?" Porter said.

"Don't remember…" Ferguson rubbed his forehead. "Only that I gave them to the Secretary."

"Who was he?"

214

"No idea…Had his face hidden, didn't say a word, and put the files inside a massive wooden chest. It got rolled away and I never saw them again."

Porter scoffed. "You must reckon we're idiots? Incriminating documents like those you refer to, wouldn't be kept in a wooden box. They'd be stored in a secure location, like a bank vault..."

"No, these men don't trust bankers. Only each other."

"Fair enough, I don't trust bankers either…But reckon you're full of shit if you're saying you don't know who these blokes are…"

"Believe what yar want…Only a few bosses knew the identities of all members. They had hundreds of followers, soldiers as they called them. It was too risky to trust them all. I made good friends in the organization but never knew their real names or where they lived."

"Did you take any photos?"

"Weren't allowed."

Lionel squinted at him. "Who would know the files' current whereabouts?"

"Only the Secretary, who vows to protect them with his life. He would destroy the files and sacrifice himself if necessary, rather than allow police or others to obtain them."

"Why not burn 'em from the start?" Porter said.

"Yar not listening… These files form part of their history and traditions. Only as a last resort can they be destroyed."

"You reckon this organization will kill you. What makes you think they're still operating?"

"Aye yar right, I can't be certain. It's been fifty years…But they grew stronger, larger in numbers, and were always expanding their business networks and assets. If they're still active, I'll find out soon enough when yar leave…"

Lionel huffed, convinced Ferguson had more precise information to divulge. "Alec, it's imperative we find these files…They can lead us to those responsible for much suffering."

"Don't blame yar for doubting it, but trust me, have told yar all I know. And find the Cumal Files? Yar never will…"

"A trustworthy pedophile?" Porter sniggered. "Don't trust you one bit…But at the same time, I don't know why you'd fabricate such a story?"

Lionel nodded. "And why are you certain we'll never find these files?"

"Yar answered yar own question a minute ago…" Ferguson smirked. "Aye, the files will lead yar to those who profited from the sale of Koori girls, and papers within them contain the signatures of once powerful and important men. Signed contracts between the organization and the government, agreements for brokerage fees. Famous family names and legacies will be humiliated if those files make it into the public domain. Yar think they'll let that happen? No, the organization aren't the only ones protecting the Cumal Files. Others will stop yar, long before yar even close…"

Lionel glanced to Porter. Nick Galios, Shirley, and John Rhodes. Were they too close already?

"You were forced to resign from the AWB…Why?" Lionel said.

"Was young and naïve. I hoped if I went to the top and told what's happening, that they'd put an end to it."

"Who'd you tell?"

"I had a secret meeting with the Prime Minister in '67. Told him those Koori girls weren't only sold to white men in Australia but were being sent all around the world. Thousands, more than government archives and Welfare Board records would ever show, were taken from their families. The Prime Minister seemed shocked, to have no knowledge of it…Or maybe he did, who knows? Word got out that he planned to abolish the Protection Act and all the power it gave us."

Porter gave a bemused smirk. "He would've known it was going on. Sounds like he tried to save his own arse?"

Ferguson shrugged.

Lionel shifted in the chair. "Either way, the organization wasn't pleased to see it abolished. Right?"

"Aye, they weren't... Hundreds of brokers were doing deals with the Welfare Board and dragging girls from every corner of the nation. For some reason they suspected me as the snitch but couldn't prove it. Fortunately, the PM kept his word and never exposed me. In '69 the organization's High Council ordered all brokers to a meeting. We were made to resign from the AWB and vow never to speak of the trade. And banished from the organization…"

"I'd guessed you weren't the only broker acting for the organization and the AWB," Lionel said. "But all other missions have records filed in government archives that cover those years, and members of the 'organization' must've filed them…Why were you told not to file Crooked River's records, when brokers for all other missions filed theirs?"

Ferguson frowned. "Never thought about that…Like I said, orders not to file the records came from up high and weren't for me to question."

Lionel's shoulders slumped. He'd hoped Ferguson would give him another clue as to why Shirley had directed him to Crooked River. What had he missed?

Porter cleared his throat. "Bent politicians were raking it in because of the Protection Act. I reckon they weren't keen on the PM's plans to abolish it either?"

"Aye, and then he disappeared…" Ferguson clicked thumb and index finger together. He pointed them at Porter in the shape of a gun.

"Bullshit. It's common knowledge he drowned…"

Lionel sensed that Ferguson was about to reveal the darkest secret yet. "You're saying 'they' the 'organization', or other politicians, got rid of him? Because of what he knew, and because he threatened to end their profitable business…?"

Ferguson beamed like a four-year-old with candy. "He might've drowned, as 'they' say. A mystery that might never be solved. Or, is it another national, fucked-up secret? Another lie for men in power to protect?"

Porter laughed. "Come on, get fair dinkum. You're talking in riddles now…"

Lionel's mouth gaped. Could Ferguson be closer to the truth than he realized? He turned to Porter. "I've heard crazier theories…"

Ferguson yawned. "It's time for afternoon whiskey and the missus will be home soon. I'd appreciate yar being gone before then..."

Lionel checked his phone. "Yes, we need to leave anyhow if we want to make our flight. One last question?"

"Aye, what?"

"Did Crooked River police officers help you remove girls from their families? Forcibly, against their will?"

Ferguson hesitated. "Aye, they did."

"You must've spent a lot of time in their company?" Lionel pressed him. "You must remember those officers' names?"

Ferguson looked to the ceiling. "I don't, was long ago..." He stood. "Forgotten more than I remember."

Lionel took a business card from his briefcase. He handed it to him as he stood. "My contact details in Crooked River. If you remember more, please get in touch."

Ferguson led them to the front door and opened it. He flicked his head towards the police car parked in the driveway. "You coppers may as well draw the target on me chest, or shoot me yarselves..."

Porter dawdled outside with cell phone held to ear.

Lionel stopped on the porch. "Thanks for speaking to us, Alec. You've helped, and acted admirably..."

He grunted. "If only yar the one to judge me..." He closed the door.

Lionel stared at it and tried to make sense of the past half hour. He approached Porter, who'd finished his phone conversation. "Everything okay?"

"Yeah mate, just checked up on Jane and Amber. Both as stubborn as usual but all's good down on the farm."

"Wonderful…" Lionel ran a hand through curls. "Can you believe what we just heard in there?"

"Dunno why, but yeah, most of it. Although he lied through his teeth when you asked about the Crooked River cops who'd helped him…"

"I sensed that too…Who's he protecting? Still, we know much more than we did before. These Cumal Files are definitely the key."

"Be careful how much weight you give 'em…Can we rely on evidence that we're not sure actually exists? And finding the files sounds simple but will be far from it…And our suspects? A secret group of blokes, who again, we're not sure actually exists…"

"I see your point, there's much uncertainty…But remember the information from Interpol in Singapore?"

"Which part? About the abductions being an international problem, around the globe?"

"Yes, and this secret 'organization' are likely the ones responsible…We're on the right track." Lionel dropped his head. "Sadly, with three dead friends to show for it."

"Yeah there's a fair chance they're doing it, that they're this KA mob we're after. But as you say, they're dangerous blokes who've killed to protect their secrets, and will again. We'll get no support from the government, even if we did know who to trust. Or Crooked River cops…"

"We're alone in this?"

"Guaranteed…And will more die, searching for answers we don't know questions to? You heard

Ferguson. He reckons that even if the Cumal Files do still exist, we'll never get to 'em…"

"You want to give up? Never saw you as a quitter…"

"Nah mate, we've come too far and lost too much for that…But I reckon, right now, your inquiry's the best chance of stirring the pot and securing the resources we need to find the girls. And there's a faster way to get the inquiry…"

"Which is?"

"We do the historical checks. We interview Bill Thompson, Barrett, and the others. We identify the cops who raped those girls in the '60s, and prosecute. Get your inquiry on that basis. Resume Azelia then widen your scope later. If you ignore that tact in favor of trying to find these files, you risk running out of time and coming out with nothing…"

Lionel smiled in admiration of Porter's passion. "You recall the first time we met?"

He grinned. "Bloody oath. I came close to knocking you out…"

"I told you Carinya would lead us to Sydney's missing girls and asked you to trust me…"

"Knew you were full of shit but needed to believe in something."

"Maybe I was back then…But the answer's stared me in the face and I've been too blinded by anger to see it. Shirley told me that the past will explain the present…"

"And you've preached it to me every bloody day…History repeats, learn from it."

Lionel chuckled. "I've ignored my own advice…Remember what 'cumal' means?"

"Yeah…"

Lionel's eyes searched the sky. An epiphany made him shiver. "The girls Ferguson sold are much more than missing records from a government archive. Much more than numbers to be added to statistics of the stolen generations…" He looked at Porter. "They were a slave generation, same as these abducted girls being shipped around the world as rich men's toys are today's slave generation."

"Bloody hell…Not sure how, but you're making sense."

"I'm certain of it, Dan. If we can find these Cumal Files and identify traffickers of the past…We'll find the despicable bastards who are doing it now."

TWENTY-EIGHT

Inspector George Barrett sat on the Thompson homestead's rear veranda and gazed towards Crooked River. He'd just delivered a batch of his wife's famous scones and joined his long-time friend Kathleen Thompson for a cup of tea, as he did most Friday afternoons around 4pm. He chewed a scone and savored its butter and salt flavor.

"Still not sleeping well, are you George?" Kathleen said.

He gasped in mock consternation then gave his usual reply. "What's my dear wife Mary told you this time?"

"That your screams wake both of you in the night…We're all concerned, George, you never seem relaxed…Like now, sitting with that ugly frown on your face."

"I'm fine." He faked a smile. "Spoke with Jim earlier…He said he visited you today?"

"Yes, he did."

"What time?"

"Close to midday…He had lunch here and then said he had to leave for a job." She smirked. "Why, are there problems with my big baby boy?"

"Oh, no, Jim's okay…But a few hours ago he found John Rhodes dead at the bottom of Bunyip Hill. He's one of the Carinya chaps..."

She raised a hand to her open mouth. "My, that's terrible. What happened?"

"Jim says Rhodes fell off the cliff, was an accident…Lyn Foster disagrees, thinks it's suspicious, possibly murder, and wants it investigated as such. When I supported Jim, she went over my head and contacted Rhodes' boss at the Feds."

"Like I told the girls at bingo, that Lyn's a troublemaker…And?"

"It's sorted itself out." He grabbed another scone. "Federal Police Commissioner Watkins is an old friend. I explained Jim's decision and told him not to bother sending federal investigators. We don't need more cops and journalists running around…"

"My god, Bill would have a fit…He hasn't stopped cursing those Carinya boys since they arrived."

Barrett straightened in the chair. "Who's that?"

"Where?"

"Coming up from the river, near the irrigation lines." He pointed. "See him? Koori chap with no shirt, moving towards the hills."

"Goodness, your eyes are better than mine…Oh yes, I see him now."

Barrett stood and marched towards stairs that led from the veranda.

"Where you going?" she said.

"To ask what he's up to…" He faced her. "We've had a few residential break-ins lately and he's probably the culprit…"

Kathleen came alongside him. "I've seen that white hair and beard before…It's my friend."

"You know him?"

"Well, I don't 'know' him. I screamed the first time I saw him standing here on the veranda, all dirty and disheveled. He seemed sorry for scaring me, so I gave him cake and a bottle of whiskey. He thanked me and scampered into the hills. Comes back each fortnight for more. He's harmless, George, leave him be."

He watched the Koori trot through straw-colored paddocks towards a forest of eucalypts near the base of Bunyip Hill. "How old is he? How long's he been coming here?"

"Hard to say with the blacks…Seventy, maybe? He's been visiting a few months now…"

"A few months, and you've never said anything? And giving away Bill's whiskey, your game…"

She scoffed. "He won't miss a few bottles. Besides, the less he has, the less he flogs me…"

He avoided her eyes. He and most residents of Crooked River knew that Bill Thompson battered his wife. And like most tragedies in the small outback town it would never be discussed. "Do you know where that old Koori lives? I'll send detectives to search his house…"

She chuckled. "His house? Look at him…Bare-chested with bare feet. He goes into the hills and disappears. They're his home."

He squinted as the man got further away. "He might live on Bunyip Hill?"

"You know the blacks never go up there." She took him by the elbow and led him to the table. "Sit down and finish your cuppa."

"They're unpredictable those wild kooris…Don't let him near the house when you're alone, he could try to molest you."

She broke into laughter. "Oh George, don't be ridiculous. Who'd want a piece of this old girl…?"

225

He kept his gaze on Bunyip Hill, not trusting himself to look at her. "You're still an attractive woman…"

She bowed her head and filled his cup.

They sat and watched sunburnt paddocks. A shrieking cockatoo broke the painful silence.

Barrett glanced sideways at her. "Keep him away, Kath…Promise?"

She didn't reply.

He smiled at her stubbornness. "I haven't seen Bill since Wednesday. Where is he?"

"Sydney, another developers' meeting, is due back tonight…Always trying to make a new sale. I saw more of him when he was a Sergeant on shift work. You used to travel to Sydney with him quite a bit…Why have you stopped?"

"I still go with him now and again, mainly to buy toys for the grandkids…" He pointed towards land to his right. "Is Bill selling off more acreage over there?"

"No, not that, further along River road. Who'd be silly enough to buy it? It floods every year…"

"Bill didn't become Mayor to fulfill a sense of civic duty. I doubt that land is still part of the flood zone on council maps…"

"Hmm, true, never enough money that man."

"Mary's been his accountant for fifteen years. She's brilliant with numbers, but not the most confidential…" He sniggered. "I know more about Bill's financial matters than he does."

"Yes Mary's lovely, but a few reds do loosen her tongue."

"Even still, there are secrets of his we'll never kn--." He stopped himself too late and dropped chin to chest. His face burned.

"Secrets?" Her tone chilled him. "What 'secrets'?"

"Oh, Kath…" He tried to laugh away her inquisition. "What I mean is…Men like Bill, they never tell us everything."

"No George…What, secrets?"

"I was joking..." He sipped tea and avoided eye contact.

She stood and took the plate of scones from the table, then dropped it and leaned towards him. He averted his eyes from her glare but she moved to follow them.

"No, the joking's over. Tell me, what do you owe him? Why do you always protect him?"

He shrugged. "He's been my mentor, my Sergeant. He's been good to me, you both have."

"Good to you?" Her head rocked back as she laughed. "He treats you like a fool, always has…But why do you take it? You're ten times the policeman, and the man he'll ever be."

"He saved me."

She bent lower, scowled face inches from his. "Yes, he saved your life. Once. And you've served him well as a friend ever since. But it's time to stand up for yourself. You're the commander of Crooked River for Christ's sake…"

"You're always telling me that, Kath. You'll never understand. You should be grateful too, for the good life he's provided."

She yelped. "The good life he's given me? You're as delusional as he is…I wanted to leave him years ago…Then he got sick."

"And you didn't leave…"

"I couldn't, but he knew I'd planned to and has never forgiven me for it. I've stayed through drunken beatings, affairs, lonely nights…And you damn well know it…I owe him nothing." She straightened and placed a soft hand on his shoulder. "Please George, stop protecting him. Surely your debt's been paid?"

He looked up into pleading eyes. "All the joys of being, my children and grandchildren, I've had because he saved me that day. I'm forever in his debt. I'd do anything he asked of me."

"You're serious?"

His jaw clenched as he nodded. "Anything..."

TWENTY-NINE

Porter parked the Landcruiser in front of the Carinya residence at 5.30pm on Friday as the sun sank into the horizon and cast a peach colored hue over the house. He and Lionel strolled towards the veranda and exchanged banter about the upcoming rugby game they planned to watch on TV. His team, the Dragons, were up against Lionel's Rabbitohs.

Porter stopped. He blinked rapidly in fading light and tried to focus. Were his eyes playing tricks? Was Fred Klose standing on the veranda near a pool of blood? Holding a…?

Porter ran up the stairs. "Bloody hell, what happened?"

Lionel shouted from behind then stopped alongside him on the veranda.

Klose grinned. "Glad you guys returned from Broken Hill safe and sound, look what I came home to…" He held a severed cow's head aloft in one hand. Flies clung to its glazed eyes. Black blood trickled from its tongue and splattered on timber.

Porter read the message that'd been written in blood on the front door. "**City dogs – leave now, or die**…Good to see the locals have finally welcomed us…" He sniffed the air. Smoke? "What time did you find this?"

"I stayed here all morning doing paperwork then went out after lunch to look for Tommy," Klose said. He tossed the cow's head onto the gravel driveway. It rolled then stopped. "Lyn called me, around 2pm…?" His voice quivered. "She told me about Rhodesy, and that Tommy was at the mission. I was in town and dropped in here on the way out there. Lucky the fire hadn't taken hold and I got it under control. Pricks must've left minutes before I arrived…"

Lionel pushed the front door open. "Fire?" He ran inside.

Porter and Klose followed him down the hallway and into the kitchen. Porter inhaled smoke and coughed.

Lionel stopped with hands on head. He stared towards the fire-damaged office and staggered sideways into the kitchen table. He closed eyes and pulled his hair.

Porter stepped into the office. He moved towards the charred filing cabinet that had stored Carinya's paperwork, careful not to fall through damaged floorboards. Piles of ash fell from each drawer as he opened them. "They targeted your files, Lio."

"Can't believe this…Evidence collected over five years…Gone." Lionel kicked a chair out from under the table and dropped onto it. "You okay?" he asked Klose. "Didn't burn yourself?"

Klose's white t-shirt was covered in smoke stains. His sneakers were black with soot. He sat next to Lionel. "I'm all good, bud."

Porter pushed a burnt desk into the corner of the office and used a sofa to cover a hole in the timber floor. He joined them at the table.

"Don't worry, it'll be alright," Klose said to Lionel. "Bit of blood and fire won't scare us off…You've made copies of your reports, right?"

Lionel's chest deflated. "Never had time. They were the originals…" He cupped his forehead in two hands and stared at the floor. After a minute he raised his head, eyes wide as though a revelation had slapped his face. "It's fate, the wise men sending a sign that those reports were a waste of time. We must pursue the information regarding corrupt practices of the AWB and Crooked River police during the '60s. That's the path we'll follow, and trust to lead us to success."

Porter rubbed his chin. "I thought that after speaking to Ferguson we'd already agreed on that?"

"Yes, we did, but any doubts regarding putting all of our efforts into it have been…" Lionel smirked as he glanced at the blackened office, "extinguished…"

Porter groaned. "Don't give up your day job…"

Klose frowned. "I know you've already spoken to Lyn about Rhodesy, but did she tell you why she'd been at the mission?"

Lionel shook his head.

"Uncle Simpson's dead. Drowned…"

"What? No?" Lionel's forehead wrinkled, his face almost white. "Another one?"

Porter grinded teeth. Simpson hadn't drowned on his own, he never went in the water. But who had motive to kill him? The same blokes who'd burned Lionel's files and left the death threat in cow's blood? Tommy Davis? Or others, who didn't want him giving more information to John Rhodes?

"Tomorrow the three of us should head up Bunyip Hill and take a look around," Porter said.

Lionel nodded. "I was thinking the same…What did Uncle Simpson tell John? What was he looking for up there?"

"Dunno, but he was murdered to stop him from getting to it," Porter said. He turned to Klose. "You reckon you would've just missed the blokes who broke in…Were any cars going the other way as you came from town?"

"No, I'd say they went south when they left here, towards the mission."

"Why didn't they take the files and destroy 'em elsewhere? Or just throw 'em in our fireplace? These blokes are fair dinkum, no half measures…"

"Yep, the whole house could've burned down."

Lionel faced Klose. "This fire needs to be investigated. Have you notified Inspector Barrett?"

"Barrett's a moron…Said the Crime Scene staff aren't here and he can't call them back. Lyn said she'll come out tomorrow and make a report. She's not a happy camper right now…"

"Don't blame her…" Porter said. "She told us Jim Thompson's treating Rhodes' death as an accident." He flicked a hand towards the fire-damaged room. "Reckon he'll call this one too…"

"Lyn will keep fighting, she's tenacious," Lionel said. "She's demanding the Feds do a proper investigation into John's death."

"She's already tried and failed," Klose said. "Our boss promised her that he'd send a forensics crew over tonight. Not long after, Lyn got a call from Commissioner Watkins himself. Told her he supports Barrett's decision and considers the case closed…"

Porter's guts churned. A fellow cop had died in suspicious circumstances and not one boss gave a flying fuck. "Unbelievable…"

Lionel tut-tutted. "Fred, we got juicy information out of Alec Ferguson today... And what's very clear after several deaths, this fire, and the not so subtle warning, is that we're all in great danger...Dan wants to stay here with Carinya and is obviously not too concerned because he's allowing his girls to visit, but you should consi--"

"That is bold, letting the girls come out here," Klose said to Porter. "When?"

Porter sighed. "I haven't told Jane the full extent of what's going on but did say it's too risky...In typical fashion she dismissed it and accused me of making excuses." A vision of Jane entered his head. She prodded his chest. Her words echoed. "Stop me from coming to Crooked River, she said, and I'll kill you myself." He laughed. "They arrive next Friday arvo for the weekend...That woman terrifies me more than these thugs ever will..."

The others laughed with him.

When the laughter stopped, Lionel frowned at Klose. "Dan and I can handle the investigation from this point on. It's okay if you want to leave."

Klose scoffed. "You fucking serious? Local cops don't give a fuck about finding the pricks who killed Rhodesy, but I do, and I'm staying on. Christ, Lio, why'd you even ask?"

"Sorry...Never doubted it but had to give you a choice."

Porter chuckled as he stood. "Alright you blokes, that's enough man love for one day...Help us clean this office. Let's open windows and get the smell out, we've gotta sleep in this house tonight."

"Shit, forgot to tell you..." Klose said.

Lionel's mouth gaped. "What now?"

"Broken Hill detectives called on the landline just before you got back…"

"And?"

"You said Ferguson gave you good info. Well, it must've really got to him after you left..."

"How's that?"

"Wife came home and found half his head blown off…Did himself in."

Porter shook his head. "Nah, wasn't suicide…This 'organization' he spoke of have left us in no doubt…They're still active, powerful, and very fucking deadly."

THIRTY

Bill Thompson drove his Range Rover towards Crooked River township on a straight, flat road. A half-moon hung in the star-speckled sky and shone opaque light on the endless highway. His phone's ringtone sounded through the car's speakers. The Eagles played Hotel California. He slowed to 60km/h, glanced to the visual display on the dashboard then pressed a button on the steering wheel to answer the incoming call.

"Hello, Kathleen," he said. "I should be home by nine...Miss me, love?"

"You fucking pig of a man!" Kathleen's high-pitched squeal blared through the speakers and reverberated throughout the car. "I know all about you...Got tired of your pathetic secrets and went searching for them." She hiccupped. "I found your hidey hole, you sick, sick bastard!"

Bill winced and hesitated. "Kath, what the hell are you talking about? Pissed on Penfolds again, aren't you?"

"Fuck you," she screeched. "Fuck your family name and its history...What history? Where you manipulate others for your own good? I'll destroy you, the way you've crushed me."

He stopped on the side of the road. "Darling, calm down...We'll discuss what's bothering you when I get home."

Her frantic gasps crackled through the speakers. "I'm calling Paul Burdett, to tell him what's in your secret little room, and about your fraud of a life. You can read his story in The Tribune…And don't bother coming home. I hate you, Bill Thompson," she slurred, "hate you..."

"You don't mean that, love. Be home soon, we'll talk then."

He closed eyes when she hung up and took a deep breath. He opened them, searched his phone and selected the contact. The call connected.

"Where are you?" a male said.

Bill stopped shaking his head. "Forty-five minutes from home."

"Been trying to reach you. Got some bad news today..."

"What, son?"

"Lionel Roberts and his team have made progress. Elders at the mission talked, and Carinya is going after historical evidence. They might find enough for a Royal Commission…"

"You're pulling my leg?" Bill raised his voice. "Christ, son, Carinya being here's bad enough. But a Royal fucking Commission would send us all broke…And we could say goodbye to investment in the new resort..."

"That would be a disaster. This town needs the money and jobs…Carinya might interview all of us? Even you?"

Bill grunted. "They can't, son. I'm the fucking Mayor...Yes those boys are gamer than Ned Kelly, but they're getting too big for their boots. Porter's a treacherous dog, and Roberts is just a cocky black kid who doesn't know his place. I'll take care of

Carinya…Now listen, you once said you'd do anything to protect my reputation. Did you mean it?"

"I did."

"Good, son, 'cos I've got a job for you. Listen up…"

THIRTY-ONE

Most single women in Crooked River headed to the pub on Friday night to fight off brazen advances from horny jackaroos and drunken shearers. But Detective Lyn Foster sat at home watching 'Pretty Woman' for the hundredth time when Inspector George Barrett called. He told her to meet him at the Thompson homestead immediately and didn't say why.

As she drove there, she recalled seeing Kathleen Thompson in the bakery a fortnight earlier. Kathleen's over-sized sunglasses had failed to hide yellow bruising around her eyes. Had Bill punched her too hard this time, and killed her?

At 10.05pm Lyn parked under the Thompson's carport, next to Barrett's car. Why was the Crime Scene Unit's van parked nearby? And why was Jim Thompson's red ute there? A uniformed police officer guarding the front door told her to enter at the rear of the house. She walked to the back. She ducked under yellow crime scene tape then climbed timber stairs to the screened veranda.

She found Barrett sitting on a recliner in the adjoining rumpus room. Her two girlfriends from the Crime Scene Unit sat on a sofa and watched TV. She acknowledged them with a smile. Barrett stood and ushered her to the far side of the room. Hands trembled. His voice quivered. Kathleen Thompson was dead.

Barrett relayed what he'd been told.

Bill had arrived home from Sydney close to 9pm and had last spoken to Kathleen about an hour before that. She'd seemed tipsy on the phone but okay. He came in via the rear veranda as he always did and saw the screen security door had been cut and left ajar. He found Kathleen lying near the front door with severe head injuries, already gone. He'd called Barrett first, who'd rushed to the scene from home.

Barrett said he'd never seen Bill so distraught. Paramedics had treated him for shock and he was now settled by a fire in the family room with Jim Thompson. The police chaplain consoled them.

Lyn followed Barrett to the entry foyer. Kathleen's naked body lay in a shallow pool of blood. Her hair was tangled, as though it had been wet when she died. There was a towel on the floor next to her.

Barrett said the bloody footprints leading away from her were most likely Bill's. Her depressed skull suggested she'd been struck several times with a blunt object. No murder weapon had been found but the Dog Squad and others were still out searching the yard and surrounding paddocks.

He led her down a hallway. At the end of it he pointed to a locked door and said that Bill's darkroom lay beyond it. He hurried into the master bedroom and pointed to Kathleen's empty jewelry box on the floor. Bill had told him she'd kept family heirlooms and other expensive pieces inside it. Four bottles of whiskey and cash from bedside drawers had also been stolen.

"I've no doubt theft was the motive," Barrett said softly. "Tragically, Kath got in the way."

Lyn watched a tear well in the corner of his eye. He and Kathleen Thompson had been close friends for many years, and according to police station gossip, might've once been lovers. She wanted to hate him because he'd dismissed John Rhodes' death as an accident and blocked Federal police from investigating it. But as she watched him crumble, she didn't see an arrogant Inspector in a freshly pressed uniform and shiny shoes. She saw a shattered old man who'd lost a loved one and needed time to grieve.

"It's okay, boss." She rubbed the side of his shoulder. "Why don't you take off? I've got this…"

He rubbed a bloodshot eye, his face flushed beetroot. "Tell anyone you saw me like this and you'll be transferred to Timbuktu tomorrow."

She smirked. "Timbuktu sounds nice compared to this place. If I'd known it's that easy to escape, I would've spread nasty rumors months ago."

"I'll leave when I know how the search for the suspect's panned out..."

"There's a suspect?"

"A homeless Koori chap's been coming here. Kath gave him whiskey and food." He sighed. "Silly old girl. I warned her but too stubborn to listen…He's burgled a few homesteads. This is his first use of force."

"How did you learn about him?"

"I visited Kath this afternoon, saw him walking towards Bunyip Hill and asked her who he was. Hopefully the dogs will track him and he'll be locked up tonight."

"Sounds promising…" She pictured John Rhodes winking at her and shuddered. She spoke her mind. "You're using a lot of resources here. I noticed the

Crime Scene girls have been called back to town...A shame you didn't do the same for John Rhodes."

Barrett scowled. "I'll ignore your tone, Constable. Once. Because I like you, you're a good worker." His face relaxed. "I know your upset about Rhodes but Jim's my senior detective and I have to trust his instincts."

"Instincts? I tend to favor a more scientific approach to homicide...Resources were available that could've proved the cause of death. Why'd you allow Jim to write it off on a hunch?"

"The girls only got back an hour ago...And as I've already explained, I won't waste time and money on such an obvious accident." His voice grew louder. "This tragic incident, however, is a definite homicide. And yes, I'll utilize everything at my disposal to find Kathleen's killer."

She shook her head. "Thought you old-school cops prided yourselves on looking after your own? Why is John Rhodes different?"

Disgust filled his glare. "That matter is finalized, Constable. Understood?"

She bit her lower lip and avoided eye contact. "Sir. Understood..."

"Good...I'll leave you to get on with it and have Crime Scene start their examinations. Anything else?"

"When can I take a statement from Bill? And won't he, his shoes, and the clothes he was wearing need to be examined? I'd also like to check his phone's call activity..."

"Oh..." Barrett's forehead wrinkled. "Best I take care of all that later tonight or in the morning when he's feeling up to it." Before she could ask why, he said.

"Bill's hostile towards female officers. He's always said they shouldn't be in the job…"

She exaggerated raised eyebrows. She stepped past him into the hallway and stopped in front of the darkroom. "What's in here exactly, and where's the key? We'll need to look inside…"

"Bill said it's always locked." He dawdled down the hallway. "The intruder didn't open it."

"But Sir," she called after him, "every room must be searched."

He turned to face her. "Not that one…Now get to work Constable, and stop being such a pain in my arse."

She waited until he was out of view. She scoffed at his audacity to call Kathleen stubborn then tried the door handle. Definitely locked. Could she force her way in without anyone knowing? Doubtful, and what would an intruder want with a darkroom anyway? Nothing of value to steal…

She decided the risk of incurring Barrett's wrath far outweighed the slim chance of finding evidence behind the locked door. Or did it? Barrett seemed confident the homeless Koori man had murdered Kathleen and was their only suspect. She didn't agree. Bill Thompson had history as an alcoholic wife-beater and was her main suspect. She turned away from the darkroom and hoped the forensic investigation would prove her right. Did Bill have motive? And was her boss, George Barrett, protecting a murderer?

THIRTY-TWO

Porter chuckled to himself, because he couldn't remember when he'd last exercised on a Saturday morning. He ran in the shade of river gums and watched birds bathing in Crooked River as he followed the road alongside it. He sucked crisp air into lungs and savored the earthy fragrances that wafted to his nose. He'd been a keen runner once and was glad he'd rediscovered it. It relaxed him, and gave him time to clear muddled thoughts.

At breakfast earlier, Lionel had warned him about venturing out alone. He considered it too dangerous after Rhodes' death and the threats they'd received, and had urged him to postpone his fitness regime. But Porter felt healthier than he had in years and was prepared to take the risk.

He reached a bridge that connected the eastern stretch of Crooked River Road to the west and slowed to check his watch. 7.55am. He felt strong and had made good time, so decided to run the full loop back home. He adjusted the iPhone holder's strap against his bicep and pushed the earbuds in further to listen to U2's greatest hits.

The phone shuffled to the next song and he mumbled the opening bars of 'I Still Haven't Found What I'm Looking For.' He frowned as the faces of abducted girls floated before his eyes and haunted his conscience. Would they be found alive? He pictured a wooden treasure chest surrounded by sharks at the bottom of the sea. Would they ever find the Cumal Files? In his mind, Jane eyed him sideways. Suspicion soured her face. He'd already found what he wanted in a life partner. But, had she?

He ran off the bridge and down a slope, then turned right towards Bunyip Hill. He recalled last night's phone conversation with Jane. She'd accused him of getting cold feet about marriage. And she'd been spot on, because he was having doubts.

He decided that she needed to hear about his past, and what she was signing up for, prior to the wedding. And she deserved to hear it face to face, not over the phone. Despite safety concerns, he wouldn't cancel her visit to Crooked River. He would see her on Friday night and tell her everything then.

He rounded a bend where the canopy of river gums thinned overhead. Bunyip Hill appeared ahead to his left. He squinted towards it and for the first time noticed the granite boulders on top. John Rhodes had told him about the bunyip, the mythical creature that slept on the hill by day then descended as its evil spirit at night to punish those who'd angered it.

When he reached the base of the hill he brushed stinging sweat from eyes and gazed at the rock formations high above. Loud music blasted his ears. He didn't hear the car that sped up the road from behind. It was meters from him when he sensed the danger and glanced over his shoulder. He jumped to the left, towards a shallow ditch at the side of the road.

The car's front end slammed into his right ankle. He winced as he landed in the ditch then rolled and pressed up onto knees. The black SUV skidded to a stop fifty meters away. He hopped to his feet. A searing hot knife sliced his ankle. The steep sloping Bunyip Hill was behind him, the river in front. He scanned one-eighty degrees and searched for an escape route.

The ground near his feet erupted in a puff of red dust. Then another puff, behind him. He spun left towards the black SUV, certain the shots had been fired from it. But its windows and doors were closed. No-one had left it. He had to think fast but couldn't, not while the bloody music blared in his head. He ripped the earbuds away. Another bullet whizzed past then ricocheted off granite behind him.

He heard rocks crunch under footsteps from the direction of the abandoned quarry. He spun towards the noise and squinted eyes to focus. His mouth fell open. Two men in black combat uniforms and balaclavas sprinted towards him, pistols in hand.

He gritted teeth and swiveled to face the hill. His natural instincts had always favored fight over flight. But he was injured and unarmed, chased by men with guns. He leaped onto the dirt path that led up Bunyip Hill and limped up the steep slope. He would climb and hide amongst rocks then call for backup.

Despite the injured ankle he moved at a good pace. Another bullet whizzed past his head and he turned to watch the attackers. One stood at the base of the hill. He held a pistol in one hand and shielded eyes with the other.

The second man held a portable radio to his mouth. He lowered it then raised the pistol and fired. A bullet whizzed past Porter's head. The men ran towards him.

He limped upwards and used clumps of mulga bush for cover and anchor points to pull himself forward. Bullets thudded into red earth, closer and closer each time. His ankle was numb. His body ran on autopilot. His lungs should've ached and his legs should've tired from the climb but they didn't. He was a hunted animal fuelled by adrenaline and a powerful will to survive drove him on.

The path leveled when he reached the top. His attackers fired. He ducked behind a granite outcrop and glanced at the iPhone strapped to his arm. Should he phone for help? He peeked around the rock. The men had gained on him and were only thirty meters behind. No time for phone calls...

He looked to the sheer cliff face on his right. No escape route there...A giant boulder blocked the path behind him, so he limped to the left. He came to a rock ledge that ran across the cliff face and led to the other side of the hill. He looked down and saw the quarry below. A bullet slammed into rock beside his head. He scampered across the narrow ledge and stumbled when he reached the other side. He followed the dirt path, pulled himself over a boulder then dived into a thick clump of mulga bush.

Porter fought his way through the bush until he came out into a gorge with high rock walls on both sides. He peered down to his left. Slits in the rock face formed entrances to dark caves. He contemplated sliding down and hiding in one but doubted he could squeeze through the narrow slits.

Boots pounded on dirt behind him, just beyond the mulga bush. He hobbled towards an opening at the end of the gorge. If he could reach it there might be a place to hide? But could he make it fifty meters before the men entered the gorge behind him? Would he be stuck in the middle with nowhere to go?

His attackers swore. Loud. They were close. He peered along the gorge. Visions of being shot in the back froze him with terror. This wasn't how he wanted to die. Jane's face flashed before him. Her gorgeous smile willed him on and he vowed to survive.

He glanced back. Balaclava covered heads bobbed through the bush. The men would emerge from it within seconds. He sucked a quick breath, turned, and braced himself.

THIRTY-THREE

Inspector George Barrett arrived at Crooked River mission close to 8.15am on Saturday. He stepped from the Ford sedan and yawned. He stretched, used both hands to straighten his uniform then bent to brush red dust from black shoes. There'd been another 'suspicious death.' Of who?

He'd avoided the mission for years and had hoped to never return. But Lyn Foster was at the Carinya residence regarding a fire, Jim Thompson mourned his mother, and all other detectives were away hunting for the weekend. He had no choice but to investigate the death himself.

Smoke from cooking fires spiraled into the air as he trudged towards houses. The smell of burnt kangaroo meat assaulted his nostrils. A baby's distressed cries churned his stomach. He came to a group of elders huddled around a body on the riverbank. Younger ones watched from the safety of front porches.

Aunty Mel told him she'd found Tommy Davis at sunrise. He'd floated face down in the river. Everyone thought it strange because Tommy had been a strong swimmer. One elder said Tommy had been drinking till late. Another had heard splashes. Those gathered around his water-logged body shuddered.

"Have to be rollin' drunk or mad to swim at night," Aunty Mel said. "It's when that evil bunyip comes out, even idiots know it…"

The Crime Scene Unit girls arrived and performed a swift examination. Tommy had vomited before entering the water then choked and drowned. Even in death he reeked of gin.

Barrett took a notebook statement from Aunty Mel and told the elders to take care of the corpse by usual means. The investigation was over within fifteen minutes. Death by drowning while intoxicated. Simple.

He scurried up the path to leave when it came to him, a sense of being followed. He quickened pace and scanned his surroundings. No-one behind, to the sides or in front of him. Something, someone, urged him towards the river. He stepped onto dry mud near the edge and gazed into the brown water. He jumped back when the serpent spirit from his nightmares hissed. Its copper-toned body coiled as it reared up and bared fangs.

Barrett stared and trembled. "What do you want?"

"You know what I want," the serpent answered in a voice rich with the wisdom of time. "You must deliver..."

Barrett gulped. "What?"

"Redemption...For your crimes against this sacred land and its people. You continue to ignore me, at your peril."

"I'm trying...I'll do it soon."

The serpent's blood-red eyes glared. "You have a week. Take the lives of ten evil men as penance, or...I take your loved ones."

Barrett's grandchildren sang nursery rhymes. He squirmed. "I will, but I'm not to bl--."

"Oh, Inspector..." The serpent gave a mocking laugh. "Are you still in denial after all this time? As a young cadet you swore to protect the innocent. You've failed miserably..."

Barrett slowed his breathing, tried to still shaking hands. "I'll do it."

The serpent sprang up from the water and hissed inches from his face. "Yes you will, or I'll be eating your grandkids for dinner." It hissed again, then curled downwards into the river.

Barrett fell to knees, mouth open as he watched the serpent disappear. He staggered to stand and spun in all directions. No-one. Had a lack of sleep made his imagination run wild? Or had the serpent spirit, his conscience, haunted him again?

"You alright fella?" A female said.

He faced the path.

Aunty Mel watched him. She scratched her head, a bemused smirk on her face.

"Yes, I'm fine..." He fumbled keys as he hurried towards his car then turned to her when he reached it. "Didn't you see it too?"

"See what?"

"That giant snake in the river just now. It spoke to me..." He pleaded. "You must've seen it?"

Aunty Mel shook her head. "I saw nothin', 'cos there weren't nothin' there...Evil spirits talkin' to ya, Mr Barrett?" She laughed as she walked away. "And you white fellas reckon us kooris are always imagining stuff..."

THIRTY-FOUR

Porter's attackers would emerge from the mulga bush in a matter of seconds and shoot him dead. As he pushed off his left foot to run towards the end of the gorge, strong hands covered his mouth and pulled him to the ground. He slid on his back, downwards. The same hands cushioned his landing against a rock wall then hauled him into a pitch-black cave.

He gasped in the cold, stale air. He sensed there was someone close to him but resisted the urge to speak. Daylight beamed into the cave through a small hole in the rock. He put his eye against the hole and peered towards the gorge.

His attackers stepped from the mulga bush, panting and grunting. They stopped above the cave. With the upward angle, Porter could only see the lower half of their bodies. They wore black GP boots, black cargo pants, and black utility belts. Black gloved hands gripped pistols.

One of them swore. Was the voice familiar? Porter strained to hear their conversation. Their voices faded as boots disappeared from view. He slumped with his back against rock. Lungs burned. His ankle throbbed.

He opened eyes wider to adjust to the light. Was that a person sitting in the opposite corner of the cave? He unstrapped his iPhone and pressed the 'home' button. The backlight cast an eerie glow over the area. He saw nothing. No-one.

"Hello?" he whispered.

251

Only a quiet echo.

"Where are you?"

"Shhh…" came a reply from the dark. "Aint safe yet, them bad fellas still about…"

The man's voice sounded like that of a Koori elder. Porter was about to ask where he came from when he heard footsteps in the gorge above. He peered through the eyehole and saw black boots. He listened.

"Shit, we've lost him," one of the men said. He sounded young but cruel.

"Lost him how?" The second man said, his voice a high-pitched squeal. "There's one way up and down, with a fucking cliff on the other side. He's hiding, keep looking."

One of them squatted less than three meters away and looked towards the cave. Porter jerked his head away and pressed his back against the wall. He sucked in a breath, held it, then moved slowly back to the eyehole. Dull brown eyes stared at him through slits in a black balaclava.

"He might be down in these caves…?" The brown-eyed man pointed towards Porter. "Got a torch?"

The other man scoffed. "It's daylight…Why would I have a fuckin' torch?"

"I'm going down for a look," the brown-eyed man said. He unclipped the portable radio from his belt. As he handed it to his partner it beeped twice. He spoke into it. "Yeah?"

"What's taking you so long?" A gruff male voice crackled through the radio.

"G'day boss." The brown-eyed man stood. "We can't find him…"

"Fucking useless wankers," the boss said. "Listen, there's a detective car at the mission, just across the river…Get down off the hill. Now!"

"Shit!" The brown-eyed man clipped the radio onto his belt and ran towards the mulga bush.

His partner growled and followed. Out of sight…

Porter sat still for a minute. He checked his phone. The battery was low but the signal was almost strong enough to make a call. He sent a silent thank you to Lyn Foster, grateful he'd followed her advice and had switched to Optus mobile.

He whispered to the Koori man. No answer. He waved the phone's torch from left to right. Nothing, no-one. He waited ten minutes then left the cave.

He climbed up the rock face and pulled himself into the gorge. He saw the signal on his phone was stronger and called the '000' emergency number. He told the operator to broadcast an alert for a black SUV and cursed himself for forgetting its registration number. He then called Lionel and told him what happened. Lionel said he'd come immediately and bring Lyn and Klose with him.

Curiosity led Porter to the end of the gorge, to the opening he'd run for earlier. He stood in the middle of a natural amphitheater and shook his head at what he saw on the rock walls. Tens of colorful murals portrayed goannas, kangaroos, eagles, and emu. And other animals, mythical and not. In some pictures the animals were drawn whole. In others, as half man-half beast. He'd seen Aboriginal art before, cave drawings that depicted the Dreamtime, but nothing like this. He scanned the walls. One section caught his attention and drew him closer.

He scratched the rock face. Paint. He stepped back to see the complete story. It had larger, detailed figures in bright colors. The first picture showed the main character – a fat, white policeman with red horns jutting from the sides of his head. He wore a navy-blue tunic, and trousers. His black eyes were wide. He snarled as he wielded a baton overhead.

The next picture showed a row of white houses and six Koori children swimming in the river. Happy, smiling faces. In the next picture, the policeman lay on top of a girl. Blood, fear, violence…In the final one, five children sat by the river. So many tears.

He studied the picture of the red-horned policeman and remembered that elders on the mission said the 'White Devil' had raped their girls. Had John Rhodes discovered these same paintings? Had he taken photos or sent messages with his phone? Would that explain its missing sim card?

Porter took photos then wandered from the amphitheater. He stopped at a series of pictures he'd missed on the way in. The colors were thick and vibrant as though recently painted. He gasped as he realized...The pictures were very recent. They told the story of John Rhodes' murder.

He took more photos then limped back along the gorge. He stopped above the cave where he'd hidden and shouted towards it. "Hello? Tell me about your paintings…Who are you?"

"Don't matter," the man said from the cave. "Don't know meself no more."

Porter squatted and peered down. "Mate, who's that fat policeman you've painted? Who's the bloke hurting the girl?"

"We called 'im the White Devil. He's the fella ya want…"

Porter's pulse quickened. "Can you remember his name?"

"No, wiped it from memory long ago…Now piss off."

The man in the cave had knowledge of Rhode's murder and other terrible crimes. Porter had no intention of leaving. "Mate, help me to punish these bad men. Come to the town and let me write your story on paper. We'll get justice for those girls…"

"From a white fellas court? Hah, be dead before I said me first words..."

"I'll bring Koori blokes to speak with you. Up here, where you feel safe."

"Don't feel safe up 'ere no more…Not since last night when you fellas sent ya dogs and tried ta sniff me out."

"Please tell me what you've seen, and I promise to put these blokes away. They'll never hurt Koori girls again…"

"No!" The man's voice trailed away. "Told ya too much already..."

Porter prodded a finger at red dirt. The man had saved his life and if his only wish were to be left alone, he'd grant it. "Last question, then I'll leave and no-one else will come…The picture story where the white man is pushed off the cliff…Who are the men in black? And who's the Koori with the blue truck?"

Ported waited several minutes for an answer. When none came, he frowned and limped towards the mulga bush.

"Them fellas chased ya today aint the same who pushed that fella from the cliff yesterday..." The man's voice echoed. "Don't know 'is name, but a yella fella drives that same blue truck every day...Now whitey, piss off and leave me alone!"

Yella fella? Porter knew a half-caste who drove a truck in Crooked River. The pub had a blue delivery truck, and Ronny Goodwin drove it...

THIRTY-FIVE

Wednesday morning, four days after escaping assassins, Porter sat at the kitchen table and rested his bruised ankle on a chair. He sipped coffee while he waited for the others to join him for the daily briefing and reflected on the past few days.

Crooked River cops hadn't responded to his call for assistance from the top of Bunyip Hill. The black SUV and his attackers had vanished from the area. When the others arrived to help him down the hill, he showed them the rock paintings. All had agreed they depicted heinous crimes, including John Rhodes' murder. When they'd questioned Porter's knowledge of the artist, he kept his promise to the Koori man who'd saved his life and made no mention of him. He told them he'd come to his own conclusions about the painting and Ronny Goodwin being the driver of the blue truck.

On Monday, possessing photos of the paintings from Bunyip Hill, Lionel and Klose had questioned most residents of Crooked River about the 'White Devil.' A few of the older residents had flinched on hearing the name but denied all knowledge of it. According to locals, a fat policeman with that nickname had never worked in Crooked River.

On Tuesday morning Porter had submitted a request to the New South Wales Police Force's administrative offices in Sydney. He asked for personnel records of all police officers who'd worked the Crooked River district during the 1960s. Getting their names and rank would be easy but he would need to put faces to them. Klose had suggested they search the employee archives for photos. Such a search might take months Porter had told him. Once the list came back from admin, they would question all ex-officers about their service in Crooked River, including Bill Thompson and George Barrett. But he doubted they'd answer questions, let alone provide old service photos, so they'd have to do without them.

Lionel and Klose had visited the pub on Tuesday afternoon and questioned Ronny Goodwin's whereabouts on the day of John Rhodes' death. Ronny denied being out near Bunyip Hill and told them to check the pub's delivery book if they didn't believe him. Klose had asked Gary Rowe to see the book, to check the deliveries Ronny had logged. Rowe had returned empty handed with a confused frown on his face. He couldn't find it. According to Patto, the barman, it'd been missing for days.

Klose thumped the kitchen table.

Porter shot upright in the chair, jolted from the daydream. His ankle thudded into a table leg and he grimaced. "Cheers Fred…"

Lionel sat and flicked through a diary. "Sleep well?" he asked in a cheerful tone.

They mumbled replies.

Lionel beamed. "Well, let me tell you…I had another wonderful dream."

Porter grinned at him. "Here we go…What'd your wise old men tell you this time?"

Klose's head rocked back as he chortled.

Porter sniggered. They'd been subjected to a daily summary of Lionel's dreams and their suffering had become a not-so-private joke between them.

"Fine, mock my spiritual guidance..." Lionel smiled. "And the fabulous news I received this morning..."

"Please, tell us Lio," Porter said. "We're dying to hear it."

Klose laughed.

Lionel waited for him to stop. "You know I've had concerns about remaining in Crooked River, after the death threats and so on...But I'm pleased to say, the wise men have allayed those fears and will protect us. We're still on the right path..."

Porter winked at Klose. "Thank the sacred 'roo turds for that."

Lionel's face wrinkled into a frown. "Secondly, the Attorney General's approved our request for more investigators. Begrudgingly no doubt...We'll have four new members starting in a fortnight. Also, support for our investigation continues, with most political parties behind it. Guys, Carinya's far from dead."

Porter gave an exaggerated cheer. His phone vibrated on the table. He glanced at the screen and answered. "Steve, good to hear from you. How goes it in the city?"

Superintendent Steve Williams grunted. "Still a shitfight...Heard you've had dramas too?"

"Nothing we can't handle." Porter hadn't told him about the recent attempt on his life but suspected he already knew. "What's up?"

"I'm calling about the missing girls' case...Have spoken to an Inspector Keyes with the South African DEA. They raided a farm near Cape Town early this morning, our time. Drug shipment they'd hoped to find was gone, and the farm deserted. But they discovered unusual cargo in a safe room under the house..."

"Yeah?"

"Twenty-three teenaged girls...Most were African and Asian but one's a thirteen-year-old Aboriginal girl from Sydney. Bianca Taylor. Port, she's one of our missing girls..."

"Yeah, Bianca..." Porter saw her pretty face. She was a surfer girl from Maroubra. "I remember her...That's bloody great news. They all okay?"

"No, nine didn't make it. Wasn't much air in the room..."

Porter grimaced. "Mongrels... And Bianca?"

"She's dehydrated, but no major problems. They're keeping her in hospital for a day for tests, then she's coming home."

"Beauty..." Porter winked at Lionel and Klose. "You said the traffickers had cleared out...Tipped off?"

"Yes, and Keyes is ropable."

"He suspects one of his own?"

"No, he trusts his staff and keeps intell tight. Mostly...He informed local Interpol guys of his operation. Wishes he hadn't, certain it's where the tip-off came from."

"Bloody hell, Interpol strikes again...That mob's got more leaks than my old man's tinny... Do the DEA reckon the drug smugglers and slave traffickers are working together?"

"No, they think they're separate, linked by use of the same shipping company. Evidence at the farm suggests shipping containers were emptied from trucks. Discarded ramps etcetera... Containers were gone when

260

they got there, so he's no wiser what shipping company they used."

"If they're separate groups, why use the same farm?"

"It's owned by one of South Africa's most notorious crooks. Keyes said he has over forty properties and makes them available to business associates for a fee. He throws armed security guys into the deal…Keyes thinks it coincidental that the drug smugglers and traffickers used it on the same days…"

"He's interviewed the owner?"

"Not yet. But he's got plenty on him and is confident he'll sing."

"Good…Did Bianca talk?"

"I had a productive chat with her…But she's refused to talk with South African cops, black or white."

"Don't blame the poor darlin'…"

"She wants Lionel to call her when he can. I'll send him the number…"

"Cheers…What did she tell you?"

"Have a full-page scribbled in front of me… She's a smart, brave girl to remember what she has. The men were --."

"Sorry, mate…" Porter glanced to Lionel and Klose. "Can I put you on speaker? Got Lionel and Fred from Carinya here in the room, and since Bianca wants to speak to Lionel, it's best he hears this."

"Yes, bring them up to speed and tell me when…"

Porter gave them a summary of what Williams had told him then switched the phone to speaker mode. "Cheers, Steve. Go on…"

Williams cleared his throat. "Bianca can't remember much of her actual abduction but did say it was a white van…She was loaded into a shipping container with thirty other girls and treated relatively well…After a few days they let her walk on the deck of a cargo ship…" He paused. "I questioned her about markings or flags but she couldn't remember any…Said she changed ship three times and lost track of how many days she was at sea. They covered her head whenever they got close to port. But, she says that one of the ports was definitely Singapore."

"How's that?" Porter said.

"There were Chinese girls with her. They overheard dock workers, who spoke of being in Singapore, with Singaporean accents…"

"That makes sense…Need to find Singaporean cops we can trust."

"Onto it…I spoke to the Interpol boss there. He seems switched on, and already has teams searching every shipping terminal on the island."

"Reminds me, any luck with the stolen van in North Sydney, where the girl got away? What's the company again?"

"Kennard Atkins Mining…" Williams said. "No, nothing came of it. My boys and customs searched their containers at the international terminal and checked all manifests. They're above board. Their top CEO's, based in the UK and Europe, checked out okay too…"

"Who ran the checks?"

"Aah…Interpol in London, I think. Will ask Claire…"

"Interpol?" Porter scoffed. "I'd trust a tripping junkie more than those blokes…"

Lionel chewed a nail.

Klose huffed.

"I know where you're coming from, because Claire told me what they've been up to," Williams said. "And I don't completely trust this guy in Singapore either, but he's the only contact we've got…"

"You're convinced that no-one at Kennard Atkins is connected to the abductions in Australia?" Porter said. "Or any form of trafficking?"

"Absolutely…In fact, there's no evidence linking them to criminal activity of any sort."

Porter scratched his chin. "Bianca got taken in a white van…Same as Nadia, same as the girl in North Sydney…"

"I see what you mean…But, the fact that Kennard Atkin's business logo is 'KA' and they own a fleet of white vans, and we're searching for psychos branding girls with the same abbreviation, is in my opinion, pure coincidence…"

Porter frowned. There was a lot of 'coincidence' going on. "I just reckon they shouldn't be discarded as suspects, not yet…"

"Don't worry, they won't be…Now, Bianca's description of the abduct--."

"Mate, was she branded?"

Williams sighed. "Afraid so... Shit, I forget to mention earlier…After her abduction, she woke up in a cell complex with no idea where she was. Let me check my notes…" He paused for a few seconds. "Okay, she spoke of a ritual in a cave-like place where hundreds of these sick bastards watched on. They stripped her naked, tied her up and burned the mark into her back. Same as Nadia…Every girl they found at the farm has it…Bianca must've been drugged when taken to the shipping container because she can't remember getting to it from the cell complex…"

Porter pictured Nadia's purple corpse and the welt marks on her wrists. He shuddered and swallowed bitter bile. "Would love to brand these mongrels the same way, watch 'em squeal and squirm..."

"You and me both, Port…"

Lionel rocked back and forward in the chair, trance-like.

Klose knuckled his jaw.

"Sorry Steve, I interrupted you again…" Porter said. "Bianca described her abductors as…?"

"Her description of them is consistent with what the girl in North Sydney told us. They dress and act like soldiers, and seem to follow a rank structure…"

"That's a worry…Means they're well-disciplined and less likely to make mistakes."

Klose leaned towards the phone. "Sir, it's Fred Klose…How's a thirteen-year-old girl make the assumption these guys have a rank structure?"

"Fair question," Williams answered. "Bianca befriended one them. Said he wore the same black uniform and balaclava every day."

"Sounds like my mates from Bunyip Hill…" Porter whispered to Lionel and Klose. They nodded.

"She asked him about the gold shield pinned to his chest. It had the letters 'KA' on it, followed by three digits..." Williams paused, as though allowing the revelation to sink in. "He told her it's his service number. 'KA', followed by that number, is how they addressed each other. Never by name."

Porter glanced to Lionel. "Ferguson said that about the blokes he'd worked for. No names, total anonymity…"

Lionel nodded. "We suspected 'KA' and this 'organization' to be the same. Bianca's information all but confirms it…"

"They have to be, too many similarities…"

"Silly, how obvious it is now…KA never stopped trading in sex slaves. They've continued on since the '60s and would've made a fortune doing it."

"No doubt they're the ones to focus on," Williams said. "And you're right, they're dealing in slavery. They told Bianca she'd be at the farm until her new owner collected her."

"That's brutal…" Klose said. "Did she ask him what the KA's an abbreviation of?"

"Didn't say…It could be what she wants to discuss with Lionel…Anyhow gents, we're back in the saddle. Let's pray the shipping terminal searches in Singapore and Cape Town prove fruitful, and the farm's owner co-operates with the DEA…"

"I'll be in touch once I've spoken to Bianca," Lionel said.

"Very good…" Williams ended the call.

The three of them discussed the phone conversation for five minutes. Porter checked the world clock app on his phone. "It's close to midnight in Cape Town…Too late to call Bianca?"

Lionel pressed his phone's screen and studied it for a few seconds. "Steve's already sent the number through…She wants me to call, so I will." He pressed the screen several times. The phone went into speaker mode and a ringing tone sounded from it.

"Lionel Roberts, calling from Australia. Your patient, Bianca, is expecting my call," he told nurse Beckett when she answered.

No immediate reply.

Then nurse Beckett said, "Hold please, Mr Roberts."

Lionel waited. Classical music blared from the phone.

"Doctor Hamilton speaking..." His accent was thick Afrikaans.

"Yes, Doctor, it's Lionel Roberts...The nurse was putting me through to Bianca Taylor. Inspector Keyes has cleared me to speak with her..."

"Sorry, that won't be possible...Bianca has passed away."

Porter listened as Doctor Hamilton explained the circumstances of Bianca's death. She'd died in her sleep from a blood clot on the brain. When he questioned the doctor regarding possible foul play, he responded in the negative. Toxicology tests showed no evidence of poisoning. And no-one could've got into the room and suffocated her because it'd been guarded the whole time.

Lionel ended the call, face blank and eyes dull.

"Don't fucking believe it..." Porter scratched the top of his head. "Who's leaking this info? He spun to face Lionel. "They knew what Bianca planned to tell you..."

"Are you saying KA have guys on the inside?"

"No doubt. Most likely plenty of 'em...But who, and where?"

"Like you mentioned before, Interpol's the common denominator," Klose said. "Lio's informant in Scotland, our request for assistance with her interview…Keyes at South African DEA suspects their operation was compromised by Interpol guys…"

Lionel clicked fingers at Porter. "You said Claire's been running her intell searches through them too. It could've been how she found Alec Ferguson. And we know what happened to him…"

Porter groaned. "Suspected they were crooked from the minute Claire said they'd ignored the multiple incidents of 'KA' brandings. I should've acted then…Because of those bastards, worldwide abductions were never linked and investigators haven't given 'em due priority."

"I've overlooked the obvious too," Lionel said. "So, where do we go from here?"

Klose turned to Porter. "Cease all contact with Interpol for a start. And recommend that Williams and Claire do the same."

"Will do…It's a given that KA's bribing Interpol, but who're the blokes making the payments? Who are KA's bosses, these so-called powerful blokes Alec Ferguson spoke of?"

"If only we knew…" Lionel said. "And don't forget what else Ferguson said, that KA aren't the only ones prepared to kill while protecting the Cumal Files."

"No doubt…The bastards who've profited, and those who still do, would all be keen to protect 'em. Corrupt politicians included…"

"What are Cumal Files?" Klose said.

Lionel smirked. "I'll tell you later. It's complicated…"

Porter leaned forward. "At this stage we reckon KA's murdered Bianca, Lio's informant in Scotland, and Alec Ferguson…Maybe John Rhodes too…"

"And Uncle Simpson. And Tommy Davis," Lionel said. "Nick Galios?"

"Yeah, if they reckon those two elders were giving us info, there's motive…But why would they do Nick Galios? He got bumped before we knew about KA, or the files, or the slave trade…"

"You said the guys who chased you the other day matched the description Bianca gave," Klose said. "Were they KA too?"

Porter wobbled his head. "Could've been…" He recalled what the Koori man on Bunyip Hill had told him. "But either way, I reckon they're a different mob than the blokes who murdered Galios. With separate motives…"

"Such as?" Lionel said.

"Blokes who see Carinya as a different type of threat."

"Like who?" Klose asked.

Porter leaned back. "Bloody hell, we've had a heap of enemies from the start, and the list grows. I mean, Lio blackmailed the bloody Attorney General for fucks sake…There's just one vindictive member of the elite with reason to kill us…" He glanced at Lionel. "Rothwell might be backing Carinya in the media, but behind the scenes his blood would be boiling…And then there's the retired judge you disgraced…"

"Charles McKinlay…" Lionel said. "Yes, you're right, we've made powerful enemies."

Klose whistled low-pitched, with eyes wide as he nodded.

"Thousands hated Galios," Porter said. "Radicals opposed to his pro-immigration policies were top of the list…When he backed Carinya and questioned the government's priorities this close to an election, he had to go."

"I agree," Lionel said. "His assassination was political."

"And KA's only possible motive for killing Galios, was his link to you..."

"Ah, do you forget, that Ferguson said he'd heard rumors of KA being linked to a political party?"

"Yeah, rumors... But we can only afford to deal with facts, mate. I don't reckon KA killed Galios..."

"Well, I still think that their men attacked you...They know what Ferguson told us, and can't risk us getting to their files...And if not KA, then who?"

"Blokes wanting to protect their interests here in Crooked River..."

Lionel frowned. "Locals?"

"Yeah mate...Think of that message on our door yesterday. City dogs, leave or die...Jim Thompson and his lackeys don't want us sniffing around. The way he wrote off Rhode's murder proves his contempt...And Bill Thompson sure as hell doesn't want us here."

"Yes, Bill's made veiled threats but he's what, close to 80? Isn't he just a cranky, money hungry Mayor protecting his town? Would he really want us, dead?"

Klose rubbed his jaw. "Greed's the ultimate motivation, bud. I heard the Thompson's stand to lose millions if we stay out here."

Lionel pursed lips. "Well, we'll know after the interviews next week if Bill's got a past to hide...There's a strong possibility he aided Ferguson in the '60s."

"Those Thompson blokes and their detective mates are loose cannons," Porter said. "I reckon they're involved in Rhode's death, and that their puppet Ronny Goodwin knows plenty about it…We're a threat 'cos we'll keep asking questions. A threat they won't hesitate to kill off…" He threw his hands up. "Fuck, to be honest, I've no clue who tried to kill me…All I know is, they're bloody dangerous."

A mask of dismay covered Lionel's face. "Indeed…Their influence is certainly strong and far-reaching." The mask vanished to reveal a wry smile. "And if it's as we suspect, and they're protecting secrets contained in the Cumal Files…Those files must be a truly fascinating read…"

THIRTY-SIX

KA1, the organization's Supreme Leader, stood at the head of a table in a dimly lit meeting room below the abandoned army barracks. He let his blood-red gown drop to the floor and raised a pewter cup. "Gentlemen, what a rare occasion to have all nine High Council members present..." His resonant voice belied the fail body it came from. Eyes sparkled through holes in the ivory mask covering half his face. "And at such short notice…"

KA4, Lord Adjudicator, scoffed. "Short notice indeed. Three hours, on a Thursday night, and having to travel from Sydney to Newcastle in peak hour traffic…"

"Come now, my dear friend, I consider attendance in such circumstance to be proof of your commitment."

"I can assure you, my Lord," KA2, the Chief of Staff said, "our commitment to the cause is stronger than ever."

"Excellent, then I declare this special meeting open…May the gods protect our kingdom."

"For the Kingdom of Alba is great!" the men seated around the table chanted. Their collective voice bounced off damp stone walls. Each wore a mask to cover eyes.

KA1 sat and shuffled papers. A hush fell over the room. "As you are well aware, we are only two days away from a very important anniversary. This coming Saturday marks an important milestone for our organization...Fifty-five years in Australia. The ceremonial celebrations will be our grandest yet, and the party to follow our most debauched..."

The others cheered.

"I'll drink to that," KA8 declared then gulped from his cup. "And, as Chief Abductor, I promise to find us the loveliest of virgins...A sacrifice worthy of the occasion."

They cheered and drank then called out to naked slave girls. The girls filled their cups with wine and retreated to dark shadows.

KA1 turned to his left. "Tell us, KA7, are preparations on track?"

KA7, the Master of Ceremonies, fiddled with a blue hat on the table in front of him. "They surely are, my Lord," he said with exaggerated grandeur. "We have three hundred members arriving by bus on late Saturday afternoon. All will be wearing full ceremonial dress. The location is already secure and locked down. Thanks to KA6 and his wonderful accounting skills, our funds are plentiful. We will provide our soldiers with a fine feast, much to drink, and generous bonus payments."

"Ah, yes, plentiful indeed..." KA1 turned towards the Secretary, KA6. "I read your latest financial report and see that slave profits have doubled this year. How wonderful that our oil-rich friends in the Middle East now share our appetite for fresh dark meat..."

KA6 inclined his head.

KA2 sniggered. "And as reports from KA5 suggest, they've enjoyed the samples we've sent from New Guinea as well."

KA1 looked to the ceiling and put hands out with upturned palms. "Praise the gods, for providing these girls and the riches they bring. Our coffers overflow through their sacrifice..."

KA3, Lord of War, leaned forward. "A good thing they do overflow..." His voice growled, stern and guttural. "We'll need every cent to continue paying off High Commissioner Davidson at Interpol and the like...The Cape Town debacle would've been much worse without his involvement..."

KA9, Master of Espionage, nodded. "If not for Davidson our men would've been caught. His warning gave them time to clean up and escape."

"That our men went undetected with nothing for South African cops to trace back to us, is vital," KA3 said. "We lost twenty-three girls...So what? Having Davidson on our payroll is money well spent..."

"Agreed. His men in Cape Town have eliminated the farm's owner, a decent crook in his own right, before DEA agents could interview him...And they've taken care of that young Koori bitch in the hospital, the one who tried to talk to Lionel Roberts..."

"It has always been one of our beliefs that the more money we have, the safer our interests become," KA1 said. "However, let this incident in Cape Town be a reminder to remain vigilant and professional. They have been given a sniff, and law enforcement will swarm all over it..."

"Aah, they should, but will they?" KA4 said. "And speaking of the vermin in blue, I have an update regarding their investigation into Kennard Atkins and our 'stolen' van...Superintendent Williams and his crew have come up empty-handed. Again...And, as

South African authorities have failed to find any links back to us, I see no reason to stop shipping goods under the Kennard Atkins name…"

"Excellent…" KA1 smiled. "Williams and his dogsbody Porter, once again exposed as the incompetent buffoons they are…I have rather enjoyed the ridicule that Sydney's abductions have brought to them."

KA2 turned to KA1. "Just as our South African problem disappears, an old one rears its ugly head and threatens more than ever…Is it true that Carinya's getting more investigators?"

"Yes, our sources at the AG's department have confirmed it... They started out as annoying bugs to be squashed under heel. They have become fat cockroaches, who no matter how many times we stomp them, refuse to die."

"They're a pain in our arses," KA3 said in a growl, "and although we hate to admit it, a real threat to the Cumal Files…A threat that I've failed to nullify. But, let me swear before this High Council, Carinya will be squashed soon enough…"

KA1 chuckled. "KA3, my dear friend, do not be concerned with the security of the files. Yes that fool Ferguson said too much, but they are in a safe place, under the excellent care of our magnificent Secretary. Police will never get to them. And do not be too hard on your men. Others have also failed to eliminate Carinya…"

KA3 huffed. "How so?"

"KA9, tell him…"

"Carinya knows they're under threat but seem ignorant of just how many want them dead," KA9 said.

"I met with the leader of WOO yesterday, and he says th--."

"WOO? What are they?" KA3 said.

"White Only Oz. A group of white supremacists more radical than we'll ever be. Think Neo-Nazis with hair…Anyhow, one of them was charged with Galios' murder late this afternoon. They did us a favor there and seem eager to do another..."

"Meaning?"

"WOO's been in Crooked River trying to get at Carinya. They see Roberts as a mouthpiece for the Greens' pro-immigration policies and fear they'll gain support from minor parties as a result. While Carinya remains under the media spotlight, so does Galios' multi-cultural message. He's become a martyr…"

KA3 scoffed. "Others want them gone but I want it more." He turned to KA1. "This is the last time we discuss Carinya at such a meeting, I assure you."

KA9 faced KA3. "Do Roberts and the others show caution?"

KA3 nodded. "They barely leave the house, and in numbers when they do. And the female detective…Foster? She's often with them and I believe she can't be harmed?"

"Correct. Foster lives," KA1 said.

"Well, that limits your options of attack…" KA9 said to KA3. "I can see why you're struggling..."

"Never mind…" KA3's forehead crinkled above the mask and deep lines spread over the visible corners of his face. "I know how to flush those cockroaches out of their hole. Come the ceremony on Saturday we'll have another reason to celebrate…Dead Carinya scum."

THIRTY-SEVEN

Porter opened the Carinya residence's front door.

Lyn Foster stood on the veranda in front of him. "Pizza?" She presented a plastic bag containing three pizza boxes.

He smiled as the aroma of smoked pepperoni tickled his nose, and took the bag from her. "Good job. How'd you know?"

"Fred told me during the week, that Saturday's pizza day..."

He turned and strolled down the hallway.

She followed him. "You're walking better. Ankle's coming good?"

He placed the pizzas on the kitchen table then turned to her. "Yeah, a bit of rest did the trick. Be running again tomorrow..."

Klose rushed in from the office. "Smells good..." He smirked at Lyn. "Late lunch or early dinner?"

"Well, dinner...But if you're hungry, go for it."

"You know me, always hungry..." Klose scrambled to sit at the table and ripped open a box. Lionel joined him a few seconds later.

Lyn sat. "Hey, you two, leave some for us."

Porter flicked the jug on then plucked the coffee jar from a shelf. "And leave some for Amber, she loves pizza..." He thought about the night before while he waited for water to boil.

Jane and Amber had arrived in Crooked River late Friday afternoon. He'd introduced them to the Carinya team during dinner at the pub. Jane and Emma Rowe had chatted like long lost friends over a few bottles of red wine. Emma told Amber about her horses and invited them to join her for a ride. Porter had pulled Jane aside and suggested it unwise for them to go. But Jane had ignored his warning and accepted the invitation.

Later, as Amber slept on a trundle bed in the corner, he and Jane had sipped Irish coffee by the fireplace. She'd asked how he'd been feeling. He told her the truth…Better. She'd asked how he'd been sleeping. He'd lied, not wanting to burden her with his nightmares, and said he'd been sleeping well.

She'd asked about the wedding and if he still wanted to go ahead with it. Her chocolate-brown eyes had warmed his heart, the coffee's whiskey his mind, and her seductive perfume his loins. He'd kissed her without answering. Her eyes had sparkled in firelight as she asked if that was a yes. He'd kissed her again, afraid to answer, and led her to the bed.

The jug boiled and Porter recoiled from hot steam in his face. He made coffee for everyone then grabbed a folder from the office and joined them at the table.

Lyn turned to him, her face crumpled in a frown. "Why didn't you go riding with the girls?"

"Wanted to, but Jane reckons my ankle's not up to it. Danced a jig in the bathroom trying to prove her wrong. She still said 'nah, you're not coming.'"

Lionel swallowed pizza. "I fell asleep with a book after lunch and didn't know they'd gone. You're not worried, Dan? After what's happened?"

"Bloody oath I am, and tried talking her out of it all morning. She told me I was being silly, to stop letting crooks rule our lives and ruin our fun…She said they've got Emma, Gary, Patto, and two shotguns for company. Reckons no-one will mess with 'em."

"Hope she's right…" Lyn said. "You obviously haven't told her about your adventure on Bunyip Hill? I'm surprised you let them go…"

"You wouldn't be, if you knew Jane like I do." Porter grinned, opened the folder and took a few pages from it. "They'll be right, no worries…" He cringed because he'd done it again. He'd tried to reassure others, despite his own doubts.

Lyn pointed at the pages. "What you got there?"

"Came via fax this morning, from the personnel section in Sydney. Lists of cops who worked Crooked River during the '60's…" Porter handed a page to Lionel. "Exactly what we needed."

Lionel studied it. "Names and addresses…Have you been through the whole list already?"

"Yeah…Nineteen still alive and kicking. Five live in Crooked River, the others are scattered throughout the state. Will send requests to the relevant commands to interview them. We don't have time to travel about."

"Indeed…And next week we'll start interviewing those still residing here."

Porter checked his watch. *4.06pm. They're late...*

"What time did the girls leave?" Lyn asked him in physic mode.

"Emma picked 'em up…Ah, around two o'clock."

278

"When are they due back?"

Worry sparked in Porter's gut and ignited flames of panic. He was about to answer when Lyn's phone ringtone blared. Adele sang, 'There's a fire starting in my heart.'

She took the phone from the table and stood. "Sorry, I'll take this over here..." She wandered into the office.

A minute later Lyn ran into the kitchen. "Dan!" Her shrill tone shocked Porter. She opened her mouth to speak but nothing came out.

The flickering flames inside him became an inferno. "What?"

"I just spoke to Grimes, a new detective who started this week...He's at an accident scene on Crooked River Road, five k's from here. Jane and Amber, the horses..."

Porter stood and shook her by the shoulders. "Spit it out. What's happened?"

"Jane and Gary are in ICU. Patto was knocked out but is okay. Emma hit her head in the fall..."

"Jane's in intensive?" Porter struggled to speak. "Fall? How?"

"Two cars drove into the horses. Those not killed got spooked, bolted for the river and threw their riders..."

"How bad is Jane?"

"Grimes only said that she's got head injuries..."

Porter staggered sideways. Lionel and Klose held him up. "Bloody hell..." Eyes ached as he yelled at the ceiling. "I shouldn't have let my girls come here." He stared at Lyn. "And Amber?"

"She wasn't at the accident scene. Current whereabouts unknown..."

"Fuck me, it's those sick KA bastards. Gotta get a search team together…"

"Get to the hospital, bud," Klose said. "Jane needs you."

Lionel punched Porter's shoulder, as though to shock him into action. "Let's go, I'll drive." He nudged him towards the front door.

Porter held his ground. "Nah, wait…Gotta find Amber."

"We won't get assistance from Barrett and co," Klose said. "I'll contact the boss at Broken Hill and request search teams, a tactical squad, and dogs. I'll wait for them to arrive then coordinate the search from here…We'll find Amber, bud."

Lyn held Porter's wrist. "I'll head to the scene and check on Grimes' investigation."

He grunted with gritted teeth. "Champions, the both of you…" He ran towards the front door and Lionel followed. He yelled over his shoulder. "Be back soon to help out…"

Ten minutes later, Porter hurried into the hospital's ICU room. He saw Jane and gasped at the sight. Her head was bandaged, face bruised and swollen, and a plastered arm hung across her chest. Emma sat next to her bed.

He rushed to Jane and sighed when she opened an eye. She tried to smile. He held her as tight as the injuries allowed and kissed her forehead. "Babe, I'm so, so sorry…Was crazy to leave you alone…"

She sighed and closed the eye.

He bent closer, ear against her cheek. "Babe? Hear me?" He straightened with moist eyes, afraid to blink.

280

He noticed blood-covered gauze above Emma's eye. "You okay, sweet?"

Emma stood. "Yep, just a few stitches…"

"How about Gary, and Patto?"

"Dad's in the operating room for a broken nose. He'll be fine. Patto was too stubborn to stay, said he needed to get back and take care of the pub…"

"Have you spoken to Jane? Does she remember what happened?"

Emma looked down at her. "She's drowsy…The doctor said there's no permanent damage but she'll be in pain for weeks. I'm glad she blacked out…" Her sweet voice trembled. "She won't remember what they did."

Flames scorched Porter's gut. He bent to kiss Jane's cheek.

Her eye opened. "Don't you worry about me," she whispered. "Amber…Those bastards have my baby." She grabbed his forearm, jaw clenched, and met his gaze. "Promise you'll find her. Don't care what you have to do, just find Amber."

He squeezed her hand. "On my life…"

Jane's eye closed. She sank lower.

Porter ushered Emma away from the bed and they joined Lionel near the doorway. He didn't want to ask her the questions but knew he had to. "What don't you want Jane to remember? What happened out there?"

"When the cars forced our horses off the road I fell and hit my head. When I came to, I lay on the road with a guy pointing a gun at me. The bastards held Jane down and they…" She stopped, cheeks striped with tears, and her eyes asked Porter if he wanted her to continue. He nodded. She gulped. "They stripped her naked and I thought they were going to…I, I started to stand but Jane told me to stay down. She protected me, knowing they'd kill us both if I tried to stop them."

Porter gulped. "How many of them? What they look like? Sound like?"

"Six. All in black, faces hidden and wearing gloves, like those SWAT teams in the movies. They didn't speak loud enough for me to hear, and everything was a bit blurry…Jane was covered in blood," her voice crackled as she sobbed, "and I was ready to kill the bastards if they laid another hand on her."

"Stop," Lionel told her. "Don't make yourself re-live it."

Porter glared at him for saying it. He addressed Emma. "Where was Amber?"

"Gone. We screamed out for her. Nothing…"

He sighed, loud and desperate. "Sorry, it's hard for us both, but I have to know what they did to Jane…They held her down…And?" He sucked at the disinfected air. "Did they…?"

"No, they didn't…But after they'd tied us, five gathered around her, and the sixth guy did the sickest…"

"What?" he prodded, crook in the guts but needing to know.

She hesitated. "He took photos while they posed with her, and they all laughed. One guy, their boss guessing by the way he acted, picked her up like a doll. Arsehole smiled into the camera and held her while the others…Took turns licking her breasts." Her shoulders slumped as she sobbed.

Porter winced then shuddered. A tingle of hate ran down his spine. "And?"

"He put Jane down on the road, and threw me this..." She took a crumpled piece of paper from her shirt pocket and handed it to him. "I didn't show it to that new guy Grimes, because you guys don't trust local coppers…"

"Good job…" Porter spread the paper in his hands. A ruptured heart threatened to break in two as he read the handwritten message.

'YOU SHOULD'VE LEFT CROOKED RIVER WHEN WE TOLD YOU TO. NOW IT'S TOO LATE, AND YOU'LL ALL DIE. WE'VE ALREADY TASTED YOUR SOUR BLACK WHORE. BUT WE'RE SURE THE YOUNG ONE WILL BE MUCH, MUCH SWEETER.'

"What does it say?" Lionel said.

Porter scrunched the paper in his fist. "They've got Amber…" He turned to Emma. "Did you see these blokes leave? Which way? What were they driving?"

"They drove away from town. Two black four-wheel drives, a bit like yours. One had damage to the front, from where it hit…My horses…"

Porter juggled his phone. "Gotta call Klose and get the vehicle descriptions circulated. Make sure they're search--" The phone vibrated and he glanced at it. Incoming, from an unknown caller. He put a finger to lips to hush the others then answered. "Yeah?"

"Dan Porter?" The voice sounded like a robot from a B-grade sci-fi movie.

Porter frowned. Someone disguising their voice was never a good sign. "Who's this?"

"Listen carefully, don't interrupt, and do as I say."

His dry throat croaked. "Listening..."

"Your girl's in extreme danger. Go to the abandoned Cobb mine on Bull Cart road. Go unarmed, hide your face, and dress as they do. Hurry, or she'll die." The call terminated.

"Who was that?" Lionel said.

"No idea…" Porter ran to Jane, pecked her cheek then moved towards the door. "Emma, how far to Cobb mine? I reckon me and Lio drove past it the other week…"

"Close to thirty k's. Why? What's going on?"

"Amber…Come on Lio, I'll explain in the car."

Emma followed them out the door. "I'll come and show you the way?"

Porter turned back to her. "Nah, we'll find it, please stay with Jane…Tell Foster what's happened when she arrives but not to follow us. And tell no-one but her where we're going…Trust no-one."

THIRTY-EIGHT

Porter drove the Landcruiser like Sebastian Vettel on speed and they reached the Bull Cart road intersection within fifteen minutes. He started to turn onto it, then braked. Forty meters ahead, men in black hooded cloaks guarded a roadblock at the entrance to Cobb mine. Dozens of buses lined the red dirt road in front of it. Men in the same black outfits stepped from the buses then hustled past the roadblock towards the entrance.

Porter reversed around the corner and out of view. "Bloody hell…" He checked the rear vision mirrors. "What's going on?"

"A huge gathering, and I don't think we're invited," Lionel said from the passenger seat. "Let's leave the car, cut across to the entrance driveway through the bush and hope they didn't see us…"

"Good idea…" Porter parked the Landcruiser off-road and hid it amongst thick mulga bush. He removed the shoulder holster and threw it into the glovebox. "Let's go."

"Won't you need your gun?"

"Told you, the person on the phone said no weapons, and to dress like 'em. Now I know why…We'll separate two, take their outfits and hide our faces with those masks." Porter smirked. "Best we cover all your parts, mate, 'cos I don't reckon there'll be any other black fellas at this party. Come on, move your arse."

They sprinted through undergrowth until boots crunched on gravel, not far ahead. They slowed into a crouch, approached the driveway then hid behind bushes. Hundreds of hooded men marched towards the homestead like black ants to sugar.

Porter winked at Lionel and gave him a hand signal to wait. Dead leaves crinkled to their right. They lowered themselves, chests pressed against red dirt. A hooded man walked thirty meters into the mulga forest and stopped to urinate.

Porter signaled for Lionel to stay put then rose to a crouch. He grabbed a fist-sized rock from the ground, crept behind the man and clubbed the back of his head. He caught the limp body and lowered it to a bed of dry leaves. He changed into the man's uniform and boots, pulled the cloak's hood over his head and tightened the full-face mask. Once he'd covered the body in leaves he crawled back to Lionel.

Lionel's eyebrows jumped. "Shit," he whispered. "Scared the --."

"Shh…Wait here."

Lionel nodded and flattened himself against dirt.

Porter returned five minutes later and handed him a uniform. Lionel changed into it and pulled on the gloves and boots. Porter looked him up and down. He straightened the gold shield on his chest then adjusted the uniform and mask so that none of Lionel's skin showed. Satisfied they would blend in, they walked to the gravel driveway and joined the march towards the sandstone homestead.

Porter peered ahead. Winter sun had sunk into the horizon. The homestead's tin roof glowed pink as day became night. He glanced from side to side and flicked a sticky tongue against the roof of his mouth. Were these KA soldiers he marched alongside, the men responsible for multiple murders and abductions? It was a risk to follow the anonymous phone tip and he might've been marching into a trap…But he'd promised Jane he would find Amber. What choice did he have?

The line halted when Porter was twenty meters from the entrance doors. He peered to his right. A six-seater helicopter with a blue stripe down its side sat idle in a clearing. Two black SUV's were parked to his left, one with a crumpled front end. The cars used in Amber's abduction? She had to be inside the homestead, but where exactly? Where were all these men going? Before he could find out, he and Lionel would have to make it past the guards up ahead.

He reached the doors and a burly guard called him forward. He trembled under the cloak as the guard told him to raise arms to the sides. The guard swept a metal detector wand over him, frisked his torso and legs then waved him towards the doorway. He took one step into the large foyer. He hesitated and turned to watch Lionel approach the entrance.

The guard gave the same instructions. Lionel slowly raised his arms. Would the cloak conceal all of the black skin underneath it? Porter held a breath…It did. Barely.

Lionel dropped his arms. The guard tilted his head from side to side, as though he couldn't see clearly in the dim light, and stepped closer to him.

Porter froze.

"You, in the doorway," a guard yelled at Porter from the foyer. "Too fucking slow…Get inside."

Porter turned and shuffled forward. He allowed men to overtake him in the line. A door off to the side of the foyer slammed shut. He peered over his shoulder and sighed. Lionel had made it past the guards and hurried towards him.

The guard who'd yelled ushered them through a sandstone archway then loaded them into a caged elevator with twenty others. Machinery above them whirled into action. The cage descended through a mine shaft. After fifty-metres the shaft opened into a gigantic cavern. Porter looked down and saw it full of KA soldiers, a black army of evil. He noticed a second elevator operating on the far side of the cavern and assumed the homestead had more than one entrance. He kept his head bowed as the elevator neared the end of its journey and avoided eye contact.

The cage slammed into the cavern's rock floor and wobbled to a stop. Porter stepped into the black army and Lionel followed. All soldiers faced the same direction, towards a section of the cavern that'd been blocked from his view on descent. He headed that way and pushed men aside to maze through the crowd.

A gap opened, he rushed forward and squeezed through it. Twenty meters ahead at the bottom of a sunken amphitheater appeared the object of the soldier's fascination. He gasped. Vomit scalded his throat as he stared at the scene before him.

THIRTY-NINE

Porter's heart thudded against chest as he watched Amber. She lay spreadeagled atop a marble bed at the bottom of the sunken amphitheater. She started to writhe and scream. Golden shackles attached to metal stakes secured her hands and feet to the bed. Fiery torches hung from rock walls and shone a flickering light over her oil-sheened nakedness.

A giant in a white, hooded-cloak stood next to her. He raised an axe above head as though it were a toothpick.

The black army chanted. "Axeman, axeman."

Porter pushed past soldiers and made his way down steps to the bottom of the amphitheater. He stopped five meters from Amber when the dense mass of bodies stopped him from going further. Eyes darted left and right. Even if he could push through the crowd, he'd still have to get past the two rows of guards circling the bed.

The axeman stepped closer to Amber and raised the axe. The black army cheered.

Porter's pulse raced. His body trembled. If he waited another second she could die. A gap opened ahead and he started towards it. A hand grabbed his elbow and held him back. He turned to lock eyes with Lionel and knocked his hand away. He prepared to lunge forward when a voice boomed throughout the cavern.

"Quiet! Calm down…Quiet!" The voice came from a man standing on a raised platform to Porter's left. He wore a blue gown with a matching peaked hat. A white mask covered his whole face. Soldiers of the black army jostled for position as they turned to watch him.

Eight masked men, wearing similar gowns and hats to the man in blue, sat on throne-like chairs behind him. Seven wore purple. A diminutive man in the center wore a red gown with sparkling gold trim.

The man in blue raised a hand then dropped it. Chatter ceased. "On this grand occasion, please make welcome members of the High Council…" His tone was theatrical, like that of a world championship boxing announcer. "And, our Supreme Leader, K…A…One!"

The black army cheered.

KA1, the frail man in red, walked to the platform's edge and stood alongside the man in blue. He dwarfed him with his presence, despite his short stature, and raised a hand to acknowledge the black army. They roared in a thunderous crescendo. He lowered it and the storm subsided.

An eerie silence fell over the cavern.

Amber's pleading sobs tortured Porter's ears. He glanced about, desperate to find a way to her.

"Thank you, KA7…" KA1 turned to the man in blue. "Our magnificent Master of Ceremonies has done a wonderful job preparing the festivities. As always..."

KA7 bowed his head.

"Well here we are, still going strong," KA1 told the soldiers in a deep, powerful voice. "I can hardly believe it's been fifty-five years since our humble beginnings…Our enemies once tried to divide us, and the fools think they succeeded…But very soon they will see what a rich and powerful organization we have become...And down in the sacrificial pit, what a beautiful, unblemished creature our men have secured for the occasion. Si diis placent!"

"Pleased be the gods!" The black army chanted.

Porter gasped under the mask. *Sacrificial pit?* He tried to push through the men in front of him. They growled and blocked his path.

KA1 threw his voice across the cavern. "When our ancestors first arrived from mother Scotland, this great southern land was a haven for those of pure Celtic blood. For decades we controlled governments and maintained their vision. But, at the start of this century came a change for the worse. Unimaginable numbers of Chinese, African refugees, other ethnics, and Arabic terrorists invaded us. Weak politicians allowed them to buy our land, infiltrate the government, and destroy our culture. Those politicians should be hung for treason..."

The soldiers booed, swore and shook fists.

Porter tried to shuffle forward but the masses jammed tight around him.

"However," KA1 continued, "we will make this nation great again. Your hard work has enabled us to position one of our own high up in the government, one soon to become leader of the ruling party. And, my brothers, laws will be made and enforced that protect us from the hordes of brethren. Impure, lesser beings will be banished. We, the Nemed, the true ruling class, will rise again. This southern land will be great again!"

The black army cheered.

KA1 pointed down to Amber's limp body, where the Axeman stood over her. "On this auspicious occasion we sacrifice a black virgin to please the gods..." He threw arms out and faced the darkness above. "Our

Lords, we ask that you accept this virgin…May her sacrifice appease you, and her blood quench your thirst." His gaze lowered to the pit. "Axeman, see it done. Caelicolis placent…Sanguis!"

"Pleased be the gods…Blood!" The black army roared as one. "Pleased be the gods…Blood!" They roared louder.

Porter lunged towards the pit and Lionel pushed from behind. They drove a wedge through the crowd until they'd reached the guards. Porter stepped right and caught a glimpse of Amber. She lay less than three meters from him. Her eyes were closed and tears streamed down her face. He grabbed a guard by the shoulders and pulled him forward. He hoped to break through but the guards linked arms and the line held.

The Axeman held his weapon aloft.

Amber opened her eyes and screamed, loud and chilling.

Porter's heart shattered into a million pieces. He would yell out and offer himself, delay them, anything…He opened his mouth. Another yelled first.

"Stop! Axeman, do not strike." The command came from a High Council member dressed in purple. He rushed down the platform's stairs and waved guards aside to enter the sacrificial pit. He stood over Amber, with body curved as though protecting her. "Put it down," he ordered the Axeman.

The Axeman lowered his weapon. The black army murmured.

KA1 stepped down the stairs, towards the pit. Three High Council members followed him.

"KA6, our dear Secretary, what is the meaning of this?" KA1 stopped at the last stair. "Why have you spoken so?"

"Stop! Come no further," KA6 yelled.

Porter's ears pricked. The Secretary? The bloke Ferguson had said protected the Cumal Files? Who was he?

Guards parted to allow KA1 and the others into the pit.

KA6 produced a pistol from inside his gown.

The black army gasped.

Porter watched in awe.

KA6's hand shook as he aimed the pistol at KA1. "Have the Axeman untie the girl, cover her and leave the pit."

"And why, KA6, would I?" KA1 said in a calm voice. "You have one gun and may kill ten of us, but the rest will tear you apart."

KA6 reached inside the gown with his free hand and pulled out a remote control. "Because this will set off the eighty kilos of TNT I've rigged to the ceiling. One press of the button buries us for eternity..."

KA1's narrow shoulders collapsed. Air seemed to rush from him.

Soldiers looked upwards. Whispers of fearful disbelief echoed throughout the cavern.

"Order the Axeman. Now," KA6 yelled.

KA1 signaled to the Axeman. The Axeman unshackled Amber, caught her as she slid from the marble bed and folded her into a sitting position. She steadied herself, wrapped arms around naked breasts and gazed wide-eyed at the army. The Axeman covered her with his cloak then marched bare-chested to the edge of the pit and stood behind KA1.

"Good..." KA6 leveled the pistol at KA1. "Now...Dan Porter, come forward."

Porter stared at KA6, his mind numb. Had the Secretary called out to him? Or had he finally lost it completely? Was he imagining the whole scene?

"Where are you, Porter?" KA6 yelled above the black army's chatter.

Porter was about to call out then stopped himself. Did KA6's voice sound familiar? Was he the bloke who'd given him the phone tip-off? Or, was this bloke the enemy, who'd used Amber to lure he and Lionel into a trap?

FORTY

Porter's guts churned as he watched Amber. She sat on a marble bed in the cavern's sacrificial pit and sobbed, her eyes wide and fearful.

KA6 swiveled in his purple robe, towards the row of guards surrounding the pit. "Dan Porter," he cried out, "come forward now."

Porter took a deep breath then let it out through gritted teeth. He threw a hand up. "Here," he shouted. "We're here."

The black army spun towards him. Hateful snarls filled the cavern.

"Guards, let them through," KA6 ordered.

The guards looked to KA1, who dipped his head, then parted to allow Porter and Lionel into the pit.

Porter ran to hug Amber. He sat and took her trembling face in hands. "It's okay, sweet, we'll get you out of here."

She nodded. Lionel stood beside the bed.

Porter removed the mask, black hooded cloak, and gloves. Lionel did the same. They were left wearing black t-shirts and cargo pants. A murmur of intrigue spread throughout the KA soldiers.

KA6 pointed to the bed. "Don't touch them," he told the guards.

Porter glanced towards the platform and saw that the other High Council members had vanished. Beyond the platform, in the far corner of the cavern, a caged elevator ascended into the mineshaft. Some of the men inside it wore purple costumes. If those KA bosses managed to escape, would they then sacrifice their army to protect themselves?

The blue-clad KA7 stood on the edge of the pit. "KA6, what do you hope to achieve?"

"Put the gun down, KA6," KA1 said, "I do not understand…Why do you betray your brothers? It is the ultimate sin…"

KA6 stepped towards him. "Standing by while you and these other demented fools destroyed countless lives, that's been my greatest sin…My miserable shame." He stopped two meters from him.

KA1 scoffed. "You wish to kill me? Then at least remove your mask and reveal yourself to our soldiers…" He swept a hand over the black army. "Show them who would dare harm their leader."

KA6 kept the pistol aimed while he removed his hat and dropped it to the stone floor. He ripped the white mask off and threw it away.

Shockwaves ran from Porter's head to toes. He stared at the Secretary's wrinkled face. The face of Inspector George Barrett.

The black army snarled as one.

"How wonderful, to be free of that hideous disguise…" Barrett said as he eyed KA1. "And now, for you to reveal yourself…"

KA1 mocked him with a condescending snigger.

"As you wish…" Barrett aimed the pistol at KA1's head. His finger hovered over the trigger.

A thick-set High Council member stepped between them. "Stop, KA6…Have you lost your mind?"

Barrett raised the remote control. "Come no closer, KA2. All of you stay back, or I'll blow this place apart...." He retreated a few meters then turned to Porter. "Come here."

Porter swooped Amber up and carried her to him. Lionel followed.

Barrett leaned close to Porter and whispered. "The door to the left, past the platform. See it?"

Porter's eyes scanned the area. He saw a wooden door thirty meters away. A path led to it from the pit, between the platform and a high metal fence. "Yeah..."

"I'll distract them. When I do, go through it into the tunnel. It's your only way out of here."

"I knew you're an alright bloke..."

"No, I'm the same as these others, a monster..." Barrett said with a frown. "Will you promise something?"

"What?"

"Expedite to my house. My wife will give you what you need, what you've been searching for...And then get her to safety."

A tingle of hope ran along Porter's spine. Did Barrett refer to the Cumal Files? "Will do..."

"Now get to the door and wait for my word..." Barrett glared at KA1 and held the remote control aloft. "Let them through, or we all die."

KA1 made a hand signal. Guards parted to clear the path from the pit to door.

"Go!" Barrett yelled.

Porter carried Amber from the pit and ran towards the door. Lionel followed. The path narrowed between the platform and the metal fence. Soldiers spat, shouted obscenities and started to climb the fence.

"Get down...Harm them and your leader dies," Barrett yelled. The soldiers dropped back to the ground.

Porter reached the door. He sucked at damp air, tried to ease the burning sensation in his chest. Lionel stopped alongside him.

Amber opened her eyes. "I'm okay, Dan."

He put her down then spun to watch the platform.

Barrett stood on the edge of it. "KA1, will you come up here and join me?"

"Very well…" A silent minute passed while KA1 shuffled from the pit to the top of the platform.

Barrett leveled the pistol at him. "Remove your mask or I shoot you dead now."

KA1's laughter echoed throughout the cavern. His frail body shook. "You, cannot demand such a thing, of me..."

"Ah but Aboriginal spirits, the rightful owners of this land, they demand it. I've failed their daughters, and your deaths will be my redemption. It is them I must appease, not you…"

"Black spirits? Redemption?" KA1 scoffed. "You are insane..."

"Madder than a meat-axe some used to say…" Barrett waved the remote control above his head. "Reveal yourself to save your army. Or are you too much of a coward?"

Gasps of dismay from the black army.

"Very well, I will show myself," KA1 said in his regal tone. "But I do it for my loyal brothers, the Knights of Alba, so you will spare their lives…And not, dear Secretary, because the imaginary torturers of your soul demand it..."

Porter frowned, unsure if he'd heard correctly. Had McKinlay just called the soldiers…Knights of Alba? He'd never heard of them, but that had to be what the

'KA' stood for? And if so, Alec Ferguson had been correct. The 'organization' did have another name...
He kept eyes on Barrett, stepped backwards and placed a hand on the door handle.

"Do it now, KA1..." Barrett yelled above the soldiers' jeers. "Who is the tyrant hiding behind the mask?"

KA1 sighed then removed his high hat. He had a head like a chihuahua, covered in white hair. The cavern fell silent as the crowd hushed. He lifted the mask from face, slow and upwards, and revealed his true identity.

The black army gasped in unison then buzzed like bees in indistinct chatter.

Porter squinted and tried to focus on KA1's face. "I recognize him...From where?" he said to Lionel. "Fuck, who is that bloke?"

"McKinlay?" Lionel's voice shook as he shouted. "Charles McKinlay?" He pointed an accusatory finger at the platform and marched forward. "Your resistance to Carinya makes even more sense now...You despicable, corrupt son of a bitch!"

Porter ran after Lionel, grabbed his arm and hauled him back to the door.

Retired Judge Charles McKinlay, the Knights of Alba's Supreme Leader, turned towards them. "Roberts, you naïve fool..." his voice was loud yet calm. "I gave you enough hints and opportunities to quit, and you should have taken them. You will never beat me, or the system..." He shifted his gaze. "And you, Porter, are far from blameless in all of this. You have been fortunate thus far but have taken too much to get out of here alive..."

"Enough!" Barrett advanced, the pistol leveled at McKinlay's head. "Your time has come..." He turned towards the door. "Go, Porter! Now!"

Porter kept one eye on Barrett and nodded.

Lionel pushed the wooden door open. Amber rushed through the doorway and he followed.

"Run. Fast," Porter shouted.

"Knights of Alba..." McKinlay yelled from the platform. He pointed at Porter. "Set upon them!"

The black army roared. One group swarmed up the platform's stairs towards Barrett. Another group headed for the door.

Porter ducked into the tunnel. As he turned to shut the door a gunshot sounded from the cavern. He peeked towards the platform. McKinlay crumpled to the ground, hands clutched to chest. A frenzied pack of KA soldiers ran at Barrett, who fired into them. Three more gunshots boomed. Men screamed. The pack retreated.

Porter slammed the heavy door shut. He picked up a wooden bolt and dropped it into place between steel brackets. He gripped the bolt's iron handle in both hands then jammed it to the left. Secure...Men shouted and pounded on the other side of the door.

Porter sprinted along the dank tunnel over a cobblestone floor. Candles mounted on sandstone brick walls flickered and showed him the way. When his eyes adjusted to the dim light he saw Amber and Lionel in front of him. They'd slowed to a walk.

He pictured Barrett standing on the platform with the remote control held high. Explosives inside the cavern could blow any second. When they did, would the tunnel collapse too?

"Keep running," he yelled. "Don't stop."

He caught up to Amber, looped an arm around her waist and urged her on. They ran up the slope. The light in the tunnel got brighter. He saw Lionel waiting twenty meters ahead and stopped to listen. Were those footsteps behind them? Getting louder?

"There're stairs, an exit," Lionel yelled. "Hurry, they'll be cha--."

The explosion whooshed through the tunnel; a giant, flaming bowling ball. Porter tumbled over the floor like a battered pin then crashed into a wall. He staggered to his feet and searched for Amber through smoke and dust. Grit in the air tickled his throat and made him cough. Searing heat stung his face. More explosions. The tunnel shook. The Earth rumbled and the ceiling began to fall.

Porter rushed to Amber. She groaned and stood. She brushed dust from the cloak, her eyes dazed like those of a shell-shocked Syrian child. They ran up the slope together, shielding faces from falling debris and wheezing from the thick smoke. They came to a wider section of tunnel with a higher ceiling and stopped.

Lionel stood atop sandstone stairs, ten meters above them. "Hurry, there's a hatch door." He shoved it open. Moonlight beamed through the opening and illuminated the tunnel in shades of silver. "These stairs are starting to break up. Hurry!"

Porter pushed Amber up the stairs ahead of him. She stumbled and squealed. Lionel leaped down and stopped her from falling. Earth shook, the tunnel's walls threatened to collapse. Stairs wobbled and cracked under Porter's feet. He picked Amber up in a fireman's lift and carried her towards the hatch door.

Lionel released her then leaped to the highest stair. He grabbed the hatch door's timber frame with one hand and used it as an anchor while Porter pushed her towards him.

Lionel hauled her upwards. She scrambled over his back and through the opening. He followed her out of the tunnel. They peered down at Porter. Looks of dread spread across dust-caked faces as they reached for him.

Porter swayed then tried to balance on crumbling stairs. As the tunnel ahead collapsed he jumped to the highest point. Rubble cascaded towards him, pounded the stairs and threatened to sweep him along the tunnel with it. He reached for a beam in the timber wall frame and gripped it. Stairs fell away beneath him. He hung from the beam one-handed, high above the ground, still two meters from the hatch door.

Muscles in his forearm bulged. Neck veins threatened to burst. He reached for another beam higher up. The timber wall frame splintered and his grip on the beam slipped. He strained and extended his arm as far as he could. Aching fingers felt for the hatch door. *Fuck, can't reach it...*

He gazed up into Amber's tear-streaked face. She told him to find strength, but he weakened and his hand slipped. He closed eyes and saw Jane. She kissed him and told him to keep fighting. He opened them and saw the tunnel collapse around him. *Sorry babe, can't hold on...*

"Dan!" Amber screamed. "No...!"

FORTY-ONE

At the peak of survival mode a rush of adrenaline flooded Porter's body. A tingling sensation rose from feet to throat. He gasped as he shook, then relaxed like a junkie after a shot of heroin. He beckoned all strength, clung to the last remaining timber beam, and growled as he climbed.

The beam splintered and began to slide away. He swung in the air then lunged for the hatch door's wooden frame. He gripped it with fingers and hung high above a dusty chasm. The frame cracked under his weight. He glanced down, ready to fall.

Lionel grabbed under his armpits and heaved him upwards. He dragged him through the opening and out into the moonlit night.

Porter slammed the hatch door shut as the tunnel imploded below. He rolled away from it then lay on dry leaves and watched stars in the clear sky. Amber and Lionel collapsed beside him. All three of them panted and let out high-pitched sighs. After a minute they sat up and laughed.

Cool air soothed Porter's face. He hugged Amber and told her that Jane would be okay. He turned to Lionel. "What the hell just happened down there?"

Lionel wobbled his head. "Amazing events. Beyond insane…"

"Not wrong…Can you believe Barrett was KA? And who else belongs to their High Council? They're the blokes we've been looking for, the ones writing the cheques to Interpol and so on…"

"Yes, you're right. And Barrett's involvement shocks me too…" Lionel snarled. "But not as much as Charles McKinlay's…And there are hundreds of others buried down there whose identities we'll never know."

Porter stood and helped Amber to her feet. McKinlay's speech echoed in his head. "What you reckon he meant? McKinlay, when he said I've taken too much?"

Lionel frowned. "I've no idea, but he made it sound as though he's intent on retribution against you rather than the entire police force. Why?"

"Dunno, I've never met the bloke. And you're spot on, it seemed personal. Strange…"

"What's even stranger, is why did he allow Carinya to proceed? Considering KA's presence in Crooked River and the risk of us exposing it…"

"Maybe the arrogant old fool didn't reckon we'd find anything?"

"Perhaps. And without Shirley's emails I doubt we would have…"

"I don't reckon that Rothwell gave McKinlay any say about whether you got your investigation phase or not…But McKinlay's done everything in his power, as leader of KA and a retired judge, to put an end to it…"

"Everything in his power, and more…" Lionel smiled as he stood. "But he failed."

Porter remembered the conversation with Barrett and the promise he'd made to protect his wife. He checked his watch. 6.33pm. They had much more to discuss but expediting to Barrett's house took priority. He'd heard footsteps behind them in the tunnel…Were their pursuers trapped when it'd collapsed? Or had they found a different exit? Were they out in the bush right now and searching for them?

"Let's go, gotta move fast," he said. "Which direction's the car you reckon?"

Lionel gazed at the sky as he ran. "It's this way…"

Porter supported Amber's weight and they followed him through dense bushland. After a few minutes he signaled them to stop and lowered himself to the ground. Porter did likewise and pulled Amber down with him. Wheels spun on gravel nearby.

Porter crawled to Lionel and whispered, "What'd you see?"

"The roadblock's just up ahead. I counted five guards. Three are still here. Two have walked to the left, towards the dirt track where we hid the car. A dark SUV just turned right and took off down Bull Cart road."

"I don't reckon they've found the Landcruiser yet…We'll cut back to our left, get ahead of the guards and hopefully come out of the bush near it."

They crawled back through the undergrowth for ten meters then stood and dodged mulga bush as they ran. They'd covered a few hundred meters when a sharp crack pierced the still night.

Porter froze, a dead branch wedged underfoot. Amber squeezed his arm. Lionel stopped up ahead.

Excited voices called from the road, got louder then faded away. They waited for a minute then started to run again. Five minutes later they reached the dirt track.

"Bloody hell, it's still here..." Porter sprinted towards the Landcruiser and pulled Amber with him. "Get in, sweet, quick."

He leaped into the drivers' seat while Amber moved into the back. Lionel sat in the front passenger seat. He grabbed the Glock and cell phones from the glovebox.

Porter snatched the Glock from him and dropped it in the center console. He accelerated. The Landcruiser fishtailed as its wheels spun in the dirt then gripped. He squinted, guided only by moonlight, and increased speed as the dirt track crossed over Bull Cart road.

"Shit," Lionel shouted above the roar of the diesel engine. "They're onto us."

Porter rammed the accelerator to the floor. "Who? Where?"

"It looked like the damaged SUV from the homestead. Was coming down Bull Cart road towards the intersection when we went through it." Lionel turned. "Faster, they're behind us."

Porter pushed the Landcruiser to its limit. He told Lionel to phone Lyn Foster and have her send navigation coordinates for the Barrett homestead. After five minutes the pursuing SUV had fallen far behind and out of sight.

Lionel turned back to the front. "Well done, we've lost them."

"They weren't gunna keep up for long with that damage…" Porter glanced to the back seat and saw Amber asleep. "We're nearly at Crooked River road, which way do we turn?"

Lionel played with the Landcruiser's bright Navigator screen. "I've entered the coordinates that Lyn sent…Wait…" A pause of five seconds. "Okay, turn right onto Crooked River Road then follow it for five k's. Why are we going to Barrett's place?"

"Remember what McKinlay called him?"

"Yes."

"And what Ferguson told us?"

"Regarding the Secretary?" Lionel's tone rose, as though he'd come to a realization. "That he protects the Cumal Files…"

"Spot on…And I reckon Barrett's wife will give 'em to us…"

"Amazing…We'll have access to KA's entire network, names of their members and associates."

"Including those of the bosses who escaped the cavern before the explosion…"

Lionel turned to the rear. "Still no sign of them…I'm thinking, with what we now know about McKinlay and Barrett…Might it be possible to find KA's associates without the files?"

"Was just thinking the sa--."

An SUV came from the side road at such speed that Porter didn't have time to brake or swerve. It rammed into the Landcruiser's rear drivers' side and sent it spinning across the road. He fought the steering wheel and struggled to regain control but they slid sideways into a tree trunk and came to a crunching stop.

The SUV flipped then rolled and crashed through bushland.

Porter blinked to focus dazed eyes. He scrambled into the back.

Amber tried to sit up but slumped onto the seat. Blood trickled from a cut on her forehead. She looked at him like a baby deer in a hunter's crosshairs. "What happened?" Blood splattered on her cloak. She sobbed. "I'm bleeding?"

"You're okay, sweet." Porter ripped a strip of cloth from the bottom of the cloak and wrapped it around her head. "Hold that and stay here, be back in a minute."

She put a hand to the makeshift bandage and closed her eyes.

He grabbed his Glock and a torch from the console then leaped from the Landcruiser. He shone the torch to search surrounding bushland for the men who'd chased them. The crumpled SUV lay upside down. Wheels spun. Its headlights illuminated the area between it and Porter.

Lionel stepped towards the SUV.

Porter tugged him back by the shoulder. "Where you going?"

"I smell smoke, a fire..." Lionel frowned. "They could be alive?"

"Dangerous, mate. Watch Amber. I'll check it out."

Lionel ignored him and strode forward.

Porter cursed his stubbornness and ran past him, Glock aimed at the wrecked SUV. He sniffed the air. Petrol. Small flames spread from the wreckage, fuelled by dry undergrowth. He snapped arms out straight and tracked movement to his right.

A blond KA soldier limped from behind the wreckage, found cover behind a small tree and fired at him.

Porter dropped to the ground and rolled to his right, hidden by low scrub. The blond soldier left cover and headed for a larger tree. Porter took aim and fired. The soldier's head exploded and he fell hard against red dirt.

Porter jumped to his feet.

Lionel pointed towards the wreckage. "Look, one's still trapped..." Black eyes pleaded with Porter. "The flames are getting closer. We can't let him burn?"

Porter aimed the Glock at the SUV and stepped towards it. The soldier lay with his upper torso outside the car. He wore a cloak, face hidden by a black mask. His legs seemed trapped in the wreckage, encased by twisted metal. He moaned quietly and appeared to be barely conscious of the rising flames crackling around him.

"We have to get him out," Lionel shouted.

Porter stepped closer, through a gap in burning undergrowth. He squinted and shielded his face from the intense heat. "I reckon we don't..." He sucked a breath and let it hiss from him through gritted teeth. "This bloke tried to kill us. And Amber..."

Lionel stood in front of Porter, his back to the SUV. "He might give us information and identify the bosses?" He glared, eyes defiant. "I'm getting him out..."

Porter peered over Lionel's shoulder. He opened his mouth to yell a warning.

Lionel buckled as the bullet struck him in the back. He gasped and gurgled. His mouth flopped open. He collapsed to the ground.

The soldier inside the wreckage raised his gun again but Porter shot first. The bullet struck him in the upper arm and the man yelped. The gun fell from his hand and tumbled out of reach.

Porter ran to Lionel and bent to cradle the back of his head. "Gutless bastard..." he yelled towards the SUV.

Lionel coughed and bright blood spewed from his mouth. A tear dribbled from an eye as he focused on Porter. "Hey," he whispered, "what's with all the commotion?"

Porter straightened. There was still hope. "Getting you to hospital, mate. You're gunna be okay…"

Lionel moved his head from one side to the other like a turtle. "Go, get Amber away. Leave me here."

"Nah, I won't…"

Lionel's right hand trembled as he dug nails into dirt. He scooped a handful and brought it to his nose. He sniffed it then smiled with bloodied teeth. "I'm happy to die here," he whispered. He grimaced, agony etched across his face. "I'm home and at one with the land, at peace amongst my people. They'll come for me…"

"Nah, you're not gunna die." Porter lowered Lionel's head to the ground. He placed hands under him and prepared to lift.

Lionel clawed the earth. "Leave me…" His chest shook as he wheezed. "Save Amber…"

Porter lowered him to the ground. He ignored the trapped soldier's pleas for help.

Lionel convulsed. "You're a good friend…" He gargled blood. A tear ran down his cheek. "Please, Dan, finish what we started…"

Porter's jaw clenched. "Will do…" He watched his mate die.

He strode towards the burning SUV, a gladiator determined to end the contest. He needed to see the coward behind the mask. The face of Lionel's killer. He stopped in front of him. Flames licked his boots.

The soldier looked up and cleared his throat as though about to speak. Porter ripped the mask away before he could make a sound.

Porter recoiled.

The soldier stared back. A wicked grin spread across his face.

"Klose?" Porter stumbled backwards. "You're with them? You're KA?"

"KA129 to be exact," Fred Klose replied, tone of voice grand as though proud of it.

Porter struggled to focus, mind numb. "But…Why? Lio loved you like a brother."

"He was no brother…" Klose scoffed. "He stole the only girl I'd loved. Used her as his plaything then threw her out like a dirty whore…Never forgave him. Wish he'd been the first one I killed…"

"You mean before you murdered all the others? Who'd also trusted you…"

Klose smirked. "Trust is a game for fools…Lio was nothing but a pest to be exterminated. Same as Rhodes when I pushed him from the cliff. Uncle Simpson and Tommy Davis...Same as you…"

"Rhodes?" Porter yelled above roaring flames. He pointed a shaking finger. "And why'd you help to blackmail Rothwell, against KA's interest?"

Klose's face wrinkled. "Get me out…" His voice croaked with panic. "I'll tell you everything."

Porter grunted. "Reckon I've heard enough..." He turned away.

"I'll give you names," Klose blurted. "Yes I helped Lionel to blackmail Rothwell. I wanted to discredit McKinlay…"

Porter faced him. "Why?"

311

"My father was KA2, the Chief of Staff. He always did the dirty work, what McKinlay lacked the balls for. He deserved to lead us...But now, because of that fruit loop Barrett, he's dead, buried in that explosion."

The movie projector in Porter's head flicked through all the events that'd sabotaged Carinya. "You and your mates have caused a lot of grief, aside from the victims you've already mentioned...Shirley, Lio's witness in Scotland. Bianca, murdered in the South African hospital. Alec Ferguson? And fuck knows how many others..."

He tightened his grip on the Glock and contemplated shooting Klose between smug eyes. But justice from a bullet would be too swift. He turned and strode towards Lionel.

"Porter?" Klose yelled. "Porter!"

Porter knelt beside Lionel and for a milli-second considered going back to free Klose. But his moral code, harder than concrete after things he'd seen and done, believed compassion worked both ways. It had to be given before received. And Fred Klose, who screamed in terror for the last time, hadn't earned the right to ask for it.

Men shouted nearby. Porter glanced towards the Landcruiser. In the time it'd take him to carry Lionel to it, the men would find them. He couldn't put Amber's life in danger, and couldn't leave his dead mate in the dirt either...But he had to make a choice. He closed eyes and drew smoky air deep into his lungs. When they opened, he'd made it.

FORTY-TWO

Porter drove the damaged Landcruiser fast towards the Barrett homestead while Amber slept on the back seat. He phoned Lyn Foster. He asked her to meet him, then followed the Navigator's directions. His head rattled as he shook it, a box of scrambled puzzle pieces. Had he done the right thing by leaving Lionel behind? He'd told him to save Amber. He had. And he was on his way to collect the Cumal Files. Lionel would be happy…Wouldn't he?

Porter braked and the Landcruiser skidded to a stop at the junction of Crooked River road and the Barrett homestead's driveway. Three meters ahead at the side of the road, Lyn leaned against an unmarked police sedan. He left the headlights on and moved to Amber in the back seat. The cloth bandage around her head had stemmed the bleeding. He carried her towards Lyn.

"Oh, god." Lyn's sweet face soured. "What happened?"

"She was knocked out." He indicated the sedan's rear door. Lyn opened it.

He laid Amber across the seat. "You'll be fine, sweet, Lyn's taking you to mum." He lowered his voice. "What do you remember?"

Amber frowned. "You mean, before our car crashed? Nothing…"

"That's beaut…" He swept hair from her forehead. He hoped she'd never be haunted by her abduction and the horrific events she'd witnessed in the cavern.

"When people ask you what happened tonight, that's all you need to tell 'em. Got it?"

She nodded and closed her eyes.

He closed the door and turned to Lyn. "Any cars head to Barrett's place while you waited?"

Her forehead crinkled. "No."

"Is backup, and the search team from Broken Hill coming?"

"Not sure. Klose was organizing it…"

"Fuck! Call Broken Hill and organize it now."

"But why didn't Klose do it? And where is he, anyway? He's not answering his phone or the Carinya landline. It's like he's disappeared…"

Klose's last scream echoed in Porter's head. "He has, kind of…"

Her eyebrows arched. "Meaning?"

He wanted to protect her from the truth. He gambled and hoped KA would dispose of Klose's remains and they'd never be found. "Klose's corrupt. On the run…"

"What? What's going on? Why are you visiting Barrett?" She peered past him and squinted in the glare of headlights. She frowned. "Where's Lionel?"

He said nothing.

"Dan, where's Lionel?" Her voice became frantic. "What happened at Cobb mine?"

He locked eyes with hers and shook his head.

A hand covered her mouth as she gasped. "Wha-. No?" she shrieked. "How?"

"Sorry mate, don't have time. Later…"

"But is he--?"

"Arrange the backup and search teams. Get Amber to Jane and tell her I'm okay. I'll speak to Barrett about the search then meet you at the hospital. Alright?"

Her face turned pale. Her bottom lip quivered. She opened the car door. "I can't believe it…"

He ran to the Landcruiser then turned to watch her. "Lyn," he called out. She looked towards him. "Lio's okay, mate. He's where he wants to be…"

She tilted her head to the side, gave a weak smile. She closed the door and drove away.

Porter parked under the carport at the front of Barrett's house and sighed with relief. Barrett's private car was the only other vehicle there. He got out, fanned the torch beam over the gravel driveway and saw no evidence that a car had left in a hurry. He ran to the front door, knocked and called out. No answer. He pulled the door handle. Locked. He called out again. No answer. He ran down the veranda to a glass sliding door. Open. How about the mesh screen door in front of it? He tried the handle and swore. Locked.

"Mrs Barrett?" He shouted through the screen door then listened. No reply, only the piercing song of cicadas. *Why isn't she answering? Gotta get the files, quick, and get her out of here...* "Mrs Barrett?"

He pressed his hand against the insect screen and peered inside. An empty bedroom. Was she in the shower, or out the back? There was no time to waste, KA soldiers might arrive at any minute. He kicked in the screen door, held the Glock out in front and stepped into the bedroom. He tiptoed towards a hallway and listened for her. "Mrs Barrett, it's Dan Porter. Your husband sent me. Mrs Barrett?"

No reply, only a loud whirring noise that came from behind the house. He ran down the hallway towards it, through the open back door and onto a timber veranda. The noise got louder, more familiar. The sound of

315

whirring rotor blades. He spun to his right. In the paddock, not thirty meters from him, a helicopter swayed and left the ground. Lights flashed and illuminated a blue stripe along its side. He'd seen the same helicopter earlier at Cobb mine.

He jumped from the veranda and shielded eyes from downforce as he sprinted towards the helicopter. He fired at it. Bullets bounced off the undercarriage. It rose out of range, killed its lights and disappeared into the night.

Porter rushed inside the house. He found Mary Barrett in the study. She lay in a pool of blood with a golf ball sized gunshot wound in her forehead. A false wall covered in bookshelves had been pushed to the side. Behind it, a hole had been blown in a concrete wall. The hole revealed a safe with its door ajar. A massive safe, big enough to store a wooden chest. His hands searched inside the safe. Empty.

"Shit." He whacked the safe with an open palm. "Fuck," he screamed at the hole in the wall. He noticed a message below it. It was still wet and he assumed it'd been written in Mary Barrett's blood.

MORE BLOOD ON YOUR HANDS, PORTER
GIVE UP, FOOL, YOU'LL NEVER GET THE FILES

FORTY-THREE

Porter yawned in the passenger seat and glanced at Lyn Foster as she drove them to the abandoned Cobb mine. The rising sun flashed between gaps in the river gum canopy along Crooked River road. He squinted, rubbed eyes then slurped the stale coffee he'd brought with him from the hospital cafeteria.

She turned to him briefly. "You look knackered…"

He shifted in the seat. "My back's stiffer than an old bloke who's popped five Viagra." He chuckled as she rolled her eyes. "The chair in that hospital room's a shocker…"

"Aww you're a good guy, staying with Jane and Amber all night. And you were worried sick…There's nowhere in this world you would've slept well."

"True, but I've only got myself to blame. I was a bloody drongo to let 'em come out here…"

"You tried to stop her, but Jane's a strong-minded woman."

"I should've tried harder…And shouldn't have taken Lio to the mine yesterday." He shuddered as he remembered cradling Lionel's head and watching him die.

Silence for a minute.

"Tell me the truth, Dan. What happened to him? And who abducted Amber?"

Lyn and Lionel had become good friends, and she deserved to know how he died. But Porter decided he wouldn't tell her about Amber's abductors, the Knights of Alba. "He was killed during Amber's rescue."

"Her rescue from who?"

"Don't know," he lied. "We found her inside the house, alone, and thought the crooks had gone. But they came back, chased us, and we crashed. Lionel got shot…"

"How?"

"Doesn't matter, but his sacrifice got Amber to safety. He said he'd found home and that he'd be looked after…I couldn't get it out of my head. That I'd left him. Last night I called Aunty Doreen at the mission and told her where to find him…"

Lyn stopped the sedan on the side of the road. She placed a soft hand on his forearm. "You did the right thing telling Doreen. And you can't blame yourself for all of this. Your girls survived, and Lio would make the same choices again."

He broke eye contact. "Reckon so…Doesn't make it easier."

"He knew he was dying but wanted you to survive. He knew you'd finish the job and fulfill his legacy." She leaned forward and forced him to meet her sympathetic gaze. "The elders will take good care of him…Right?"

"Yeah…Let's go and see wh--" An announcement on ABC radio caught his attention. He increased the volume.

"It's a bit lou--."

"Shoosh! Hear that? Something about a crash near Crooked River…"

They listened to the female radio announcer - "It's 8am Sunday, and repeating news just in…A helicopter

318

transporting retired Judge Charles McKinlay and Federal Police Commissioner Kevin Watkins has crashed. It came down two-hundred-and-ninety kilometers south-east of Crooked River, in the north-western part of New South Wales. Police say the helicopter exploded on impact, and despite no remains being found as yet, have confirmed the death of both passengers and a pilot. A Federal Police spokesman said Judge McKinlay, head of the National Human Rights Commission, and Commissioner Watkins, were heading to Crooked River to meet with Aboriginal leaders and local officials over concerns about neglect in the district. They were also due to meet with police attached to the controversial Carinya investigation. The pilot is believed to have been a Crooked River local, whose identity is yet to be confirmed. More updates as they come in..."

Porter scoffed. "Bullshit…" The realization struck him flush across the nose, like a head-high tackle. Federal Police Commissioner Watkins had been a member of KA's High Council. It explained his resistance to Lyn's request for a proper investigation into John Rhode's murder. It explained why Fred Klose had been assigned to Carinya.

McKinlay and Watkins had been killed when the cavern exploded. The helicopter crash was a cover-up, an attempt to explain the sudden disappearance of two high profile men. Had it been done by a KA associate, one high up in the Federal Police?

He did the math in his head. Barrett, Fred Klose's father, McKinlay and Watkins were confirmed dead. Up to five High Council members could still remain. How many of them had died in the explosion? How many had got away? For the nightmare to end he'd have to find them all. The Cumal Files held the answers. But where had Mary Barrett's killers taken them?

Lyn turned down the radio volume. "What's bullshit?"

"McKinlay and Watkins weren't gunna meet with Carinya, the bastards hated us...That crash wasn't an acc...' He winced as paranoia stabbed his gut. He was unsure who to trust and worried he'd say too much.

She squinted. "Not an accident?" She faced him, mouth and eyes wide. "You know what happened, don't you? And now Barrett's missing too...It's all related, isn't it?"

He looked into her intelligent blue eyes. He saw a great lady and an excellent cop who he trusted more than most. But he didn't trust her enough to reveal the truth about Charles McKinlay. Or about her boss, George Barrett, and the insane events he'd witnessed in the cavern. And he doubted she'd believe him anyway...Who would believe the tale of a sacrificial, pagan-like ceremony with hundreds of men in strange costumes? She'd probably accuse him of watching too many conspiracy theory documentaries on Netflix...

He'd made an important decision during his sleepless night. He would trust no-one with what he knew. Not until the very end, with the try line in sight.

"Nah, I've got no idea what happened..." he said. "Just reckon it's too early to write it off as an accident...It might be another political assassination? Terrorism? Who knows in the current climate...?"

Her head rocked from side to side. "Okay, sorry, maybe you don't know where Barrett is..." He said

nothing. "And yes, terrorism is a definite possibility..."
She smirked then steered the sedan onto the road.
"Lucky it didn't crash in our area, imagine the
paperwork..."

He sighed under his breath. He'd survived the
interrogation.

Twenty minutes later they arrived at Cobb mine,
produced ID's for the police standing guard at the start
of the driveway, and parked the sedan. Porter saw that
the roadblock from the night before had gone, as had
the multitude of buses. They ducked under crime scene
tape and walked towards a column of smoke. Dust and
ash filled the air. He grimaced, rubbed his nose and
swallowed the grit in his throat. A smell he knew too
well attacked his nostrils. The putrid stench of burnt
human flesh.

They stopped five meters from the edge of the
gigantic crater that'd swallowed the Cobb homestead,
alongside two men in white coveralls and face masks.
The men removed their masks. They gave polite smiles
to her and suspicious nods to him.

Lyn turned to Porter. "Senior Constable Dan Porter,
meet Detective Senior Sergeant Ray Wilkes, the boss at
Broken Hill Crime Scene."

Wilkes, wiry and bald, shook Porter's hand. "With
Inspector Barrett's sudden absence, we've taken over
the investigation."

Porter grunted. "You're bound to do a better job..."

"And," Lyn indicated the second man, "Inspector
Ken Crowley, boss of the Disaster Victim Identification
Unit."

Porter offered a hand to Crowley, who shook it once
with a weak grip.

Crowley stepped to the crater's edge and beckoned them to join him. "Constable Porter, I've read a report filed by Detective Grimes, and the statement you gave him last night. You and Lionel rescued Amber from the homestead, right?"

"Yeah…"

Crowley's eyes narrowed while he fingered a white mustache. "Tell me about the explosion…"

Porter stood beside him and looked at the smoldering crater. Nothing remained of the homestead but a jumbled mess of charred timber, blackened sandstone blocks, and molten metal. He crouched and stared into the crater. Any body parts? A head? Couldn't the others detect the same foul smell of death? He turned to Crowley. "Found anything?"

"No chance," Crowley said. "It would've been a cauldron after the explosion, a giant incinerator. And it might collapse again at any moment. It's too dangerous for my staff. I doubt we'll ever know what, or who is buried here…"

Wilkes cleared his throat. "You didn't answer the question, Porter. Regarding your knowledge of the explosion…"

Porter stood. "Like I told Grimes, it must've happened after we left. The crooks covering their tracks, to destroy evidence? A black SUV chased us, we collided and came off better than they did. Amber was concussed and can't remember anything…I shot and killed one offender. The other, I reckon he died in the accident…We didn't have time to hang around for any fireworks." He smiled at his own sarcasm. "Did you find Lionel?"

Wilkes frowned. "No, but we'll keep looking…"

Porter glanced at Lyn, who dipped her head. Koori elders had collected Lionel's body. "How about the crooks? They been found?"

"That's one of several things puzzling me..." Crowley said. "We found the burnt-out SUV, and evidence that supports a collision and an exchange of gunfire. Why haven't we found dead suspects?"

Porter shrugged. "I reckon more bad guys returned and took the dead'uns away...To protect their identities."

"Plausible...Any clue who these men were?"

"Nah...Carinya's received multiple threats, from multiple groups." Porter's jaw clenched. "I've got no idea who abducted Amber..."

"You need to give us more, Porter," Wilkes said. "A tactical response team remain on standby in Broken Hill. Give them targets to go after..."

"Stand 'em down, it's a waste of time..." Porter pictured the helicopter with the blue stripe as it disappeared above Barrett's house. "The blokes who did this could be anywhere by now..."

Crowley squinted at him. Wilkes scoffed.

Lyn must've sensed the friction. She flashed her eyes at Crowley then stepped closer to him and flicked her head. Golden hair flowed behind her in the slight breeze. "Sir, who owns the Cobb mine these days?"

Crowley smiled at her. He glanced to Wilkes.

Wilkes studied a page on his clipboard. "Here...The mine was decommissioned in '93. It's listed under, Kennard Atkins Mining corporation." His eyes darted to Lyn then Porter. "Mean anything to you?"

She shook her head.

"Nah," Porter said. "Never heard of 'em."

"I have…" a man said from behind them.

Porter turned towards the familiar voice. Bill Thompson wore a loose-fitting grey suit and tie. Jim Thompson ambled alongside in his Sergeant's uniform. They joined the group to form a semi-circle.

"Oh joy…" Lyn whispered.

"Bill," Crowley said. "It's been a while…"

The Thompson's shook hands with Crowley and Wilkes. Bill acknowledged Porter with a nod and ignored Lyn. Jim stood with arms folded across broad chest, face frozen in a scowl.

"Kennard Atkins is a fine company that brought much work to our district," Bill said. "A damn shame when the mine closed."

"And the homestead's been uninhabited?" Crowley said.

"Far as I know…" Bill turned to Jim, who grunted.

"Good enough for me, and it's what I'll be telling the Coroner."

Bill faced Porter. "Glad to hear your missus and kid are okay, son. Young Grimes gave me a heads-up this morning."

Porter noticed a glint in his eye. One of concern, or contempt? "Cheers…"

"And I'm sorry about your friend. You know I didn't want Lionel Roberts in my town but he died a hero by all accounts…"

Porter watched smoke waft from the crater. "Yeah…"

"Sadly, another tragedy struck our town last night." Bill stepped towards him. "I hear you found Mary Barrett dead?"

Porter hesitated and reminded himself to be careful with the answer. George Barrett had been a KA member. Bill had been his mentor and close friend for half a century. And with Bill's probable links to Alec Ferguson and human trafficking, he suspected him of being a KA member too. But how to prove it?

"I went to ask Barrett's assistance for the search," he told Bill. "He wasn't answering his phone…"

"And now old George's gone walkabout…" Bill frowned. "Hate to say, but wonder if he finally lost his marbles and did poor Mary in? And has he now gone off to finish himself?"

"Nah…" Jim unfolded arms and placed hands on hips. "Our suspect's the same homeless Koori that murdered mum…We'll get the bastard. He's been spotted near Bunyip Hill again."

Bill bowed his head. "Rest in peace, my love..."

Jim glared at Porter. "There's been too much strife 'round here since you arrived. Shit follows you like a bad smell, doesn't it?"

Porter resisted the temptation to reply.

"Not to mention the judge and federal police boss killed in the crash this morning." Bill sighed. "Absolutely terrible…"

Porter had held his tongue for long enough. He glanced at Jim. "Shit didn't need to follow me to Crooked River…This place already had plenty of its own variety, with a very unique smell."

Jim snarled at him.

Lyn put a hand to mouth, too late to muffle a laugh.

"Apparently, McKinlay and Watkins were coming to grace Carinya with their presence," Porter said.

"Being the Mayor, Bill, you must've known those blokes were coming?"

"I expected them today, son, yes."

Porter sensed uneasiness behind his confident façade and pressed him. "Did you know Charles McKinlay? Or Watkins?"

Bill huffed to make his annoyance clear. "Watkins? No…Met McKinlay once, briefly. He spoke at a local government conference. A damn shame, he seemed a good man. I've heard he was a bastion of human rights?"

Porter gagged on his tongue. He looked at Crowley, then Wilkes. "Gents, I need to speak with the Mayor in private, a Carinya matter…Give us a minute?"

Crowley nodded. "Certainly, it's time we got back to it."

Porter waited for them to leave. He asked Lyn to walk out of earshot then told Jim to do the same.

"No, Jim stays," Bill said. "As a witness to whatever crap's about to spill from your gob."

Porter grinned. "No worries…" He winked at Jim and enjoyed the sight of his flared nostrils. "Boofhead can stay."

Jim lunged. Bill held him back.

"There something you wanna know, dog?" Jim seethed. "Or you just trying to piss us off?"

Porter smirked. He wanted to have more fun but it wasn't the time. "I need to clarify a few facts, about the years Bill was Senior Sergeant in Crooked River…"

"Such as?" Bill said.

"There've been claims that police officers had inappropriate relations with young Koori girls…That ever come to your notice?"

His head rocked back in laughter. "Been speaking to those pissed old idiots on the mission, haven't you, son? After a lifetime of gin, you think they've got a fucking clue? Think they know what's real, and what's not?" He laughed again. "They're all as crazy as Barrett and his ghosts…" His face lost all expression and voice became stern. "Son, during my time as Senior Sergeant, the blacks were respected, and well taken care of."

"You're prepared to put that on paper? Next week?"

Bill stroked the jacket, near his heart. He grimaced. "Certainly, I've nothing to hide, son. Nothing…"

Porter studied him. He'd spent a career detecting liars, and Bill was either a brilliant actor or had told the truth. "Did you…" He flicked through the folders of questions in his mind and selected the most important one. "Did you ever know a bloke named Alec Ferguson?"

Bill stared at him, face and eyes blank as though he didn't hear or understand the question. Then he seemed to flinch.

Porter repeated the question.

"Alec Ferguson?" Bill said with a bemused frown. "No, doesn't ring a bell. Who is he?"

Porter watched him for clues of a lie. Again, he wasn't sure. A brilliant act? Or the truth?

"Ferguson worked for the Aboriginal Welfare Board in the 1960s," he stated. "He told us that officers from Crooked River, where you worked, aided him in the illegal removal of Koori girls from the mission. Remember that?"

Bill ignored him.

"Bill?" Porter stepped forward. "What do you say about that? About the claims by Alec Ferguson?"

Bill locked eyes on the ground. Jim fumed, and reminded Porter of Queen Cersei's gigantic bodyguard in 'Game of Thrones'.

Porter sensed that Bill had known Ferguson, but maybe, just didn't remember the name. "Okay, you don't know Ferguson…Ever heard the name - White Devil?"

Bill's face flushed red. "What the hell?"

Jim stepped between them. "Piss off, Porter. Stop harassing an old man…"

Bill's mouth gaped open and he grabbed at his heart. "Son, take me to my medicine."

Jim held his elbow. "Let's go." He helped Bill take a few steps down the driveway. He steadied him then marched back to Porter and glared down at him. "Listen dog, he's lost his wife and he's sick. And he sure don't need your ugly mug in his face."

Porter stood his ground, shorter and lighter but far from afraid. "Just doing my job, mate. Police work. Try it sometime…"

"Well, fuck off back to the city and do it. There's plenty of coppers for you to dog on…"

Porter returned the hate-filled stare. "Bill should give a statement. If he's nothing to hide?"

Jim stabbed a finger into his chest. "Hassle my dad again, and I'll come lookin' for ya. And I swear, dog, you'll have nowhere to hide…"

FORTY-FOUR

Porter spent Sunday lunch at the hospital with Jane and Amber. He ate like a sparrow, unable to stop thinking about Bianca Taylor. She'd been in a guarded hospital room when KA had murdered her and they could get to his girls too. He managed to convince Jane and her doctor that she and Amber weren't safe in Crooked River. At 4pm he drove them to the airport and put them on a flight back to Sydney.

He returned to the Carinya residence at dusk and threw Landcruiser keys onto the kitchen table. Caffeine had replaced beer as his favored remedy for stress so he flicked the kettle on. His phone vibrated. He fished it from a trouser pocket. He looked at the caller ID and swore, tired of talking shop.

"Steve," he said, "good to hear from you."

Steve Williams laughed. "Doesn't sound like it..."

"Sorry mate, I've been flat out like a lizard drinking..."

"Port, relax, I'm kidding. I heard what happened...Are your girls okay now?"

"All's good, they're on their way to Sydney." Porter leaned against the kitchen bench and ran a hand across stinging eyeballs. "Had to get them out. It's the fucking wild west this place..."

"Sorry. Should've called soon as I heard but shit has hit the fan here too."

"No worries, mate. I saw a bit on the tele, that the riots have kicked off again?"

"Kicked off is an understatement…We knew kooris would be pissed when Betts got bail, but not like this. Anyhow, we'll handle it…Why didn't you fly back with Jane for a bit of a break? Have you got urgent leads to follow up?"

Urgent leads? Porter considered telling him all he knew - that KA had abducted Amber, about the insane ceremony involving McKinlay and Barrett, about Watkins, about KA's confirmed links to Kennard Atkins and their ownership of Cobb mine. He contemplated revealing what he knew of the Cumal Files because Williams had allies in high places who'd pay a fortune for such information. Allies with access to resources that would help him find the files and arrest KA's bosses. But could they be trusted?

Porter began a reply then stopped. Sudden paranoia choked him, a giant python around his throat. He said nothing, and in that moment doubted Williams' motives for enquiring about the investigation. His attitude towards Kennard Atkins had confused Porter from the start. He'd been hesitant, almost resistant to label them a suspect in Sydney's abductions. Despite the evidence…

And it was Williams who'd urged him to join Lionel's investigation team. Why? To keep tabs on him and monitor Carinya's progress? Why? Was he an associate, or member of KA? Steve Williams had changed…Did Porter still know him? Had he ever?

"I can't fly back to Sydney yet, 'cos Lionel's burial's on Wednesday," Porter told him. "Will head back on Thursday, then return next week when the new Carinya blokes start…"

"Oh, shit…Lionel. His death saddened us all. A gentleman, one of the good guys."

"Yeah…"

"His funeral's on Wednesday? I'd hoped to go but they're having state funerals for McKinlay and Watkins that morning."

"It's not a funeral for Lio…An Aboriginal burial ceremony," Porter said. "Local elders have prepared a plot near the mission, sacred ground or whatever…He'll be happy there rather than forgotten in some overgrown graveyard, next to a church he'd lost faith in…" He paused and heard Lionel's infectious laugh. It made him smile. "Koori elders reckon I'm the only white fella invited…"

Williams chuckled. "Hey, I forgot to tell you…Claire's spoken to Interpol analysts in Singapore and Cape Town. Nothing came from the leads concerning the shipping containers. And the crook who owned the farm, he's dead…"

"Expected as much…Azelia, now Carinya. It's been one dead end after another."

"Yes, and it's doing my fucking head in…Listen, I asked if you had leads or suspects for Ambers' abduction. You didn't answer…"

"Nah, zero suspects or leads. I killed two crooks but their bodies were gone when local cops arrived at the scene."

"What have Jane and Amber said?"

He hesitated. "They can't remember a thing. Both were knocked out."

"I can hear it in your voice, Port…What aren't you telling me?"

Porter didn't want to lie but stuck to his vow to trust no-one. "There's nothing more, mate."

"Why'd they take Amber? They must have links to the traffickers? Or this, 'KA' organization we're looking for?"

"What's with the interrogation?" Porter shouted into the phone. He wasn't angry but wanted to sound it, in the hope Williams would back off. "I don't fucking know…Alright?"

"Hey, careful, I'm still your boss…" After a few seconds Williams sighed. "Shit, Port, I didn't call to argue with you…I just hoped for the slightest clue, something to pull us out of this quagmire. And if you don't have it, I'm worried these pricks will get away with every abduction and murder they've committed."

"Your blokes need patience until more leads develop overseas…I've gotta focus on Carinya for now, and getting Lionel's inquiry…International media coverage and political pressure – it's the best hope for these girls."

"Understood…Well, at least the abductions have stopped. But I worry Sydney's lost interest in those still missing and they'll soon be forgotten…"

"Not if Carinya can force a public inquiry?"

"Yes, I guess so…In the meantime, you need to find the historical evidence that Lionel was convinced exists in that outback shithole."

Porter saw himself raise the lid of a wooden chest and gaze upon the Cumal Files. "That's the plan, mate... And for the record, I reckon you're spot on, that this KA mob did hurt my girls. And when I find the mongrels, I'll be dishing out my own form of bush justice…"

FORTY-FIVE

"Bloody hell, dad, turn your frickin' phone off will you," Jim Thompson said with a slur. He pointed to writhing naked bodies on the television in the corner. "Between it and your porn, how the fuck can we concentrate on cards? And it's ten-thirty, who the fuck keeps calling you this late?"

Bill Thompson took a cigar from his mouth. He blew smoke towards the cloud hanging over the dining room table then leaned back in the chair. "It's Dan Porter…The prick hasn't left me alone since Sunday at Cobb mine…He wanted to interview me tonight and I told him to fuck off, 'cos Wednesday night's poker night. Right boys?" He raised a whiskey-filled glass to the four men around the table.

Jim guzzled beer from a bottle. "If Porter turns up, I'll kill him…"

"I know it, son," Bill said with a frown. "And you wouldn't have to if these useless turds had finished him off on top of Bunyip Hill…" He pointed to the three-man assassination team sat opposite. They wore black t-shirts and cargo pants. "It'll take a Thompson to finish the job…" His face lit up as he slammed cards onto the table. "Now, beat that beauty."

"Fuck, another straight?" Chubby KA72 scratched his red beard. "Very suss…"

"Now, now, 72, stop whinging…I've given you boys refuge in my home, and it's only fair I take your money."

KA72 threw cards into the air. "Your deal, 256," he said to the muscular man in his mid-twenties seated next to him.

KA198 swore. He was the team's third member, of similar age and build to KA256. "I'm out, broke…"

The doorbell buzzed, louder than the moans coming from the television. The assassination team jumped to their feet and drew pistols from shoulder holsters.

Jim pulled a Glock from the utility belt slung over his chair. He glared at KA72. "Get down the hallway and hide in the bedrooms. Porter's here."

"Fucking relax," Bill said. "It's Ronny from the pub, delivering beer…Don't freeze like you've pissed your pants. Let the boy in."

Jim strolled towards the front door while the other soldiers sat. He returned carrying two cartons of beer.

Ronny Goodwin stood behind him holding two more cartons. He wore khaki bib and brace overalls, too tight at the shoulders and ample gut, over a red flannelette shirt he'd rolled to elbows. He greeted them with a shy smile.

Jim peered at Bill. "Okay if Ronny stays for a beer?" He placed the cartons on the kitchen bench. Ronny did the same.

Bill waved Ronny towards him. "Pull up a chair, son. Have a drink."

KA72's face turned crimson. "Wait…Who's this guy?" He stared at Ronny. "Can we trust him?"

Jim pushed Ronny into a chair, slapped his back and handed him a beer. "There's no-one I'd trust more. Ronny's one of us…" He slapped him again. "Aren't you, mate?"

Ronny coughed and swatted cigar smoke. "Yep, that's what you always ta, ta, tell me."

"Fuck me." KA256 sat back in the chair. "You sharing our secrets with a retard now?"

Jim cuffed him across the back of the head. "Enough," he growled into his ear. "Don't forget, it's Ronny who saw you and Fred Klose with Rhodes at Bunyip Hill...Carinya hammered him, but Ronny never said a word...So lay off."

Bill pointed to the assassination team. "Ronny, these are mates of ours from the city."

Ronny rocked back and forward towards the table. He sipped beer then rested the bottle on his gut and turned towards the television. A dark-skinned girl kissed a fat white man. "Wow," he said, "she's pretty hot."

Jim laughed. "But not as hot as Lyn Foster, eh?"

"No other girl is like Lyn..."

Jim punched his shoulder. "Too bad she wants me, mate."

Ronny winced and pretended to throw a jab. "Hey, Lyn's mine."

Bill chuckled in between puffs of his cigar. "Ronny, you think the skank in that movie's a good sort?" He wobbled and burped. "Down the hall on the right's my darkroom." He signaled for Ronny to stand. "There're two boxes on the bench, bring me the smaller one. And no need for a sticky beak...Go on son, I've something to show you." His glazed eyes swept around the table. "All of you."

Ronny wandered down the hallway.

"That reminds me..." Jim took sheets of folded paper from shirt pocket. He handed a page to each man.

Two spares fell to the floor. "I printed these today, as a memento. Thought you'd appreciate them..."

KA72 laid the sheet on the table. It was a photo, of a group in black combat fatigues and balaclavas. They posed outdoors with a naked woman. "Hmm...Jane. Gotta say, she did have amazing tits." He winked at Jim. "Ta, one for the album..."

The others giggled at their photos. They hid them from view when Ronny returned with a blue shoebox.

"That's the one," Bill said as he took the box from Ronny. He dropped bundles on the table. He removed the rubber bands that bound them and spread the photos in front of him. Tens of them, all in black and white. Some depicted white men in sexual acts with young Koori girls. In others, girls posed naked, barely in puberty.

Ronny sat back and sipped beer while the others sifted through the photos. They grinned and whistled.

Bill glanced sideways at Jim. "These pics are what your mum found, bless her soul...Wish she hadn't..."

Jim grunted then sculled beer.

Bill plucked a photo from the table and handed it to Ronny. "Now, she's a beauty...Not bad eh, son?"

Ronny cringed. "She looks ta, ta, too young."

KA72 scoffed. "That's the best part, dickhead." He held a photo in front of Bill's face. "This one looks a bit older?"

Bill nodded.

"There're some stunners in here, boss," KA198 said as he studied a photo.

"Yep, I had plenty of scrumptious black bunnies in my day..." Bill pulled a bundle covered in black plastic from the box and unwrapped it. "But this one was by far my favorite girl from the mission…"

Ronny sipped beer and watched the porn movie.

Bill held the photos in two hands. His eyes sparkled while he flicked through them. "Hmm, hmm." Head tilted, he licked lips. "Had fun times with this one..." He handed photos to KA72.

KA72 studied some then passed them around the table. "Gorgeous..." He let out a low whistle. "She's well-developed. Must've had some whitey in her…" He looked at Ronny. "Same caramel color as our friend here..."

"She was a teenager in those pics, but only eleven the first time I had her...Crazy bitch fought like hell." Bill made a devious sniggering sound. "Had to whack her to stop the screaming. Cut her open and she didn't flinch. She was prouder than a stallion's cock and had more balls than any of the Koori men, who never once tried to stop us."

"Stop, 'us'? How many of you went there?" Jim said.

"Oh, more than twenty over the years. Most have already dropped from the perch…"

"And Barrett?"

"George would drive me out there, but never partook. Was too smitten with Mary…Plus he got spooked out there one time and…" Bill hesitated then frowned as he glanced at Ronny. Ronny stared at the TV and seemed oblivious to the conversation around him. "Did you boys hear what George said in the cavern before we escaped?"

"Yeah, the fucking lunatic…" Jim said.

"He'd been talking about those Koori ghosts for years…" Bill laughed before his smile vanished and he continued like the melancholic drunk he was. "Shame about George and Mary, they were good friends of ours…" He turned to KA72. "When you took the files, did Mary suffer?"

"Nope, it was a clean hit…"

"Good, and speaking of cleanliness…When you put the helicopter down with our boys in it, are you certain the explosion would've incinerated them? We can't have investigators finding their gun-shot wounds…"

"Don't concern yourself, boss, that bird exploded hotter than Vesuvius. Felt it as I landed a hundred meters away…Forensic cops will be lucky to find a bone, let alone flesh…"

"Who'd you put in as the pilot?"

"Fred Klose. He was already half cooked when we took his body from the car wreck. Cops are saying his identity can't be confirmed. All the flight records have been destroyed."

Bill dipped his head and sucked the cigar.

Photos of Bill's favorite girl made their way to Jim. His face screwed as he studied one. "Ewh, fuck me, dad, you could've said that you're in some of these…Really didn't need to see your fat guts and wrinkly little cock…"

Bill smirked. "Pass them to Ronny then if you don't appreciate true beauty…"

"Is this favorite of yours still around?" Jim grinned. "Still a good sort?"

"Christ, son, she'd be well over sixty now. Heard a rumor in, shit, '68 or thereabouts, that she was up the duff with my kid. She would've been aged thirteen or fourteen by then…"

Jim's eyebrows furrowed. "Fuck, what happened to her and the baby?"

"No idea…She disappeared and was never seen around here again. Searched the city for a bit, around Redfern, and spoke to the locals. No-one knew of her."

Jim grunted and passed photos to Ronny.

Ronny held one at arm's length and turned his head away.

"Go on, son," Bill said, "look at her... None these days do what that firecracker could." He pumped a fist at shoulder height. All except Ronny joined him in a chorus of laughter.

Ronny thumbed through more photos. His forehead wrinkled. Others shouted and cursed and started a new game of poker. Bill sorted photos. Jim filled beer cartons with empty bottles and soggy cigars.

Ronny threw the photos of Bill's favorite girl onto the table and dropped his bottle to the timber floor. The raucous banter stopped. All eyes fixed on him.

Bill chortled. "Christ son, I know they're raunchy pictures, but didn't think you'd get that excited..."

Ronny picked the bottle from the floor. "Sa, sa, sorry."

"What's up, Ron?" Jim yanked a thumb towards KA72. "You've gone whiter than ginger here. Feeling crook?"

"Yeah, bit dizzy from the beer." Ronny rubbed his gut. "Haven't had dinner yet." Hands trembled as he drew the photos into a pile.

"Ronny, I'll pack those away in a sec," Bill said. "Grab a cloth and clean up the beer." He burped and wobbled to his feet. "Going for a piss…"

"I'll throw a few pies in the microwave. Ronny can eat with us." Jim strolled into the kitchen. "Feeling a bit peckish meself..."

Bill returned five minutes later, scooped photos from the table and wrapped them in plastic.

Jim put a plate of meat pies on the table. "Tucker time..."

Ronny stood when he'd finished cleaning the floor. "Thanks, but I gotta go. Emma wants me back there…"

Bill squinted at him. "Alright, son…But as Jim said, you've been loyal to our cause. Stay a minute to help us toast old friends."

Ronny said nothing.

"We'll have the blue, son," Bill told Jim.

Jim grabbed a bottle of Johnny Walker blue label from a side cabinet. He filled six glasses and handed one to each man. They stood.

"Unfortunately, for obvious reasons, we couldn't attend their funerals today…" Bill said in a voice tinged with sadness. "But those boys know we're thinking of them all the same. Here's to lost brothers. Chuck McKinlay and Boozer Watkins." He raised the glass. "Leaders, friends, and great, great men."

"To brothers lost," four of them said.

Ronny pretended to drink.

"As you boys know," Bill continued, "the highest-ranked, remaining High Council member is yours truly." He grinned. "From this moment forth I will hold the title of KA1, a Regal Lord, Supreme Leader of the Knights of Alba..."

340

"To our new leader," Jim led the toast. "Si Diis Placet."

"Pleased be the gods," all but Ronny replied.

"Thank you, boys, thank you," Bill said. "Sadly, inexplicably, in the madness of the past week, we've also lost our Secretary, KA6." He stepped closer to Jim and his blood-shot eyes scanned his face. "Jim, my son, you've made me a proud old man." He took a brass skeleton key from breast pocket. "Take care of this key and the history it protects...Fellow Knights, I present to you," his arm extended towards Jim with upturned palm, "our new Secretary, KA6, keeper of the Cumal Files..."

"To KA6," all but Ronny said.

Jim embraced his father. "I'll protect them with my life."

"Damn right you will..." Bill thumped a fist against Jim's chest. They separated and he handed him the key. "No son of mine will be the first to lose them." He sculled whiskey then sat and continued sorting photos.

Ronny placed his glass on the table. "Thanks for the drink. Have ta, ta, to go. Emma will kill me." He moved into the kitchen, towards the front door.

Jim slapped his back as he went past. "Give my love to Lyn..."

Ronny hurried through the kitchen and front foyer then tugged the door open. He stepped through the doorway and began to close the door behind him.

"Stop!" Bill yelled from inside. "Get back here you black bastard. Right now!"

Ronny's shoulders slumped. He froze for a few seconds then shuffled back to the dining room.

Bill sat with palms on the table. He breathed loud and labored. Jim and the other KA soldiers stood behind him with arms folded.

Ronny stopped in front of Bill and bowed his head. "Yes, Mr Thompson? Sa, sa, something wrong?"

"Well, son...You tell me."

Ronny's eyes searched the ceiling. "What do you mean?"

"Look at me!" Bill waited until Ronny did. "I've always had fifty photos of my beauty. But just now I've counted only forty-nine..." He snorted as he stood, an enraged bull ready to charge, face redder than a matador's muleta. "So, tell me son, where's the missing photo? 'Cos if I don't get it this minute, you're a dead man."

FORTY-SIX

Ronny stood in front of a livid Bill Thompson. He kept his head bowed and gulped for air like a fish on a jetty.

"Well?" Bill slurred. "I asked you a question, son...Did you take one of my photos or not?"

"No, I never," Ronny blurted.

"Bullshit." Bill turned to Jim. "The bastard's stolen it. Search him."

"No, look." Ronny turned all pockets inside out and held his palms open.

Bill moaned. "Christ, son, think I'm a fucking idiot? Do a proper search, Jim." He fixed eyes on Ronny. "Last chance…"

Ronny blinked. Tears welled. "Got no photo, Mr Thompson. Promise."

"Fuck me, dad, give the fella a break," Jim said. "I aint searching him..."

Bill glared. "Jim, do it. He's stolen my girl."

"You're pissed and can't remember how many photos you had…" Jim placed an arm around Ronny's shoulders. "And why would he take one? He only looked 'cos you forced him to…"

Bill's brow furrowed as he watched Ronny in silence. "I'm drunk as ten men, and it's been an emotional day…" He dismissed him with a flick of a hand. "Go on, fuck off back to the pub…And if you tell anyone what you've heard here tonight, I'll kill you."

Porter and Lyn Foster sat on stools along the Crooked River Hotel's main bar, two of the four remaining patrons. The barman Patto, in his mid-thirties and resembling the wild pigs he liked to hunt, poured beers. Emma Rowe bent next to him and chatted with Porter and Lyn while she tapped a keg.

Ronny Goodwin rushed to the bar and panted as he leaned on it.

Emma straightened and scowled at him. "You took your time…"

"Sa, sa, sorry. Bill made me have a beer."

"Well, Bill Thompson's not your frickin' boss, and Patto's got more deliveries for you."

Ronny stepped towards Porter. "Can we ta, ta, talk?"

Porter noticed his flushed face. Couldn't he have a few quiet beers without some jealous drongo looking for a scrap? "What's up, mate?"

"Sa, sa, something important." Ronny glanced at Lyn. "In private…"

Porter huffed. "No worries…" He put the beer down and led him away from the bar. "What?"

Ronny spun in all directions as though worried someone would hear. "Remember when Lionel asked me about that cop who died at Bunyip Hill?"

Intrigue wiped Porter's bemused grin from his face. "John Rhodes…And you told him you didn't see anything…"

"Well, I lied. I did sa, sa, see them fellas who killed him...And I just sa, sa, saw one of them now."

Porter grabbed his biceps in both hands and pulled him in. "What?" He'd said it louder than intended and turned towards the bar. Patto had moved closer and stacked glasses on shelves. "Where?"

Ronny gulped. His eyes darted to the bar and back.

Porter read the fear in them. "C'mon mate, tell me. No-one can hear us, you're safe…"

"I delivered beer to Bill Thompson's house…" Ronny pulled a piece of crumpled paper from his overalls. "I sa, sa, stole this picture and hid it in my undies," he whispered. He laid the paper on a table and flattened it. He pointed to the only man in the picture without a balaclava over his face and head. "This one with the red beard was there when Rhodes died…And he's at Bill's house now."

Porter ripped the picture from under Ronny's hand and studied it. His mouth fell open, chest sagged. Five men posed for a photo. All were dressed the same as those who'd chased him up Bunyip Hill. A red-bearded man nuzzled Jane's naked breast while a much taller one held her in bulging arms.

The taller one wore a tight black t-shirt that exposed a tattooed forearm. Porter squinted and brought the picture closer. A tattoo of a green and red Celtic cross. He gritted teeth to stop bitter vomit spewing from his mouth. He'd seen the same tattoo before. On the same muscular forearm.

He knew from his first day in Crooked River that the tattooed man, Detective Sergeant Jim Thompson, despised him. He'd labeled him an internal witness 'dog', and made his suspicions obvious. And, as heir to a property portfolio threatened by Carinya's negative influence on investors, Jim also had financial reasons to force him from the town.

But when Porter realized the chief motivation behind Jim's hatred, it jabbed him between the eyes. He shook his head like a stunned boxer. The men in the picture, Jim included, were KA soldiers. He'd suspected that Bill was a KA member too. He now had zero doubt.

He scoffed at his own stupidity, that he'd missed what seemed so obvious. The Knights of Alba had been active in Crooked River for decades. Bill Thompson and George Barrett had led the way. Lionel's witness Shirley had known it, suspected their involvement in present-day human trafficking and sent Carinya to stop them. He'd finally identified KA members. But did they hold the evidence he'd need to destroy their entire network? Did they possess the Cumal Files?

Porter stared at the picture and focused on Jim and the bearded man who'd humiliated Jane. Nostrils flared. A shudder of loathing ran down his body. He stored their cruel faces in the front of his mind and vowed to kill them both.

He nudged Ronny. "How many blokes inside the house?"

"Umm…Five."

"Guns?"

"Yep, in their belts. And rifles in the corner."

"What did they talk about?"

"Umm..." He looked at the ceiling. "Fellas who died. Bill called them…Chuck? Boozer? And other things I forget and didn't really understand…"

Porter frowned. He'd heard the name Chuck not so long ago. But who'd said it, and where? He searched the name registry in his brain for a clue. Nothing. "What else you see?"

"A box."

Porter's pulse quickened. "What kind?"

"A sa, sa, small blue one." Ronny's face turned crimson. "Bill keeps his photos in it. I got it from his darkroom and th--"

"Darkroom?" Porter recalled a conversation he'd had with Lyn regarding Kathleen Thompson's murder. She'd been denied access to Bill's 'darkroom.' "Was it only the blue box in there?"

"Yep."

Porter sighed. He'd hoped for more.

Ronny's eyes flashed. "Wait, there was another box…"

"What did it look like?"

"Bigger. Kind of a brown color."

"Wooden?"

"Yep, a wooden box. Like the ones pirates keep treasure in…"

Porter's heart jumped. *The Cumal Files?* He jabbed Ronny's shoulder. "Good man..." He turned to call Lyn and flinched when he saw her next to him.

"You guys okay?" she said. "I heard you getting excited."

"All good, no worries..." Porter winked at Ronny then turned to her. "Stay here and secure the pub. Gotta go…" He juggled car keys and hurried towards the exit.

"Where you going?"

"Bill Thompson's."

"What?" She ran ahead to block him. "Why?"

"To arrest the blokes who took Amber…" He stepped around her and yelled over his shoulder. "Have Broken Hill send a tactical response team asap. These blokes are well-armed. Call out PolAir and block all air

347

traffic in and out. I'll phone Steve Williams en-route and have more troops sent from Sydney..."

"Thompson? Amber? Well-armed?" She followed him outside. Ronny was close behind.

Porter got into the Landcruiser and wound the window down.

"You can't go alone?" Her eyes pleaded. "Dan, wait for backup."

"There's no time."

"At least use local GD crews to set up a perimeter. It's suicide..."

He scoffed. "What, and trust Crooked River coppers?"

She moved closer and wrapped a hand around his forearm. "I'm coming with you..."

He removed her hand. "Cheers, but I've gotta do this alone." He turned the key and the Landcruiser roared. He looked past her. "Ronny, come here mate."

She shook her head and went inside the pub.

Ronny stepped up to the window. "Yep?"

"Stay here, lock yourselves inside, and protect Emma..."

He nodded, his chest puffed like a peacock.

"Tell me this, mate, quick...Why are you helping me now?"

Ronny took a photo from a pocket and handed it to him.

Porter studied the black and white photo. A Koori girl stared into the camera with black eyes full of contempt. She looked to be in her early teens. She had a doll-like face, its only blemish a scar that ran from mouth to chin.

"Who's this?" Porter said.

348

"I sa, sa, stole that picture too. It's Bill's favorite girl...He has more photos of him doing ta, ta, terrible things to her." Ronny's chin dropped to chest.

The Carinya team had considered Bill their main suspect for the historical rapes on Crooked River mission. Ronny's evidence confirmed it.

Porter noticed his trembling hands. "Seeing those photos has upset you, mate. I understand..."

Ronny glared. "No, you don't..." He thrust the photo in front of Porter's face and pointed to the girl. "I've sa, sa, seen that scar on her chin since I was a baby." Veins at temples quivered, his head a purple balloon ready to burst. "I'm helping you 'cos Bill Thompson's a rapist pig...And I'm his bastard sa, sa, son."

FORTY-SEVEN

Porter turned into Bill Thompson's driveway and killed the Landcruiser's headlights. He drove at walking pace towards the house, guided by silver moonlight. A hundred meters from the house he parked and continued on foot. He reached the carport, ducked to his left, found cover behind its brick wall and peered into the dark parking space. Empty? He cursed. He'd forgotten the torch.

He ripped the Glock from its shoulder holster and aimed at the front door as he crept towards it. Stairs creaked, he climbed to the veranda. He stopped to listen. A cicada choir broke the still night. He rushed to the front door and saw it ajar then listened for movement inside. Nothing. His denim jacket scraped against sandstone as he pushed the door open and slithered through the gap. He stood in the dark entry foyer and waited for his eyes to adjust.

He recalled his previous visit to the house and remembered that the bedrooms and darkroom were down the hallway to his right. The kitchen and dining room were straight ahead and led to a rumpus room and rear veranda. The living room, with the bar and Bill's photos, was off the hallway to the left.

Curiosity urged him to head for the darkroom, but instinct overruled and told him to first find and eliminate any threats. He stepped forward into the dining room. His nose twitched, cigar smoke and stale beer fumes attacked it. He tuned ears to the clock's tick-tock, and dripping water. Too quiet…

His fingers found the light switch and flicked it on. Beer bottles and playing cards covered a table. Cigars smoldered in ashtrays. Half-eaten pies spilled open on plates. He felt the bottom of a beer bottle. Still cold…They'd been in the room less than half an hour ago, as Ronny had said, and left in a hurry. He ran to the rear veranda. Eyes searched the yard and paddocks further afield. Nothing. He swore. He'd lost the Cumal Files. Again...

He trudged back into the dining room like a footballer who'd missed a penalty in a World Cup final. He reached for the ceiling, stretched and exhaled. A tapeworm of failure chewed his gut. A voice of self-doubt urged him to quit, told him he'd done his best but wouldn't succeed. He clenched fists. He'd risked too much to give up now. Self-doubt could go fuck itself…

He walked towards the front door, decided he'd call Lyn from the Landcruiser and wait for the Crime Scene Unit. When he reached the entry foyer he stopped and listened. A noise from the hallway on his right? Yes. The unmistakable sound of a crackling fire. He crept down the hall towards it and saw an orange glow coming from the living room.

He stopped outside the room. Why hadn't he heard or seen the fire earlier? He aimed the Glock at the door and visualized what lay beyond it. Sofas at the far end to the left, in front of the fireplace. Bar and shelves on the far right. Knight in armor, and photos, against the left side wall…He readied himself with a deep breath, pushed the door open and stepped into the room. He swiveled and swept it with the Glock.

In dim firelight he saw a human shape stretched across a sofa. He stepped towards it with Glock aimed and opened his mouth to yell. Bright lights came on. He froze, eyes trained on the sofa, then frowned. The 'human shape' was a cushion.

"Hello, Porter…"

He spun towards the opposite end of the room and aimed the Glock at Jim Thompson.

Jim tapped a wooden box sat on the bench top. "Is this what you're after?" His crooked smile personified evil. He wore a black t-shirt and matching cargo pants. "I've been looking forward to this day..."

"Not as much as I have…" Porter eyed the pistol beside the box. "Go for the gun, you're dead…"

Jim sniggered. "Come on, where's the fun in that? I could've finished you already…But you don't deserve a bullet in the back. You're gunna die a lot slower than that…"

Porter stepped right and pressed his back against the wall. He aimed the Glock and shuffled towards him, mindful of the knight in armor blocking his path.

Jim moved towards the door.

Porter darted forward to stop him and tripped on the knight's steel boot. He tumbled forward. His right hand opened in reflex as he landed on his elbow and the Glock clattered onto the timber floor. He got to his knees.

Jim stood over him with the Glock aimed down. He grunted and told Porter to stand. "Well I'll be…" He kept the gun aimed while he straightened the knight and returned a steel lance to its gloved hand. "Dad's old piece of junk came in handy after all."

Porter glanced at the wooden box. "The new secretary, eh?" He whistled, low-pitched. "You must be chuffed that Barrett went mad?"

Jim smiled as though enjoying the game. "Barrett was a treacherous leech. I'm glad he's dead." He sneered. "And yeah, I'm the new Secretary, keeper of the files."

"Why didn't you run and hide like your daddy has?"

"He's the Supreme Leader now…I've stayed behind to protect him."

He pointed to the wooden box. "But you've risked the files?"

"There's no risk…I'm not the one who dies tonight."

"You seem confident for a weak bastard who hurts innocent women? I don't reckon you're the hard man you pretend to be…"

"That's rich, coming from a grub who shoots unarmed kids and rolls over on his mates." Jim's grey eyes twitched. "What innocent women?"

Eddy Tindall and Ian Betts' faces flashed through Porter's mind. He swallowed sour guilt. "I know what you did to Jane…And Amber at Cobb mine."

"Prove it..."

He raised arms above his head. "Proof's here, in my jacket pocket."

Jim stepped forward and snatched crumpled paper from the pocket. He kept one eye on Porter and unfolded it. A mask of perversion covered his face. "Ah, selfies and tattoos, eh? The nemesis of modern bad guys…" The mask changed to one of contempt. "This picture proves nothing, there're thousands of guys with similar tattoos. And Ronny's a simple fool who thinks he saw something. No-one will listen…If he's still alive…"

"I've got plenty of evidence, more than I need." Porter scowled, hands curled into fists, teeth ground his jaw. He wanted to lunge and take him down, but not with a gun pointed at his head. He ignored the tinderbox of hate that sparked deep inside and willed patience.

Jim grinned like a deranged child torturing a kitten. "A damn shame when young Amber got away, she would've been sweet." He paused, as though awaiting a reaction. "Sweet as honey, just like little Tilly Johnson was…"

Porter huffed. "Tilly Johnson? You're the paedo Tommy Davis protected?"

"Tommy was loyal to our family. He respected the Thompson name."

"Yeah? Too bad your sons are gunna grow up ashamed of it...I know plenty about Bill's dirty past, and present. Can't wait to show the world what a perverted and cowardly bastard he is."

He laughed and waved the gun in Porter's face. "Got nothing on him and you know it. The only witnesses were the black bitch in Scotland and Alec Ferguson. Both have been taken care of. You failed to protect 'em, just like the Tindall girl…"

Porter heard Nadia's giggle. He cringed. "You're the one who took her from the park?"

"Nup, but I saw her die after we'd had our fun…"

Porter fumed. His throat burned. He willed himself to remain calm. "Other victims will come forward. You can't kill 'em all…"

Jim scoffed. "I've killed plenty to protect our name and the organization. My mother included..." He locked cold eyes on him. "Think I'll stop? Wrong. I'll do whatever it takes."

"You're fucking sicker than I thought...Murdered your own mother? But you let Jane and Amber live. Why?"

"Wanted to see the look on your face..." His mouth formed a savage grin. "When I told you how much I loved licking the sweat of fear from Jane's chocolate tits."

Porter shook as the volcano inside him erupted. He ducked onto haunches and swayed to his right. A bullet whizzed past his left ear. A second shot missed again. He sprang up like an NFL linebacker and drove his shoulder into ribs.

Jim winced. His giant frame doubled over.

Porter reached for the gun and managed to wedge his right index finger behind the trigger. He tried to rip it from Jim's grasp. They struggled chest to chest, two bulls refusing to give ground as they wrestled for control of the gun. He dug his left thumb into Jim's eyeball.

Jim howled then responded with a headbutt.

Porter's nose crunched. He yelped. Jim shoved fingers up his blood-filled nostrils and ripped at them.

They grunted. Snot blew forth like steam. When they released their grip on each other at the same time, the freed hands grappled in a wrestling match of their own.

Porter's muscles ached and lactic acid burned as he lost the battle of sheer power. Despite its risky nature – it would leave him vulnerable if it failed – he decided it was time for his 'last ditch' move. He dropped his weight and leaned back to open a gap between them, then used his right hand to twist Jim's left wrist. He tugged Jim's arm down and extended it to expose the elbow joint. At the same time, he pulled his left hand free of the grapple and swung it across his body. Its flexed palm drove into Jim's elbow.

Bone cracked. Jim screamed. The gun fell to the floor.

Porter snatched the Glock up and aimed it at him.

Jim stood wide-eyed. His disfigured arm dangled.

Porter rushed to the bar and kept the Glock aimed at him. He removed the magazine from Jim's pistol, emptied all its bullets into a whiskey bottle and racked the barrel slide to eject the last one. He repeated the process with his own Glock. He left both pistols on the bench top and carried the empty magazines to the fireplace.

"Let's do this the old-fashioned way?" He inhaled to slow his racing heart then threw the magazines into the fire. "A fair fight…"

Jim studied him as though analyzing the odds of winning a fight with one arm. He moved to the knight in armor and took the steel lance in his right hand. He juggled its weight then pointed the sharp end at him. "Now it's a fair fight..."

Porter threw his jacket off. He stepped into the middle of the room and crouched into a southpaw boxing stance.

Jim raised the lance and came forward to meet him.

They circled, stares intense.

Porter feigned a move to his left and ducked under the swinging lance. He smashed his right fist into Jim's injured arm then spun away out of range.

Jim gritted teeth and looked down at his elbow.

Porter lunged again.

Jim swung the lance lower this time. Porter's legs were swept from under him and he landed on his back.

Jim seized the advantage and dropped his full weight onto him. He held the lance across his neck and rammed his fist against Porter's throat.

Porter tried to wriggle from under him but couldn't move. He felt hot breath on his face and saw maniacal eyes. He tried to force his hands under the lance and push up. Hopeless. His head filled with blood. The lance's cold steel crushed his windpipe and he gasped for air. His consciousness slipped, dizzy without oxygen. He pounded fists against Jim's temples but he didn't flinch.

He closed eyes, mustered the last of his strength and aimed a punch.

Jim swayed his head to avoid it. His injured arm swung towards the floor.

Porter grabbed its elbow with his right hand and yanked it down. Ligaments popped.

Jim yelped. His right hand released its grip on the lance and reached for the mangled elbow. The lance clattered onto timber floor then rolled across it.

Porter gasped to fill his lungs. He threw Jim off then rolled onto his stomach and reached for the lance. Fingers brushed steel.

Jim grabbed Porter's calf and pulled him away from it.

He pushed hands into the floor, desperate to stop the slide.

"I'm gunna finish ya, dog." Jim released his grip.

Porter heard a click and flipped onto his back.

Jim rose, a Bowie knife in hand. "Gunna cut your soft, bleeding heart right outta ya."

Porter watched him advance. He'd be stabbed if he tried to stand. He dug heels into the floor and pushed himself across it. His right hand reached back and felt for the lance.

Jim stood over him with the knife gripped like a dagger. He fell onto him, chest to chest. His massive weight pinned him to the floor.

Porter's fingers searched for the lance. He pushed his left hand against Jim's shoulder and tried to stop the knife but its jagged blade inched towards his chest. Adrenaline flooded his shaking body. Every muscle strained. Every sinew twitched.

Jim snarled and grunted. The blade pierced Porter's t-shirt and sliced skin.

Porter grimaced. His eyes watered as he watched bright blood bubble through his shirt. His left arm went numb, unable to resist any longer. He saw excitement in Jim's flushed face and realized he had seconds to live.

He pictured Jane's beautiful face and heard Amber's playful laugh…And then his right hand felt steel. He gripped the lance like a javelin thrower. He swung it out to the side then slammed its blunt end against Jim's temple.

Jim groaned and slumped off him. He lay face down on the floor. Still.

Porter winced as he pulled the knife from his pectoral muscle. He dropped it, then used the lance to stand. He held it one hand with the sharp end pointed forward.

Without warning Jim rolled onto his back. He grabbed the knife and stabbed at Porter's knee.

Porter jumped back to avoid it.

Jim lunged again, missed and left his chest exposed.

Porter speared the steel lance into it. Flesh tore. Ribs cracked.

Jim stared. Blood spewed from his mouth.

Porter panted as he stood over him. He pictured Jane, Amber, Lionel, and Nadia. The faces of the abducted girls and countless others Jim had made suffer. He leaned on the lance and plunged it deeper into his black heart. The ease with which he ignored whimpers for mercy shocked him, yet he smiled as Jim Thompson took a final breath.

He released the lance and hurried to the bar. The wooden box was a meter wide and almost as deep. A padlock secured its front. A padlock too thick and strong for a bullet to shatter. Could he lever the box open with the lance? No, that might damage it…Where's the key? He rushed to Jim and turned his pockets inside out. A worn skeleton key fell to the floor. Would it unlock the Cumal Files?

He inserted the key in the padlock. He sucked a breath and sent a prayer to any god who'd listen. He turned it. The padlock clicked open. He sighed and removed it, then ran his hands around the box's rusted edges. He tilted it and heard objects move inside. Were they files sliding from side to side? Files containing the secrets of powerful men?

The heavy lid creaked open.

FORTY-EIGHT

Porter stared into the wooden box and realized he'd been fooled. He pulled a pile of hard-plastic folders to the side, searched for anything hidden beneath them, and found zilch…He opened a folder and skimmed over photos of Bill Thompson fishing and playing rugby. The box stored nothing but old photo albums.

Jim hadn't risked the security of the Cumal Files, because Bill had already left with them. He'd stayed behind to buy KA's new Supreme Leader more time. Time that would allow him to escape and take the files further away.

Porter slammed the lid shut then punched it. "Fuck!"

He heard his phone vibrating and picked it from his jacket. "Yeah?"

"Dan?" Lyn Foster said, her voice shrill. "Where are you?'

"Still at Bill's house. What's wrong?"

"Ronny's been bashed. I'm in the ambulance with him," she yelled above wailing sirens. "Patto got him alone in the cellar and has done a runner."

"Patto? How bad's Ronny?"

"Unconscious, but he'll be okay. Patto would've killed him. Luckily Emma heard and pulled a shotgun…"

"Bloody hell…" Porter frowned, remembering that Patto had hovered in the background when he'd spoken to Ronny inside the pub. "Bill and the others cleared out before I got here. Patto must've tipped 'em off."

"What others? What exactly, is going on?"

"We're looking for Bill and three other men. Well-trained military types. One's stocky with a red beard. Tell the search team from Broken Hill. Circulate descriptions of Bill's Range Rover, and Patto's ute too…"

"How'd you go with Steve Williams?"

"He's sending tactical response blokes from Sydney. They'll arrive early morning."

"And where's Jim Thompson?"

He glanced at the giant corpse on the floor. For a millisecond he considered telling her the truth. If he left the house intact, fingerprints and DNA might identify the men who'd fled with Bill. But wasn't it more important to destroy evidence of his own crime? Yeah, he would burn the house to the ground.

"Dunno where Jim is," he told her. "But reckon he'll be feeling the heat sooner than later…"

"He's on the run you mean?" Her tone grew impatient when he didn't answer. "You need help there? Are you okay?"

He wriggled his broken nose then checked the cut to his chest. Blood oozed from it and stained the shirt. Not enough to worry about. "All's good, gunna leave here soon…Will meet you at the hospital and make plans from there."

She agreed and ended the call.

He ran to the darkroom, found it unlocked and turned the light on. Bill's photos covered the walls. He searched shelves and under benches. No wooden chest…Nothing of interest except the Australian flag that covered the far wall. A strange place to hang one?

He switched the light off and turned to leave the room. Was that a faint light coming from behind the flag? He tore it from the wall to reveal a timber door. He pushed it open and stared at what lay beyond it.

The closet-like room had one piece of furniture. A desk lay on its side. Broken drawers hung from it. Manila folders and magazines littered the floor. He glanced at his watch. It was after midnight and Bill got further away with each passing minute. He picked a folder from the floor and flipped through it. Mayoral paperwork?

He scanned the photos and newspaper clippings on the walls and leaned towards a photo he hadn't seen before. Bill fished in a creek. A timber cabin in the background. He took it down and tucked it into a pocket.

He stepped quickly along the wall then stopped to examine a newspaper clipping. It had a black and white photo attached to it. He realized that a larger version of the same picture hung from the living room wall. He'd seen it when he'd visited for lunch and had asked Bill about the short man posing with him. The man had looked familiar.

He scoffed and cursed his failing memory. When Ronny had mentioned the name 'Chuck' earlier, he couldn't think where he'd heard it before. Now he knew. The short man was Charles 'Chuck' McKinlay, the man who'd become KA1. But the pimple-faced twenty-something in the photo looked nothing like the frail old man Porter had seen in the Cobb mine cavern ceremony.

He read the caption below the photo. It named the third man in it as Joseph Klose. Fred's father. A few more pieces of the jigsaw puzzle in his head came together.

He ripped the clipping from the wall and would read the full story later. He started to leave when a color photo caught his eye. Charles McKinlay and Bill Thompson posed with a much younger man. A young man dressed in army officer's uniform. He moved closer and squinted to study the officer's proud face.

Porter's eyebrows leapt. His mouth fell open. He knew the face too well, because it haunted his dreams.

FORTY-NINE

Porter opened Carinya's front door. He greeted Lyn Foster in his favorite purple pyjama pants and a wrinkled white t-shirt. She grinned. He rolled eyes at her perfect hair and ironed blouse then poked his tongue out and led her to the kitchen. They'd worked together until 5am co-ordinating the district-wide search for Bill Thompson. They yawned as they sank into chairs.

He closed his laptop and tidied the pieces of paper strewn across the table into a pile. He pulled the pile towards him, unsure of how much he wanted Lyn to know.

Her face screwed. "Your nose is still a mess but at least the bleeding's stopped."

"Cheers…It was just starting to heal after Neilsen had mistaken it for a baseball…And frickin' Jim's head, it was hard as a bowling ball when he butted me last night…"

"You might have a nasty scar where he cut you too?"

He rubbed his chest. "Nah, it didn't go too deep. A few stitches..."

She pointed to the pile of papers on the table. "What are you up to?"

He pretended not to hear. "Want a coffee?"

"I've had three already... How long you been up?"

He sipped coffee then checked his watch. "Half an hour. Woke up close to eleven. Spoke to Steve

Williams then dozed off until Jane rang. Lucky, or I'd still be crashed out. You?"

"Grimes called me out to the Thompson fire at seven. Couldn't sleep anyhow...Went to check on Ronny at ten."

"How's he going?"

"Much better...Was sat up in bed ready for lunch when I left. And Emma finally managed to contact his mum. She's on her way out from Sydney."

"What's happening with the fire investigation?"

"Just a pile of ash... But we did find charred remains."

"Bloody hell. Whose?"

She frowned. "Aren't we beyond these silly games yet? I know you torched that house with Jim inside it. His wife ID an inscription on his wedding ring..."

He kept a blank face. "And?"

"As the most senior detective left in Crooked River, I signed off on Grime's report to the Coroner. Jim was paralytic drunk and fell into the fireplace. An accident...No further investigation. No autopsy."

He blew hot air through buzzing lips. Jim's actual cause of death would never be revealed. "Cheers..."

"No need, I did it for John Rhodes. Call it karma."

"You can close your Kathleen Thompson murder case too...Jim confessed to it."

She cringed. "Jesus, his own mum? What an animal..."

"Got that right...Steve Williams had good news, for once."

"What?"

"Sixteen girls were located this week... Alive and well, from all parts. It seems the corrupt Interpol bosses have been spooked, and have stopped hampering investigations…"

"Excellent."

"Yeah, except for the girls we'll never find…"

"I know, it's terrible…" She watched him. "And your eyes go dull whenever you mention them…"

He exhaled. The force's fuckups weighed heavy on sagging shoulders.

She took a singing phone from her pocket, glanced at the screen and answered. "Sergeant Nees. Hi."

Porter straightened and listened. Nees, attached to Broken Hill command, led the Operations Support Group that conducted the search for Bill Thompson and co.

"Wow, really? Sarge, please hold a sec…" She held the phone against chest. "Four men have just been shot dead trying to break through a roadblock," she told Porter. "They sound like the ones y--."

He reached across the table and snatched the phone from her. "Sarge, Dan Porter…Is Bill Thompson one of the dead'uns?"

"No, he aint," Nees answered in a labored drawl. "We got the Patterson fella who works the pub, and a few fellas I aint seen before. Dressed in black, special forces types…That red-bearded fella you circulated, he's one of 'em…"

Porter smiled. Mission complete. The men who'd hurt and humiliated Jane were both dead. "Any ID on red-beard?"

"No…But we did find one of them USB stick thingys on him. We've got some Broken Hill D's with us, and they've watched a few files off it on their laptop. They reckon the sick bastard had more than ten videos showing girls being abducted. Same MO, same fellas in black, same white van with some logo on it. Every time…"

"Good job. Book it up, it's important evidence. It confirms what the located girls have said."

Nees grunted.

"What happened exactly?" Porter asked. "Where were those blokes heading to?"

"Dunno, but we've got the highway blocked to the south…Crazy bastards tried to drive straight through in a ute, and took us on when they got stuck. They had some high-powered weapons with 'em. But we had more…"

"Any sign of Bill Thompson's Range Rover?'

"Nope."

"Get your blokes to search the car and surrounding area. Thoroughly. They're looking for a large wooden box. It's like a chest…"

"Job's done," Nees said. "Searched the car meself. Aside from that USB stick, there's nothin' but dead crooks and weapons. My boys have combed the whole area. Aint no wooden box here…"

Porter's gut wrenched. "Bill's wanted for multiple serious offences. He can't slip through."

"We've got all the roads blocked. No helicopters or planes have been sighted since Lyn called last night, and PolAir choppers are searchin' too. We'll keep goin' until we find the bastard. Thompson aint goin' anywhere but the slammer."

Porter thanked him and ended the call.

Lyn frowned and took her phone from him. "Bill's still on the run? And what's this wooden box you keep asking about? I heard Ronny mention it last night too. Asked him this morning but he wouldn't tell…"

He smirked. "Losing your charms?"

The frown hadn't left her face. "Dan, I'm serious…What's with the box?"

He'd realized during the night that he needed to trust at least one person with what he knew. He needed support, and insurance should anything happen to him. Lyn could provide both. "You know that me and Steve Williams have tracked this international sex slave syndicate, the blokes abducting girls from Sydney?" He waited for her to nod. "The wooden chest contains evidence that'll name, shame and help us lock up every mongrel associated with 'em. I reckon Bill has it. But no idea where."

She squinted. "Call me stupid, but from the bits and pieces you've told me I still can't make sense of it. Why are you so certain of Bill's involvement?"

He took the newspaper clipping he'd found in Bill's secret room from the pile of papers and handed it to her.

She read the photo caption aloud. *"Founding members of the Australian National Socialist Party, Sydney branch. Bill Thompson,"* her eyes widened, "Charles McKinlay and Josef Klose. Men protecting the values of white Australia. ANSP national convention, Melbourne, 1965.*"* She dropped the paper to the table.

"That's one hell of a threesome, isn't it? Crooked River mayor Bill Thompson, Judge McKinlay, and Josef Klose. As in, Fred's old man…"

"Unbelievable…No wonder Fred took off…"

He nodded and pointed to the clipping. "I've been searching the internet, trying to find who else might be involved with this mob... Most of the ANSP's early members were Scottish immigrants. Girls abducted from Sydney were branded with the initials 'KA'. Took a while, but we now know what it stands for...Knights of Alba."

"What? Alba? Never heard of it..."

"Amazing what you find on the net...Alba's a name for ancient Scotland. The ANSP called their henchmen, The Knights of Alba. The military arm of their party."

"McKinlay, retired high court judge, was head of a white supremacy organization?"

"Crazy, but yeah."

"Is the ANSP still a political party?"

"Officially, no, the government disbanded them in '75. But in reality, they've been active since '63 and are still very active today."

"How do you know all this?"

"Me and Lionel interviewed a bloke named Alec Ferguson...He mentioned this mysterious organization, blokes with power in high places. McKinlay kept it going after '75, just changed its name to the Knights of Alba and made it very secretive." He pointed to the photo. "Bill Thompson and his mates are more than just puppets in a multi-million-dollar human trafficking syndicate...They run the bloody thing."

"Amazing...And Jim Thompson?"

His pulse quickened when he heard the name. "He was a member too. A murdering rapist. Like father, like son."

"There's evidence that Bill's a rapist, in addition to the human trafficking links?"

370

"Yeah, Bill and other cops raped girls back in the '60s…Lionel said if we found the blokes who hurt girls in the past, we'd find the ones doing it now." Porter heard Lionel whistle a Bruno Mars tune and smiled. "He was spot on…"

"Meaning?"

"Time moves in circles…Powerful blokes will always abuse power, and it'll always bring 'em undone."

She frowned as though unconvinced. "But how does any of this, prove, Bill's involvement? How does it prove he's with this 'organization' that's abducted girls?"

A shiver of doubt ran over him. "Like I said, the evidence is stored in a wooden chest, in documents called the Cumal Files. And you're spot on…If we can't find 'em we'll have next to nothing, and a lot of evil bastards will go unpunished."

FIFTY

Porter had spent the second half of Thursday looking for Bill Thompson's Range Rover. But, just like the multiple search teams that swept across Crooked River district, he found nothing. When he'd knocked off at 1am and spoke to Sergeant Nees, there'd been concern all around. Bosses in Sydney wanted to call off the search. The cost of the operation had soared they said, and the likelihood of finding Bill Thompson diminished with each passing hour.

Porter arrived at Crooked River hospital just after nine on Friday morning. He stopped at the canteen to buy bottles of Sprite and a rugby magazine then made his way to Ronny Goodwin's private room. He hovered in the doorway and peered inside. Ronny already had a visitor.

The thin Koori lady in a lilac dress turned towards him. Her black eyes twinkled. She wore grey hair in a tight bun. A few strands fell over a walnut colored forehead. He guessed she was just past sixty.

"G'day..." he said to the lady then strolled to the opposite side of Ronny's bed. He handed him the drinks and magazine. "I know you love your footy, mate."

Ronny sat up. "Thanks."

He studied Ronny's bruised face and a nail of guilt pierced his chest. Ronny had risked his life to expose the Thompson's. But Porter had been too caught up in his own vengeful obsession and had failed to protect him. He glanced to the lady. "You're mum?"

"Yes, Margaret…And you're Ronny's friend?"

Ronny stopped guzzling Sprite. "He's Dan Porter, mum, my new bro. I used ta, ta, to hate him, but we're all good now."

"Good to meet you," Porter said. "Margaret...?"

"Goodwin, same as Ronny." She smiled, then frowned at Ronny. "Why'd you hate such a nice man?"

Ronny shifted. "Remember when Ben Neilsen got shot in the city? People blamed Dan. He never did it."

"Oh..." She turned to Porter. "You're, that, Dan Porter?"

He met her gaze for a second then dropped his to the bed. The question put a lump in his throat every time. "That's me…"

"Only that Betts fella is a bad one, mum." Ronny yawned and slipped down in the bed. "Dan's a good fella. Sa, sa, same as his mate Lionel was…Before the spirits ta, ta, took him away."

"Lionel?" she asked Porter. "Lionel Roberts, the human rights lawyer?"

"Yeah."

She swayed on her feet and gripped the bed rails. She steadied herself then bent to run a hand over Ronny's forehead. His eyelids flickered closed. She straightened and wiped a tear from her cheek. "Poor darling, the medicine's made him sleepy."

Porter noticed her trembling hands. "You knew Lionel?"

She shook her head. "It just upsets me, seeing Ronny like this." She watched him sleep. "I didn't know Lionel Roberts but heard what he'd done for kooris. Saw nothing in the media regarding his death. How did he die?"

Did she already know the answer? He searched her face for a clue. "We chased suspects. He died in a car accident."

She closed her eyes. Her chest rose and she opened them. "Awful, so young...Did you work with him on the investigation I've read about?"

"Yeah, Carinya...And you're spot on, because Lio was a champion of the Koori cause. Don't worry, we'll finish what he started. We won't let him die for nothing."

Her head fell to the side as wise eyes studied him. She reminded him of the way his Aunt Sue would judge 'best poodle' at the South Coast annual show.

She kissed Ronny's cheek. "He's fast asleep...I have questions, Dan, regarding what happened to Ronny. Let's talk outside, so we don't wake him?"

He followed her from the room, down a corridor and into a courtyard. They sat on a wooden bench.

She smiled at him. "I told Ronny once that our ancestors had lived in this district for many years. But when he went missing, I didn't think he'd come out here..."

"Why'd he leave Sydney?"

"My husband found out he was dealing drugs with Neilsen and other bad ones around Redfern. They had an argument. Ronny said I'd taken my husband's side, and ran away. Last night is the first time I'd seen him in a year..."

"Well, you've got him back now..."

Her moist eyes met his. "Yes, and there's more to tell."

He recalled what Ronny had told him. *Bill Thompson's a rapist pig, and I'm his bastard son.* He had an idea what Margaret wanted to tell him and decided to save her the pain of saying it. "I'm sorry, that Bill Thompson hurt you as a child."

Her mouth fell open, and eyebrows formed a valley. "Why would you say that?"

He realized his mistake. She hadn't intended to reveal herself as a victim. He watched a tear fall from her eye and gave himself a mental uppercut. He waited while she composed herself.

She squinted at him sideways. "How dare you assume to know what's happened to me…"

He scratched his forehead with a thumb. "Ronny told me."

She clutched a hand to chest. "Ronny told you what?"

"That Bill Thompson raped you…Sorry you've found out like this. Ronny saw photos that Bill had taken of you…"

She shuddered and raised shaking hands to her face. Her eyes were closed when she took them away. "Yes, it's true…" She opened them and turned to him. "Sadly, I was one of many."

"Again," he said, "I'm sorry…" He waited for half a minute in respect of her need to reflect. "Elders told us what police did to Koori girls in the '60s, but none gave names. Too scared. Bill being the boss back then had made him our main suspect. Ronny was brave to come to me and he's evidence confirmed it."

She sat upright and stared at him, the same way a felon given life imprisonment stared at a judge. "Please, tell me that Bill doesn't know…" Fingers spread across her throat. "Does he know that Ronny's his son?"

His head tilted. "Nah, I don't reckon he does…"

"Oh, thank God." Her eyes darted over his face. "Were you and Lionel friends?"

"We had a rocky start but ended up as good mates…"

"And you worked closely? He would've shared everything with you?"

"Reckon so…Why?"

Her expression went blank. "You may know me as Shirley...Shirley McMahon."

The revelation punched Porter in the face. Shirley had been Lionel's best informant. He'd told him she'd been murdered in Scotland, betrayed by Interpol agents loyal to the Knights of Alba. But she lived. And she was the mouse-like, courageous Koori women sat next to him.

He scowled when he thought of Fred Klose the KA mole. Lionel had been wise to keep Shirley's survival a secret. "It seems that Lio didn't tell me everything after all…"

She dropped her gaze to the paving stones. A tear slid down her cheek and she wiped it away. "I went into hiding after they murdered Colin, with friends in the north of England. Lionel said it was safer to let them think they'd killed me too."

He dipped his head in agreeance.

"When Lionel didn't reply to recent emails, I just assumed he was busy and that he'd get in touch when safe for me to come home. I've been keeping off social media and the internet as much as possible. I had no idea he was dead."

He swallowed grief. "There was stuff all mentioned about it here, let alone in the UK…"

"I arrived back in Sydney on Tuesday. Two days later I'm getting a phone call from Emma saying Ronny's close to death."

He had read Shirley's emails to Lionel. "You told Lionel of a girl named Rosie. You said to ask the elders about her, but not when Tommy Davis was present. Why?"

She hesitated before answering. "Because I'm Tommy's niece. My real name is Rosie Davis."

His head rocked back. "What? Wait…Now I'm bloody confused…Didn't you just say you're Shirley?"

"I am. It's complicated."

He smiled. "Not wrong…Rosie." Then he noticed the thick scar that ran from her mouth to the bottom of her chin, and frowned.

"It's okay, you can call me Rosie. I like it…" She sighed, as though resigned to a long explanation. "Where to start?"

"Beginnings are always good…"

"Okay…" She fiddled with fingers. "When I was thirteen, the Welfare Board officer, Ferguson, planned to sell me to a man in Germany. You know of Ferguson?"

"Yeah, from your emails…Me and Lionel interviewed him."

"Well, I was about to leave for Germany when I became pregnant with Bill's child. Ronny. Bill stopped the sale, wanting to keep me for himself. And then I began to show…"

"Bill found out you were pregnant?'

"No, thankfully…But I couldn't stay. The minute he saw me with child I would've been dead. Was no way he'd let his bastard half-caste into the world, it would've destroyed him." She scoffed. "I also knew of payments he received from Ferguson and corrupt politicians. Bill had contacts overseas and helped them with the sales. It would've ruined his precious family name if I ever talked…"

He laughed at the irony. "And now Ronny has helped to ruin the Thompson name. And Bill, the silly old bastard, doesn't know it."

She smiled. "Yes, I suppose you're right…Anyhow, Doreen from the mission put me on a bus to Sydney and I never came back. Until now. Changed my name to Shirley Goodwin, sure Bill would come looking for me. Then I got married, took Colin's surname and became Margaret McMahon to make it even harder for Bill to track us down. I still use Shirley now and again, like a nickname…"

She paused to watch him, as though she gave it time to make sense.

He frowned. Most of it did, but not all. "Why didn't you tell Lio everything from the start? You could've named Bill and the other rapists. Could've uncovered the corrupt government officials and the blokes who'd sold Koori girls as sex slaves…Why didn't you end it long ago?"

Her shoulders slumped as she let out a long sigh. "Everything I've done, and how I've done it, has been to protect Ronny. From Bill, from the truth. I was very scared and I still am…I hoped the elders would tell my story to Lionel and name the men involved. And I prayed that if they did, Bill wouldn't be able to find me and Ronny."

"The elders didn't tell us much about you..."

"They've always feared Tommy, because of Bill, but it was worth a shot. I hoped they'd give Lionel enough information for a successful investigation. And hoped they'd never be named as informants and would be safe from Bill and the others."

Porter pictured Old Man Simpson and John Rhodes, and he smiled. He scowled in disgust at a vision of Tommy Davis. All three had been murdered for knowing too much, and he doubted that elders on the mission would ever be safe. He considered asking if she knew about the Knights of Alba but chose not to. There was no need to endanger her with the knowledge. Her life seemed complicated enough.

"Doreen and the other elders protected your secret when we spoke to 'em," he said. "They told us you disappeared from the mission but said nothing of sending you to the city. They did mention your cousin. Malcolm?"

"Malcolm was Tommy's adopted nephew...He was two years older than me."

"Where's he now?"

"Who knows? He followed me into the city and fell into the wrong crowd. Drugs and crime."

"When was that?"

"Hmm...Late '68?"

"He lived with you?'

"No, for various reasons...I distanced myself from him then cut contact altogether. After ten years or so I heard he'd got a girl pregnant. Poor thing died giving birth. Malcolm got caught stealing, and with his record went to prison for three years. No-one's seen him since. I heard he'd moved to Queensland..."

"And his baby?"

Her eyes twinkled. "The church adopted the baby...You see, Malcolm is Lionel's father...And I'm his aunt..."

The washing machine in Porter's head kicked into spin mode. Could it all be true? Or was she taking the piss? He decided on the latter and was about to accuse her of telling porkpies when he recalled a conversation with Tugger Walford. Lionel had been raised by the church and didn't know his parents. An unknown benefactor had supported him through school and university.

He waggled a finger at her. "You sent Lionel money. You put him through school..."

She bowed her head. "I apologize for lying earlier when I said I didn't know Lionel...Colin and I supported him until the day he graduated. He just didn't know it."

"Why didn't he live with you?"

She groaned. "Not proud of it, in fact, I'm ashamed. But he couldn't, to protect Ronny."

"I don't get it..."

"When word got back to Crooked River that I'd had Ronny, Bill came looking to kill us. He asked all over the city for me. Fifteen years he kept looking and I lived in constant fear. He even had men follow Malcolm, hoping he'd lead them to us."

"That's when you ceased contact with him..."

"Yes. And I wasn't sure if Bill knew that Lionel lived at the church...If I'd taken him in, it could've led Bill to us and placed Ronny at risk. I couldn't..."

"Must've been hard watching Lio grow up, and not being able to reach out…"

"Terribly frustrating. But Colin and I worked hard to ensure he wanted for nothing. Always been proud of him, especially when he went into human rights. And when they started abducting those girls from Sydney a few months back, instinct told me they were the same men who'd done it in the '60s. I trusted Lionel with the information."

"And you gave him just enough…Too much and too precise, and it's obvious to Bill that you're Lionel's informant. Bad guys come looking for you and Ronny again…"

She closed eyes. "Exactly…I was torn between helping Lionel find the missing girls and a need to protect Ronny." She opened them and smirked. "Imagine my reaction when I heard that Ronny's here in Crooked River, right under Bill's nose…"

He shook his head. "Wouldn't read about it…I still can't believe you're Lio's aunty." He paused and thought back to Lionel's burial ceremony. "He preferred to die out here, away from the city. I'll take you to see him if you like?'

"That would be nice…"

"I should tell you this too…Tommy Davis died recently."

Her face showed no emotion. "How?"

"They reckon he drowned."

"Unusual, he was always a strong swimmer. Can't say I'm saddened by it."

"Don't reckon you would be…What kind of a man turns his back on helpless children the way he did?"

Rosie scoffed. "Tommy wasn't a man. Only a gutless drunk who never tried to stop men from raping me, or bashing Malcolm. He was happy to turn a blind eye to get his gin and smokes. He's always been a gofer for the devil and them other coppers."

He spun to face her. "Did you just say, the devil?"

"Yes."

"The elders mentioned a 'White Devil.' We asked around town and everyone denied knowing the nickname. Are they one and the same?"

"Yes, and the elders know his real name but it's bad luck to say it. Bill Thompson's the White Devil."

"I suspected that…But part of it still confuses me. I saw paintings of this bloke. Wasn't he fat?"

She winced, as though the memory caused her pain. "All those coppers were fat back then but Bill was huge. I heard he got sick and lost a lot of weight. He was the White Devil. But then again they all were..."

Porter saw himself shake Bill's bony hand and remembered the loose skin at his neck. It reminded him of the photo in his jacket pocket. The picture of Bill fishing in a river with a timber cabin in the background. "We can't find Bill, there's no sign of him." He handed her the crumpled photo. "Found this in his house...Any idea where it was taken?"

She held it. Her hand shook. "Yes. It's his winter fishing cabin."

His heart thudded against chest. "Serious? Remember where?"

"Not too far from here. Off Crooked River road, maybe five k's past Bunyip Hill."

He realized why they hadn't found Bill and scolded himself. The search had started too far from town. "Can you show me the way?"

Black eyes bored into him. "Yes…But on two conditions."

"Name 'em."

"One…Ronny's told nothing of this, or of anything we've discussed just now. He's to be left out of any future investigations and never called as a witness."

"Done."

"Two…We go alone. You and I. No-one else."

"Rosie, you have my word…C'mon, we're off." He stood and helped her up. "It's time to end this."

FIFTY-ONE

Twenty minutes after they'd left the hospital, Porter obeyed Rosie's direction and made the turn off Crooked River road. He knocked the visor down to shield eyes from the rising sun. The steering wheel vibrated as he drove the Landcruiser down a bumpy dirt track lined with towering eucalypts. His heart pounded. Guts churned. Would they find Bill Thompson up ahead? Would he finally get his hands on the Cumal Files?

They came to a thick screen of mulga bush and could drive no further.

Rosie shifted in the passenger seat, her facial expression apprehensive. "We have to walk from here…"

He parked across the track then peered ahead through red dust. The track became a path that sloped downwards and out of sight. He glanced at the car's Navigator screen. "We're close to the river. This path leads to Bill's fishing cabin?"

"Yes, I'm pretty sure it's the one…But the cabin might be gone?" Her voice quivered. "And he may not be here?"

He smiled and tried to ease her fear. "I can't believe you remembered how to get here…"

"Have tried to forget for fifty years but I never will…It's a place in my nightmares."

"I know what you mean…" He paused to contemplate the task ahead. It was a risk to take Bill on without backup, one that'd place Rosie in extreme danger. But she'd insisted she would go all the way to the cabin with him. He had to respect her wishes. And if he found the Cumal Files, the fewer people present, the better. "Did Bill keep guns in the cabin?"

"Yes."

"Then it's probably best you stay here. He's still a dangerous bloke..."

"No. I want to see him go down. I deserve to..."

Porter had fought alongside hardened police veterans and battled tough rugby men, but he respected Rosie Davis more than any of them. He removed his denim jacket, then tucked a white t-shirt into cargo pants.

She removed her sandals and wriggled bare feet.

He jammed the Glock into its shoulder holster. "Let's go."

Porter crept down the path and Rosie followed. He scoured the ground for fresh footprints or any other sign of human activity. Cockatoo screeched overhead from the river gums' highest branches. They'd covered a hundred meters when the path leveled out.

He saw the river fifty meters ahead. He stopped and sniffed at the air. Smoke? He pulled Rosie down to the ground with him and they hid behind low scrub. A crisp smell wafted to his nostrils, rich with the raw fragrance of native flowers. He inhaled and smelled smoke again. From a nearby fire?

He glanced up to his left, north towards the town, and saw Bunyip Hill through a gap in the tree canopy. Five kilometers away? Ahead of him black smoke spiraled above the river. From a campfire? Or a cabin's chimney? He tried to see what lay ahead but the track turned to the right and bushes blocked his view. He listened and heard nothing but sounds of nature.

He stood with caution. He helped Rosie to her feet then aimed the Glock to the front. He crept towards the bend in the track and kept his head lower than the bushes. When he reached the bend he kneeled and peeked around the corner.

He froze, but his pulse raced like the little drummer boy on fast forward. Bill's grey fishing cabin stood close to the river. Less than thirty meters away. A small boat floated on brown water in front of it, shaded by gum trees. Smoke rose from a campfire.

Porter scolded himself. When he'd searched a storage shed at the rear of Bill's property, he hadn't realized a boat was missing. On the night Bill disappeared, Jim must've helped him put the boat in the river and he'd escaped to his cabin. Porter cursed again, because he'd also failed to check the riverbank for tire tracks.

He turned to Rosie and signaled for her stay put. He watched the cabin for movement. None. A row of mulga bush behind the cabin would provide cover. He dropped and crawled towards it.

When he reached the mulga bush he stood and listened. Nothing. He shuffled to the end of the row and peered around it towards the cabin. He saw no-one. No windows facing him. He ran five meters to the cabin's rear wall and pressed his back against worn timber panels. He listened again. Only the sound of waterfowl as they splashed in the river.

He shuffled left to the corner closest to the campfire. He spun to face the wall and stepped to his right to look around it, then scanned the ten-meter wide strip between the cabin and river. No-one. Nothing but a wooden chair next to a campfire, and a window on the side of the cabin.

He stepped back behind cover. His nose twitched. Smoke caught in his throat and he suppressed a cough. A bead of sweat slid down his forehead, over his cheek and welled in the corner of his mouth. Was Bill in the cabin? Or was he out hunting or fishing nearby?

He duck-walked around the corner and stopped under the window. He scanned the riverfront in both directions. Nothing. He stood and held the Glock in one hand while the other shielded eyes from the sun. He peered through the dusty window. The rear section of the cabin was in shadow. Still. Bright sunlight shone through the front door.

He shuffled past the window towards the door then straightened to full height. He took a deep breath and rushed around the front corner. He gasped and jumped back, grateful he'd rested his finger against the pistols' trigger guard.

Rosie covered her mouth with a hand and stared at him.

"Bloody hell, I nearly shot you in the face," he whispered quickly. "Get back over there…"

"Sorry, I saw the boat and wanted to warn you. Can't stand it, I need to know if he's he--." Her eyes expanded as her mouth fell open. Her warning came too late.

Bill Thompson's rifle butt slammed into Porter's face. The Glock slipped from fingers and he crashed to the ground.

Rosie's screams brought Porter back to consciousness, the piercing noise louder than the shock waves that bounced from one side of his skull to the other. He raised his chest from the ground and rotated his head to the right, towards the screams. He willed his eyes open but only the left one obeyed. Two blurred figures moved somewhere near the river. He tried to prise his right eye's lids apart but couldn't. His face fell towards the ground. Fell, then rose. Fell, then rose. Over and over, in time with the violent clash of cymbals ringing in his ears.

He rotated his head to the left and saw the cabin's front door a meter from him. Where was his Glock? More screams. He looked towards the river. Blurred images came into focus. Rosie thrashed arms and legs as Bill dragged her through shallow water in a headlock.

"Rosie," he tried to yell but whispered. He rolled onto his left side and dug his right hand into the ground for support. "Rosie…" He winced, slumped against mud and watched her. Hopeless.

Bill dragged her up the riverbank by the hair. He dumped her next to the campfire, five meters from Porter. He dropped knees into her gut then grinned like the big bad wolf. She wheezed underneath him.

Porter pushed both hands into the ground and tried to press himself up. He got halfway before the spirit-level in his brain tilted too far to the right. Cymbals crashed, arms buckled, his chin thudded into hard mud. He urged himself to try harder. Rosie needed him.

He tried again and fell down again. Experience told him it'd take a few minutes for his brain to re-calibrate and restore balance. But he didn't have a few minutes…He watched Rosie fight for her life.

Bill straddled her chest and pushed knees against her elbows. A white-haired praying mantis pinned a lilac butterfly to the ground. She squirmed, snarled and spat. He laughed and wiped saliva from his face.

She rolled her head and squinted towards the cabin. Tearful eyes pleaded for Porter's help.

Bill glanced at Porter. "Forget it, bitch," he roared. "That lame dog can't help you now...I'll put him down in a minute, but first let's have some fun." He bent and licked her from chin to forehead.

She flung her head from side to side. "Fuck off devil. Get off me!"

Bill reeled away from her and straightened. "Devil?" He cradled her chin in one hand then smirked. "Well, how 'bout that, little Rosie's come back to papa." He swept a hand over her jawline, down her neck and across the top of slight breasts.

She freed her right arm and slapped the side of his head. "Get your filthy hands off me…"

Bill grabbed her arm and shoved it under his knee. "Ah, my black beauty, still feisty as ever."

She grunted and wriggled. After a frantic minute her shoulders sagged into the ground and she whimpered as though realizing resistance was futile.

Bill grinned, a dingo with a fresh carcass. "You always did put up a good fight." He ripped the front of her dress. Buttons flew into the air and she shrieked as he reached under it. "Do you still fuck like you used to?"

Porter ignored his throbbing head. He dug knees and elbows into the ground and crawled towards them.

Bill grabbed her throat and rubbed his chest against her bra. He seemed oblivious to Porter's presence.

The fog in Porter's head dispersed and he reached out to drag him off her. But the spirit-level in his brain tilted too far again and he slumped onto chest against mud. He tried to move but couldn't. His whole body numbed. He watched in futile desperation as Bill choked her less than a meter away.

Rosie's eyes rolled back in her head. Her body relaxed. She would die if Bill didn't let go, and Porter could do nothing to save her.

Another man flashed past him and hurled himself onto Bill's back. A Koori man, black as charcoal, with a knotted beard that hung to a bare chest. White hair fell down his back to a dirty loincloth. He wrapped arms around Bill's neck, an anorexic boa-constrictor.

Bill gagged and released his hold on her. He reached both arms over his head and tried to pull the Koori from his back. The man hung on.

Rosie gasped for air. She yanked arms from under Bill's knees and clawed at his face. He slammed a fist into her jaw.

Her head flopped to the side. Eyes closed. She lay still.

Bill wheezed as his face turned crimson. He threw himself to the side and off her. He pulled the Koori man to the ground and twisted both bodies. When they stopped rolling he held him in a headlock from behind and lifted him to his feet.

Porter swayed to his knees and dived at Bill's legs, much slower than he'd wanted to.

Bill avoided him and drove a heel into his nose.

It crunched. Porter grimaced and fell against mud. He watched Bill drag the Koori man over the grey riverbank.

Bill held him in a headlock and walked backwards into the river. "You think you can stop me, dirty black bastard?"

The Koori's heels submerged. He squealed like a toddler who hated bath time.

Bill dragged him until the water was waist high then pushed his head under. "Time for a scrub…"

Porter crawled to Rosie and found a pulse at her neck. Her eyes flickered open. Blood trickled from her mouth but she managed a weak smile.

Water splashed. The Koori man screamed.

Her forehead crinkled. "Help him," she pleaded.

Porter glanced to the river. Bill dunked the Koori underwater, pulled him up then pushed him under again. He scanned the ground for his Glock. Nowhere. Had Bill hidden it?

He pressed up to his knees. "Who is he?"

She shook her head. "But help him…Please?"

Porter stood, relieved that the cymbals had stopped crashing. He swayed, dropped his iPhone onto the ground and stumbled towards the river without falling. Self-calibration complete. He ran into the water.

Bill glanced over his shoulder and his mouth fell open. He dragged the Koori through water to face Porter's approach.

"Let him go," Porter said. "He's nobody, innocent…"

Bill scoffed. "Innocent? Hardly, son, he's the bastard who killed my Kathleen."

"Bullshit, we both know who murdered her…"

Bill said nothing, just glared at him then dunked the man under water.

Porter lunged forward and placed his left arm under the Koori's armpit. He squatted underwater then exploded upwards and lifted the man's head above the surface. His left arm extended as his right hand balled into a fist.

Bill froze with eyes and mouth wide, an easy target.

Porter slammed a fist into his temple.

Bill wobbled then fell face first into the water. Unconscious.

Porter pulled the Koori man and Bill from the river. He laid them on their sides.

Bill spluttered and groaned and clutched the side of his head.

The Koori coughed up water.

Porter spotted his iPhone and bent to pick it up.

Rosie stood by the campfire. One hand massaged her jaw while the other hugged her soaked body. "Goodness, Dan, your eye's bleeding. Are you okay?"

He removed his t-shirt, ripped a bandage from the bottom of it and wrapped it tight around his head. He noticed her torn dress and threw the t-shirt to her. "Put that on…"

Her smiling eyes thanked him. She put the shirt on then kneeled behind the Koori man and lifted his head from the ground. "Who are you?" She swept matted hair from his eyes. "Why are you here?"

Bill convulsed. Brown water spilled from his mouth.

Porter watched him writhe on the ground, a pathetic antithesis of the intimidating Crooked River Mayor. He saw a weak but cruel old man, to be despised and never pitied.

Rosie held the Koori man's head in her lap. She locked eyes with Porter then nodded towards Bill. "You should've let that pig of a man drown..."

He stopped beside her, looked down and smirked. "I don't disagree, but it's not my decision to make...Besides, men like Bill struggle with defeat. Reckon he'd rather be dead than lose to you..."

The Koori man coughed then gazed into Rosie's face.

"Thank you, friend," she said.

He grimaced as though it were painful to talk. "Could'n stop the Devil from hurtin' ya when youse a little one, cousin. But I told meself he'd never hurt ya again..."

Rosie's bottom lip dropped. "Malcolm?" She shook her head. "Malcolm Davis?"

His black eyes twinkled.

"Where'd you come from, out of nowhere?" Porter said.

Malcolm pointed to his left.

Porter peered in that direction, towards gumtrees that lined the river bank. He saw Bunyip Hill beyond them.

"I was walkin' through the bush to this hut, thinkin' to steal some food," Malcolm said. "Then I run 'ere when I heard a lady screamin'."

"I know your voice...You're from the caves on Bunyip Hill?"

Malcolm nodded then returned his gaze to Rosie.

"I, I'm stunned..." She stroked Malcolm's forehead. "I thought you lived in Queensland. But all this time, you've been here, in Crooked River?"

"Since I got outta jail…Weren't stayin' in no white fellas' city."

"You're not the only one who owes him your life," Porter told her. "He helped me hide when blokes tried to kill me." He smiled at him. "Cheers mate…"

Malcolm said nothing. He made brief eye contact then looked away.

Rosie beamed at Porter. "Have you forgotten, Dan?"

"About what?"

"That Malcolm is Lionel's father…"

He rolled his good eye towards Malcolm, tried to say to her – 'you tell him.'

"I already know Lionel's dead," Malcolm said. "Was at 'is burial…"

Porter frowned. "Didn't see you there."

"Because I did'n wanna be seen."

"Fair enough… And for what it's worth, he was a top bloke…Shame you never met him. You can be proud."

Malcolm raised his head from Rosie's lap. He moaned as she helped him to his feet then stared up into Porter's face. "I am proud of 'im…And no, he never knew me as 'is dad but we spoke all the time."

Rosie smiled as though she understood.

Porter heard Lionel's voice, and listened to him speak about Aboriginal spirits and the wise elders who'd guided him. Had they sent him to Crooked River to find his father? He started to tell Malcolm when Bill spluttered and convulsed. His line of thought jumped from Bill to the Knights of Alba, to the reason he'd come to the cabin…The wooden chest. The Cumal Files.

He glanced towards the cabin and tightened the cloth around his head. "Watch Bill…I'm gunna search it."

She nodded, stepped forward with tear filled eyes and hugged Malcolm.

Porter rushed to the cabin and stepped inside the dank room. He swept his phone's torch from left to right, back and forth. Fishing rods against a wall, tins of food and empty whiskey bottles on a bench top, a wooden rocking chair, mounted rifles, work boots, a jemmy bar and other tools on the floor, overalls hanging from a hook, a stack of newspapers in the corner, a pile of kindling and an axe by the door. A cow skin rug…

But no wooden chest…

He crawled around the room's perimeter. Hands probed the timber wall and he hoped to uncover a hiding place. He found his Glock in a dark corner and holstered it. His injured eye throbbed and bones ached. The pain became unbearable. His lungs craved air. He left the cabin to let the sun warm his face and sucked in rapid breaths.

When he'd filled his lungs and heartbeat had slowed, he cleared his throat and spat at the ground. He'd had a gutful of unfair rules. It was time to play dirty, same as the crooks did. One way or another he'd make Bill Thompson tell where he'd hidden the Cumal Files. He strode towards the campfire.

Rosie stood alone on the riverbank and gazed into the cloudless sky.

He stopped, spun and scanned all directions.

Bill and Malcolm had disappeared.

FIFTY-TWO

Porter ran past Rosie to the spot where he'd left Bill
Thompson lying on the riverbank. He saw two blood-
covered rocks. Thin splatters of blood fanned the
ground and a thicker trail of blood led towards the
shallows. He followed it to the water's edge then
looked out across the brown river. Bill Thompson
floated face down in the middle of it. A bright-red
cloud billowed from his head.

Porter spun towards Rosie and noticed her blood
covered hands. He pointed at them and charged
forward. "What have you done?"

She met his glare, chin raised. "You said it wasn't
your decision to make if the White Devil lived or not."
Her voice shook. "Malcolm and I invoked the ancient
laws of these lands. We decided…"

He gritted teeth and hissed. "Fuck!" Bill was likely
the only person who'd known the whereabouts of the
Cumal Files, of where they'd been hidden. With him
dead he'd never find them. "Where's Malcolm?"

"Gone…Said he's leaving this district and never
coming back." She trudged to the river and bent to
wash her hands.

Porter said nothing as he watched Bill's limp body
bob up and down in the river. He'd just heard a
confession to murder. But if ever questioned regarding
Bill's disappearance he'd deny any knowledge of it. If
anyone had earned the right to administer their own
justice, as judge and executioner, it was Rosie Davis.

He turned to her. "I don't reckon we should leave him in the river…His body might be found…"

She shook her head. "He'll float close to the edge soon enough…Dingos will wait till dark, drag him from the water and tear him apart. They're very efficient eaters, and don't leave any bones or scraps…"

He thought it a fitting end to an evil existence. "No worries…It's your call."

She walked towards the cabin. "Did you find what you're looking for?"

"Nah…" He followed her. "Were there other places he'd go? Other cabins?"

"Not that I know of..." She stopped in the doorway and pointed at the floor. "Did you look under there?"

He stepped past her into the room. "Where?"

"He hid guns in there, beneath the rug."

He cursed his stupidity. He dropped to knees and pulled the cow skin rug aside. Loose timber floorboards underneath it ran in opposite directions to the others. He yanked the boards away to reveal a dark space below. He shone the phone's torch towards the cavity. His heart jumped to throat when he saw it. A wooden chest.

She leaned towards it. "What's that?"

He reached down and grabbed the metal handle on top. Then the one on the left side. "It'll be heavy…Please grab the other side and help pull it up..."

She nodded.

He waited till she moved into position. "One, two, three…"

They grunted and groaned as they lifted the chest out and placed it on the floor. He noticed metal wheels on the bottom of it and rolled it out the door into bright sunshine. It was a meter in length and half as deep and wide. Made of dark oak. Coated in a matte finish. He fingered the rusted brass corners.

The chest was beautiful. Solid. He admired the genius craftsmanship. It looked and felt antique. How old was it? He chuckled as he remembered how Ronny Goodwin had described the wooden box inside Bill Thompson's house. This wooden chest was just like those pirates had kept their treasure in. He ran a hand over the smooth lid. Did this pirate's chest contain the treasure he searched for? Or would he be disappointed again?

Rosie stood beside him. "What's inside?"

He fumbled with a thick brass padlock on the front of the chest. Should he search for a key? Use the jemmy bar inside the cabin to force it open? Nah, he'd shown enough patience for one day...

"Step back..." He took the Glock from its holster and waited for her to retreat to a safe distance. He knelt beside the chest, aimed at the padlock and fired. The lock flew away. He holstered the pistol.

He examined the chest. Undamaged and unlocked. He raised its heavy lid with both hands then pushed it back. It squeaked open on metal hinges and stayed there. He gazed into the sky for a few seconds. He returned smiles from Jane and Lionel then took a deep breath. He stared into the wooden chest and let the breath out slowly.

The chest contained brown folders stacked to the top in neat piles. He took one out and studied it. A4 in size, three inches thick and weighty in his hands. A cover made of soft leather. White, bold font on the front read: CUMAL FILES – 2016.

He returned the folder and a thunderbolt of relief shocked him to his core. From the moment Alec Ferguson had mentioned the Cumal Files and said what they would reveal, he'd wanted to believe in their existence. And now he'd found them. For the first time in a long time he slapped himself on the back. He'd persevered…

"What are Cumal Files?"

Her question jolted him from the daydream. "Information." He stood. "Evidence…"

"Of what?"

"Of crimes that me and Lionel had been trying to prove. Historical, and present day. Crimes that you helped us uncover…" He closed the lid.

"And will you? Prove them?"

He placed a hand on her shoulder. "For you, and for Lionel, and a heap of others…I'm gunna make sure of it." He realized the need to protect her. "Tell no-one about this. Alright?"

Her eyes narrowed. "I won't…"

He gripped a handle and pulled the chest over hard mud towards the dirt path. "Let's get out of here, and get this pirate's chest safe and secure."

Porter placed the last of fifty-four brown folders into the wooden chest and secured the lid. He yawned, stretched in the chair and glanced at his watch. 9.28pm. He'd returned Rosie to the hospital, had his eye treated, and arrived back at the Carinya residence close to 2.30pm. It'd taken him seven hours to sift through fifty-four years of Cumal Files and write a report that summarised their contents.

After studying lists contained in the files, he knew that no KA members or associates remained in Crooked River. He was finally able to place full trust in Lyn Foster. He called her and asked if she would secure the files in the police station's evidence safe. She agreed to, and as the acting boss of Crooked River command, she possessed the only set of keys to it. He told her he'd take the wooden chest to the station at 11pm and they would discuss its contents then.

He selected 'Print' then strolled into the office. His mind wandered as the report spilled out. How could he best use the evidence contained in it? What would achieve the best results for victims like Rosie Davis? For the families of recently abducted girls? What actions would secure a better future for kooris and guarantee the changes to legislation that Lionel had fought and died for? The Cumal Files implicated numerous influential men and women from all parts of the globe. Who could he trust with his demands? And who had the power to see that they were met?

By the time the last page printed he'd committed to a course of action. He took his phone from the table, skimmed through the contact list and called a number.

"Hello?" A female answered, her tone annoyed. "Karen Flintoff speaking..."

"Karen...It's Dan Porter with the Carinya investigation. Got a minute?"

Flintoff huffed. "It's late...And how did you get my private number?"

"Lionel Roberts...He told me to call you if ever in need. I am..."

"Fucking Roberts...Still a pain in my arse from the grave..." She sighed. "What do you want?"

"A meeting with the AG. Canberra. 4pm tomorrow."

"Tomorrow? Impossible...Won't happen."

"Karen, listen to who else I want to be there, and make it happen...It's in everyone's best interest, including yours, that it does."

FIFTY-THREE

At 8am Saturday Porter boarded a flight from Crooked River to Broken Hill. Not long after landing he took another flight to Sydney. There he waited two hours before a connecting flight to Canberra. He rented a car from the airport then drove to a nearby hotel to freshen up. In the afternoon he made his way to an obscure government building in Barton, Australian Capital Territory.

At 3.59pm he strode into the foyer of the Attorney-General's office. He took a deep breath to prepare himself, the same as Maximus Meridius always did. He was going into battle, entering a political Colosseum, and for his plan to succeed he would have to claim the most rousing victory of his gladiatorial police career.

A brunette receptionist welcomed him with a brilliant smile.

"G'day…Dan Porter…" He placed the briefcase on the reception counter, straightened his tie and brushed lint from the sleeves of a black suit. "Rothwell's expecting me."

"Certainly, Mr Porter," she said. "Ooh that's a nasty bruise. I bet you can hardly see through that eye you poor thing…An accident?"

He fingered the swollen side of his face. "Yeah, a bit clumsy sometimes…"

She waved a hand towards the door behind her. "Mr Rothwell said to go straight in."

He took the briefcase from the counter, knocked and accepted the invitation to enter.

Attorney-General Rothwell sat behind a mahogany desk in the center of the room. Drab curtains covered windows along one wall. Horrendous artwork lined the other. Bright downlights reflected off his bald head and thick glasses. He wore a long-sleeved shirt that hung from a middle-aged body, and a loosely knotted tie. Shelves behind him housed books, framed certificates and photos.

Porter recognized the second man in the room and resisted a smile. To Rothwell's left sat Jeremy Tate, the Prime Minister of Australia. He'd seen him on television, with chiseled features made for the camera. But in the flesh Tate looked all of fifty-five years. His hair seemed greyer, frown lines more pronounced, and ears pointier.

Rothwell stood to shake Porter's hand and commented on his bruised face. He introduced him to Tate.

Tate rose to shake hands then sat. "I've delayed an important meeting. This had better be worth it…"

Rothwell scowled then gestured for Porter to sit opposite. "Let me be clear, I've only agreed to this on such short notice because I'm told Carinya has uncovered pertinent information. Regarding a matter of national integrity..."

In Porter's mind he heard an angry Karen Flintoff curse his blackmail. He smirked.

"There's nothing amusing about this, Porter. We're extremely busy…You've got ten minutes to tell us what you know."

He rubbed his jaw. "You'll wanna give me more than that…"

Tate leaned forward. "Listen, I'm the big dog here, so let's not waste time sniffing each other's arses…What's this about?"

Porter took two documents from the briefcase and handed one to each of them. "Read it."

Tate thumbed through the five-pages. "I don't have time." He stood and dropped it on the desk. "My legal people will examine it and get back to you."

"Nah, sit down and read it. Now."

Tate eyed Rothwell and sat. "You're going to tolerate this?"

Rothwell shrugged.

"Dismiss what's in the report," Porter said, "and you won't be PM by next week…"

Tate scoffed. "A bold prediction…What am I reading?"

"A report that summarises historical documents and financial records uncovered by Carinya. Evidence of major criminal activity. Here, and internationally. Past, and present."

Rothwell tilted his head. "Criminal activity by who?"

Porter pointed to the report. "Read it."

He watched their expressions change as they read the reports. From mild amusement to concern. To shock. And lastly, when they'd finished, to one of horror. They dropped the reports on the desk, as though they were alight and would burn their hands.

After a half-minute silence, Rothwell spoke first. "Cumal Files? Where on earth does the 'cumal' come from?"

"The Knights of Alba organization practices the rituals of ancient Celts. A cumal is what they called female slaves. They eventually became a measure of value, and it's why they applied the term to financial records. Another of their beliefs is to never destroy such records. In this case, they should have…"

"Ludicrous…" Rothwell said. "To accuse Charles McKinlay, one of our hardest working human rights advocates, as being the leader of this…KA? I knew Charles well and to suggest he led a white supremacist group and was a founding member of the National Socialist party…" He glared at Porter. "Absolutely ludicrous."

Porter grinned. "You sure you knew the real man at all? If he was such a wonderful human rights advocate, why did he hamper Carinya?"

Rothwell scoffed.

Tate cleared his throat. "Rothwell's right, this report's an insult. I don't for one minute believe, that this, KA as you call them, actually exist. There's no 'secret' organization masterminding the international sex slave market. Not in these times and not in Australia. It's pure fantasy…"

"Evidence in my possession says otherwise," Porter said. "Are you blokes that stupid? You reckon racial supremacists and human traffickers don't exist?" He glanced at Rothwell then back to Tate. "From what I've seen and the files confirm, they're more prevalent than ever."

"Seen?" Rothwell said.

He told them of KA brandings on abducted girls, Amber's rescue during the ceremony at Cobb mine, about the death of Charles McKinlay and others in the explosion.

Tate chuckled.

Rothwell peered at Porter over the top of his glasses. "I'd heard you're a loose cannon, a bit of an Elliot Ness wannabe. But you're more than that, with these, fairy tales…You're fucking insane."

"Charles McKinlay died in a helicopter crash..." Tate said.

Porter cocked his head. "Sure about that? There was no autopsy…"

"The Coroner said he'd been incinerated on impact."

"Believe what you want. The Knights of Alba exist, and I've got evidence to prove it..."

Rothwell leaned forward. "Where is this, evidence?"

"Original files are in a secure location. Copies are with a colleague…Anything happens to me, or the originals, those copies get sent to the media."

Tate winced. "Okay, let's say KA does exist…Go on."

Porter allowed himself an indulgent smirk, he had their full attention. "KA's run by a High Council. Of the original nine members named in my report; McKinlay, Bill Thompson, Josef Klose, George Barrett, and the Fed's Commissioner, Watkins, are dead. Three others, all retired judges, are missing. Reckon they died in the mine explosion… Leaves one of their High Council, Alexander, alive and wanted."

"Another ridiculous accusation..." Rothwell pointed to the document. "To suggest Commissioner Watkins was a member of this, High Council. And a retired Supreme Court Judge, Ian Alexander, now leads this imaginary, army? As I said, you're a madman."

"Again, the proof's in the files…They're all named, members and associates. Payments made and all other financial records. Ledgers, if you wanna call them that…"

Tate frowned. "Associates, in what way? And how many?"

Porter paused to study him, saw a face etched with worry that hadn't been there a minute earlier and nervous fingers that tapped the desk. "The list of KA associates is in there, hundreds are named." He nodded to the briefcase in front of him. "Most of KA's members, their soldiers and assassins for hire, we'll never identify. And without leadership and funds, they should fold. But with Alexander still out there, who knows?"

Tate's forehead crinkled. "Without funds? Yet your report says they hold capital of 1.2 billion dollars?"

"You see, Porter…" Rothwell waggled a finger at Tate, as though he'd proven a point for him. "That's exactly why I think your theory, your story, is a concoction. Personal bank accounts of these men you accuse, judges and the like, come under intense scrutiny. Money laundering prevention and anti-terrorism strategies demand it. They're not keeping money here in Australia, and we can't freeze assets that we can't find."

"Spot on," Porter said. "Their money isn't here in Oz. And isn't in personal accounts…"

"Then where? In whose?"

"Scotland. Kennard Atkins Mining Corporation…Glasgow, London, Cape Town, Singapore and Sydney. Global exporters of specialist mining equipment since 1966."

Rothwell gave a condescending smirk. "Let me guess, it's in the files?"

"Did you even read the report? It's some serious shit we're talking about here…But are you grasping it?"

Rothwell's face flushed red as he shouted obscenities.

Tate stopped him with a raised hand then turned to Porter. "Kennard Atkins is a shell company? Explain…"

"Their financial records for the past ten years show container movements and invoices, shipping manifests, and names of company directors at Glasgow headquarters." Porter turned to Rothwell. "Land titles from hundreds of property purchases, like the Cobb mine they managed to buy from the National Lands Trust, aided by the AG's department…"

Rothwell huffed, sat back and folded arms.

"Containers? Shipping manifest?" Tate said.

"KA transported the abducted girls in shipping containers. Fake manifests listed the cargo as drills and other mining equipment. The girls went from Sydney to Newcastle, then to Singapore, and onto Middle Eastern, European, American and African clients. For Asian customers they went via Hong Kong."

"I remember seeing a memo regarding missing girls in Sydney. Have the abductions ceased?"

"They'd dwindled, and have now stopped completely after McKinlay's death…"

Rothwell whacked the desk. "How'd our Customs people miss this? How many girls are we talking about?"

"From Australia, well over a hundred. Worldwide, thousands. KA have bribed customs officers, shipping inspectors, local cops, the lot. And corrupt Interpol bosses, all the way to the top, hampered all efforts towards international co-operation. My boss, Steve Williams, had his crew check out Kennard Atkins in Sydney. They found nothing. KA shipped the girls out of Newcastle and covered their tracks each time."

"And their bosses in Glasgow? Why haven't they been investigated?"

"They have, with nothing adverse found at that time…Big money buys big protection. But them, and all other Kennard Atkins executives based in Europe are on the list of KA's international associates. They'll be picked up in our sweep…"

Tate picked at his chin. "Again, you mention these, associates. Precise details and names will lend credence to your story."

Porter studied his beady eyes. "It's no story, mate. It's all fact…" He turned to Rothwell, unimpressed by his smug face and arrogant snarl. He didn't like him, let alone trust him. He turned back to Tate. "Rothwell should leave. You'll wanna be alone when you hear this…"

Rothwell threw hands up. "What? Fuck you, Porter." He glared at Tate, as though daring him to throw him out.

"He stays," Tate said.

Porter rubbed his neck. "Is he loyal to your party? 'Cos he'll need to be…"

Tate's eyes darted to the report, to Rothwell, to Porter, then back to the report. "Rothwell, leave us."

Rothwell snarled at Porter. "You'll pay for what you've done, and you know damn well what I'm talking about…Fuck you, you'll pay." He thumped the desk with a flat hand, stormed from the office and slammed the door behind him.

Porter took a piece of paper from the briefcase. He offered it to Tate then pulled it back and held it against his chest. "The list of KA associates...Convince me, why trust you?"

Tate smirked. "Who else do you have? And what have you said that links me to KA?"

"Had you heard of 'em before today?"

"One hears many things in my position...Years ago, when I first heard whispers of a secret organization that'd supposedly stemmed from the defunct NSP, I dismissed them, as most in politics did. Seemed the stuff of Masons, conspiracy theories..."

"KA hasn't recruited you...Why do you reckon that is?"

"Are you certain they haven't?" Tate laughed. "It's simple... I'm pro-immigration and pro-refugee. I disgust white supremacists..."

Tate hadn't been mentioned in the Cumal Files. But did that mean he couldn't still be somehow linked to KA? Porter had to gamble and trust him, as the only man capable of delivering what he wanted. And if he lost the bet he'd most likely pay with his life.

"Spot on," Porter said. "You represent everything the Knights of Alba hate." He handed him the list. "You're a threat, and they're paying your mates to remove you from office."

"What? To replace me with who?"

"They're backing Jenkins for leadership...He's a KA puppet, who'll promote their anti-immigration policy and legislate it. And he'll have the numbers in a slip when Alexander decides to move you on..."

"Surely he won't?"

"Why not? KA don't know I've got the Cumal Files. I wouldn't have made it here today if they did…They probably reckon the files got destroyed in the Thompson's house fire, or are still out there somewhere..."

"You're saying that Jenkins and Alexander have no idea they've been compromised?"

"They don't, and if allowed to, they'll oust you. Then they'll be in the clear and able to steer party policies toward KA objectives…"

Tate read. Eyebrows jumped. "Moorecroft's on their payroll? Jesus, I considered Ken to be a good friend. Unbelievable…And what makes you think Jenkins will have the numbers?"

"I've only included high ranking officials and public figures in that list of associates. You've got another twenty-three corrupt members. Sleepers in parliament sympathetic to KA's cause. You'll lose."

"Unless?"

Porter considered spelling it out for him. "You lock 'em all up."

He gasped. "Have my own members arrested? Impossible…It would end the party."

"That's only the start…"

"Meaning?'

"We'll get to that…Take out Alexander, Jenkins and these KA associates. That's your first move. Today."

Tate blew air through pursed lips. "Jesus, you're right..." He scanned the page, his hand shook. "It's quite a list... High ranking Interpol officials, police bosses, judges, and lawyers. And the sex slave clients named…They're rich and influential men and

411

women…Wouldn't it be very embarrassing if we move against these people and you're wrong?"

"I'm not…And your failure to act, if the files get to the media and become public knowledge, would be worse. Embarrassment's the least of your worries."

"That a threat?"

"Nah, sound advice…"

Tate broke eye contact when Porter stared back. "Let's say I take your 'advice.' Watkins was crooked, and there are still corrupt Police Commissioners and Ministers in office. We can't trust the cops…So who'll round up these hundreds of KA associates?"

"I spoke to Steve Williams this morning. He suggest-"

"Wait…He knows what's in your report? Knows about the files?"

"Nah, only the names in front of you, of associates to be arrested…"

"Thank Christ…" Tate leaned closer. "If I'm to trust you on this, I need your complete confidentiality. No-one else can know of the report. We clear?"

Porter almost laughed. Tate wanted to know if he could trust him? "Yeah…And works both ways, right?"

Tate nodded.

"Beaut…Now, Williams suggested that ASIO investigators arrest the members of parliament and police commissioners. Their blokes are clean, not mentioned anywhere in the files. Sell it to them as being a breach of national security…Tell 'em the truth, that KA's a bunch of homegrown terrorists, who can be incarcerated under provisions in your new legislation. NSW Crime Commission blokes will grab Judge Alexander and Jenkins first, followed by a co-ordinated swoop for the others. When all suspects are in custody, I'll forward evidence to relevant investigators, for applicable charges to be laid…"

"Good, that should avoid conflicts of interest. Who'll arrest Ken Moorecroft?"

Porter grinned. "I'm back in Sydney tonight. Me and Steve Williams will handle Moorecroft."

"I see that pleases you. Because he's the Police Minister?"

"Nah, because his KA mates abducted and murdered girls on my patch, and he shut down all efforts to find 'em. He's as guilty as any bastard in all of this, not to mention being a condescending arsehole. I can't wait to take him down…"

"Don't hold back…Now tell me this, who makes the international arrests of corrupt officials and KA clients? Surely not Interpol?"

"Nah, not with their High Commissioner Davidson being first on the list…Every nation with an interest in this have a Crime Commission similar to ours. They have no links to KA and will jump all over this. Anti-human trafficking agencies independent of Interpol will assist as well...We'll forward the info asap."

"I must brief Rothwell and others I still trust, to initiate some damage control...The fallout will be immense." He passed Porter a business card. "Email me names of those loyal to KA, the twenty-three others you mentioned."

"Will do…"

Tate slid the list of associates onto the desk.

Porter snatched it up. "I'll keep a hold of this and put those we've discussed to work on it…" He placed the list inside his briefcase. "With your authorization?"

Tate squinted at the briefcase. "Yes of course…Is that all?"

"Nah, we still need to cover the second part of my report…"

"The neglect of Aboriginal children in far western New South Wales? Look, we haven't got time for that now."

"Make time."

Tate mumbled incoherently. He opened the report and read for a minute. "I'm confused…How did Carinya's investigation in the Outback lead to this evidence of international human trafficking? Where's the link?"

"Glad you asked…" Porter sucked a long breath and readied himself for the final blow. "Lionel Roberts, the bloke behind Carinya, uncovered sexual abuse at Crooked River Aboriginal mission going back to the early 1960s. Young Koori girls were raped by police and others, and sold as sex slaves." He paused and watched the look of bewilderment spread across Tate's face. He wanted his words to whack it hard. "And the men who profited from sex slavery back then, profit from it today. The Knights of Alba's members, and corrupt politicians…"

Tate chortled. "You're serious?"

"Very…"

"Profited? How?"

"Through manipulation of the Aboriginal Protection Act, for a start..."

Tate groaned. "This, again? I heard good things of Lionel Roberts and imagine he'd want more from Carinya than simply re-visiting the stolen generations?

Those Aboriginal children were taken legally, under the Protection Act, for their own good."

"Not all…And the government of the day profited."

The sarcastic smile on Tate's face disappeared. "That's potentially an extremely damaging accusation. Thankfully," his smile returned, "it's a false one…"

Porter leaned his head to the side. "Lionel discovered that Aboriginal Welfare Board records for girls taken from Crooked River mission between 1963 and 1969 were never filed in the State Archives…"

"An honest mistake?"

"Nah, because the missing records are contained in the Cumal Files. I left that out of my report on purpose…"

"Welfare Board records that list what?"

"Already told you…Names of four-hundred and fifty-six girls, between nine and seventeen years of age, who were sold into sex slavery by government officials."

Tate's nose scrunched as though a foul smell had wafted to it. "Sold? Be very careful, Porter." His face flushed. He clawed the desk. "It's a fucking lie. Names on a list prove nothing."

"Nah, but original bills of sale, and receipts of payments made by Welfare Board officials to the girls' families…They do. And I've got 'em."

"It's the most ridiculous claim I've ever heard…To suggest the government made money from the Protection Act. I should have, you, arrested. For slander…"

Porter smirked. He pointed to the report. "But, you won't…"

Tate sank into the chair. "What do you want?"

"I don't trust your government to honor the promises you're gunna make."

"I'm making promises?" Tate scoffed. "To you?"

"Yeah, and like I said, I don't trust the current mob. That's why you're gunna have the Governor-General dismiss them. Then bring in a new government that'll act on our demands…"

"Our demands?"

"Well, Lionel's, mostly…"

"Jesus, what are you on? You have any idea, of the ramifications of dismissing a government? It would be the chaos of '75 all over again…"

"See it as a fresh start. A chance to weed your garden..."

"Federal elections are very close…Can't we do the clear out then? Tell me who you want in, and where?"

"Nah, there could be KA sleepers not named in the files. It's too risky to leave 'em in place."

Tate's eyes whirled. "This would be catastrophic for my party..."

"Compared to releasing evidence showing its involvement in sex slavery?"

Tate snarled. "Go ahead, release it. I'll simply brand it the work of a few rogue officials who profited themselves. Nothing you've shown can directly implicate that government."

Porter removed a page from his briefcase and held it up. "This, top-level directive, does…"

"I'm losing patience with your games, Constable. What is this nonsense?"

Porter slammed the page onto the desk. "A stamped directive, signed by the Prime Minister in March of 1965…You said the dismissal of government is the worst scenario for your party and this nation. Still sure about that?"

Tate ripped at his jaw. "Yes."

"How much does Australia's history mean to you? Are you proud of it?"

"Of course, I am…What's your point?"

Porter slid the page across the desk. "Read that. And then tell me how proud."

Tate read. His hands trembled. He forced a laugh as though trying to shake himself from a bad dream. "It's a photocopy of a fake…It's easy to forge old documents…"

"The original is safely tucked away. It's no fake."

"That Prime Minister was a magnificent, honest man, who'd never approve such a farce. It's an absurd allegation…"

"He approved the acquisition, and sale, of young Aboriginal girls. That's his signature. He had full knowledge of what those corrupt Welfare Board blokes were doing."

"Nonsense."

"Is it? Face reality, mate, your mob has profited from sex slavery since the 1960s. Maybe longer? Working hand in hand with a bunch of racist pricks calling themselves the Knights of Alba. Dismissal of your government aint the worst scenario. Far from it…"

Tate crossed arms and closed his eyes. Five seconds later he opened them. "The stolen generations were shameful enough…But sex slavery? Christ, if this got leaked we'd never recover from it…And I'm not only speaking of my party. Our nation…Australia would become a cancerous mole on the face of humanity…"

Porter inclined his head, lips pursed. "Our greatest shame no doubt...And one that, for the sake of millions of decent people, I'm prepared to keep a secret. But my terms are non-negotiable..."

"Understood...Name them."

The night before, Porter had recalled the various conversations he'd had with Lionel over recent weeks and made a list of demands based on them. He took a crumpled piece of paper from his trouser pocket. "Now, in brief...The full details I'll email later."

Tate nodded and readied a pen to paper.

Porter read from the list. "You agree to dismiss your government, and authorize the arrests we've discussed?"

Tate sighed. "I do...I mean, I'll push the Governor-General for it."

"Alright, good. Be sure to push hard...Now, I've spoken to one of the Crooked River rape victims...She believes that, since the main offenders are all dead, an inquiry into those historical rapes would do nothing but revive terrible memories for the victims. But she's compiling a list with my help, and they'll be well compensated..."

"By who?"

"Your politician buddies riding the KA gravy train...The millions we'll seize from their accounts will be the compensation..."

"But we ca--"

Porter held up a flat palm. "Nah, ah, ah. Non-negotiable…"

Tate moaned, face glum.

"Righto, next…" Porter eyed the page. "The seized assets of Kennard Atkins Mining Corporation, owned by the Knights of Alba. 1.2 billion dollars. Half of it will go to the families of girls named in the Cumal Files, the ones whose daughters were taken and sold as sex slaves. The other half goes to families of those Australian girls recently abducted by KA..."

"Anything else?"

"Lots...Like I said, I'll send a complete set of demands later. There's one priority..."

"What?"

"Your new government will pass new legislation to be known as the Carinya Act. You'll allocate a higher percentage of the Federal budget to Aboriginal health, education, and housing, with tough penalties for government departments found to be negligent..."

"Such penalties already exist..."

"Yeah, but they're never enforced...A full-time squad of Koori investigators, trained and funded by the Attorney-Generals' department, will have powers to investigate any breaches. They'll continue Carinya's work..." Porter skimmed over his list. "This one's a biggy too..."

Tate scoffed. "What, bigger than a new act of parliament?"

"Yeah, I reckon it is...You'll begin the process of constitutional recognition for Australian Aborigines and support it." Porter smirked. "Lionel was passionate about that one. He would've bloody haunted me till death if I forgot it..."

"I can't make any promises..."

Porter frowned. "Then I can't promise to keep all this from the media..." He waited for him to concede with a dull nod. "And, you'll set up the Lionel Roberts Foundation."

"For?"

"Tertiary scholarships. Koori kids to study law. Twenty million dollars a year."

"But we already spe--."

He raised a palm and gave him the 'stop' sign. "No buts, just do it…"

Tate watched him. "You're enjoying yourself, but tell me this…Considering how wicked and corrupt you deem all politicians to be, are you entirely convinced I'm not KA? Do you know which High Council members escaped the explosion you mention? Said yourself, there could be KA sleepers and associates who aren't named in the Cumal Files…" He leaned forward. "Am I one of them?"

A corkscrew of doubt plowed Porter's gut, he swallowed sticky bile. The sudden devilish glint in Tate's eyes and the hint of deception in his voice suggested he'd been a fool to trust him.

He hoped to call his bluff. "Nah, don't reckon you are…"

Tate sniggered. "The look on your face…Priceless. For a second you weren't sure, were you?" He paused. "What if I've changed my mind?"

"Regarding…?"

"Your demands…They're excessive. And damaging…"

"Again, compared to what, the files going public?"

"Even so, I very much doubt the Governor-General will agree to dismiss the government…"

"You're the Prime Minister, make him…Let him know what'll happen if he doesn't. I don't reckon the Commonwealth will be too keen on such a scandal?"

"You make a valid point but it's not so simple…And I'm to just take your word that you have hard evidence against my parliamentary colleagues? As I said earlier, it'll be embarrassing if you're wrong, and would destroy the careers of some fine politicians."

"Don't you mean, dodgy politicians? The ones named in that list are more corrupt than FIFA bosses…They must be arrested."

"The 1.2 billion dollars we'll seize from Kennard Atkins could be put to great use in our fight against terrorism…It's one we're currently losing, and that sum of money would turn the tide. And haven't the stolen generation's victims been well compensated already?"

"Nah, they haven't, and you're speaking as though you have a choice…" Porter plonked a clenched fist on the desk. "You don't."

Tate leaned forward. "Ah, see that's where you're wrong, because I've just realized I do…What's to stop me from having you arrested and locked up? It would give my agents time to find and destroy these files you're talking about."

The corkscrew in Porter's gut tightened. He analyzed him, noticed his sweaty forehead and the nervous twitch at the corner of his mouth. "Don't take up poker, mate…You'll agree to the demands."

Tate rocked back in the chair. "I've worked fucking hard to get where I am. Why risk my career, my legacy, to pay for the sins of imbeciles who've gone before me? Why?"

"A good mate used to say, 'history repeats but we never learn from it'. He was spot on…Be the one who heeds past mistakes. Wanna discuss your legacy? Do what's right, implement what we've discussed, and you'll have a decent one…If you don't? Well, you can figure that out yourself…"

Tate scoffed. "History's shrouded in grey. It's not always as black and white as you make it sound…" He sighed and pulled a phone from breast pocket.

Porter watched him push a button and wait with the phone against his ear. His pulse quickened. What was he up to? He sensed he wouldn't be leaving Canberra any time soon and hoped Lyn Foster would act as he'd instructed. He hoped she'd forward the Cumal Files to the media before federal agents could reach her and destroy them.

Porter kept one eye on his briefcase, the other on Tate. "Do we have an agreement? Or are you willing to risk Australia's place in the world to protect your own?"

A muffled male voice sounded from Tate's cell phone.

He placed a hand over it then replied to Porter. "The shocking nature of your allegations has clouded my better judgement…I'm unsure of my earlier decisions made in haste and need time to think…" He took the hand away and spoke into the phone. "Inside. Now."

Seconds later the office door flew open. Two thick-set men in suits burst into the room. They drew pistols and ran to stand behind the desk, either side of Tate.

Tate snarled. "You really think I'm the only sitting Prime Minister to be told of government-backed slavery in the 1960s? How naïve…" He eyed him with contempt. "Tell me…Why would I, half a century later, be the first to act?"

Porter shrugged.

"It would be much easier for me, my colleagues, and the nation's conscience, if you just disappeared...Our guilty secrets and shame would simply disappear with you."

Porter swiveled and searched for an exit. He stood.

Two more agents ran into the room and blocked the doorway. Same suits, same buzzcuts, same 'don't fuck with me' snarls.

Porter sat. "Your call...But it's the wrong one."

Tate stood and pushed his chest out. "Gentlemen, take good care of him."

The four agents rushed to Porter and pinned him to the chair.

Prime Minister Tate took Porter's briefcase from the desk. He looked down at him, his expression cold but calm. "Am I the enemy you speak of? Or am I merely showing you who's in charge? Either way, you'll find out soon enough..."

Porter stared after him. "You're making a mistake...."

Tate stopped in the doorway, turned and raised the briefcase. He grinned like a junkie who'd stolen a doctor's prescription pad. "Thanks for the chat, Porter. It's been...Enlightening."

FIFTY-FOUR

Porter smiled because he'd finally reached a decision and knew what he had to do. He sipped chilled beer in celebration and let its sweet malt flavor slide down his throat. He sighed, sunk deeper on the wicker lounger and gazed at the scene in front of him.

Amber chatted with lifeguards near the shoreline, hair flowing in the breeze. Kids played in white sand and laughed as they destroyed castles. Couples linked at elbows strolled through crystal-clear tidal pools. And on the turquoise ocean beyond them, surfers danced with rolling waves.

He reclined the lounger so palm trees shaded him from the midday sun and took a breath of tropical air. A hectic fortnight had passed since his initial meeting with Prime Minister Tate in Canberra, and with much work still to do, he'd been reluctant to take a week off. But Jane had insisted. And for that he was grateful. The Whitsunday Islands were heaven on Earth and his beautiful angel sat beside him.

A newspaper rustled in Jane's hands. "I can't believe what I'm reading here, babe."

He sipped beer and closed eyes, lulled by the sound of waves breaking on the shore.

"Dan?" She flicked his bare shoulder. "Hear what I said? Today's paper, it's unbelievable..."

He shook his eyes open and turned to study her. Her full lips glistened, covered in balm. Designer sunglasses. Hair in a playful ponytail. Her yellow bikini

424

accentuated smooth, dark-mocha skin. She had the 'look,' minus the 'bitch,' with a heart bigger than Pharlap's. "What's so, unbelievable?"

"Here on da front page, it says they're changing da whole government. Endemic corruption at all levels…Over forty politicians removed from office, federal and state, with more arrests to come…" After a few seconds she gasped. "And the Police Minister's one of them…"

"I'm not surprised Moorecroft's involved. Always reckoned the bloke was more crooked than Sepp Blatter. They name any others?"

"Da new immigration guy, Jenkins. Da list is long."

"Sounds like a shakedown was well overdue…"

"It's incredible…And how does Tate remain as Prime Minister? He must've been aware of this level of corruption? I mean, what da?"

"Who knows…?"

She tut-tutted. "It says here that Tate's shocked and angered…He said da evidence presented by investigators gave him and da Governor-General no choice but to act as they did." She paused. "Then he mentions changes to national human rights legislation…Increases to Aboriginal health funding..." She turned to him. "Lionel would be happy…Did Carinya have anything to do with these arrests?"

He smirked. "A little…Crime Commission blokes and ASIO made most of 'em… But we did have a big say in getting changes to legislation that Lionel wanted...And Tate's sudden interest in constitutional recognition, that came from us."

"Well done, babe. Who is it that always says da little guys can't make a difference?"

"I'm glad to be wrong…"

She turned a page. After a minute she said, "Ah, I was wondering why Interpol wasn't involved, it's da next big story in here…" She read for a minute then spun in the lounger to face him. "You didn't think I'd wanna know?"

He frowned. "About what?"

"About da corrupt Interpol guys…And girls kidnapped from Sydney being found all over da place. Da low-life scum…Are they da ones who took Amber?"

"Nah, I don't reckon…"

She removed the sunglasses. Brown eyes darted over his face. "Then who?"

He gazed at the ocean, hoping to disguise the lie he would tell to protect her from the truth. "I've no idea, babe…Amber still can't remember anything, and all other lines of investigation came to nothing. Don't reckon we'll ever know…"

She watched him for a few seconds then put the sunglasses on and returned her attention to the paper. "Interpol's High Commissioner's been thrown in jail…"

"Yeah, and many others who worked with 'em. Their Sydney boss got shafted and Steve Williams has been seconded as the interim one. He's setting up a squad to target the mongrels running the child slavery syndicates. He wants me to join it. Lyn Foster's already started there…"

She dropped the open paper onto her chest. "You have to take that job…Protecting kids is your passion."

"I told Steve I'll go and have only just now decided for sure. Still a bit wary of working at Interpol after all the pain they've caused, but Steve's convinced me the corrupt bastards have all been weeded out…I'll be away from home weeks at a time, babe. You gunna be okay with that?"

She caressed his forearm. "Yes, Amber and I will be fine…Da police force has never appreciated you. Take da job, babe. Be happier at work."

He put the beer down and asked her to make room. He moved to her lounger.

She pushed sunglasses onto the top of her head then nestled her chin against his chest.

He glanced down at her. "The really good news…We still have two whole days left here together."

"Hmm…" She combed fingers through his chest hair. "I'm proud of you, babe. And Lionel would be too, with da new legislation."

In Porter's mind, Lionel gave him a thumbs-up sign. He smiled. "Yeah, reckon so…But he'd have done more, just by being around. And nothing's certain until the new government passes that legislation. I've gotta make sure they do…"

She prodded him. "That reminds me of da lady I met at Lionel's memorial service last week. Rosie? Amazing how she could only help Lionel from a distance and began a whole new life to protect her son…" Her eyebrows arched. "Makes you wonder, how do people keep such secrets?"

He hesitated, aware she referred to him. "Who knows? But Rosie's was an important one, very well kept."

"Speaking of which…" She rolled onto her stomach to face him. "You're supposed to tell me your big secret. Before we get married…"

He laughed it off and hoped she'd laugh too.

She scowled. "I'm serious, Dan. We won't be like other couples. No secrets…" Her eyes pleaded with him.

His chest burned and he swallowed to douse flames. The time had come. Jane deserved the truth. "Alright. Here's the first…"

Her nose scrunched. "There's more than one?"

"I've told you I was army before joining the cops, right?"

She sat up with legs crossed. "You were a soldier at eighteen…You've never said much else."

He straightened against the backrest. "At the end of 2001 I was with the SAS in Kandahar, Afghanistan. Our platoon leader was a kid straight out of Duntroon academy, raw as hell…We were on patrol one night. He led us into an ambush and panicked during the firefight…" He forced saliva into a dry mouth and swallowed it. "He ran straight into my line of fire…I killed him."

She stared and said nothing.

He took his phone out. He opened a photo then handed her the phone.

She squinted. "It's blurry. A photo of a photo?"

"Yeah, it's of a picture I found in Bill Thompson's house."

She pointed to the screen. "Was he your platoon leader? This young guy in uniform?"

"Yeah, the bloke I shot. Lieutenant Andrew Dawes."

428

"And who's da short, older guy with him? Actually, he looks kinda familiar..."

"His face has been in the news lately...The photo was taken at Dawes' graduation from Duntroon. The short bloke with him is Charles McKinlay."

"As in, da judge that died in that helicopter crash?"

He sucked a breath. "Yeah...Turns out he's Dawes' father. I had no idea, 'cos Dawes always used his mum's maiden name."

"I don't understand...Why was this picture in Thompson's house?"

"Won't tell you too much for your own sake. But McKinlay and Bill Thompson were best mates who'd led an international sex slave syndicate since the '60s."

"Oh, my god. That's...That's insane."

"You're not wrong...When I saw this photo and realized that McKinlay was Dawes' father, other things I'd stewed over for ages started to make sense."

"Like?"

"That McKinlay blamed me for Andrew's death and was motivated by revenge from the start. I finally asked Steve Williams some questions I'd been avoiding."

"And?"

"It's no coincidence I ended up in Crooked River. Moorecroft, not Delaney, ordered my secondment to Carinya. He acted on McKinlay's request."

"Amazing..."

"When McKinlay had no choice but to approve Carinya, he used the abducted girls to get at me, as bait to lure me in... I'd assumed they wanted to lay blame on the whole force, but nah, he targeted me personally and wanted the guilt on my conscience. For Nadia and all the other girls. And Andrew..."

She leaned towards him. "But hey, he's da one who died in disgrace... He didn't win, babe. You did."

"Ah, it wasn't about winning..." he lied. "But I reckon you're spot on, 'cos all the bastards linked to their syndicate are either dead or will rot in the slammer...Their organization's been dismantled and shut down for good..."

"Thanks to you and Lionel."

He gave her a tight smile.

She held his hand. "Listen babe, that shooting in Afghanistan wasn't your fault."

"And the military inquest ruled that way...It hasn't stopped me from blaming myself though..."

"But you can't..."

"Easy to say, babe. Much harder to do..."

She kissed his cheek. "I wish you'd told me earlier."

"I'd only told Steve up till now...When the guilt got too much, I quit the army and lost it big time. Drank a heap, got into fights. Every night I saw myself shooting Dawes. I was a physical wreck...Went to see a private psych because I didn't trust army doctors..."

She gulped. "What did they say?"

He looked into the sky. Hairs on neck bristled. Skin on his hollow chest tingled. He opened his mouth to speak then stopped. He wasn't ready. "That's something I'll tell you soon. Before we get married."

She frowned. "You have three months. Or like I said, there won't be a wedding. I can't live in a relationship with secrets...Okay?"

He nodded.

"Please babe, don't blame yourself for da force's fuckups," she said. "Be proud of helping all da girls you have, and of da lives you've saved..."

"It aint easy being part of the system that failed them…But Carinya gave me hope, and I guess anger drove me on. I had to arrest those mongrels abducting the girls…I had to find Amber…Had to hunt down the bastards that'd hurt you…Had to get justice for Lionel, and Rosie Davis. I just had to…"

"Redemption…" She nodded. "As our pastor in London used to say, it's been da savior of many great men."

"I'm hardly a great man, and not sure if redemption's the right word…But am I feeling less guilty? Yeah…"

"Well, I think you're great."

He kissed her bottom lip.

She flashed a gorgeous smile. "You excited, babe? About your new career starting soon…"

"Yeah, and Steve's not wasting any time. We get back to Sydney on Saturday, and on Monday I fly out on my first job."

"Fantastic…Where to?"

"He hasn't said too much but I've got a fair idea...He sent me a crash course in basic Thai yesterday."

"Ooh, my cunning linguist is off to Thailand…Need practice?" She giggled. "Been studying?"

"A bit…" He grinned then attempted a Thai accent. "Pom rak koon," he said, the words stilted. "Samuur..."

Her eyes sparkled as she frowned. "Did you just call me a raccoon?"

"Nah…" Porter held her angelic face in two hands. "I terribly tried to say…I love you, Jane. Always."

Dear reader,

We hope you've enjoyed THE CUMAL FILES as much as we enjoyed bringing it to you. If you have a spare moment, kindly leave a rating/review at the merchant site you obtained the novel from.

Visit **www.jameskeeganauthor.com** for news about the upcoming release of 'Oriental Illusions', book 2 in the Dan Porter series.

Thanks for your support, it's much appreciated,

SLEUTH HOUND BOOKS

Printed in Great Britain
by Amazon